LESSER OF TWO EVILS?

She looked around the great hall. It seemed as if they were all casting glances her way. Glances that were filled with consternation and sorrow.

Eric had returned with some news regarding her, obviously, and they were all talking about it.

Sounds could be picked up and echoed, and heard across the room. She caught whispered syllables of their words.

With mounting horror, she put them together.

She is to be murdered.

Weakness filled her limbs. Murdered. Her death was to be one of the "events" taking place at Langley tonight. This was a drastic measure. Not even King Edward had executed his female hostages. And now, Eric wanted her to go upstairs so that he could tell her alone, so that she could get some dignity together, compose herself so that her screams wouldn't create an uprising within the castle.

"Igrainia," Eric said, "Jarrett will escort you up."

She shook her head, facing him. "No. Find the courage to tell me here and now."

"The courage?" He arched a brow.

"Tell me now," she said, her limbs like ice. "Am I to be killed?"

"Killed?" Eric repeated, frowning and startled. He shook his head, lowering it, a dry, curious smile curving his lips. "No, my lady, I have not returned with any intent to do murder, legal, royal, or other."

"I overheard the men talking. You don't need to disguise what is happening to me. If I am to be executed, *murdered,* simply say so."

His smile deepened, and once again, he shook his head. "So you hear them speaking, but I'm afraid you didn't hear correctly. You're not to be *murdered.* You are to be *married.*"

KNIGHT
TRIUMPHANT

SHANNON
DRAKE

ZEBRA BOOKS
KENSINGTON PUBLISHING CORP.

ZEBRA BOOKS are published by

Kensington Publishing Corp.
850 Third Avenue
New York, NY 10022

ISBN 0-7394-2450-5

PROLOGUE

Once upon a time . . .

There lived a good king, and the land grew in peace and prosperity.

But the king grew older. Anxious to secure the succession, he remarried, because after the loss of his beloved wife and son, only the infant female babe of his daughter was left to inherit the crown. His new bride was young and beautiful, and his task—to procreate and give his country strong sons to rule after his death—should have been a pleasant and easy one. Indeed, in his eagerness to rejoin his lady after a council meeting one dark and stormy night, he rode the high cliffs and tors of his native land with abandon, despite the warnings of his advisors.

Along his way on that deep and tempestuous night, the king's horse lost its footing, or the king himself lost his horse. He plummeted down the ragged hillside, and perished before his time—and before his task could be complete. The land mourned.

The king's young granddaughter inherited the throne. Hope remained. The land would still thrive, all thought, for the Guardians of the country would protect their young queen well.

She was Margaret, known as the Maid of Norway. But alas, the child queen of Scotland died before ever reaching the shores of the land she should rule.

The land lay in loss and confusion, for after her death, the claimants to the crown were many. The strong, powerful, and rightful king of a neighboring country was called upon for aid and advice. He would listen to the claims of all, and help the Guardians decide who should rule. Of the many claimants, three were predominant: John Balliol, John Hastings, and Robert Bruce, the Competitor. All three were descendants of the daughters of David, Earl of Huntington, grandson of David I, another good king who had given the land strength and prosperity.

The wise men of the country were sadly unwary and indeed, unwise.

Their neighboring king had eyes upon the country himself.

Before the death of the young heiress, he had planned that she should marry his son, and thus unite the two countries.

Now, he helped to choose a puppet king, a man to rule the country, yet bow to him as an overlord. With his eyes in truth, upon the prize for himself, he chose John Balliol.

King John was at first acclaimed and accepted. But the overlord made the demands, and when the puppet king disobeyed, he was brought low. The great neighboring king folded his hands and nodded with pleasure. The prize, he thought, was his.

The land was cast into years of war.

Years of hell.

A desperate purgatory, at the very least.

Heroes rose to fight in the name of their absent king when he was broken by the overlord, dishonored, and forced to abdicate. They fought for freedom from the overlord's brutal rule for they were a country of their own people, proud and separate. The greatest of these heroes was a man named William. He brought the would-be conquering army low. But in time, the great wrath of the neighboring king fell upon them, and William Wallace, champion of the people, fell to treachery and lost his life—head, limbs, innards, and more—to the fury and vengeance of the English king.

Two men would now vie for the questionable treasure of the Scottish crown: John Comyn, kinsman of John Balliol and a powerful baron, and Robert Bruce, grandson of Robert Bruce the Competitor, who had made the original claim.

The two would make a pact, the one giving the other his lands and riches in exchange for the other's support in his quest for the crown. The neighboring king was now growing old and ailed, and, they thought, they could seize back their own country at his death. The churchmen knew of this plan, and they were pleased.

But treachery again struck: The one betrayed the other, seeing that the neighboring king knew of the plan. Edward, self-proclaimed "hammer" of the Scots, failed to die as all had hoped, and instead, vowed his wrath and vengeance once again.

John Comyn conspired against Robert Bruce, telling the neighboring king of Bruce's compact with him and great churchmen.

The neighboring king was again in a fury.

And Robert Bruce, hearing of the betrayal, rode hard in his wrath to find the man who had betrayed him. They met within a church, and there, upon the altar, Bruce spilled the blood of Comyn. If he did not murder his distant kinsman with his blow, it did not matter, for his men finished the deed.

In 1306, Bruce was crowned king of the Scots at Scone. The English king had stolen the great stone of Scone, upon which Scottish kings had been crowned for eons, but still, Robert the Bruce was anointed in the ancient tradition. He was crowned not just once, but twice, for Isabel, a daughter of the house of Mar, came rushing to perform the hereditary duties of her family at a coronation as her brother, the earl, was a lad, and held by the neighboring king, Edward of England. She was but nineteen and married to the earl of Buchan, an ally of the English king, but in her devotion to her land, she was heedless of her marriage. And the consequences.

She arrived for the coronation a day late, and therefore, so that tradition and propriety might be maintained, the ancient rites were performed again on Palm Sunday, the twenty-sixth of March, 1306. Now none of the people might doubt that Robert Bruce was king.

And so, in name, he had risen at last to claim his great quest.

But the new king had many enemies, among them the kinsmen of the slain John Comyn, powerful barons of the land.

And then there was Edward I of England, who had ruled long, and hard, and brutally.

And who, most annoyingly, had failed, thus far, to die.

When he heard of Bruce's coronation, Edward I had his son honored as Prince of Wales. Hundreds of hardy young Englishmen were knighted at the ceremony, giving vows before the altar of chivalry and valor.

The English king's wrath was such that no such vows might be maintained. There would be few prisoners taken by the English, for all men captured who supported Robert

Bruce were to be treated as outlaws, executed without trial, hanged, beheaded, drawn and quartered, or dragged through the streets to meet various forms of torture, humiliation, then a grisly death. Heralds proclaimed throughout the land that the women—the wives, sisters, even daughters of the valiant patriots—should be treated little better. The English knights were given leave to rob, rape, and murder as they saw fit. They were the outlaw kin of an outlaw king.

Within months of his coronation, Bruce had met savage defeats, and many of his finest men had been captured and executed, including three of his brothers. His wife had become a hostage of the vengeful English king, along with two of his sisters and his daughter. Only his great prowess, at times against incredible numerical odds, kept patriotism and loyalty alive among those who would serve him. He was not a ruler with a great army, but a tattered bandit fighting from the rich forests in which he could find shelter. Troops had to be raised from those loyal to this new king, and to the dream of freedom. Help was sought from abroad. The highlands of Scotland were far from the English, but the lowlands had been brought to their knees.

The borderlands remained a form of Hell on earth. In this purgatory and chaos, men and women, the great and the small, struggled to survive.

Robert Bruce was king of Scotland.

But it was treachery that reigned.

Once upon a time . . .

There lived a man who would be a great king.

But in the year of our Lord 1307, his battle for the land, for the freedom of his country, had only just begun.

CHAPTER 1

They were surely madmen.

From the hill, Igrainia could see the riders coming.

They flew the flags of Robert the Bruce.

They had to be mad.

She rode with a party of twenty men, selected carefully for their skill and courage—and, of course, the simple fact that they were still alive and well. They wore full armor and carried well-honed weapons with which they were very adept.

There were less than half that number coming toward them, a pathetically ragtag band, racing up the hill.

"My lady . . . ?" queried Sir Morton Hamill, head of her guard.

"Can we outrun them?" she asked.

Sir Morton let out a sound of disgust. "Outrun them!" He was indignant. "They are but rabble; their so-called king runs to the forests while his family is slain in his stead. The

Bruce is aware that he is an outlaw to most of his own people. My lady, there is no reason to run.''

"No reason," she said, her eyes narrowing, "except that more men will die. I am weary of death.''

The riders were still gaining on them at a breakneck pace, racing from the site of the castle, where surely even they had realized that the black crosses covering the stone were no ploy of the enemy, but a true warning of the situation within.

Sir Morton was trying hard to hold his temper. "My lady, I am aware of the pain in your heart. But these are the very renegades who brought the terror to your home, who cost you . . . who cost you everything.''

"No man, or woman, asks for the plague, Sir Morton. And indeed, if you ask Father MacKinley, he will tell you that God sent the sickness in his anger that we should brutally make hostages of women and children, and execute our enemies so freely. We were warned of the sickness; we refused to believe the warnings of our foes. So now, if we can outrun the renegades, that is my choice. It was not my choice to leave Langley. I want no more death laid at my feet.''

"Alas. We cannot outrun them," Sir Morton argued then. "They are almost upon us.''

She stared at him angrily. "You would fight them rather than do your duty to bring me to safety.''

"My lady, you are beside yourself with grief and cannot think clearly. I would fight such upstart rebels, aye, my lady, for that is my duty.''

"Sir Morton, I am in my full senses, quite capable of coherent thought—''

"My lady, watch! Your position here on the hill is excellent; you may view the carnage as I take my revenge on these knaves!''

Furious, Igrainia reined in her horse as Sir Morton called out an order to his men. He did not intend to await the enemy. He meant to attack first.

"Sir Morton!" She raged with fury, her heart sick as she watched the men spur their horses to his command. In seconds, the liege men of her late lord, Afton of Langley, spurned her order and took flight down the hill.

They seemed to sail in a sea of silver, armor gleaming in the sun. The colors they flew, the rich blue and red, noble colors, created a riot of shades along with the silver stream. Down the hill, a display of might and power . . .

Bearing down upon a sad rabble, scattered horsemen on fine enough mounts, some in tarnished armor, most in no more than leather jerkins to protect their hearts from the onslaught of steel that would soon come their way.

At her distance, she could see their leader. She frowned, wondering what madness would make a man risk certain death. She narrowed her eyes against the sun, studying the man. A small gasp escaped her.

She had seen him before. She knew, because he rode without protection; no helmet covered his head, and the length of his tangled blond hair glinted in the sun with almost as much of a sheen as the steel helmets worn by her own people. She had seen him dragged in with the other captured men, shackled in irons. He had looked like a wild man, uncivilized, a barbarian, yet despite the dirt and mud that marred his clothes, she had seen his eyes once, when they had met hers, and she had read something frightening in that glance. She had the odd feeling that he had allowed himself to be taken prisoner, though why, she didn't know. Or perhaps she did. Castle Langley, as her husband's home was called, had just been turned into quarters for the king's men when they had come through, bearing the families of

Scottish outlaws to London, where they would be held until their rebel kin surrendered.

And offered their own necks to the axeman's blade.

Sir Morton's men were nearly upon the riders. In the glittering sunlight, it was almost a beautiful spectacle, the gleam and glint of steel and color . . .

Until the riders came together in a hideous clash, horses screaming, men shouting, steel becoming drenched in the deep red of blood. Tears suddenly stung her eyes; Afton had wanted no part of this. He had been furious with the order to welcome the king's men, to house renegades who were his own people. He had demanded that the hostages not be treated as animals, even when they spoke with their highland language and strange burrs, and looked like wild creatures from heathen times. He had stood, a proud voice of reason and mercy, until he had fallen . . .

And neither her love nor her prowess with herbs had managed to save him.

He would have been furious at this bloodbath, had he been with her.

Had he had his way, they would never have come to this . . .

She gasped, bringing her hand to her lips as she saw that a rebel had met Sir Morton head on, ever ready to do battle. The rebel was the wild man with the tangled blond hair.

Sir Morton's sword never made contact with the rebel's flesh.

Sir Morton's head fell to the earth and bounced as his body continued through the mass upon his horse, until that part of him, too fell to the ground to be trampled upon.

Bile filled her throat. She closed her eyes, and lowered her head, fighting the sickness that threatened to overwhelm her. Dear God, she had just left plague victims, nursed the sick and the putrid and the rotting and . . .

With her eyes closed, she could still see the head, bouncing.

The clash of steel seemed to rise in a cacophony around her; she heard more cries, shouts, the terrified whinnies of warhorses, animals accustomed to battle and mayhem. She forced herself to look up.

The finest armor to be found had not protected the men of Langley from the fury of the rebels' wrath. Men lay everywhere.

Armor glinting in the sun. The shining intermittent, against the bloodstained field. Some had survived. Unhorsed, the men milled in a circle. There were shouts and commands; the blond giant was on his feet as well, approaching the eight or so men of Langley who remained standing. Watching, appalled, she didn't realize her own danger. Voices carried on the air.

"Do we slay them now?" someone inquired.

The blond man replied, then shouted at the survivors. Swords fell to the ground. One man fell to his knees. Did he do so in absolute desolation, or in gratitude for his life?

Were they to be executed? Or were their lives to be spared?

She couldn't tell. Others were talking, but they spoke in softer voices.

One of the rebels pointed up the hill.

Then, suddenly, the blond man was staring at her.

She couldn't see his eyes in the distance. She could only remember them.

He started toward his horse.

Only then did she realize her own situation, and that he was mounting to ride once again, after her.

She spurred her horse, praying that she knew this region better than he, that her mare was a fresher mount, ready to take her to greater bursts of speed . . .

For a far longer period of time.

She prayed . . .

There had been a time, not so long ago, that she had wanted to die. When the death and despair had seemed so great that she would willingly have taken Afton's hand, and entered the afterlife with him. That moment when she realized that she had lost him, that he had breathed his last, that his laughter would never sound again.

And yet now . . .

She did not want to depart this life at the hands of a furious barbarian, bent on some form of revenge. She thought of how Edward I had killed Wallace, of the horrors that had taken place, of the English furor at the crowning of Robert Bruce.

And she rode as she had never done before, flat against her mare's neck, heels jamming the beast's haunches, whispers begging her to ever greater speed. The rebel's horse had to be flagging; their animals had been foaming when they first met with the men of Langley. If she could just evade him for a distance . . .

She galloped over the hill, through the thick grasses of the lea to the north. The forest beckoned beyond the hill, a forest she knew well, with twisting trails and sheltering oaks, a place in which to disappear. She could see the trees, the great branches waving high in the sky, the darkness of the trails beneath the canopy of leaves. She could smell the very richness of the earth and hear the leaves, as she could hear the thunder of her horse's hooves, the desperate, ragged catch of her own breath, the pulse of her heartbeat, echoed with each thunder of a hoof upon the earth. There . . . just a moment away . . .

She was never aware that his horse's hoofbeats thundered along with those of her mare; the first she knew of him was the hook of his arm, sweeping her from her horse in a deadly gamble. She was whisked from the mare and left to watch as the horse made the shelter of the trees. And for a moment, she looked on, in amazement, as she dangled from the great warhorse, a prisoner taken by a madman.

She began to twist and struggle, and bite—a sound enough attack so that he swore, and dropped her. His horse was huge; she fell a distance to the earth, stunned, then gathered her senses quickly and began to run. She headed for the dark trail, desperately, running with the speed of a hunted doe.

Yet again, she was swept off her feet, this time, lifted up, and thrown down, and the next thing she knew, he was on top of her, smelling of the earth and the blood of battle. She screamed, fought, kicked, yet found her hands vised above her head, and the barbarian straddled atop her, staring at her with a cold, wicked fury that allowed no mercy.

"You are the lady of Langley," he said.

"Igrainia," she replied.

"I don't give a damn about your name," he told her. "But you will come with me, and you will demand that the gates be opened."

She shook her head, "I cannot—"

She broke off as he raised a hand to strike her. The blow did not fall.

"You will," he said simply. "Or I will break you, bone by bone, until you do so."

"There is plague there, you idiot!"

"My wife is there, and my daughter," he told her.

"They are all dead or dying within the castle!"

"So you run in fear!" he said contemptuously.

"No! No," she raged, struggling to free herself again. Afraid? Of the plague? She was afraid only of life without Afton now.

Not quite true, she realized. She was afraid of this man

who would carry out his every threat, and break her. Bone by bone. She had never seen anyone so coldly determined.

"I am not afraid of the plague for myself!" she managed to snap out with an amazing tone of contempt.

"Good. We will go back, my fine lady, and you will dirty your hands with caring for those who are ill. You will save my wife, if she is stricken, or so help me, you will forfeit your own life."

Dirty her hands? He thought she was afraid to dirty her hands after the days and nights she had been through?

Her temper rose like a battle flag, and she spat at him. "Kill me then, you stupid, savage fool! I have been in that castle. Death does not scare me. I don't care anymore. Can you comprehend that? Are such words in your vocabulary?"

She gasped as he stood, wrenching her to her feet.

"If my wife or my daughter should die because of the English king's cruelty against the innocent, my lady, you are the one who will pay."

"My husband is dead because of the sickness brought in by your people!" she cried, trying to wrench her arm free. She could not. She looked at the hand vised around her arm. Huge, long-fingered, covered in mud and earth and . . .

Blood.

His grip seemed stronger than steel. Not to be broken. She stood still, determined not to tremble or falter. His face was as muddied and filthy as his hand and tangled blond hair. Only those sky blue eyes peered at her uncovered by the remnants of battle, brilliant and hard.

He either hadn't heard her, or he didn't give a damn. His command of language seemed to be excellent, so she assumed it was the latter.

"Hear me again. If my wife dies, my lady, you will be forfeit to the mercy of the Scottish king's men."

"Mercy? There is no mercy to be had there."

"At this point? Perhaps you are quite right. Therefore, you had best save my wife."

"I, sir, have no difficulty doing anything in my power to save the stricken, though I can assure you—their lives are in God's hands, and no others. I was forced to leave Langley. I did not go of my own volition."

He arched a brow skeptically. "You were willing to serve the plague-stricken and dying?"

"Aye, I would have stayed there willingly. I had no reason to leave."

"You *are* the lady of Langley."

"Indeed."

He didn't seem to care why she would have stayed.

"Then, as you say, it will be no hardship for you to return."

"Where I go, or what is done to me, does not matter in the least."

"You will save my wife, and my child."

She raised her chin.

"As I have told you, and surely you must understand, their lives are in God's hands. What, then, if I cannot save them?"

"Then it will be fortunate that you seem to have so little care for your own life."

He shoved her forward.

With no other choice, Igrainia walked.

Yet her heart was sinking.

If your wife is among the women stricken, then I am afraid that she has already died! Igrainia thought.

Because she had lied. She had thought herself immune to fear when she left Langley. Immune to further pain. Now, she was discovering that she did fear for her life, that there was something inside her that instinctively craved survival.

She wanted to live.

But if she failed, so he proclaimed, he would break her. That was certainly no less savage than the commands given by Edward in regard to the wives and womenfolk of any man loyal to Robert the Bruce.

Break her. Bone by bone.

It was all in God's hands. But maybe this filthy and half-savage man, no matter how articulate, didn't comprehend that.

"I will save your wife and child, if you will give me a promise."

"You think that you can barter with me?" he demanded harshly.

"I am bartering with you."

"You will do as I command."

"No. No, I will not. Because you are welcome to lop off my head here and now if you will not barter with me."

"Do you think that I will not?"

"I don't care if you do or do not!"

"So the lord of Langley is dead!" he breathed bitterly.

"Indeed. So you have no power over me."

"Believe me, my lady, if I choose, I can show you that I have power over you. Death is simple. Life is not. The living can be made to suffer. Your grief means nothing to me. It was the lord of Langley who imprisoned the women and children."

She shook her head. "You're wrong! So foolishly wrong! What care they received was by his order. Those who will live will do so, because he commanded their care. And he is dead because of the wretched disease brought in by *your* women and *your* children."

"None of this matters!" he roared to her.

She ignored his rage, and the tightening vise of his fingers around her arm.

She stared at his hand upon her, and then into his eyes,

so brilliantly blue and cold against the mud-stained darkness of his face.

"I will save your wife and child, if you will swear to let your prisoners live."

Again, he arched a brow and shrugged. "Their fates matter not in the least to me; save her, and they shall live."

She started forward again, then once more stopped. She had spoken with contempt and assurance. A bluff, a lie. And now, her hands were shaking. "What if I *cannot*? What if it has gone too far? God decides who lives and dies, and the black death is a brutal killer—"

"You will save them," he said.

They had reached his horse, an exceptionally fine mount. Stolen, she was certain, from a wealthy baron killed in battle. He lifted her carelessly upon the horse, then stared up at her, as if seeing her, really seeing her, perhaps for the first time.

"You will save them," he repeated, as if by doing so he could make it true.

"Listen to me. Surely, you understand this. Their lives are in God's hands."

"And yours."

"You are mad; you are possessed! Only a madman thinks he can rule a plague. Not even King Edward has power over life and death against such an illness. Kings are not immune, no man, no woman—"

"My wife and child must survive."

He had no sense, no intellect, no reason!

"Which of the women is your wife?" she asked. She wondered if she could kick his horse, and flee. She was in the saddle; he was on the ground.

"And if I give you a name, what will it mean to you?" he inquired.

"I have been among the prisoners."

It seemed he doubted that. "Margot," he told her. "She is tall, slim and light, and very beautiful."

Margot. Aye, she knew the woman. Beautiful indeed, gentle, moving about, cheering the children, nursing the others . . .

Until she had been struck down.

She had been well dressed, and had worn delicate Celtic jewelry, as the wife of a notable man, a lord, or a wealthy man at the least.

Rather than a filthy barbarian such as this.

But it was said that even Robert Bruce, King of the Scots, looked like a pauper often enough these days. He was a desperate man, ever searching out a ragtag army, reduced to hunger and hardship time and time again.

"Who are you?" she asked

"Who I am doesn't matter."

"Do you even have a name, or should I think of you as Madman, or Certain Death?"

His eyes lit upon her with cold fury. "You must have a name when it doesn't matter, when your life is at stake? When Edward has decreed that Scottish women are fair game, no better than outlaws to be robbed, raped or *murdered*? Wouldn't you be the one who is surely mad to expect chivalry in return for such barbarity, and test the temper of a man whose rage now equals that of your king? You would have a name? So be it. I am Eric, Robert Bruce's liege man by choice, sworn to the sovereign nation of Scotland, a patriot by both birth and choice. You see, my father was a Scottish knight, but my grandfather, on my mother's side, was a Norse jarl of the western isles. So there is a great deal of *berserker*—or indeed, *madman*—in me, lady. You must beware. We are not known to act rationally—and by God, no matter what our inclination at any time—*mercifully.*

Now, tell me what I ask. Does my wife live? You do know her, don't you?''

''Aye. I know her. Father MacKinley is with her,'' Igrainia said. ''She lives. When I left, she still lived.'' Aye, she knew his wife. She had spoken with her often when the disease had brought them together, forgetting nationalities and loyalties, fighting death itself.

And she knew his little girl. The beautiful child with the soft yellow hair and huge blue eyes, smiling even when she fell ill. The little girl had gone into a fever with a whimper.

But the woman had been so ill, burning, twisting, crying out . . .

She would die. And then . . .

Igrainia suddenly grabbed the reins and slammed the horse with her heels, using all the strength she had.

The huge gray warhorse reared, pawing the air. Igrainia clung desperately to the animal, hugging its neck, continuing to slam her heels against its flank. The man was forced to move back, and she felt hope take flight in her heart as the horse hit the ground and started running toward the trees.

Yet nearly to the trail, the animal came to an amazing halt, reared again, and spun.

This time, Igrainia did not keep her seat.

She hit the ground with a heavy thud that knocked the air from her.

A moment later, he was back by her side, reaching down to her, wrenching her to her feet. ''Try to escape again, and I will drag you back in chains.''

She gasped for breath, shaking her head. ''No one will stop your entry at the castle. Only the truly mad would enter there. I cannot help your wife—''

''I have told you who I am. And I know who you are. Igrainia of Langley, known to have the power to heal. Daughter of an *English* earl, greatly valued by many. My God, what you could be worth! There will be a price on your head, my lady, and you will save my wife.''

Once again, she found herself thrown onto the horse, which had obediently trotted back to its master.

This time, he mounted behind her.

Even as he did so, he urged the horse forward at a reckless gallop.

She felt his heat and his fury in the wall of his chest against her back, felt the strength of the man, and the power of his emotion.

And more . . .

She felt the trembling in him.

And suddenly understood.

Aye, he was furious.

And he was afraid.

And dear God . . .

So was she.

CHAPTER 2

He was excellent at the art of killing. Eric knew it well. Against superior forces, he and his men always had the advantage of extreme training, experience, and the cold hard fact of desperation. But none of their expertise had ever wielded such a blow against the English as that of the strange disease that had seized their little band of rebels. One moment, they had been the most dreaded of the English king's enemies; the next moment, they were a group of outcasts, shunned and feared by their captors. But even after their capture by the English, Eric had been confident of escape. He had allowed his own incarceration, planning on escaping walls and chains, to return for the others. He had known his ability to fight, to elude the strongest of his foes. He had never imagined that there would be an unseen enemy against whom all the prowess in the world was utterly futile. For all of his determination and strength, he had no power whatsoever against the illness that had ravaged their number.

There was no enemy he had ever wanted to best with such passion, and no enemy who had ever had a greater power over him.

As they neared the great gates to Langley Castle, he was barely aware of the woman on the saddle before him, or even of his own men, as willing as he to risk their own lives for the return of their women, children, and compatriots. Of course, they had all already been exposed to the disease. It had come upon them when they returned from the sea with the lone survivor of a shipwreck. None of them had known, when they plucked the unlucky survivor from the waves, that they had taken death itself from the brine, and that the man's ship had gone down because none aboard his damned vessel had been able to fight the onslaught of the storm. The man had never regained consciousness. Within hours after coming aboard, he acquired the dreaded boils.

None had thought to return him, still breathing, to the sea whence he had come; they knew that they had brought death aboard. Only when the fellow had breathed his last, had he been returned to the water.

Soon after they had brought their own small boats back to shore, the English had come upon their camp, not knowing then that they had just captured the promise of certain death. Though Eric and many of the others had been apart from the band when King Edward's men seized hold of the group, they had allowed their own capture, aware in their depleted condition and poor numbers that their only sure chance to rescue their women from the grip of the enemy was to come among them and discover the weaknesses among their captors and their prison. They had gone so far as to warn the English as to the manner of prisoner they were taking. The enemy had not believed them.

Now, they did.

Even as they rode the last stretch of distance to their

destination, they could see that black crosses had been painted here and there around the walls, warning any who might venture too near that death lay within.

"Tell the guard to open the gates," he commanded his captive, reining in.

Castle Langley rose high before them. A Norman fortification, it had high, solidly built stone walls, and a moat surrounded the edifice. It was an excellent estate, one that stood on a hill surrounded by rich valleys. It was near the vast hereditary Bruce holdings, except that Robert, recently anointed king of Scotland, now held less than he ever had as a first earl of the land. Edward of England had come to lay his heavy fist of domination with a greater vengeance and anger than ever. The Scots had a king they could admire, one behind whom they could fight for a free Scotland. But being crowned king, and becoming king, in Scotland were far from one and the same.

"You will but have me open the gates of death," she said softly.

"Call out; have them open the gates," he said. "We are a band of dead men riding already."

"Guard!" she called. "It is I, Igrainia, lady of Langley. Cast down the bridge."

There was motion on the parapets high above them, and a reply.

"My lady, where is your guard? You must be away from this place; you must not reenter here!"

"Open the gates; lower the bridge."

"Sir Robert has said that you must not return—"

"I am lady here; open the gates."

"You ride with madmen; you come with rebels—"

"The guard will die if you do not open the gates."

"Oh, my lady! For your own dear life—"

"I am commanding you. Open the gates. Let down the bridge."

For a moment Eric feared that the woman might not have the authority she should wield; despite his desperation, he had not come here ill prepared, without knowledge regarding the situation at Langley. The lady here was a woman of greater importance than the lord. Though her husband had been a Scottish peer in his own right—one who had maintained a loyalty to Edward of England—this woman, wife of the perished lord, was the daughter of an English earl, a man who had gained his title some years back through an ancestor born on the wrong side of the English royal blanket.

The sound of gears and pulleys creaked against the stillness of the day. The gates began to lower to span the moat. Here, near the sea, it was an oddly clean body of water, for the moat joined a stream that cut a blue ribbon across the green plain toward the rocky coastline where the land joined the sea. Moments later the gate was down, and entry to the castle was but yards away. He spurred his horse and entered into the courtyard.

A pathetic show of troops came mustering from the tower keep as his band of men came clattering over the bridge. Though clad in mail and the colors of their late lord, the group that greeted them did not draw weapons, but formed a semicircle around their horses, waiting. They seemed to be leaderless, strangely adrift.

"Set me down!" Igrainia said, "if you would manage this without bloodshed."

He didn't like her tone, it was as rasping as her mere existence. But her words made sense toward his one driving goal, that of reaching Margot, his daughter, Aileen, and the others. It was all he could do to keep from throwing the woman down from his horse. She was anathema to him, hair pitch black when he sought a woman with a head of hair as golden and glowing as the sun, eyes a curious dark shade of violet when his world had come to rise and set in a gaze as soft and blue as the most beautiful spring morning.

Alive and well and walking while Margot lay dying . . .

He lifted the Englishwoman with a forced control and set her to the ground before dismounting behind her.

"Where is Sir Robert Neville?" she asked.

One of the guardsmen stepped forward.

"My lady, he is . . . he is abed."

"Does anyone tend to him?" she asked anxiously.

Eric lost his patience, stepping around her. "I am Eric Graham, emissary of the rightful king of this holding, Robert the Bruce of Scotland. Lay down your arms, and your lives will be spared. The castle is now in the hands of the Scots who honor and acknowledge Robert Bruce as king."

He glanced back at Peter MacDonald, who had ridden at his heels, giving a quick nod that he should now take over as the authority. Ignoring all else, he then started across the courtyard to the door to the keep, knowing exactly where the prisoners, even though near death, were held. It might have been a foolish move; a guard with a death wish of his own might have brought a battle sword piercing through his back. Behind him, he could hear the fall of arms as his men dismounted from their horses and collected the weapons. Peter MacDonald, a man who had been his right hand since the coronation of the king, began shouting the orders. Eric had complete confidence in Peter: the Scottish nationalists with whom he rode had survived thus far by covering one another's back. They had become so tightly knit in their numbers, they nearly thought alike.

He was prepared for some sign of resistance when he entered into the great hall, but there was no one there, other than an old man hunched in a chair by the fire. The old man tried to stir at the sight of Eric, but the effort seemed too great. He fell back into the chair, watching Eric as Eric watched him.

"You've the disease, man?" Eric asked, his voice seeming to bellow across the stone expanse.

"Aye. But survived, I believe," the fellow replied, watching Eric. "You've come to take the castle, sir? You've taken hell, sir, that's what you've done. Slay me, if you will. I would serve you, if I could."

Eric waved a hand. "Save your strength. Tell me, where are the rest of those who serve the castle?"

"Dead, many dead. Sir Robert Neville fell, and the Lady Igrainia's maid tends him in his room. The guards . . . not yet afflicted, keep to the courtyard and the armory. The Lord of Langley was laid hastily into the crypt, walled into his grave, lest his sickness travel; his wife could not bear that he should be burned, as the rest of the victims."

"And what of the prisoners and their guards?"

"Fallen together below in the dungeons."

"And who tends them?"

"Those who still stand on two feet among their own number. Before . . . ah, well, the lady of the castle tended to the dying, until she was sent from here that her life might be spared."

"Rest, old man. When you've strength, you might yet be called upon to serve."

Eric strode through the hall, finding the passage that led from the hall to the winding stone stairs that led below. Hell . . . the man had said. Hell had been planned long before any disease for those incarcerated here. The damp stairs to the bowels of the castle seemed endless; the prisons here were sure to bring about disease all on their own, fetid, molded, wretched. Those brought here to the belly of the fortification were among the dead, long hallways with crypts where past lords and ladies, knights, nobility, and those who had served them well lay in perpetual silence and rot, some in no more than misty shrouds that barely hid the remnants of finery and bone, while some were walled with stone and remembered with fine chiseled monuments. The passages of dead came before the cells with their iron bars, chains and filthy rushes. The dead of the household were far more honored here than the prisoners brought in with little hope for life.

Eric passed through the crypts and knew he neared the cells again as he heard the sound of moaning. Ducking beneath an archway he came to a large, thick wooden door with a huge bolt; the bolt was not slid into place and the great door gaped. Pushing through, he saw the cells, and those who lay within them.

There were no soft beds or pallets here. The stench was so overwhelming that he wavered as he stood, but for no more than a matter of seconds. On either side of the hall, the sick and dying lay like piles of cast-off clothing. He entered to the right, where he had been kept with Margot and his daughter. He rolled a body over, saw where the boils on the man had swollen and burst. He did not recognize the dead man, who had surely been one of his own. He looked at a death more heinous than any horrible torture devised by his enemies.

The dead should have been taken away, their sad remains burned to keep the pestilence from spreading. Here . . .

''Margot!'' he whispered his wife's name, because the scene would allow for no more than a whisper, and he moved through the bodies around him on the rushes. He could not find Margot, but even in his desperation, as he searched, a burst of fury and fear gave him a force of energy that was near madness; he made some sense of the room, finding those who breathed, with signs of life, and lifted and carried them, separating the living from the dead.

"She is not here."

He started at the sound of the woman's voice.

Igrainia of Langley stood at the entrance to the cell, watching him, holding a large ewer.

"Where is she?"

"Several of the women were brought to the solar above," she told him. As if she had known what he had been about, she approached those who still showed signs of life. She seemed heedless of the scent of rot and the horror that surrounded her. Despite her elegant apparel, she came down to the rushes among the living, her touch careful as she lifted heads to bring water to parched lips.

He strode to her, catching a handful of her hair to draw her face to his, his intent at the moment not cruel but born of greater desperation. "Where is the solar?"

"Above. Take the stairs from the great hall, to the tower. There is sun there. Father MacKinley believes the sun may have the power of healing."

He still had a handful of ebony hair in his hands. His fingers tightened.

"Come with me."

"If you care nothing for these, your friends—"

"They are my life's blood. But my men will be along. They will see that the dead are burned, and that the others are brought from this deadly morass as well."

Even as he spoke, he heard footsteps along the stone flooring that led to the cells. James of Menteith and Jarrett Miller had come. The Lady of Langley stood gracefully, yet gritted her teeth. "My hair, sir. I will accompany you with greater facility if you will be so good as to release me."

He did so, unaware that he had maintained his death grip upon the black tresses.

She handed the ewer to James and pointed out where she had brought water, and what survivors remained. She stepped carefully around the prone Scots upon the floor and left the bars, her footsteps silent upon the stone where the men's heavier tread had created a clatter. Eric nodded to James, who inclined his head in return, then followed after the Lady of Langley.

Once returned to the hall, he found that they traveled up a staircase amazing in its breadth for such a fortified castle. Though this stronghold had been built to repel an enemy, some resident had taken pains to turn the place into more of a manor. The stairway he followed was not stone, but intricately carved wood. It led to a second landing with a long hallway and doors where the lady did not pause, but continued on to a smaller staircase. There, arrow slits lined the stone and she passed them all, coming to a large room filled with daylight. Makeshift beds littered the space, and light from a break in the ceiling seemed to cast a ray of hope over those who lay there. A priest moved among the beds, a young slender man in the black garment of his calling. He seemed surprised to see his lady at the doorway, and called to her with a frown. "Igrainia, you were to be away from all this!" he chastised.

She stepped inside. "This is Sir Eric, Father MacKinley," she said, and walked into the room, approaching a bed. Eric nodded to the priest and followed Igrainia.

He fell to his knees by the pallet; he had found Margot at last. She seemed to be sleeping. No boils or poxes appeared to mar the beauty of her face. Yet as he touched her face, it was as if he touched flame. He saw where the boils had grown upon a collarbone and on her neck, and he was tempted to weep.

He stared up at Igrainia of Langley. "Save her," he commanded.

She found water and brought it to Margot's side and began to bathe her forehead.

"Where is my daughter?" he asked.

"Your daughter?" said the priest.

"My child. Aileen. Young, blond hair, pale, soft as silk."

There was a silence from the priest.

"My daughter, man! There were not so many young children among our number!"

The priest nodded. "The little angel," he murmured. "Sir, God has taken her."

He rose from his wife's side, pain a blinding arrow through his heart. He approached the priest like a madman, tempted to take him by the throat and crush flesh and bone. Some sense delayed him from his purpose, and he paused before the man, who had not flinched. Eric stood before him, fists clenching and unclenching, muscles taut and straining.

"Where is her body?"

"Yonder room," the priest said quietly. "We meant to do her honor in death."

"You knew I would come and kill you," Eric said in a bitter breath.

"She was a child, and beloved by all. What fear have we of violent death, of murder, when we work here?" the priest replied, and even in his madness, Eric knew it was true.

"You," he said, pointing to the priest, "you will bring me to my child. And you," he said, pointing at Igrainia, "you will bring Margot to a room alone, and you will spend your every moment seeing that she breathes. If she ceases to do so . . ."

He let his voice trail.

"What of the others?" the lady asked.

"We are here now. And we will drop down in death ourselves before we let our kindred lie in rot and die without our care. Ready a chamber for my lady wife. Nay, the master's chamber. See that she is surrounded by the greatest possible comfort. Priest, now you will take me to my daughter.''

The priest led him quickly from the solar, opening the door to a small room in the hall just beyond. There, on a long wooden storage cabinet, lay the body of his daughter.

For a moment he couldn't move.

He felt the priest at his back.

''There is comfort in knowing that she rests with our Lord God in Heaven—'' the man began.

''Leave me!'' Eric said sharply.

The door closed behind him instantly.

He walked forward, forcing his feet to move. He looked down upon Aileen's face, and his knees sagged beneath him and tears sprang to his eyes. He swallowed and reached out for her. Her poor little body was cold. He cradled her against him as if he could warm her, smoothing his long, calloused fingers through the infinitely fine tendrils of her hair. *Aileen, with her laughter and her smile and her innocence of the cruelty of the world around her. Aileen, with her little arms outstretched to him, calling him, each time he had been away, her little footsteps bringing her to him. And he would bend down and scoop her into his arms, and she would cup his face in her hands and kiss his cheek and say his name again with such sweet trust that he knew that the world itself was worth saving, that freedom was worth fighting for . . .*

Innocence, trust beauty . . . dead. The sun had gone out of the world.

This time, when his knees failed him, he fell to the floor, cradling her lifeless form in his arms.

Alone among the sick in the solar, Igrainia looked about with dismay. Among the Scots seized and still living, there was an older woman with long, graying hair. She would survive, Igrainia thought. Her boils had broken, and she was breathing still. The pestilence here was as strange as death itself; this woman had lived many years; she appeared frail and weak. Yet she would survive.

Another younger woman seemed to slip away as Igrainia bathed her forehead. The two others in the room were young as well, both still holding on. Igrainia lowered her head to the chest of one, and heard that the rattle had left her breathing; she, too, would survive. And the other . . .

"Water!" came a desperate and pathetic whisper.

"Carefully, carefully," Igrainia warned, holding the woman's head. She was, perhaps, twenty, almost as light as Margot. Igrainia forced her to drink slowly, then nearly dropped her head back to the pallet as a cry suddenly seemed to rip through the stone walls. It was more than a cry, more like a howl of fury, despair and anguish. It was like the sound of a wolf, lifting its head, giving a shattering curse upon heaven itself, and she knew that the Scotsman had seen his daughter.

She looked up at a sound in the doorway and saw her maid, Jennie, a frightened and startled look upon her face as they both listened to the echoes of the cry.

"My God. We are haunted now by monsters!" Jennie whispered. "My lady . . ."

She ran across the room and greeted Igrainia with a fierce and trembling hug. "You did not make it away; the Scotsmen came. They are here, now, among us. They won't understand that we have done all we can. Mary was working in the dungeons, until she fell there, she lies among them still. Father MacKinley and I are all who walk now, even Garth fell ill, you know, yet survived, the boils did not come to him, he thinks he might have suffered a similar illness as a child. Berlinda in the kitchen fell ill in the scant time you were away. Sir Robert Neville stood upon the parapets watching you go . . . then took instantly to his bed. Oh, lord, this man will kill us, won't he, we might as well have all fallen to the plague! So few of us are left . . .''

Jennie was still in Igrainia's arms, shaking. Igrainia pulled away from her. Sir Eric's agony over his child would last some time, but then he would be back.

"Jennie, we must be strong. Tell me, first, who tends Sir Robert Neville?''

"I keep watch over him. Molly, Merry, John . . . Tom, the kitchen lad.''

"Where is Sir Neville?''

"In his chambers. We are doing all we can.''

"Why were the remaining prisoners ignored in the dungeons?''

Jennie stared at her, wide eyed. "How could we tend to more? We are all dying. And the smiths and merchants in residence in the courtyard . . . they all fight for their own lives. But what difference does it make now? We are all doomed.''

"This rebel doesn't know that the Earl of Pembroke ordered Sir Niles Mason to find what Bruce forces he could and bring them here for their fates to be decided. Nor does he realize that Sir Niles took his troops and left at the first sign of the disease!'' Igrainia said bitterly. "He thinks that Afton was responsible.''

"And he knows he would have been executed,'' Jennie said, her voice rising with fear. "Tied to a horse's heels, dragged over rocks and debris, hanged until half dead, cut to ribbons, castrated, and not beheaded until it was certain he could feel no pain!''

"Perhaps that wouldn't have been his fate.''

"It's the order Sir Niles said he had been given! I heard him, my lady, I heard him telling your husband what must be done. Afton argued that no executions should take place here, but Sir Niles was determined. He said that the rebel, Eric Graham, had fought far too long and too often against King Edward—first with William Wallace, and now, for Robert Bruce. He is a known outlaw, lady. He was to be an example. His wife was to be given to the troops. And as to his daughter . . . oh, Lord!'' She crossed herself quickly. ''Sir Niles thought it so amusing. The child was too young for much entertainment, but she was the spawn of a rebel and would grow to be a traitor, and if she was murdered, it would be best.''

''Afton would have never allowed the slaughter of a child.''

''Igrainia, Lord Afton had little rule over Sir Niles, not when his orders came from the Earl of Pembroke, who is following the direct command of King Edward! And Robert Bruce may have had himself crowned king of the Scots, but he hasn't taken hold of Scotland, certainly not here. King Edward's men hold almost everything in the lowlands, from the small farms and hamlets to the great castles. Igrainia, I swear, as well, that we have tended to the sick, to all of them, as Afton first said we must, then as we promised you, when Sir Robert insisted you flee. There are many alive who would not be if you hadn't had us tend them.''

''The fact that so many are alive seems to have little effect upon the wrath of this man. Perhaps he cannot see the truth now, but he must. For all of our people who remain alive, Jennie, and who may survive, we must do everything we can now for the prisoners.'' She felt her own voice rising slightly. The *prisoners!* Now, *they* were the prisoners. ''My chamber must be prepared. Clean sheets, fresh water. Fresh rushes. His wife will be cared for there. We must . . . we must keep her alive.''

''He will kill us, one way or the other.''

"Jennie!" Igrainia took her maid by the shoulders and shook her lightly. "He will not kill us while he needs us."

"But . . . your chamber. Where . . ." Her voice wavered and she gave up speaking.

"Where Afton died," Igrainia said softly. "It doesn't matter. He has said that she will be brought there. Jennie, we need to keep her alive."

"She is dying."

"She must not die."

Jennie seemed to understand then. She straightened, nodded to Igrainia, and hurried out. Igrainia turned her attention to Margot once again, trying to cool the woman and sorry once again that someone so gentle and kind, who had worked tirelessly among the others, had been stricken. But this pestilence had struck with ravaging cruelty, bypassing so very few of them. Years before, when she was in France, the village where she was staying, outside Paris had suffered a similar fate, and she and Jennie had nearly died then. She did not fall now because of that terrible time, she knew, yet this illness was so devastating she didn't know if it wouldn't sicken her in the end after all. When Afton had died, it hadn't seemed to matter.

There were herbs that would help bring down the ravaging fevers, sometimes, and there were broths that could be forced between the lips of the sick. But little done by man seemed to make a difference.

"The master chamber is prepared for my wife?"

He stood in the doorway, now as harsh and cold and pale as the ice sheets of the northern waters by winter. She might have felt a great pity for a man who had lost his child and let out such a terrible admission of pain in a single cry, but now . . . he was frightening in his steel control.

"Yes."

He walked across the room. Heedless of contagion himself, he lifted his wife with the utmost care and tenderness. "You will show me where to go," he said.

"But the others here—"

"Your priest will return. And my men are bringing the others from the wretched hell into which you have cast them."

"They were cared for, always, wherever they lay. It was my husband's order."

The scathing look he gave her did far more than infer that she was a liar. "Show me where we are going."

Igrainia did so, leading the way down the stairs and to the master's chamber. She was almost embarrassed by the richness of it as they entered, certain that the quality within was but something else that he would hold against her, Afton, and the household where his people had been brought. Langley Castle had first been built when the Conqueror had come north, and in those days, it had been stern rock and wall, loaded with weaponry, and manned to keep King William's borders against the wild tribal clansmen of Scotland safe. The Conqueror had spent his life proving his position against the Saxons of England as well, and therefore needed strongholds rather than royal residences. But over time, and in the days of King David I of Scotland, borders had changed, and intermittently, during the years, there had been times of friendship between the two countries. During the reign of Alexander, the castle had been given to the first Langley, and each succeeding lord had married well, until here, in the master's chamber, the walls were hung with the richest tapestries. Arabian rugs had been brought back from the Crusades to warm the floors, and a magnificently carved bed had been brought from France. Flemish lacework edged the sheets; pillows were made of softest down; and sleek furs scattered over the bed that stood before the great hearth. The room was furnished with trunks and a wardrobe from

France, marble-covered tables from Italy, and great shields upon the wall crossed with swords from Spain, Germany and the finest arms manufacturers in England.

He didn't notice the furnishings, only that the bed was vast and comfortable, a good place to lay his lady. When she was down, and he had smoothed the damp blond tendrils from her face, he stood back. "You will save her."

"I will do all that I can."

"You have killed my child."

Ice seemed to race along her spine. He spoke the words without malice or anger, merely as if they were a simple truth. "God, sir, has taken your child." She wanted to add that she was sorry, so very sorry, because his agony was such a terrible thing, almost palpable on the air.

But she dared not. He stared at her with red-rimmed eyes of loathing.

"You will keep Him from taking my wife," he said bitterly.

She thought he would leave the room, but he did not. He brought one of the heavy wooden chairs from the window to the bed and sat there, taking his wife's ashen hand in his own, and looking upon her face.

"She is as hot as fire."

"Then you must move so that I can cool her."

Jennie had left fresh cool water on the marble-topped table near the bed. Igrainia first set the kettle upon the hearth where a poor fire burned, then began dousing clothes in the water. When she turned back to the woman she found that he was frowning, his eyes blue blades again, so sharp as to cut into her.

"You've gone so far as to steal the rags of clothing from her back?"

"She is swaddled, sir, because the only way to ease the fever is to cool her skin from head to toe. I will brew herbs with wine as well, for some have the power to heal, as surely you know.''

''If you poison her, you will die very slowly. There are some interesting torture devices to be found in the foul dungeons below where we were kept.''

''There is no real threat you can give me. But since I pray that you don't set forth upon a bloodbath and murder the men and women who live in this castle, I can promise you, I have no intention of poisoning your wife. Nor sir, would I ever do such a thing. You malign my husband, who is now judged by God alone. If you were blessed with half the intelligence of your brute strength, sir, you would have realized that when you were brought in.''

She didn't look at him as she spoke, but gave her entire attention to the task at hand, bathing the woman to slake the fever.

As the day wore on, he saw what she did, and tried to help. When he realized her dismay at the poor flames in the hearth, he went to fetch wood, and when she dropped each herb into the mulling wine, she had to give him a detailed explanation of just what she used, and why.

During the long afternoon his men came to the door and gave him reports on what was being done to secure the castle or who had lived, and who had died. Father MacKinley came, and flagons were filled from the great kettle of mulling wine so that he could treat the others as well. Except to fetch wood and kindling for the fire when it was needed, the rebel Scot did not leave the room at all, and when he was not working to bring down his wife's fever, he sat by her side, holding her hand. What emotion he felt he did not display, other than in the ticking of a blood vessel at his throat, and in the tension in his muscled forearms, and the tightening of his hands.

"Have you suffered the fever yourself, ever?" she asked him once.

His cold Nordic blue eyes touched hers. "No."

"You are at great risk."

"We have been at great risk."

"From where had you come to bring this fever with you?"

He scowled at her, as if talking to her was an extreme bother, but he gave her a reply. "I don't know where this fever came from. We found a man at sea . . . his shipmates had apparently perished. We thought to save his life. Instead, he has taken all ours."

"Perhaps," she said, changing the cloth on the woman's forehead, "it was God's judgment."

"Perhaps it was God's judgment that the English should seize upon women and children and bring them here, and so kill many more English than Scots," he said sharply. "And what makes you think I honor your God?"

She started. "The God of England is the God of Scotland."

"But I am not entirely a Scotsman, lady. So don't think that I will stop at anything because of Christianity or a fear of Hell."

"I have no doubts that you would kill as brutally as any man alive."

"No man alive is more brutal than Edward of England."

That was difficult to argue. Not a man, woman, or child alive had not heard tales of the king's fury when he sacked Berwick. Orders had been given that none should be spared, and women, children and infants had been struck down as they ran in terror. Only the slaying of a mother at the moment of giving birth at last brought the king's own horror home to him, and only then did the carnage come to an end.

"Edward is merciless against those he considers to be traitors," she said.

"I am merciless against those I consider to be traitors—or murderers," he replied.

A knock sounded at the door and he went to answer the summons. A man he had called Patrick stood there, and spoke to him in quiet tones. A moment later, he closed the door and returned to the room, showing Igrainia a parchment.

"There lies the love of your king! It's an order delivered at the end of an arrow shot far from the gates, warning that we must not spread the plague from Langley. How intriguing. It seems that the troops who swept down upon women and children, refusing to believe in the illness, managed to depart your husband's castle at the first sign we were telling the truth. They have crossed the border, and are ordered to remain in an abbey there until they are certain they will not bring this contagion into England. It's a pity that none of the king's lackeys could have delivered it straight into Edward's bosom. The Earl of Pembroke, that illustrious battle arm of Edward, has sent word that none should leave here until all are certain that the illness will not be spread beyond these gates. There is lengthy rhetoric here, which you are welcome to read, but in truth, it says that all must die with the Scottish rebel prisoners rather than risk infesting the land. Of course, the message has been sent to your late husband. Apparently, no one has received word of his demise. But you must be grateful, of course, that I waylaid you before you were able to disobey an order from the long arm of your king."

"No reasonable man would want this plague spread. It came to Langley through your people. It is an enemy to you, and to me. Any ruler, mindful of his subjects, would give such an order."

"Madam, you are very understanding. What would your father think, however, knowing that his child must be sacrificed along with all the others!"

"My father, sir, cannot share his thoughts on the matter. He has been dead some months now."

"Ah! So the king can cast you to your fate with no fear of reparation among his greatest barons. Ah, but, surely, there is someone to claim the title now?"

"My brother."

"And, pray tell, does he fight for Edward?"

"He is expected to ride with him soon. He just turned seventeen."

"Just seventeen? Do you know how many young men of that age litter not just the battlefields here, but the farmsteads and villages as well?"

"Justin is an excellent horseman and swordsman. The king has taken a keen interest in his training, and has been intent that he should be fully prepared to command his elders."

"Oh, yes, of course. Poor lad. He is an earl. He can't be taking orders from lesser men. Yet I wonder if he is aware of what has occurred here, news can travel so slowly. And if he knew . . . what could he do? Orders have been given. So his dear sister must stay here . . . languishing among the doomed!"

"By the time my brother hears of the situation here, it will be over."

"And how shall it all end?" he asked lightly, and she realized that he didn't want an answer. He was watching his wife where she lay upon the bed. He leaned toward her, then told Igrainia tensely, "Her fever does not lessen."

"I am afraid she has fallen very ill."

"You know that you must save her."

"I know only that I can do my best."

"If she dies—"

"Aye, yes, I know, you will murder us all. Then you

must, for I can do all that is in my power, but I am not invested with magic."

Again, he did not seem to be paying any heed. His eyes were upon his wife, and though she loathed him, she felt an odd chill, wondering what great love he must have for this woman that he could think that anyone, any power, could fight death.

She was startled when he replied to her after several moments. "That is not what they say."

Igrainia stared at him, but his steady gaze remained upon his wife. He knew much more about Langley Castle, and about her, than she had imagined.

She measured her answer carefully. "If I were a witch, sir, with magic beyond that of healing herbs, I would have saved my own husband."

That brought his steady gaze to her at last, and he slowly arched a brow. "Madam, your marriage was arranged at your birth, and you have been lady here less than a year."

She felt the hot burning of her eyes, and she was furious. It was one thing that he should come here, fight her people, demand the castle, and mourn his child while demanding that she keep his wife alive. Force and power, even brute cruelty might be expected in war, and these were violent and dangerous times.

But that he should know her life, and mock her love for so fine a man, seemed an invasion that went beyond the power of a victor. She locked her jaw tightly, fighting tears before she replied. Then her anger infused her words with strength. "How dare you? How dare you suggest that . . . You did not know Afton. You could never know a man like Afton, never understand a man like Afton. The world to you is take and seize with your sword, with your violence. Fight with such fury that you will always win. There are those alive who can see the plight of others, men with minds as well as brawn, who will not practice cruelty because cruelty has been practiced against them. My husband was such a man, with both strength and gentleness, and had I been his wife but one day, sir, I would have loved him with a deeper passion, *admiration,* and *respect* than you could ever *begin* to understand.''

His gaze remained on her and she waited for—expected— mocking words in return. But after a moment he turned to his wife. "Then I am sorry for your loss. But still, this is— was—your husband's holding. And it was he, surely, who ordered that prisoners, dying and in pain, be kept in the dank bowels of a castle, there the quicker to die.''

"It was not Afton! The king's men came—''

"A lord need not bend a knee so low, even to a king.''

"You fight and bow to yours.''

"I choose to stand behind mine. He does not cross the lines of right and wrong—those lines drawn by *your* God, my lady.''

"How wondrous—when it is said that he did away with the last man to compete with him for the throne by doing a murder.''

He twisted where he sat, staring at her coldly, but not denying the charge. "Many men have betrayed one another in this struggle. But the die is cast now, and Bruce is king. King of Scotland. None of this is important now. My wife is.''

She walked to the bed, standing at his side, trying very hard not to tremble. "I have done what was in my power for your lady, for your people. I will fight to save her life. Not because you will kill me—or even others—if I don't. But because your are mistaken when you think that my lord husband did not know compassion, and what was right, and wrong, in the eyes of God. And humanity.''

"Perhaps you should give your speech about humanity to Edward of England."

"As you have said, kings are not important here, this lady is. Speak no more about my husband, if you would have me tend your wife—with you in the room."

He stood, coming to his full height and size, which sent her back a step.

His fingers bit into her shoulder, but stopped short of inflicting real pain.

"She *must* live!" he said, and in his words she at last sensed his desperation, and the weakness within the man.

"I swear to you that I will try."

He released her, and took his chair again, and in a few minutes' time, she had him hold his wife so that she could do her best to get some of the healing brew of wine and herbs between the lips of his beloved Margot.

Again, then, she began the bathing with cold cloths.

An hour later, it seemed that Margot's fever had cooled somewhat. Father MacKinley came to the room and told Igrainia that she must rest. She shook her head firmly before the Scotsman could reply to him. "I am fine for now, Father."

"Sir, I would speak with you for a moment, if you would allow me," Father MacKinley said to Eric.

The Scotsman rose and went to the door with the priest. Igrainia kept vigil at the woman's side, praying.

She was startled when Eric called her sharply. "Madam, the priest has need of you for a moment's time."

Arching a brow, Igrainia rose from the bedside and walked to where Father MacKinley stood.

"I will return her immediately," the priest vowed.

The man nodded, turning back to his wife.

Still amazed, Igrainia followed the priest into the hall. "Where are we going?"

"Sir Robert Neville tosses in a fever, but he has asked to see you. It may well be a last request, and so Sir Eric has said you may have a minute."

They hurried down the hall to Robert's chamber. Igrainia swept in, alarmed to see how seriously ill Robert had grown in such a short time. She immediately took the water by the bed and began bathing his face. Robert was a handsome man, her husband's second cousin. He was gifted with sable brown hair and deep, haunting eyes. His features were very fine, as Afton's had been, and usually, when he stood, he was lean and straight, and he both rode and fought with courage and skill.

Now his face was pale, and his eyes seemed like stygian pools. He caught her hand as she cooled his face.

"Igrainia!"

"Robert, rest."

"You're alive, safe . . ."

"Aye, Robert. I'm well."

"They have the castle. The outlaws, the barbarians . . . you must find a way to leave."

"Aye, Robert, don't worry." She glanced at Father MacKinley; they both knew she'd be forgiven any lie. "Don't worry. I will get away. They pay little heed to me."

He almost seemed to have forgotten her.

"It should have been mine now. It shouldn't have fallen . . . to this. To them. King Edward should have bestowed the castle on me. Now . . . it is death, they are death. You mustn't worry. I was Afton's kinsman, I will take the castle again, I will see that you are safe . . . that you are safe with me."

"Aye, Robert, don't worry. You must save your strength. I'm brewing herbs in warm wine, and you will drink it and sleep and fight this illness. We'll survive, we'll both survive, and the castle will be ours again."

He still held her hand, but he had no power. She slipped free from his grasp, slipping his arm back beneath the sheets. When she looked up, she saw that Eric Graham had come to the door and was watching her. She didn't know what he had heard.

"You must come," he said simply.

She nodded. Robert Neville's eyes had closed; he wasn't dead, she saw with relief, only sleeping. She hurried to the Scotsman, and walked back across the hall again.

Margot was tossing again, burning with heat. Igrainia immediately began bathing her with cool cloths, harnessing the rampaging fever.

Eric imitated her every action. At last, the fever somewhat abated. It appeared that Margot slept in some peace once again.

The Scotsman continued to pace, then paused by the mantel at last, staring into the fire.

Igrainia sank into the chair by her bedside, watching Margot.

She kept that vigil through the night.

When morning came, she stretched, having fallen into a doze in the chair. The woman still breathed.

The Scotsman was still standing by the fire. She doubted that he had taken a minute's sleep, all through the night.

Igrainia touched Margot's lips gently, then rose and told Eric, "She is still with us. I need more kindling for the fire. And now, we must get some more plain, cool water past her lips. If you would help me here . . . please."

He turned away from the mantel where he had leaned. His color had gone from the ruddy glow of health to the pale ash of illness.

"Tell me what I must do."

His voice rasped. It seemed he would walk to her, but could not manage to make his legs move.

Igrainia gasped, staring at him, then walked instinctively his way.

"You are about to—"

Even as she neared him, the great power of the man gave way, and his imperious length of muscle, sinew and strength went crashing to the floor.

She came to a halt, wincing.

Then she froze, waiting to see if he would move.

He did not.

She came to her knees at his side. His eyes were closed. They opened briefly, a deep, dark blue. He moved his lips to speak but no sound came. He reached out. His long fingers fell short of touching her face. His eyes closed once again.

Igrainia hesitated, then laid her fingers against the ashen flesh of his face.

His flesh burned with a heat like the fires of hell.

He wielded no power over any man then.

CHAPTER 3

He could hear his wife's voice.

Her tone crystalline and soft, a whisper that came to him, brushing his ear. She moved about him, telling him that he must drink, sip cool water. He seemed to live the days when the sea breezes were strong against him and the world was shaded in the blue of the sky and the kiss of the cool air. Then there was darkness. He would waken, and think again that she was near, and that he could feel the silken brush of her hair against his flesh.

There were times when he knew that his wife was dead. No woman, no witch, no healer, could have brought her back, just as his babe was gone. His child, who had been everything tender and sweet in a world of steel and blood. She had been a shimmering ray of innocence, so small. She came to him in his dreams, fingers curled in those of her mother, and they walked to him together, beckoning, and he would follow. He heard his daughter's melodic laughter, and the music of Margot's voice as she so gently chastised and taught. There had been such wonder in holding Aileen when she came into the world, his hands so big and calloused against the purity of her flesh. He seemed to live again the time when he shook, holding her, and heard Margot's voice. "You would have liked a son."

"One day, not now; she is beautiful beyond measure, she is . . . mine. My flesh, my blood, so beautiful . . . so tiny!"

"That is how they come into the world, my lord. She is not so tiny for a babe; she merely seems so to you."

"She'll be tall, as you are."

"Light, dear husband, as we both are."

"Her eyes . . . they are the sky."

"She will be beautiful," Margot agreed a bit unwillingly, for part of her own charm was an amazing humility, and she would never have a child grow into the world with too great a sense of pride. "And you will think her far too good for any man when she comes of age to marry."

"I will keep them all away. Especially . . . well, men like me," he admitted, and his own words were humble then, because she had loved him with such loyalty and for so many years before he had made her his wife. Yet once they had married he had realized, in the midst of a world filled with never-ending warfare and bloodshed, that she was a beacon of life. Few men found a life's companion to love with such passion and strength.

And still, she stood before him now, fingers touching him, cooling his brow. Yet even so . . . her image wavered. Again, he knew that she was gone. With their child. He opened his eyes. Darkness hovered over him. The hair that brushed his flesh was not the color of the sun on a summer's day, wheat reflected with a glow of light, gold shimmering against the day.

Black. There was a black-haired witch hovering over him.

He wanted to move an arm to push her away. He could not. He stared at her, then again, his eyes closed, and it seemed the world burned around him, fires blazing through a forest.

He moved his lips.

"Witch."

"You mustn't push me away. The cold cloths must stay on your head."

"Darkness . . . witch."

"If you keep pushing me away, you will die."

Death would be easy, he thought. He could reach out for Margot, for the faded image in his dreams, take her hand. Fade with her, and their little daughter, from the world.

"My wife . . ."

"Lie still."

"She is . . . gone . . . I know."

The black-haired serpent did not answer him.

Aye, Margot was gone.

He managed to catch hold of the woman, his fingers curling around her wrist. "My wife, like my child, is dead."

She drew away. He hadn't the strength to hold her.

"You should let him die!" someone whispered.

"We cannot *let* any man die. That we will all eventually pass from our lives on earth is certain, but whether we are so evil as to spend eternity in Hell has yet to be determined," came a dry and sardonic reply. "We can't let any man die."

"He is why we are all dying!"

"I don't believe the Scots asked to be captured and dragged in for humiliation and execution without trial."

"There, you have said it! He was to be *executed*!"

"But not by my judgment!"

"You would save him at great risk for the king to order his execution!"

"I say again, we cannot simply let any man die—"

"He is not a man. He is a monster. A follower of the

treacherous betrayer, Bruce. Their king would be king by
murdering his enemies! He was intended for death. And he
is dangerous—alive. You waste your time. He will live and
kill us all.''

They were gone then.

Perhaps to let him die.

He determined then that he would live.

In the week that followed, it seemed that the closed com-
munity of stricken and ill—the English, the Scottish who
were still loyal to Edward and against the coronation of
Robert Bruce, and the Scottish patriots—worked together
in pleasant harmony. For once, they were all fighting a
common enemy, one with no face except for that of the
threat of death.

There was a great discussion between Igrainia and Father
MacKinley regarding the bodies of the wife and child of the
Scotsman. For the woman had died within a day of her
husband falling ill, and the child's body, ravaged by the
illness, had set quickly into decay. They should have been
burned on one of the large pyres set each day just beyond
the courtyard walls. But since the man himself rallied and
lingered, they were fearful of his wrath should he live.

Igrainia couldn't help but think that Jennie was right;
orders had been given by the king of England that any man
loyal to the treacherous Bruce should be executed without
trial. They weren't even required to carry out any manner
of death to rid themselves of the threat of his presence; they
had only to let him die. But when the illness had become
apparent at Langley—and the king's contingent had fled—
Afton had ordered that all the prisoners must be treated in a
Christian manner. But the illness had taken flight throughout
Langley like a flock of birds in winter, and some had been

taken to the solar. Afton's death had been the most shattering blow, and even after his body had been walled into the crypt, Igrainia had not wanted to leave, but it had been Afton's wish, as he had lain dying, that she would do so. There was the possibility that she was carrying a child, and so she must take the greatest care of herself.

Sir Robert Neville still lay ill, but Igrainia saw that his fever had broken, and though he still lay weak and spent upon his bed, he seemed to rally more each day.

As did the rebel Scotsman.

Father MacKinley never fell prey to the sickness, but administered daily to the ill, the dying, and the dead. Those who had been prisoners received proper prayers and rites, that their souls might sweep to Heaven amidst the smoke that rose above the inferno of their earthly remains. But they were all afraid. Even Father MacKinley was afraid. And so, in the end, it was decided that the bodies of the Scottish rebel's wife and child would be interred in the wall of the crypt near Igrainia's late husband.

Ten days after the rebel had fallen ill, she stood upon the parapets with Father MacKinley and discussed what must be done. The rebel would live, so it seemed, and Sir Robert was doing well. No one else had fallen ill. The survivors, and those not stricken, had worked together long and well. Perhaps it was not so difficult a picture to see, for Langley stood in what had been known now for a long time as the Borders, an area ravaged by the struggle for power between the Scots and the English, or the various factions of the Scots loyal to the king of England, and those who supported Bruce. The murder of John Comyn had created a rift within Scotland itself; as the Bruces had not supported John Balliol as king, there were many who did not accept Robert Bruce's claim to the throne. Some were superstitious, believing that the reign of a king begun with a murder could not ever bring peace and prosperity to a kingdom. There were simply those, as always, who had lands in both Scotland and England, and their estates in England, held under Edward I, were worth far more than their lands in Scotland, and so their loyalties varied on an almost daily basis.

"We have to think of what is best for those of us here, now," Father MacKinley told Igrainia. "We are in a precarious position here. Again and again, by both sides, these lands are sacked and ravaged. There are many things to consider, especially in regard to the man we have saved from death, wise or not, I don't know. We have done right for our immortal souls, but as to our days here on earth . . . well. The Norse rule many of our neighboring islands, and this man has lineage back to powerful jarls, as well as the love of the man to whom he is loyal, Robert Bruce, who has been crowned king of Scotland. Langley, though Border land, is claimed by both kings. The lowlands fall prey to Edward every time; Bruce hasn't the strength as yet to hold what he would claim by word. Some here will be loyal to Bruce; most are afraid of the English; they have been beaten down far too many times. Robert Bruce has been forced to fight his battle from the forest, striking out at Edward's men when his spies let him know where they are, and when he can strike and run. But it is likely that word was sent to him when Eric Graham rode here to seize you and make his way into the castle. It is a stronghold. Perhaps he has a contingent of men he can send here, because in his quest to find Bruce, Edward will not have men to lay siege here, and Langley, though a house of death now, is a powerful fortification when manned and armed. I have spent hours of prayer on this matter. You are a pawn here for Eric Graham. You must escape before he is well, and can use you as such."

"I am afraid that if I leave, he will punish the people here," Igrainia said.

Father MacKinley shook his head slowly. He was a man she admired and liked very much. He was tall, graceful in movement, and serious in almost all matters. Born in Ireland, he had served his God in Italy, France, England and Spain before coming to them at Langley. He believed deeply that the soul of a man was far more important than his time on earth, but his compassion ran deep, as did his belief that the nobility of any land, honored by their people, were equally responsible to those people for their livelihood and welfare. As God was the great King of Heaven and all men his flock, the nobles ruled on earth, and their tenants were as their sheep, and must be guarded and tended. Murder was wrong by any measure, and he seemed to have little loyalty to Edward I as he practiced so much slaughter and wanton cruelty in his determination to crush Scotland, but equally, he was not certain of Robert Bruce, though he had been known to say that Bruce fought for his own land while Edward fought to take that of others.

"This man will not take vengeance on the people here," Father MacKinley said.

"He has said that he would kill everyone, if his wife died. She is gone, Father, and it was through no lack of effort on our part."

"He knows this. Even now, weak, spent and incoherent, he knows this."

"We're taking a chance."

"The only chance we take is with you."

"He would kill me, and spare the others?"

Father MacKinley shook his head. "You are of no use dead."

"Then I should stay."

"Then you must not. Igrainia, you must go back to your brother. You had something fine here with Lord Afton. Marriage, as surely you are aware, is not often so sweet. Go home to your brother, let him guard you, live in the estates outside London where every day is not plagued by war and death. Perhaps one day you will marry again.''

''No.''

''You will be expected to marry again, and with your brother as your guardian, you will have a choice. You don't see it now, but there can be happiness in your future. You mustn't stay here. This man could do many things. Imprison you in misery. Barter with the powers in England for your life. For your safety, your honor—your mind!—you must be away from here. What can be done to a noblewoman held prisoner can be far worse than death. Look what King Edward has done to the women of the Scots.''

Igrainia thought with unease of how Robert Bruce's sister, Mary, and the young Countess of Buchan, who had rushed to Robert Bruce's coronation, had been punished by the king; caged outside the castle walls of Berwick and Roxburgh, as if they were rare animals on display. Day after day they spent in their wooden prisons. The same punishment had first been ordered for Bruce's twelve-year-old daughter, Marjorie, but thankfully, enough men around the king thought that such a sentence upon a child was too savage, and so the girl had been sent to a monastery. The Bruce's wife, daughter of an English earl, was kept in strict captivity in the manor of Burstwick-in-Holderness.

Igrainia's own father had been an earl; her brother was an earl. But he was young and did not hold the kind of power yet that swayed kings. If she was captured by the Scots and made into an example of their retaliation, she could face dire consequences indeed.

''What if you're wrong?'' she asked softly. ''What if I am gone, and in his fury, he executes even you.''

''Few churchmen have met an axe, even in the vengeance and brutality of what has gone by.''

"The others . . ."

"He has not killed the men in your escort who surrendered to him."

"He has lain ill and unconscious most of the time he has been here."

Father MacKinley shook his head. "He gave orders before he sat with his wife that none were to be killed unless they refused to yield. Death has stricken Langley hard enough. He does not take pleasure in bloodshed, as do some. Igrainia, it is you I fear for. I beg of you, leave here."

"How can I do so? We can muster no escort, and even most of the women are ill. I cannot take Jennie, not when she is still so important here. And I cannot go with Sir Robert Neville who is still so ill, yet must be taken quickly from here. He is my husband's kinsman and surely in great danger among the Scots."

Father MacKinley looked at her a moment and then smiled slowly. "No, you cannot go with Sir Robert, for precisely those reasons. And you mustn't fear for him. Sir Robert has already been taken south. He and his squire slipped out this morning through the tunnel at the end of the crypt."

Igrainia gasped. "I wasn't even informed!"

"I thought it best to make his escape at the first moment I could, and not because I didn't trust your judgment or want your counsel. The opportunity arose this morning and I had to take it. The outlaw Scots were busy in the courtyard, except for the man guarding Eric Graham and the door to the master's chamber. No one knows that he has gone, as yet. And we must get you away in the same fashion. We cannot have the gates open, the drawbridge dropped. Soon, as soon as you can make a hasty preparation. You will go as a poor woman, seeking peace and prayer on a pilgrimage to shrines in the south. I beg of you, Igrainia. I have prayed on this matter myself. The rest of the people here will fare well. You might be of value to the Scots, and therefore, a value for them to keep in jeopardy. I have honestly pondered this long and hard as I prayed. I know that you must go. And I hope that God has given me his wisdom.''

In the first days when the fever broke, Eric was too weak to do more than lie in his bed, and listen.

He listened carefully.

Though his limbs seemed worn and painful, it was the pain of knowing all that he had lost which was the worst. His child, his wife. There were times when it did not seem worth the effort to live, to gain strength again.

But with the death of love came the birth of an idea, a fierce preoccupation. He would regain his strength and rise from the bed, for a long fight remained ahead. He would rise, because he would win.

Before they could realize that he had regained his strength, he would do so. He knew that many of his men had failed to fall to the disease because they came to the sickroom; indeed one of his own followers was in a chair at all times. The priest came and went. Women from the castle served him, but they were watched. He knew the one voice that whispered often with the others; the voice of the servant who had said they must let him die. He was grateful that he rode with so many who were wary, and careful, lest his enemies slip poison into the brews they gave him to bring him back to strength.

He knew so much, because he lay there carefully, eyes closed.

And listened.

He had lain abed more than two weeks. Margot had died the day he had fallen.

Sir Robert Neville, stricken kin of the late lord of Langley, had been spirited away by the priest who was not afraid.

And the lady of Langley was gone as well.

He understood the mind of the young priest, and he admired him, as he admired the fact that the man himself did not run. He wondered if he had been saved because of the man's reverence to God, or because his men remained in the castle and might slaughter everyone if he were to die, and they were left without direction. He thought, though, that the priest had judged them, and knew that they would not wantonly kill.

Then, again, there was the fact that Langley had long stood as a bastion in the borderlands, and loyalties here had wavered frequently. The late lord had been a product of both England and Scotland. His mother had been Celtic to the core, and in the past, it had been as if Langley stood apart. The great gates and drawbridge had been lowered at the command of those serving the king, but Pembroke's army had not been far away, and if the wrath of that army had been turned from the pursuit of Robert Bruce to the total subjugation of Langley, the castle and its people would have most likely suffered a bitter defeat. Sad though it might be, the people in the lowlands had good reason to bow before Edward of England before bending a knee to Robert Bruce.

He lay in the master chamber, in the same bed where Margot had lain. And often, the pain of her loss and his innocent sweet child Aileen lay on his heart so heavily that not even his anger, grief and hatred could stir him. But there were moments when he was alone in the room, and remembered his vow to himself that he would live. And in those moments, he began to move. To work his muscles. The priest sometimes came to watch over him, but he had passed the stage of death, and there were those who needed the priest's ministrations so much more. His men, he knew, guarded the door, and came in with the maidservants when they tended to him. But as the days passed, he began to have hours alone, and in those hours, he began to work his weakened muscles. His hands first, because in the days following the worst of the fevers and the nightmares and the dreams and illusions, not even his fingers wanted to bend at the command of his mind. Bit by bit, he struggled to create a grip, then to raise his arms, to sit up, and then to stand, and finally to walk. He forced himself to eat, for he knew that he had to do so, and he knew, as well, that his own people watched over the kitchen. He kept to the bed until he had gained a certain sense of power, then he rose, and called to Peter MacDonald to help him; he needed water, a long bath in hot, soothing water. In all the days when he had tossed and turned, he had known that he still bore remnants of the blood and mud of battle, and the sweat of sickness. He was eager to feel clean again.

As he bathed, he listened gravely to Peter, who was at a loss to know how either Robert Neville, who had been abed, scarcely able to move, and the lady—well enough, but certainly within the gates at all times—had managed to leave.

"None will speak," Peter told him.

Eric nodded.

"There is obviously a way out through the castle. And, therefore, a way in. I will discover what it is."

"But have you the strength to force out of them what you need to know?" Peter asked him. He wasn't an old man, but his features were weathered, lined and creased. Like Eric, he was a natural sailor, brought to shore, and a learned warrior.

There had been no other choice for them.

"Today, I will let them know that this castle will be kept

in the name of the Bruce. And that we will discover their secrets. But soon, very soon . . .''

''Soon . . . ?''

''We will begin to even the score in this deadly tournament,'' Eric said softly.

When he was done bathing, he donned a linen chemise and breeches belonging to the past master of the castle, found his boots, and made his way down the stairs. He drew out a chair at the head of the great long table in the hall, lifted a booted foot upon the table, startling the poor old steward of the castle into something like apoplexy.

''Yes, I am alive and well,'' Eric said. ''And very hungry for good bread and meat. Are there such luxuries to be had?''

The old fellow nodded dumbly and started to turn.

''Wait. What is your name?''

''Garth, my lord.''

''Well, Garth, it is good to see you moving, in far better circumstance than that in which we found you here.''

''And you, sir, have apparently weathered the illness as well.''

''I have. Most regretfully, I'm certain, to your number.''

The old man shrugged. ''It has made little difference here. Kings and nobles make war. Men such as I merely serve until we die.''

''Not true, Garth. The common man of Scotland is the soldier who will make her free.''

''The common man of Scotland is the one who dies, butchered by the armies, starved out by either side.''

''Langley stood unaffected for many years.''

''Langley could only fall from within.''

Eric arched a brow without replying for a moment. Aye, it was true. Without huge war machines and a massive army moving against it, this castle could not fall.

Except from within. And if there was a way for men and women to escape the walls, there was a way for traitors to slip inside as well.

"God's judgment," Eric said after a moment to Garth. "Had we not been imprisoned for the purposes of torture and demise, this death would not have come to Langley. Some might call that God's judgment."

"And some," came a voice from the doorway, "might call it the idiocy of a few stupid men with enough arms to force their way."

Eric grinned, seeing the priest at the entry to the great hall. "Welcome, Father MacKinley. I was about to send for you."

"You're looking extremely well."

"Yes. The sickness is gone."

"Is it?" the priest asked. "I have a feeling that an illness far worse festers within your soul."

"My soul is of little interest to me at the moment, if you will forgive me, Father."

"Whether I forgive you or not—"

"Let's not get into a philosophical discussion, Father, on my soul. There are other matters to be discussed. First, Garth, I am very hungry."

"Aye, sir."

He turned to leave.

"Garth."

The man paused, looking back. He was wary, but also worn.

"I have no real liking for bloodshed and death. But if I—or any of my men—are poisoned here, the retaliation upon those here will be swift and any who die at your hands will wish that they had been taken by the plague. You understand that."

"Aye, my lord. That was made quite clear at the beginning of your illness by your man, MacDonald."

Eric smiled. Thank God for Peter MacDonald. His right hand. Because of Peter, and this priest, he had lived. When he should have died. When he would have gladly died. He dared not think too long on that fact. Dark clouds seemed to fog his vision when he did so, and the dull pain would begin to thud again, and he wanted to rage, and tear the place apart stone by stone, though nothing would bring back Margot and his daughter.

"Good. Bring food. Father MacKinley, sit."

Garth left the hall, hurrying to bring food as bidden. As bidden, Father MacKinley sat, his eyes wary.

"So, Father, tell me about the state of affairs."

"The state of affairs?" MacKinley said. "War, I believe. It has been war here, as long as I remember."

"Ah, yes, it's a way of life, isn't it? Here, Father, you know exactly what I am asking you."

"I'm sure that you know everything that is going on, and that your man, MacDonald, has brought you up to date."

"Yes, but I would like to hear your assessment of the current situation at the castle."

"People have stopped dying. Most of the poor deceased have been burned in great heaps just beyond the walls."

"Most of the dead."

"Your wife and child are buried in the wall with the late Lord Afton."

Eric stared down at his hands for a moment. "There will be masses said," he murmured quietly.

"There have been masses said. All men are equal before God."

Eric allowed his mouth to curl just slightly. MacKinley was either a fool or a very brave man.

"Where is your mistress?"

MacKinley stiffened at Eric's evenly voiced question.

"Gone."

"That's evident. Gone where?"

"Back to her brother."

"The young widow, returned to England to be a pawn in another advantageous marriage."

"Gone back to the love and care of her family."

"When did she leave?"

"I don't remember—"

"When?"

"Several days ago."

"How many?"

"Perhaps five . . . or six."

"Ah. So she cannot have gotten far."

"She has been gone many days. It would be folly to pursue her."

"But she has gone on foot."

The priest frowned, and Eric knew he was right.

"How—"

"She departed through a secret tunnel, certainly, or my men would have known. So, at the least, she started out by foot. I think I will be able to find her."

"She was not responsible for the death here. She saved your life."

"I survived. She is not capable of saving lives. My wife is dead."

"She is not a magician."

"She has the reputation of a healer."

"But no man can work miracles."

"I repeat, my wife is dead. And my babe. A child as innocent of evil as any soul could be."

"But what matters here—"

"Nothing else matters. My wife and child are dead."

"But you have survived," MacKinley said, leaning forward in sudden passion. "God willed that you should survive, and so you should be on your knees in gratitude, and let go the innocent woman who aided you in that survival. Thank God, and embrace life, and the world will again begin to hold substance, there will be a reason to live, you will find a reason to live—"

"Father, you needn't speak so passionately, as if I were a lost member of your flock," Eric said dryly. "There is a reason to live. Scotland."

"A man must have more to live for, sir, than bloodshed and battle. You have lost much, but gained much. You hold this castle, and your man, Bruce, is king. Therefore—"

"Oh, he is king. But he does not hold Scotland. Where was the lady going?"

MacKinley frowned "I haven't lied to you in any way. I have told you; Lady Igrainia is on her way to her brother, the young earl."

"But there was no party to escort her; I have been abed and ill a long time, but I am aware of what goes on here. My small party of men hold the workings of the castle. Some of the poor men drawn to arms in the name of Edward of England have readily changed sides. They might as readily change back, but . . . not while we hold the power. Few of the workers and craftsmen who have survived care much who holds the castle, as long as they may live and work and continue surviving. Anyone loyal to the king of England languishes in the dungeons below where the rot of death must still permeate the stone. There was no way for you to provide an escort for the lady of the castle. Therefore, she is traveling alone, or with a maid or manservant, no more. And even on the border of England, she wouldn't dare let her true identity be known. She would be far too rich a prey for even a loyal English outlaw to overlook. So . . . She has donned some poor woolen cloak, and gone out on the road as a poor pilgrim. Am I correct?''

MacKinley didn't need to answer. His cheeks were flushed.

"You must leave her be. She is not guilty of any harm."

Eric felt a rising fury within him. "She was the wife of Afton of Langley. Langley played host to the king's men sent to murder Scottish nationalists and imprison, humiliate and torment their wives. She is as guilty as original sin, Father."

"You're wrong. You must not harm her . . . you must not . . ."

Eric cast the priest a look of total disdain. "I have no interest in your lady witch, priest. But she has a value to the cause of Scotland. You know what has befallen certain noblewomen of our country, Father. Word has gone out faster than the wind."

Garth came into the room carrying a large tray. A fresh haunch of venison lay on the tray with a loaf of bread and a ewer of ale.

Eric watched Garth as he delivered the food. "Garth of Langley, you've long been in service here. Sit and join us."

"There is no poison in the meat," Father MacKinley said. "We did not save your life to end it with poison."

"Nevertheless, you will both oblige me by dining first."

Father MacKinley kept his eyes full upon Eric's as he knifed a large section from the meat and chewed it down, then broke off bread, and did the same. Eric brought his gaze upon Garth, who also took meat and bread.

"The ale," Eric suggested.

Both men drank.

Eric then set upon the meal, suddenly ravenous, yet aware that he had to take care with meat so rich when he had been ill so long. It was hard not to wolf down every last bite. When he had finished, he realized both men were still watching him in silence.

He sat back. "You are both free to leave the castle, if you wish."

Neither man replied.

"Did you hear me? You are free to travel south, to safer ground."

"Where would I go?" Garth asked him. "I have worked here all my life."

"These people are my . . . they are my flock," MacKinley said. "And I would keep the peace between them, and you."

"You must keep the peace between them—and Peter MacDonald."

"You're leaving?"

"Aye."

"Joining the Bruce to fight on?" The priest said hopefully.

"You know that I am not. Aye, I'm leaving, but I won't be joining the Bruce—not just yet. I was sent out to solicit men for his battles, and thus was at sea where we found the man who inflicted us all with this rampaging disease. I meant to return to the king with more men at arms. And we will soon have help from many Irish chieftains. But for ourselves . . . now . . . we've lost so many. But, still, I believe that I will bring Robert Bruce a political and powerful prize, nevertheless."

"You don't mean . . ."

"The Lady of Langley? The very wealthy daughter of the late Earl of Wheaten? Aye, she is the exact prize I do mean."

"You will give her over—to Robert Bruce?"

"Indeed."

"But—but—she is long gone. You will never find her."

Eric rose and came to the priest, staring down at him. "Oh, but I will. You have told me that I will find something to live for. I have found it, Father. I am living for two things, and two things only. Scotland—and revenge. Trust me, Father, I never lie. I intend to find her. And I will.''

"But . . . then . . .''

"Then the lady will pay the price of war," he said simply. He left the great hall then with long strides.

He made his way up the staircase as if he were in complete power and control. Peter waited at the door to the master's chamber. He opened it quickly.

He managed to enter the chamber before he sagged. Peter helped him to the bed. He gripped Peter's shoulders tightly.

"They can't know that I haven't my full strength."

"They will not," Peter assured him. "But I should go after the lady of Langley. You haven't the strength yet—"

"Your strength is needed here, Peter. The castle is not secure, and it must be held against the English.''

"But, can you ride?''

"Aye, Peter. In just a few days time. Every hour now, I feel my strength returning. I need food, and aye, just a little more rest. Then I will be ready. And I will ride, and I *will* find her, and I will bring her back.''

CHAPTER 4

Igrainia traveled in a far different way from that to which she had become accustomed.

The first time she had come to the Borders, she had ridden with her father, his knights, their squires, and a dozen attendants. The knights had been beautiful in their glistening plate, mail, and her father's colors of red, black and yellow. The horses had been equally resplendent. She had been attended by Jennie and two other maids, and if they had tired, they had wagons in which to rest. They had stayed at castles and manors along the way, been greeted with enthusiasm, feasts, warm wine and rich comforts. When she had later traveled with Afton, they had always left with the same entourage, and been welcomed in fine homes along the way. She rode Menfreya, her beautiful, smooth-gaited, fast-paced mare. Naturally, there were hardships along the way. Rain, snow, sleet, wind and the mud that seemed a never-ending feature of the roads. Sometimes, in summer, there was the heat of the sun, but she loved the sun, and it always seemed to be tempered by a moist whisper of coolness in the air. She had always loved to travel, to see new places, meet new people. Naturally, it had always held an element of danger, but she had never ventured out far without an armed guard.

This was quite different.

She had slipped from the castle with John Simpson and his wife, Merry. They had both worked in the kitchen at Langley Castle as long as they could remember. They had been married as long as they could remember as well, and though they had not been blessed with children, they had maintained what Igrainia knew to be a very special love for one another. Both were old now. John was tall and rail thin, while Merry was short and round as a little ball, with bright blue eyes and silver gray hair. In the worst of circumstances, she was able to find a smile, and remark that anything bad was God's will, and man could only wonder why until the great day came when the gates to Heaven admitted them all. She was a wonderful companion, as was John, who liked to talk about the Scotland of Alexander's day, and describe how good it had been when the land had been at peace.

The difficulties lay not in her fellow ''pilgrims'' for the journey, but in the journey itself.

Of necessity, they left the castle on foot. Father MacKinley had given them directions to reach a tiny parish church just north of the ever-disputed border, and there, from an old friend of his, they were to obtain horses. Their journey on foot took well over two weeks, for though John could walk fairly swiftly with his long, skinny legs, Merry huffed and puffed and they were forced frequently to stop. They'd had to carry some provisions, and the provisions grew heavier with every footstep over the rocky terrain. At night, they slept upon their rolled woolen blankets on the ground, which wasn't much of a hardship for Igrainia—she loved the feeling of being minute in a world of a million stars and darkness—but for Merry the ground was hard, and for John as well, and they both woke each morning with a moan and a creaking and cracking of knee joints and elbows, and limped for a few minutes as they tried to get the crinkles out of their backs. They dared not light fires, lest they should be seen by marauding troops of outlaws, and so they ate berries they found along the way, and dined carefully on the bread and cheese they carried. Water was abundant, because the land was filled with beautiful little lochs, ponds and streams. The weather was extremely mild, and sometimes, at night, Igrainia would strip down to her shift and dare the chilly yet inviting waters of a stream to indulge in the longest bath she dare before her limbs began to turn blue.

They traveled carefully, and for many days, by keeping to the forest paths indicated by Father MacKinley. They walked as if the world belonged to them alone, and it was a beautiful world, with the land rich in the green and pastels of summer, sloping in the sun, falling to shadow in the denseness of the forest. They did, upon one occasion, pass by what had once been a small village, a thriving farm, and saw that the buildings remained burned and ghostly, the fields barren, the burnt out remnants of paddocks and stables nothing but eerie, skeletal chars. But the land had a way of replenishing quickly; the grass came each year where warhorses had trampled it just months before, and wild flowers grew in profusion. Even here, the grass was beginning to grow, and wild flowers—weeds perhaps, but colorful and tenacious—circled the ruins, and would, in time, cover the violence of the past.

They did, at last, arrive at the little village where Father MacKinley's friend, Father Padraic, came from his small church as children ran ahead to tell him visitors were coming.

Igrainia remained silent as John introduced them as a family on a pilgrimage, with letters asking for his help in acquiring mounts for them, and sending them on their way. In her drab gray, hooded wool cloak, Igrainia wondered what evil this gentle man would offer her if he knew the truth of who she was. Father Padraic, very old, with long white hair and beard that seemed to stream as one on his shoulders and chest, eyed her with a deep, dark, reflective gaze. She was certain he knew that she was a young woman of a certain wealth, fleeing to the south.

He said nothing regarding his thoughts, though, but set about welcoming them to the village, and telling them he would find comfortable lodging for them in the cloisters of the old nunnery. There were other pilgrims stopping by, for this was a known stop on the way to the many places of prayer and salvation to be found in England. The language most frequently spoken here was the French used at court, or the English of the Saxons, though the Gaelic of the Celts was known as well.

"Father MacKinley has asked that I provide you with mounts," Father Padraic said, reading the rolled scroll MacKinley had sent in John's care. He studied them again, dark eyes upon Igrainia. "I will do the best I can. Meanwhile, take your ease in our parish home, a poor place by many standards, but a wayside for faithful travelers. Gregory!" he called suddenly in a loud tone. "Where is that lad? Ah, there you are, my boy. Show these good people to the rectory house, and see that they receive something to eat."

Gregory, a lad of about sixteen with green eyes and wild red hair, nodded to them and smiled broadly. "The lad is deaf as stone, but a good boy," Father Padraic said. "He'll escort you, and I'll see what arrangements can be made for horses."

"Thank you," Igrainia said, speaking at last.

Father Padraic nodded, watched her closely once again, then turned away.

The rectory was little more than a large hovel made of wood and sod, the main room a large hall with battered benches and tables. At one sat a group of nuns who nodded when they entered. An ancient priest sat alone at another, and two other tables seemed to be filled with bands of pilgrims. They were seated at the table next to one group that seemed to be comprised of three couples. The other group might have been young men aspiring to be squires so that they might go on to be knights; they were young, and seemed hardy and in robust health and energy. As Igrainia sat across from John, she noted that the elderly priest, sitting alone, was casting disapproving glances toward the young men, who were imbibing heavily from the pitcher of ale that sat upon their table.

A young woman with a jagged scar down her check brought them ale, bread and a haunch of tough meat.

"Poor lass! I wonder what befell her!" Merry murmured as the girl moved about, serving them.

"War—soldiers with no mercy," John replied briefly. "Don't stare at her so, wife."

Igrainia watched the girl work with tremendous sympathy; like Merry, she couldn't help but wonder how she had sustained the terrible wound. She felt sorry for the girl, and when John gave her a small coin in payment, Igrainia called her back softly, adding to the payment they had made.

"Take care, my lady!" John warned.

"No one saw me, and if so . . . we are in a religious house."

"And you think all men who profess to be of God are naturally saints?" John said.

"She needs the coin," Igrainia said.

John crossed himself. "My lady, your welfare is in my hands."

She reached across the table and squeezed his hand. "My life is in my own hands, John, and you and Merry are dear to be with me."

" 'Tis no hardship, being with you, m'lady," Merry murmured, sawing away at her food. "But this meat! What on earth might it be?"

"We might well be better off not knowing," John warned.

"The bread is very good," Igrainia told Merry.

"Ah, indeed, fresh and filling," Merry said, finding happiness in the warm loaf and the sweet butter served with it.

"Hello, welcome!" a woman called from across the table.

"Hello," Igrainia said, noting then that John gave her a stern warning.

She decided to ignore him.

"Where are you traveling?" she asked the woman.

"Canterbury," the woman said. "I'm Anne, and that's Joseph, my husband. We're late of Berwick. Gannet is our brother, and Jacob is married to my sister there, Lizzie, and Beth . . . Beth is a dear, but we've never found a husband for her."

"I've not really been looking!" Beth, the youngest of the three, an attractive woman with a quick smile, said with an indignant sigh. "Anne thinks all women must be married, or they have no value in life."

"Well, it is the way of things!" Anne reproached.

"I have a trade," Beth told them.

"A trade?" Igrainia inquired.

Beth smiled. "I am a poet, and I play the harp."

"She needs a husband. There weren't many paying for a woman to play and sing in Berwick!" Anne said.

"I will make my own way," Beth said.

"I'm quite sure you will," Igrainia said. "Perhaps there

are hard times many places here, in the Borders, in the cities so often crossed by the armies. But in London . . .''

"Oh, child! You mustn't encourage her!" Anne protested. "She needs to find a husband, a good husband, though it won't be easy at her age. Most probably, we'll have to find her a widower in need of a good woman to watch over his children."

"Anne, we've barely met these people," Beth protested. "And I'm not interested in meeting a man who is looking for a cook and housekeeper."

"All men are looking for an able woman to cook and keep house," Anne said impatiently.

"There's always a nunnery," Beth murmured. She winked at Igrainia. Anne didn't seem to notice the irony in her sister's tone.

"Yes, there's that, of course, but . . ."

"But it doesn't fit my nature," Beth said.

"Not at all," Anne agreed. "She has an atrocious temper, you see. And a way of speaking her mind . . ."

"She makes it very, very difficult, you see," Lizzie finished.

"Lizzie!" Beth remonstrated.

"Lizzie, Beth, really, both of you might want to be a bit more discreet," the women's brother, Gannet, said in a soft, amused drawl.

He appeared to be younger than any of the women. Though the independent Beth seemed to be in her mid-twenties, Gannet was younger still, probably a year or two behind Beth, but very obviously her kin with blue eyes, shoulder length, curling blond hair and a pleasant face.

"Indeed," said Jacob, a man as slim as his wife, Lizzie, but with a sinewy, tough-looking strength to his leanness, "we've not even really met these good people!"

"Aye, and we've barely let them say a word!" Joseph said.

Then the three couples all stared at Igrainia's table, waiting for the trio there to speak.

"I'm—" Igrainia began, but John stepped in quickly, interrupting her before she could give a name. "I'm John of Annandale, and this is my wife, Merry. We're taking our niece, Isabel, south to worship at Canterbury as well, and hoping to see her wed to the son of an old friend outside of London, a fine fellow, a blacksmith's boy, with a fine future ahead."

"Well, then! We are travelers of a like mind!" Joseph said. He had a pleasant, weathered face, and a welcoming manner. He lowered his voice.

Between them all, they were quite interesting in appearance. Anne and Joseph, so plump and cheerful, Lizzie and Jacob, slender and stern, and Gannet and Beth, alike as sister and brother, pleasant faced and voiced, and of a slightly rebellious nature.

"I believe we, too, will be staying in London," Joseph continued. "Back in Berwick . . . well, years back . . . there was such a slaughter there, when the people held out against King Edward. Most of our kin are dead and buried, and there's no livelihood for a man in these parts anymore, not when his craft is metalworking, and those who desired his fine goods are all either gone or impoverished."

"We're all looking to make a new living," Jacob said. "We had a farm . . . a small farm, just outside the town, and we were tenants of a young lord who took to the hills with Robert Bruce. First, the English decimated the area. Then . . . the Scots burned us out, trying to keep the English from living off our land. Then the English came back and laid waste the land, in retaliation against the Scots. Seems London is far enough from the wars for us to find a way to manage. And we've a daughter living there, married a landed knight, she did, so she's written for us all to come and find work with them and their kin and good friends. Sorry I am to be leaving, but a man's got to make his way."

"Of course!" Merry said.

"So, Isabel, you're looking to make a good marriage, eh?" Anne inquired.

Igrainia forgot that her name was supposed to be Isabel until Merry kicked her gently beneath the table.

"Oh! Yes. Marriage, of course," she murmured.

"Poor lass! She has so little to offer," John said, shaking his head sadly.

"So little to offer!" Anne said indignantly, and looked to her husband, since she couldn't quite seem to find the words she wanted.

"Never feel that way, my girl," Joseph advised. "Why, lass, you are a beauty, pure and simple," John said. "Don't worry, girl, for though many a man is looking to better his own lot in life through his wife's riches, there's many a man as well ready to love and cherish a lass for her soul and her nature."

"And her appearance," Anne added dryly. "You'll have no problems, girl. Perhaps you're not looking high enough," she suggested to Merry. "If you could get her into a good household, she might win the eye of a young man with potential. Not nobility, of course, but she's the face and figure for an ambitious young man with a knack for arms. She could, perhaps, find a lad quick and nimble enough to ride in the king's army, and thus become a knight himself, and make her his wife."

"A blacksmith's son, safe and solid, will do," Merry said firmly.

"You will settle for a blacksmith's boy?" Gannet asked. He was looking more at Igrainia than at Merry and Joseph.

Igrainia lowered her head, hiding a smile.

"Now, there's nothing wrong in being a smith!" John said.

"Not at all!" Merry agreed.

Igrainia looked at her, still trying not to smile. She arched a brow to her. Merry shrugged, and smiled. "Aye, a black-smith's boy. Why, in London, such a fellow will never be out of work."

"You really should travel with us," Lizzie put in. "There is always safety in numbers."

"Perhaps we will ride with you," John said. Igrainia noted that he was watching the other table, the one filled with young men. He said quietly to their neighbors. "They seem an unlikely lot."

"Oh, no, they're quite charming, really!" Beth advised. "Young men who are willing to humble themselves before God! No prospects for them here, on the borders. They are mostly from old Anglo-Saxon homes in the area . . . once they've made their way and laid their sins before God, I believe they mean to volunteer for the king's forces. It's a harsh world, and there's little a man can do to improve his lot! That group, well, they will do what they can!"

"Perhaps," Merry said quietly, "we should all join with them. Though most men fear God enough to leave humble pilgrims be, there are many along the way who care for only what they can take."

"There's not much they can take from us!" Beth said.

"Unless they know—" Anne began.

"Anne!" Joseph chastised.

"We've nothing to fear from this good family!" Anne said indignantly. She shrugged, and seemed to squirm, adjusting her voluminous shift beneath the table. Igrainia looked downward quickly, certain that Anne had been about to tell them that she had hidden what few "riches" she owned in the hem of her long gown.

"We've certainly no wish to hurt anyone," Igrainia told her.

"John, what do you say?" Merry asked.

John watched Igrainia, as if he were going to hesitate. She smiled at him, offering him a silent query with her eyes. *What could go wrong with these gentle folk?*

After a moment, John agreed. "There is safety in numbers."

"Oh, lovely. We will all really get to know one another," Anne said. "We should leave quite early. Get a good night's sleep, and leave early."

Just as she finished speaking, the young men at the nearby table rose.

"Good journey," one said to Anne and her party, pausing by their table. He was probably in his early twenties, tall, and thickset, apparently heavy muscled. He spoke to Anne, but his eyes traveled to the table beyond and he nodded an acknowledgment to Igrainia, John and Merry. "And to you as well," he said politely.

John nodded in return.

"You are on a religious quest?" the young man asked.

"We travel to London, making the pilgrim's stops along the way," John replied politely. "We hear that you seek to join the king's service. Good journey to you and your friends as well."

"Oh, yes, of course. Thank you. Perhaps we shall pass along the way, and be of some service."

"You will probably travel a good deal faster," Igrainia said, a small smile curving her lips. If they joined with Anne's group, they would surely move as slowly as the seasons. Not that she had expected to make fast time with John and Merry.

And not that it really mattered. With Afton gone, with the world she had known at an end, she was in no great hurry to go anywhere.

"Well, yes, we do travel quickly," the young man told her, his brown eyes studying her with a strange intensity. "But then . . . we, too, will have our stops to make along the way. May God allow that we meet again."

"Godspeed!" Merry told him.

The four young men departed.

"Like as not, they'll all be dead in a year!" Beth said with a soft sigh. "There they are, young and in fine health, and they're off to learn to do battle, and fight the king's wars. They'll return here, and fight their own kin, like as not. They might earn a greater place in life by battling and killing, but still, they'll be nothing more than common foot soldiers when they march, and God knows, 'tis the common man who bleeds for the rich folk, and that's the way it is!"

"I think we all need a good night's sleep," Merry said, rising.

"Goodnight, then," Joseph told them.

"Goodnight," Igrainia said.

The deaf lad, Gregory, appeared in the long room then, as if intuitively knowing just when they would be ready to go to their accommodations. He smiled a lot, but seemed uneasy. Igrainia offered him a warm smile, but he still seemed rather distressed, looking around as he led them across the now darkened yard where they had to walk carefully to avoid chickens and pigs in the muck. They came to another thatched-roof dwelling and entered a hall where a small fire burned. Father Padraic was waiting in a chair before the fire. He warmed his calloused hands, then rose when he saw them. "Well, I hope that you are sated, since our food is filling, if not greatly pleasing to the palate."

"We are quite sated, and grateful," Igrainia said.

Father Padraic nodded. "We welcome all here, and ask few questions, and therefore, can give few answers when soldiers, from either side, sweep down upon us. Child, there is a very small but private room for you at the end of the corridor. Please retire when you are ready to sleep; we don't waste candles or torches here. There is an anteroom adjoining the small chamber. Merry, John, I believe you will find it sufficient. All of our rooms are small and spare, but most often, we have to fill what space we have with many pilgrims. And so many are poor, wounded and left homeless, their lands destroyed by the battles waged!" he added softly. "There are so many of God's children who must be tended."

"I need no special consideration," Igrainia told him. "If there is a common room—"

"There is, but since it is not necessary, I don't think it wise for you to sleep there. If I were not able to offer it, you would have no special consideration. As it is, I have the space this evening," he told her. "It is quiet here now . . . there are not so many travelers here tonight. The lads have a room together on the left of the hall; they have come in already and are eager to travel on in the morning. We have a large family group, and they are in the room to the right. We've a few priests moving from parish to parish . . . but we are able still to give you the small privacy. Fresh water is in the pitchers, and we ask that all guests care for their own—for their own necessities."

"He means privy pots!" Merry whispered to Igrainia.

"I believe I knew that," Igrainia told her softly.

Father Padraic was smiling. "I believe she did!" he said softly, teasing Merry.

Igrainia extended a hand to him. "We cannot thank you enough."

"Well, child, wait until you see the horses, the best I

could find, in the morning. By midday, you may be cursing me.''

''Never, Father Padraic.''

He made the sign of the cross. ''I'll bid you goodnight.''

The room was indeed small. At one time, it had been a nun's residence. There was a narrow bed that consisted of a thin mattress on taut ropes. Gregory, with his single candle, led Ingrainia to her room first, showed her the pitcher and ewer on the plain, hardwood stand, and left her. In the dark.

She felt for the water, managed to wash her face and teeth without flooding the room, then found the towel without groping too long. There was a window in the little cell, and in time, she was able to make out some of what she was doing with the bit of moon glow that filtered into the room. It didn't matter; she was very weary and ready for sleep, and afraid, that the sleep would elude her. Lying awake was always a nightmare of memory. Sleeping too often brought her bolting to wakefulness, thinking that there was someone she hadn't tended, someone who would die . . . had died, because she had fallen asleep.

Lying awake made her remember too much of the past when the walls of the castle had shielded them from the ugliness of the battle-ravaged world around them. She had known, always, what was going on—as well as anyone could know, with news traveling slowly around the country and beyond. But the news of John Comyn's murder, of Robert Bruce's coronation, of King Edward's fury, had all come to them, usually by mounted men, traveling to and from sites of battle, keen that all should know King Edward's mind.

Afton, caught between his heritage and the king whose might gave him power over the Borders, had only once been forced to take a stand between the two factions that made up his heritage. That had been when the king's men had come with the prisoners. And before that . . .

Life had been idyllic.

Lying awake now, Igrainia too clearly saw his face, his smile, his laughter. She could hear his voice, his words, always reasonable, gentle, compassionate. He had been taught the responsibility of his power, and what it meant to be a lord, a man beholden to the people, as the people were to him. He had used the law to keep his men from fighting in foreign wars, convinced the king that the knights and tenants of Langley were needed there, to hold the precarious position of the castle. And whatever call to arms came to him, he delved first into his books, always finding a point of law that Edward himself had brought to the English people, and using that point to maintain his policy of neutrality and separateness. Tall, slender and artistic, Afton had never had the burly build or stamina required of a true warrior; his strength had always lain in the power of his mind.

She could almost feel him beside her, as if he came in dreams. "Returning to England is the wisest course of action, my love. Your brother is young and will force nothing on you. Take time to heal, choose the life you'll lead. It will all come out well in the end . . ."

It was as if he were really there, the softness of his breath against her cheek, his fingers in her hair. She could feel his presence, his tenderness, yet she knew that it wasn't real, and she felt the pain of his loss rising in her again, touching within; she felt the burn of tears against her eyelids. And the sense that she was not alone.

She woke suddenly, not feeling the tenderness, but a rise of awareness and panic. A whisper broke the darkness.

"Sh . . . sh! Please, my lady, don't cry out!"

She gritted her teeth, trying to control a scream of terror. Waking in the darkness was different from its sudden fall; the moon glow still entered the room and she could see the young girl, and Gregory, the deaf boy, at her side.

The girl with the scar across the length of her young face.

"What is it?" she asked.

"I had to come, I'm so sorry I frightened you."

"It's all right; I'm all right," she said quickly.

She sat up, looking at the two in the shadows. "It's all right, really. But why have you come?"

"To warn you," the girl said.

"Warn me? Is there . . . has someone ridden here?"

The girl shook her head. She hesitated. "Gregory . . . he can't speak, but he can *see*."

"He can . . . see?" Igrainia repeated.

The girl nodded. "There's a danger ahead for you. It will come out as it should, but you must be very careful. You must watch everyone around you. Always. There's a haze . . . and a chance that you could lose your life. But if you are wary, and watch, always watch. He sees riders, and if you're not aware . . . they could . . . hurt you. He can't tell you when or where you will meet with them, only that your journey is dangerous."

Igrainia looked past the girl to Gregory. He nodded somberly.

"You can speak with him?"

"He isn't in the least stupid, my lady. He is only deaf and mute."

Igrainia smiled. "And he . . . sees?"

"He has a certain vision."

She wondered about his "vision." She knew she was in danger when she rode; her very existence created danger. But she felt an uneasy prickling along her spine, as if she were hearing a warning as real as any she might find from a messenger sent ahead to tell of armed men riding down upon the gates of a castle.

"Why should a pilgrim be in danger?" she asked cautiously.

"Why would a pilgrim give a poor lass such a rich coin?" the girl asked her.

"The poor lass needs the coin more than the pilgrim," Igrainia said.

"Aye, indeed, I'd not survive at all if it were not for Father Padraic and the bounty of the folk coming through. But few have the ability, or the kindness, to give with such generosity."

"There are many things that gold coins cannot buy," Igrainia murmured. "As to Gregory's vision, what would he have me do? I cannot stay here; I have to ride, and reach London."

"It's true, you can't stay. But you must be wary. It's your very life you must guard. That's why we came. If you are wary, you can survive. There's help that will come to you. You must only be on guard, and . . . there's nothing else we can really tell you. If you are wary and protect yourself, then you will survive. We must go now. Father Padraic is a wonderful man. But he has doubts about Gregory's visions. And there are those who would accuse him of dangerous witchcraft. There are many things he sees which he feels he can never say . . . Father Padraic has been too good to us. But you have been so kind . . . and you must understand, in the way that you speak, walk, and even in your manner, it is easy to see that you are no orphan of the poor, the landless, the luckless or the downtrodden."

They turned to leave. Igrainia caught the girl's arm. "I don't even know your name."

"Rowenna," the girl said. "And I must go now."

"Thank you. Both of you. I will repay you, when I can."

"You owe us nothing. We would give you more, if only we could. Please, just believe what we tell you. We must go. Father Padraic sleeps lightly."

They slipped from the room in a silence as deep as the darkness.

Igrainia lay back against her pillow, staring into the shadows. The strange ripple of unease seeped down her spine again.

He was coming after her, she thought.

They were warning her, because Gregory saw . . .

Why?

Why would such a man, who sorrowed so deeply and loathed her with such a vengeance, take the time and trouble to come after her now?

He had told her from the beginning what her fate would be if she didn't keep his wife and child alive.

And the poor little girl had died before they had even returned.

Margot had died in her care.

She didn't need Gregory to *see* for her.

There was no great mystery to her fate. Eric intended to hunt her down. No matter how long she was gone, and no matter how far she traveled.

And what he intended then . . .

She didn't know.

But sleep eluded her for the rest of the night.

As did her dreams.

CHAPTER 5

They had drawn up before the walls of Perth. The Earl of Pembroke had ridden hard into Scotland at the bidding of the English king, his army of six thousand men drawn from the northern counties of England and the lowlands of Scotland.

Robert Bruce, knowing of Pembroke's advance and his own dire circumstances and lack of men, had gathered forces for the country north of the Forth and Clyde. He had managed to raise an army of about four thousand, five hundred men. Having received word that Pembroke was at Perth, they had ridden there hard, ready to do battle. But he hadn't the necessary siege engines to batter down walls or gates, nor could he afford the cost in human life it would take to send a relentless stream of men to scale the walls. Bruce and his advisers had argued their tactics, many doubtful of the honor of the Earl of Pembroke, yet many equally convinced that he was a man who would not give his word lightly. In the end,

Robert Bruce insisted that he knew the Earl of Pembroke, and many silently agreed. He should know many of King Edward's men, since there had been a time when he had given his allegiance to the English king.

"I know Pembroke!" He stated firmly in the copse where they had come to talk. "And there is also the matter that we have little choice. I will challenge him, in the chivalric code, and hear what he has to say."

Old Angus spat into the grass. "It doesn't matter what he says."

Eric shrugged when Robert Bruce stared his way. "It's true, we haven't the means to lay siege to the castle. That is the only real and substantial fact we have."

So Bruce himself rode to the gates, and issued his challenge. And he was so convinced that the Earl of Pembroke would honor his promise to bring his men forth and do battle in the morning, that no guards were officially ordered to watch the camp that night.

And so, the English came in.

Many of the men had been out, searching for supplies. Many had been sleeping.

The English fell upon them in the summer dusk.

Slaughter ensued.

Eric was fighting near the king when he slew the horse of the Earl of Pembroke, the man who had broken his promise, but not even Bruce's wrath allowed him to break the sudden crowd of men around the earl. Bruce's horse was seized next, but Christopher Seton broke through, and sent Philip Mowbray, who had gotten hold of Bruce's horse, reeling to the ground. Eric pushed through then, forming the guard around Robert Bruce that allowed them to escape the English troops and bring their king to safety.

Robert Bruce survived but his army was shattered. Many of his finest followers were hunted down and later found at the castles where they had fled. They met King Edward's fury, and paid with their lives.

The handful of men who survived and still gave their loyalty to Robert Bruce knew, as he did that it wasn't time to fight, but rather to retreat, to set out into the countryside, and over the Irish Sea, to gather more followers to form a new army.

They had to build. The forces they gathered had to be passionate, about the cause of Scottish nationalism, and they had to create a body of men that was large and strong, if they were to come against the English again.

Everyone knew that there were no rules of chivalry in this war.

No mercy to be had.

And so Eric had gone to the isles—stopping for his wife and child, for riders had warned him as he made his way cross country that the English had seized Bruce's wife and women kin, after Bruce had been sure that they were safely in the care of his brother, Nigel.

Nigel, having heard that the Earl of Pembroke had arrived at Aberdeen, sent the women ahead once they had reached Kildrummy Castle.

The women, in the company of the Earl of Atholl, were captured at the sanctuary of St. Duthac at Tain.

Sanctuary had availed them little.

They had been seized and sent straight to King Edward, who had come to the monastery of Lanercost.

Kildrummy Castle had not shielded Nigel.

Nigel, a handsome young man, quick to laugh, as quick to find courage and fight, had paid the price for supporting his brother. A brutal price. And the women . . .

So Eric had determined to keep his own wife and child and the kin of his men with him. They had set forth upon the sea to find men in the rugged north and among the western isles, among them their own kin, largely Norse, and the Irish, many with a hatred for Edward as deep as that which stirred in the heart of the most maligned and bitter Scotsman.

For a moment, he felt the sea breeze, fresh and cool.

And he heard her voice, ever gentle, ever compassionate.

"It's a man, we must stop. A man, a human being . . . he will drown . . ."

"Aye, and maybe an agent of the English, better off dead!" Peter had warned.

"And perhaps a loyal follower of King Robert Bruce, in such dire condition since he chose to serve his king," Margot had said.

And so they had taken in the man . . .

And they had taken in death.

And the English, coming upon them when they were weakened and desperate, had seized the women, and knowing he hadn't the power to beat the forces bringing them to their imprisonment, he had allowed his own capture . . .

Maneuvered his escape, and come back. Too late. He came back to sickness, to death.

Faces seemed to whirl in a fog before him. Drawn, ashen, marred by plague, gray, purple, blistered, skeletal . . . faces, white beneath a flow of blood, faces, eyes . . . eyes of death, haunted, the gray of agony, the white of death, the red of all the blood that had spilled . . .

He woke with a start.

And lay there, feeling numb. His wife, and his daughter were gone. Blood, horror, battle, sickness, death, gone.

There was only the numbness . . .

He rose, restless in the night.

Aye, numbness, he felt numbness. But when he forced himself to move, he realized that there was more.

He had regained his strength.

And his fury to fight.

It was time to ride.

Before the dawn broke, they were prepared to strike out on their journey again.

They could move faster now. They were mounted.

Igrainia found little fault with the shaggy horse Father Padraic had found for her to ride. Her name was Skye, and she had a sweet disposition, even if she had a slow lope.

Skye wasn't young, but good horses were hard to come by in the area. One good way to kill a knight was to kill the mount beneath him, and slay him when he crashed to the ground with the weight of his mail and plate. Well trained warhorses were extremely expensive, but when armies vied over a territory, few were sold because war gave men an excuse to steal, and in the Borders, horses had been seized by men bowing down before both kings.

Father Padraic was there to wish them Godspeed, as all the pilgrims who found shelter in his village rose to ride at the same time. Fresh baked loaves of bread were given out, along with what smoked and cured meat could be spared.

Father Padraic had said Mass at the first hint of the pink dawn, and all that was left for them to do was to receive his final blessing, and move on.

As Igrainia mounted her horse, Rowenna and Gregory sidled near her. Rowenna offered her a cup of cool water and what should have been bread wrapped in linen.

It wasn't bread.

She had been given a dagger.

She accepted the gift smoothly and stared down at the girl.

"I wish that you were among us, you and Gregory," she told her.

Rowenna offered her a smile. She touched the ugly scar that marred what had been a pretty face.

"I will never go to London," she said softly. "This was the gift of an English earl."

"I'm so sorry."

"We all bear scars in life. Mine is not so hard. I survive here. I have Father Padraic and a dear young friend. I have lost husband, father, mother, brother and most of my other kin. I have survived to tell the tales to those who come behind us. Scotland is my home."

"There is little difference in living in the lowlands of Scotland, and in England," Igrainia told her.

"One day, there will be."

Gregory stood behind Rowenna, still appearing troubled.

Igrainia knew that he must read lips. "It will be all right," she told him.

"He's very worried. He wishes he could tell you more. And he says that you are one of us, though I have tried to explain that you are going to London to be married. But then, you're not who you say you are, so, perhaps that is not true either."

"I am going to London," Igrainia said. "Whatever comes from there, none of us really knows right now. I will pray for you both, for your lives, for your happiness, but I hope that once I have ridden away, I never return."

Rowenna said, "We will pray for you as well."

Father Padraic had lifted a hand for silence; they all bowed their heads as he offered them God's blessing for their journey.

The four young men were in the lead. They were on better horses than the others; horses they had procured themselves, before coming here.

Ahead of Igrainia, John and Merry were riding beside

Anne and Joseph. The rest of Anne's family was lining up behind them.

Igrainia offered a final wave to Rowenna and Gregory.

Gregory was mouthing words and making hand signs to Rowenna. Rowenna looked after Igrainia, a strange look in her eyes.

"What is it?"

Rowenna shook her head. "He believes that you have a stronger will and spirit than you know yourself. He knows that you will fare well, but still, he will beg God to protect you until we meet again."

"Bless you, Gregory!" Igrainia said, touched by their fervent desire to be her spiritual protectors. "God be with you both!"

She nudged her shaggy horse, and the animal jounced into a jarring trot. As the others moved ahead, the trot became a bearable lope.

They left the village behind.

England lay ahead. Death and darkness lay behind.

She did not look back.

He spoke from the old stone steps leading from the courtyard of Langley to the entrance to the great hall.

Peter had seen that the people had been assembled, from the lowliest of the kitchen help to the knights and armed soldiers who had once ruled the battlements of the castle. He had his own band of men, those who had returned with him, and those who had survived the disease within the castle, not quite fifty in all, but many of the women and children had lived as well. If they couldn't wield swords with strength and expertise, they could ferret out any plot to seize the castle back from the nationalists, and they could see to it that none escaped to seek help from the troops under the various men now in the service of King Edward. He felt with a certain assurance, as well, that the men to whom he had shown mercy, who had now sworn their loyalty to the King of the Scots, would abide by their oaths—they knew that their fates would not include simple or painless deaths if they broke the solemn vows they had given.

Since death had taken so many, there were no more than a hundred and fifty people in the courtyard, but all of them, those who were his own, and those who had been loyal to a different lord, watched him worriedly.

"You have come to know me in the past few days, and know that I am a man of my word. It is a time to rebuild here, and I have no desire for any further bloodshed or death. We have all lost far too many people as it is. Peter MacDonald, who led you through sickness and brought you through, will continue to lead you while I am away. His every command will be like the voice of God. Those who heed him will do well, and find a way from the pain and death that have robbed us all of those we loved. You have all found mercy at our hands during a time when hatreds run so deep, even little children have met the sword of the conquerors. A castle such as Langley cannot fall, unless it falls from within. And I will tell you a story that gives you fair warning. At Kildrummy, Nigel, brother of the king, Robert Bruce of Scotland, defended his fortification from constant and repeated attacks by the English. He and his men defended the castle so well that the English were nearly ready to give up. But there was a traitor within the castle walls. A blacksmith, a man named Osborne. He was bribed by a promise of great riches if he set a fire, and allowed the castle walls to fall. And so, he started a fire in the storehouse, and the fire spread, and indeed, the people within were sent to the walls, and the castle gates fell to the blaze as well, and the English were able to seize the fortification. For any thinking that they might do such a thing and reap the rewards of English gold, the story did not end there. The castle was taken. Nigel Bruce was executed. But Osborne did not prosper. The English kept their promise and gave him riches in gold. They melted it—and poured it down his throat. There is no way that any English lord, knight or warrior will believe that you have not fallen to the enemy. There is no real reward for betrayal—except death. We have kept every promise to you. This is Scotland, and you are the people of Scotland. We will have a long hard fight, but Robert Bruce is king, and will rule in the end, and what he will rule is a sovereign country. Your loyalty is not required. It is demanded. In return, we vow to protect you, at the cost of our own lives."

Silence greeted his words. He nodded toward Peter, who lifted a hand, and his horse was brought forward. The four men who would ride with him were mounted already, and awaited him at the gate and drawbridge.

As his horse came forward, he walked through the crowd that parted for him. As he mounted, he was surprised to hear a cheer arise from the crowd.

"Godspeed your journey!"

"Bless you for your mercy, Sir Eric!"

The cries arose, blended, and continued.

He wondered if he was being mocked.

He looked at the faces in the sea of people surrounding him as he moved his horse through them. And there was hope in their eyes, not mockery.

The inner gate opened.

The drawbridge fell.

And he rode out, followed by his men.

* * *

As it happened, the four young men decided that, at the least, they would start out riding with the others.

At first, Igrainia was glad. They were a strong foursome.

Then she feared that they might offer the danger that Gregory had foretold.

But each of them seemed so earnest and decent.

Igrainia found herself riding in the lead with one of them, Thayer Miller. And as they spoke, her fears abated.

He told her that his mother was English, his father was dead. They'd worked a small piece of land through Lord Denning, who had chosen to follow Robert Bruce. Not long ago, when the Bruce had gathered men to go against Edward's forces, there had been a slaughter that had become known as Methven, and Lord Denning had been killed. Soon after, English troops had come to the late lord's holdings. Most of the people had escaped to the woods, but the English had slaughtered the pigs and livestock, trampled the fields, and set fire to all the buildings. There had been nothing left to eat, and the promises Lord Denning had made, to teach his promising young tenants the ways of the warrior, were as dead as he and the land that had once been the livelihood for so many. Thayer's mother, surviving with his younger siblings in the poor homestead of an aunt, had given him letters of introduction.

"But, the English destroyed your home and everything you knew," Igrainia said. "One would think you'd rise against them."

He looked at her with a rueful smile. "You must understand this. I don't know if Robert Bruce has a right to be king; he followed Edward long enough himself, when it suited his purpose. There were many in the lowlands who supported John Comyn, and though Bruce may have done penance, it seems, if the news that covers the countryside is true, that he murdered Comyn. He struck a blow in the sanctity of a church. Perhaps God is against Bruce for such an act. But what I have heard, thought, and believed, is not really what guides my desire now to reach England. I believe that this country, especially the lowlands, will be torn by war for years to come. If I were to try to remain, I could spend my every waking moment working another's man land, growing crops, raising livestock, and waking again one morning to find that one army or another is coming, and will again slaughter every living thing, raze the buildings, and burn the houses. When I get to England, I will find the right noble to serve, and I will prove myself, as will my friends. Aye, there's much more I need in the way of training, but I have the will to learn. When I've made my place, I will be loyal until the last breath has left my body, and then I will send for my mother, my sisters and brothers, and see that they have a life in which they do not spend their days hiding in the forest, desperately searching for anything that resembles food, just to survive.''

''Perhaps, when we reach London, I can help you,'' Igrainia said, touched by his determination to help his family. ''We have some letters of introductions, and some friends there,'' she added quickly. But he was already watching her with a skeptical smile, and when she furrowed her brow in a frown at the look he gave her, he apologized quickly.

''I'm sorry. I don't believe that you're a poor farm lass, a refugee from the wars,'' he said.

''Believe me, I am a refugee,'' she said. ''And I am as desperate as any man or woman in the lowlands of Scotland to reach London.''

She saw in his face that he had decided not to pry.

"If it's only marriage you're seeking, you need go no further than this party," he told her.

She frowned again.

"Haven't you seen?"

"I'm sorry, seen what?"

"The younger man with the old folks. Gannet, the brother. He has watched you constantly. Like a great roast, ready to be devoured."

His words startled Igrainia. She looked back. Far back. Gannet was riding with one of Thayer's friends, the one he had called Reed, she thought, at the far rear of the company. John and Merry rode together, right behind her—just like proper guardians. Behind them, Thayer's two other companions rode with the rest of Anne and Joseph's party. They all seemed to be in conversation.

"I have to get to London," she told Thayer. "Our new friends certainly seem to be fine enough people, but . . . I have to get to London."

"And I don't think you're intended for such a man."

"At this moment . . ."

"At this moment?" Thayer queried.

She shook her head. "I think I'd like time alone more than anything."

Thayer studied her. "Ah. Well, there is more to your story than you are telling. I think I know the truth. There was a young man . . . probably a knight. And he rode forth to do battle—for one side or the other—and he was killed. And with his death . . . your future has changed. And you're not happy. I'm so sorry. It was someone you loved."

She arched a brow to him. "All right. There was someone. And it's true. He died. And so, everything is changed."

As she spoke, Igrainia became aware of a disturbance behind them. John and Merry had reined in and were looking back timorously. Thayer's two companions had already started riding back on the rough trail they had followed, where the others could be heard but not seen because of a twist in the path and the high trees that hedged the road, nearly growing upon it.

"What's going on?" Igrainia called to Merry.

"I don't know—there was a sudden cry from the rear," John said.

"Someone is in trouble!" Thayer cried out, and he kneed his horse, sending the animal into a swift lope back in the direction from which they had come.

Igrainia started to follow him, but John reached out and caught her horse's bridle. "No, lass, there's something amiss!"

"Has someone ridden up behind us?" she asked fearfully.

"No!" Merry said.

The air was rent by a horrible scream. The others had all moved back, and because of the twist in the trail, could still see nothing.

"John, I must see what has happened. Someone has been hurt!" Igrainia insisted.

She broke free from his hold, and her little horse made amazing speed as she raced back along the way, reining in confusion as she saw that a young man appeared to be the one in danger; he lay on the ground on the path. Anne was down beside him with her sister Lizzie while Joseph and the others hovered at his side. The others had reached his side as well, and were on their knees in the trail, questioning Anne. Thayer had dismounted from his horse.

Igrainia lost no time as well, dismounting from Skye, but even as she did so, she heard another sudden cry. Another of the young men fell to his side, grasping his stomach.

"What is it? Have they been poisoned in some manner?" Igrainia cried out. "Let me closer; perhaps I can help."

"My God, what is happening to them?" Thayer demanded, now on his knees, reaching for his friend.

"No great mystery!" Anne said with surprising cheer.

"Aye, no mystery!" a voice said from behind Igrainia. "They've been stabbed."

Igrainia swung around and saw that Gannet stood behind her smiling. She whirled back in time to see Anne slip a knife from the fold of her skirt and strike with alarming speed and determination, shoving the blade of the weapon into Thayer's midsection.

Joseph stepped closer, a huge rock in his hand. As one of the younger men began to attack, the rock was thudded down hard upon his head.

"No!" Igrainia shrieked. "No!"

He fell, joining his fallen companions on the dirt road.

Igrainia saw then that a pool of blood had formed beneath the fallen form, and that it stretched, like a strange band of brotherhood, to Thayer, who had crumpled so close behind him. She marveled at the vicious cunning that had allowed two women to bring down three healthy young males, and the horror of the situation wrapped around her at the same time.

Gannet, she knew, was at her rear.

As much as she had once thought that she cared little for her own life, she knew that she wanted to escape these people and live. She felt a fury burn through her, and a longing for vengeance against these people who were surely planning on murdering her, John, and Merry next.

She couldn't go to the fallen young men; there would be no helping them now. These people outnumbered her and they meant for the men to die. All she could do was preserve her own life.

She felt Gannet about to reach for her; she didn't need to

turn. Each member of their party had positioned themselves perfectly to bring this about.

She didn't turn and she didn't hesitate. With a sudden spurt of speed she raced the few steps to her horse and leaped into the saddle.

Gannet was instantly behind her, reaching for the bridle. She freed her foot from the stirrup and kicked him with all her might, aiming high for his face. He released the bridle, crying out and grabbing for his eye. She kneed Skye and the little horse reared a foot off the ground, found her footing, and started out.

Igrainia saw John and Merry in the path before her. "Run!" she shouted. "Run your horses, run now!"

John heard the urgency in her voice; he said something to Merry and the two moved their horses.

They were not mounts bred for speed.

But neither was Skye, though she gave good effort.

But as Igrainia rode, she heard the horse coming from behind her. She felt the thunder of hooves, and the menace that nearly hovered over her.

A moment later, she risked a glance, and saw that Gannet was at her side.

"Stop!" he shouted. "We intend you no harm. You'll come with us; we'll make you one of us. Stop, and you'll not need a blacksmith's son; we'll make you far richer. I'll make you my wife."

Her glance of horror must have assured him that she would accept no such fate.

She flattened herself against Skye, trying to allow the little horse a greater speed.

But Gannet captured the horse's bridle, and as they dangerously twisted and turned on the path, the mare was forced to slow her gait, and Gannet hurled his own form from his horse to hers, knocking them both to the ground.

They struggled in the dirt, and she remembered that the knife Rowenna had given her was lodged against her shoe.

She kicked, scratched and struggled until she had freed herself from his weight, then reached beneath the skirt for her knife. She sprang to her feet as Gannet did. He was ready to leap upon her again, to bring her down, when he saw the weapon gleaming in her hand.

"A frisky one, eh? And you think you're going to stab me?"

He circled around her, apparently amused.

She knew that in minutes, his companions would be behind them. She had to escape him now, before the rest of his murderous crew could reach them.

She lunged at him, bringing forth a startled cry as her knife ripped through his shoulder.

He grasped at the wound, stared at the blood that covered his hand, then looked at her anew, fury in his eyes.

"Now . . . now, you'll suffer!" he promised her.

As he stared at her and she stood, poised and ready to strike and fly, she became aware of the sound of hoofbeats on the road behind them. His companions were coming fast now. Any second they would be upon them.

She lunged again.

This time, she caught the man in his midsection. But his force against her was great, and they both went crashing back to the ground.

He managed to keep his weight heavy on her, and though she brought her knife up again, he caught her wrist with both hands, and exerted such pressure against her to release the knife that she screamed in pain.

Yet held on.

She twisted, bringing up a knee against his groin. He rolled to his side, bellowing in pain but still maintaining his deadly grasp upon her wrist. She lashed out with her feet, but he rolled again, leaning half his now bloodied form against her.

She clawed at his wrists with her free hand, bringing her nails desperately into his flesh. He swore, cursing at her with a fury.

The hoofbeats came near . . .

Stopped.

She could see nothing, but she knew that at any second, he would have help with his companions at his side, aiding him.

She couldn't see. There was now too much road mud and dust in her eyes, and she could only stay locked with Gannet, fighting to the end.

Then, arms wrapped around her.

Gannet was dragged away from her.

And she was dragged up.

"No!" she let out in a scream of rage and fury and desolation. She tried to claw at the hands holding her.

Her fingers did nothing. She was clawing against heavy leather riding gloves.

She brought her hand to her face, clearing her hair from her eyes, wiping away the dirt and tears that had so blinded her.

Gannet was screaming, she realized suddenly. And when she looked before her, she saw that a man in mail and a hood had taken the man and hurled him across the road with such strength that he had landed hard against the trees.

She heard the snapping of bones.

And then Gannet was silent.

The mail-clad warrior who had wrested Gannet from her side then turned to her.

"You!" she gasped.

The man behind her released her.

She had been fighting against his hold with such energy

that her own strength and determination brought her surging forward.

She would have fallen.

But she was caught against cold, hard, steel mesh.

And she was staring into eyes that were even colder, and harder.

CHAPTER 6

He didn't say a word to her, but steadied her on her feet and spoke to the man behind her. "Allan, see that she's not hurt."

Then he turned and walked to where Gannet had fallen against the trees. He stooped, turned him over. "Dead," he said briefly, and rose.

The man was dead. She couldn't feel sorrow. He had been trying to kill her.

He and his companions had plotted carefully to kill all of them.

The sounds of hoofbeats came again, and they all turned to see that Merry and John were trotting along the path in front of two more men in mail and tunics that bore the colors of Robert Bruce.

Merry, seeing Igrainia, called out, and as fast as her round bulk would allow, she dismounted and rushed to her, ignoring everyone else. "Oh, my lady!" she cried in alarm, seeing the condition of her clothing and the blood that spattered it. "You're hurt!" she said, reaching up to put her arms around her and hug her tightly.

Igrainia wasn't seriously injured, but she realized, as Merry's arms came around her, that she was sore in every muscle of her body. Her throat hurt her and she had banged a knee and her hip hard against the ground when she had fallen. But the blood spattered over her was Gannet's, not hers.

She tried to reassure Merry. "No, I am not really hurt," she said quickly as she eased herself from the caring yet tight hold around her and squeezed Merry's hands.

Eric left Gannet's body on the road by the trees where it had fallen. He remounted his horse. "I'll see to the others," he said to Allan, "if you will escort these three."

There was something utterly dismissive about the way he spoke that sparked anger in Igrainia.

She walked to him quickly. "They murdered people, simply murdered them in cold blood." She was startled when she added, "Don't be deceived by the women, they are the ones who killed first. The young men, if they are back there . . ."

"They are aware of what they face."

He started to turn his horse.

"Wait. Perhaps I can do something, help. They may not all be dead—"

"You wish to help?" he said. His eyes were still cold and somewhat scathing. "They tried to kill you. They were common thieves and murderers."

"No . . . just that family. The others were just trying to reach a new life, they were riding with us for our safety." The irony of the last filled her and her words ended on something of a high note that threatened both laughter and tears. "That you . . . that *you* should have come along to stop them . . ."

"Ah, and there's a wonderful note of gratitude!" he muttered.

"They stabbed them, and struck them . . . someone may
still be alive," she said, ignoring his words. "I can perhaps
help—"

"And perhaps not."

And she knew by his tone that he referred to the fact that
his wife was dead.

"I saved your life!" she told him.

"Perhaps a will to live saved my life."

"There's a wonderful note of gratitude!" she mocked.

She was startled as he dismounted from his horse. Perhaps
because of her very near brush with death at Gannet's hands,
she backed away.

He reached out, grabbing her hand. "What in God's name
ails you, woman?" he demanded. "We did not take the time
to follow in your thankfully slow footsteps to murder you
ourselves."

She tried not to wince as he caught her roughly about the
waist, and she managed not to cry out, or wonder too long
at his intent. He set her atop his great warhorse, mounting
behind her. He said nothing more, but nudged the horse,
and a second later they were moving at a heady lope back
along the path until they came to the place where Anne and
her party had tricked the young men.

Joseph and Jacob had apparently attempted some fight;
the two were dead, locked in a strange embrace where they
had been deposited by the side of the road. Anne and her
lethal sisters now cowered together near a tree, all but
ignored, as two of Eric's men, easily recognizable in their
mail and tunics, worked over the fallen men. Two were
prone and crumpled, but Brandon was obviously breathing;
the one called Timothy was holding his head in his hands

and trying to explain what had happened, yet still so stunned by the events that he didn't seem to be making sense.

"We never thought . . . who would have feared . . ."

"It was them!" Anne called out. "They attacked us! We had no choice. And now you've killed my poor husband!"

Igrainia cried out, "You wretched liar!"

Eric reined in. Before he could dismount or help her down, she was sliding from the horse, nearly tripping and falling in her haste. She approached Anne with loathing and hatred, seeing that Thayer remained on the ground, not moving. She started for Anne, her fury so deep she didn't know what she had intended. "You liar! You murdered good people, people trying to help you, my God, how could you—"

Anne let out a scream as if she had been gutted. "*She! She* caused this. She knew that we had coins in our hems, she bewitched the men, she told them to attack us, it was *her*! We might have all died, and now our poor men are fallen for trying to defend us—"

"Liar!" Igrainia charged, and kept coming, not at all sure of what she intended, only that she was so angry she had to strike out at the woman. But as she came near Anne, the woman let out another shriek and came tearing at her, a knife, which she must have hidden in her skirts, suddenly glittering in the sun as she moved. Igrainia saw the blade in time and sidestepped. Eric had seen the danger as well, and caught her from behind as she moved, casting her far from harm's way. She fell in the dirt, but there was no need for anyone to go after Anne. Her force brought her crashing past the place where Igrainia should have been, and she tripped upon a pothole in the trail and fell flat upon the earth. She remained where she fell, and didn't move.

"Anne!" Lizzie shrieked, leaving Beth to stand alone as she raced to the spot where her sister had fallen. She turned Anne's prone form, and Igrainia saw that Anne had unwittingly brought about her own destruction; she had fallen upon the blade of her knife. It protruded from her chest, and the blood that soaked her breast made it apparent she had managed to drive the blade into her heart.

Lizzie let out a terrible wail.

Igrainia picked herself out of the dirt, wincing as she did so, realizing more and more with each passing moment that she was bruised and sore.

Again, she could feel nothing but a terrible coldness in her heart where once she would have felt sorrow at the sight of death.

"What do we do with the other two?" one of the men asked Eric.

"I don't know—yet. But tie them—they seem to have weapons everywhere. Yorick, gather the horses you can find," he commanded, speaking to another of the men. "It seems we will have a strange party returning."

Igrainia hurried to where Thayer lay, falling to her knees and trying to ascertain just where he had been struck, and how many injuries he had received—indeed, if he had survived at all. She let out a small sigh of relief; he was breathing. Slowly, laboriously, but his chest rose and fell at regular intervals. One strike of the knife's blade had struck just beneath his shoulder, and another had gone through his side, and she could only pray that the blade had not damaged his insides. She began to rip at the hem of her linen gown for bandages to stop the flow of blood.

As she wound material and pressed it against the wounds, she realized that large booted feet were at her side. She looked up. Eric was standing there.

"He was trying to find a way to survive, and get money home to his mother and family. They were all off to make new lives ... their lord was killed, their lands were decimated ..."

She was afraid that he meant to stop her. She was startled and nearly jumped when he came to her side.

To her amazement, he took one of the makeshift bandages from her and expertly applied pressure to one of the wounds.

"He has a chance, I think," he said.

"But he can't ride."

Eric was silent. After a moment, he stood, and Igrainia realized it was because Merry and John had reached them. Merry had come to see what help they could give the fallen men.

Eric moved off. She saw him speaking with the man he had called Allan.

"He is a strong one," Merry told her, amazingly calm for the events that had been occurring around them. "If he has just a few days' time, and the rot does not set in . . ."

Igrainia leaped to her feet, gasping, as Eric strode toward them with a sudden determination. He hunkered down by Thayer's side, and Igrainia placed a hand on his shoulder, trying to stop whatever it was he intended to do. "I'm telling you, these were decent men—"

He ignored her, casting off her touch, and lifted Thayer with an amazing care. He started straight for the trees, and she found herself running after him. "What are you doing? Wait! If you mean to throw his body into the woods to hide it and leave him to die, I will not let you. You can't. I don't care about your cause, or Scotland, or the English, or . . . any of your bloody intentions. You cannot just leave a man to die!"

He stopped dead, turning on her with anger and impatience. "There is a cove with a good stream just a few feet in. If you want this man to live, his wounds must be cleansed, and if you want any of us to live, we've got to get off the roads. Do you think your evil friends are the only monsters preying on the remnants of war? Nor am I particularly willing to die myself in this wretched pursuit of you, and the health and happiness of the companions you acquired along your escape route.''

She fell silent, staring at him. He started walking again and she followed him, and realized that the path behind her was filled with soft voices and the rustling of trees as the others followed behind them.

It seemed that they walked far, yet perhaps the path seemed long and winding because her every footstep seemed a painful chore. Her shoulder ached now as well as the rest of her bruised and battered flesh and muscle. But they came at last to a break in the dense forest and brush. There was a fast rushing stream before them, beautiful as it sparkled suddenly in the sunlight that was no longer obscured by the green wealth of the trees in the forest despite the trampling of armies upon the land. The bank of the stream was richly carpeted in pine needles, and the earth here was soft with the wealth of moisture provided by the stream.

As she walked, she heard soft words.

''Pardon, my lady.''

As he spoke, Allan passed by her side, and laid down a woolen cloak at the base of a tree, and it was there that Eric paused with his heavy burden of the wounded Thayer, and set him down with the same care to his injuries with which he had first lifted him.

And then he turned to her.

''Madam, you may tend to your new friend, but one of us will be with you at all times. And if anyone makes any attempt to part company with us again, they will be slain upon the spot. If you decide that you have given your best efforts and must again leave, your friends will suffer for your actions. I don't believe that you are stupid, Igrainia, and therefore I will trust in your efforts to keep those around you alive. You do understand me perfectly, I'm sure. But I will have your word that you will not leave, and your sworn oath that you will do nothing to bring English troops down upon us should they wander down this stretch of the road.''

He stared at her hard. She drew in a deep breath. He hadn't come to murder her. Nor did he intend to explain what he meant to do with her. Nor did she think that he intended to murder the others.

''I can't . . . willingly accept whatever you may have in mind . . .''

''You can't? But you must. And will. Swear now that you will not attempt to escape or let out any cry of alarm.''

Still, she hesitated.

He took a step toward her.

She took a step back.

''The others will fall first!'' he said softly.

''I swear,'' she murmured.

''Louder, please.''

''I swear.''

She jumped back again as he came closer. But he didn't intend to touch her. He passed by her, going on to help the others bring the horses back into the small cove in the forest by the rushing brook.

By nightfall, the cove in the trees had become a campsite. A fire had been built, water had been boiled, capes and cloaks had been laid out as makeshift beds, more bandages had been made. Eric and Raymond Campbell had brought down a stag, supplying them with fresh meat for however many days they dared linger, waiting for the wounded to heal enough to ride—or to die.

Eric had sent the two surviving women from the strange party of murdering pilgrims back to Langley with Allan MacLeod, not willing to risk having them among the dangerous assortment of people then in his care or confinement: the injured men, the lady he had come to retrieve, and her two retainers.

He expected no trouble from Merry or John; both were excessively grateful to be living and to be in the company of men who might be political enemies, but seemed trustworthy, for the time, although he didn't trust Igrainia.

She would run at the first possible moment.

He chafed at the time this was taking him. There had been no choice but to come after her; he couldn't have let her go, she was far too valuable a prisoner. And there was a certain satisfaction in the fact that in their pursuit, they had happened upon a clutch of criminals who had evidently been making their way in life by preying upon the innocent and unwary for some time.

There had been occasions when they had been forced to flee from battlefields, knowing that they left men among their number wounded, perhaps mortally so, and at the hands of their enemies, and still, such was battle—men had to desert the field if they were to live and fight again to win not just the day but the war. No man ever learned to come to peace with himself for leaving a companion either dying in agony—or not dying quickly enough to avoid whatever brutal end the enemy might intend. And so, since they were not on a battlefield and not being pursued and in no imminent danger, he couldn't leave these injured young fellows to die, even if England had been their destination. They had ridden slowly to protect those they thought weaker than themselves. They had fallen to treachery, but there was a certain nobility about their behavior that appealed to Eric, and therefore, he could not leave them behind to die.

But cooling his heels in the forest was the least productive use of his time that he could imagine, and he wished that he had sent one of his men after the lady of Langley, rather than riding out himself. He had considered taking the two knife-wielding women to Langley himself and leaving Allan behind with this group, but again, he did not trust the lady of Langley. He would not let her escape again.

He studied her where she knelt by the man she had called Thayer Miller. Miller was a survivor, he noted, which was a quality that appealed to him. He had lost a lot of blood, surely enough to take the life away from most men, but still, it was as if he had determined not to die. He had yet to regain consciousness. His friend, Brandon, remained prone, his eyes opening upon occasion and closing again. He was able to whisper, and had given Eric much the same picture of the events that Eric had already heard and surmised. The man named Timothy had regained his senses, and helped Igrainia tend to his friends, but earlier, he had come to Eric when he had stood by the water, idly watching the horses drink, and once there before him, Timothy had fallen on his knees, thanked Eric and his men for his life and the lives of his companions, told his own rendition of the story, and sworn eternal loyalty, if Eric would have him in his service.

Eric had weighed the matter. After Timothy's initial confusion—natural, considering the blow he had received to his head—he had made a good appearance, speaking articulately and concisely, while also conveying just how deeply stunned they all had been by the strange twist in the intents and purposes of the "pilgrims" with whom they had been riding.

"Though, in truth, we did not linger and ride slowly for that group," Timothy had said. "Rather, we feared for the young woman riding with the older couple. They claimed that she was riding to London to wed a blacksmith's son, but Thayer didn't believe that could be the truth. He was certain that she was an heiress running away, but her kindness and courtesy to those at the priest's village impressed him deeply, and he thought that she might be in need of help. We thought we would slow our gait long enough to see her well past the border, and then perhaps, pick up some speed of movement.''

"But you were headed south. To fight with the English.''

"Aye," he admitted gravely.

"You are Scottish."

"I am from the Borders. And have no lord who remains among the living to serve. But I can say freely, for my companions and myself, that we owe you our lives. And we would gladly serve a Scotsman with the strength and will to stay alive and fight the English. There is nothing for us, anywhere, except that which we can earn for ourselves."

"We shall see," Eric had promised.

He tended to be a fair judge of men. And he judged this one as an honest man, deeply sincere. But time would tell.

Time.

The single day dragged. At Langley, Peter MacDonald would be securing the formidable walls, and strengthening the structure in any way that he could. Peter was far more fond of building than he was of war. Eric had left Langley in the best of hands, and in so doing, he knew, he was fighting the most important part of the war for his king. But now, Margot was gone. The moments of peace when he could rest beside her and talk, perhaps rant angrily until she had soothed his temper, and talk about the strategy that had worked, or what had failed, and who had rallied to the king, and who had not. Margot was gone, as Aileen was gone. There was nothing left, and to be caught here, in this forest cove with nothing but the prison of his own thoughts was worse than being held captive behind any wall of metal or stone.

Raymond Campbell strode over to where Eric leaned against one of the old oaks close to the water and far from the fire.

"They live, still. All three men."

"The one called Thayer Miller was the most sorely injured, nearest to death. How do his wounds appear now?"

"His bleeding has stopped; he is well bandaged. The lady of Langley made him a number of strange poultices from the mosses and mud at the embankment. As yet he has no fever, and his breathing is regular and deep. However, we surely have no fears of his running tonight and looking for a party of the English. Nor, do I think, will his friend, Brandon, rise to escape into the darkness. Timothy no longer seems affected by the blow to his head, and you have the lady, and her companions."

"One of us remains on guard through the night," Eric said.

"Aye, Eric, but do you think we need secure the captives in any way?"

Eric smiled grimly. "I would wager a great deal that the old couple are going nowhere. Nor would Timothy desert his friends. But as to the lady of Langley ..."

"Where would she go on her own?"

"Oh, I believe she might find another road upon which to find murderers and thieves. She is foolhardy and stubborn enough. She is not to be alone. At any time. Whatsoever."

"Aye, then, Eric."

"I'm sorry. I believe she must be watched every minute. In my present temper, I do not believe I am the right man. You'll have to share the duty."

Raymond started to smile, then sobered. "Aye, Eric."

Eric frowned. "You were about to laugh."

"I had forgotten how much we have lost. It occurred to me only that watching such a beauty is not such a hardship of duty—there are many responsibilities that are indeed drudgery ... but this ... believe me, this will not be so tiresome."

"You think not?" Eric said. "I'll be curious to hear your opinion on that matter in a few days' time. I will take the first watch, while she is still dedicated to the wounded man. Take your rest by that tree, yonder, and have Angus sleep at the next. The lady will be between you then. I'll wake you at midnight."

"Aye, Eric. And I assure you, I'll not complain of this duty."

"Um. Well, we shall see."

Igrainia was grateful, and a bit amazed, that the Scots waited so patiently for the injured men to be able to ride.

She was cautiously elated as well that her ministrations seemed to be working magic with Thayer. The injuries he had sustained had been serious and potentially fatal, but his wounds were already beginning to close. She had stitched the worst of them carefully with horsehair, packed them with moss and mud, and they appeared to be healing cleanly and well.

As yet, there was no sign of infection. Though he was still sleeping most of the day, he opened his eyes and spoke now, and Timothy had informed him with the greatest pleasure that it would be no time at all before he could rise, and at the least, make it behind a tree for personal business.

Under the circumstances, she couldn't ask for much more.

Except that the constraints put upon her were making her mad.

Perhaps Eric wanted to throttle her, rip her limb from limb, or see her eternally caged within a prison set outside a castle wall, but for the time being, he kept as far away from her as the copse allowed. He brought in the meat, conferred with his men, disappeared completely—and was yet never really gone—and never spoke a word to her.

She thanked God. She didn't think that anything would ever ease the pain of losing Afton, but being busy and useful was the sweetest balm for that kind of anguish. She knew the limitations of man and woman, and that she could only use what she had learned about herbs and the properties of the earth to help heal any man. God alone decided who would live and die.

But the longer she knew them, the dearer Timothy, Brandon, and Thayer came to be to her. She couldn't help but feel certain that she had been the target of Anne and Joseph and their family all along, and that giving the coin to Rowenna had alerted them to the money in her possession. And because Thayer and his friends had decided to ride with her to be protectors, Reed was now dead and the others would never make the journey they had planned. Like her, they were prisoners of Eric and his band.

Except that they didn't seem to feel that they were in any need to escape.

But, she realized, Timothy and Brandon would never leave while Thayer still lay dangerously prey to infection. And perhaps the Scots knew that.

By the third morning in the forest, Eric's followers and the young men who had been heading south to join with Edward's army were becoming well acquainted. Timothy was learning sword maneuvers from Angus, and being corrected by Geoffrey, who was far more slender and had determined that Timothy, being more of his own shape, needed to learn to move more lightly and depend far more on craft than on muscle.

Nor did Merry or John seem disturbed by the change in their fates. Both spent the days serenely preparing whatever catch the men brought down, smoking meat or searing it for the next meal, finding what berries they could in the nearby woods, repairing rips and tears in tunics, and helping to oil mail or sharpen swords or do whatever useful work there was to be had.

It seemed, however, that they had been warned to keep their distance from their mistress. Yet despite the fact that they slept far from her and hurried about their daily tasks with little contact, and despite Eric's remove from her proximity, she was never alone.

Never.

And it was driving her mad.

She could scarcely get either Angus or Geoffrey to stay ten feet away when she slipped into the forest.

If she dipped her face into the stream, they were there.

When she slept at night, if she turned one way she saw one face. If she turned the other way, she saw the other face. And, she knew, of course, that she wasn't trusted in the least.

She longed to shout at Eric that he was an idiot, an ass. Where on earth could she possibly go? There was no escape here unless she managed to seize one of their horses in an instant, which was surely impossible with Angus, Geoffrey, and Eric himself about. There was also the last man who remained from his party, the giant of a man called Raymond Campbell, who seemed to have the ability to bring down the fastest, highest flying bird with barely taking time to set an arrow to his bow.

There was the fact, too, that she had, at first, taken to heart Eric's threat that he would kill the others if she attempted to escape.

However, she didn't believe that he would do so. He made his decisions on what he would do to a man or woman based on that particular person, and she realized that more thoroughly as each day went by and it appeared that her young friends did not intend to leave; they weren't really held by any restrictions.

She was the only prisoner here.

And a prisoner ready to jump out of her skin.

She longed to bathe.

She could hear the trickle of the stream so near them, and she could reach it, and touch it, but she longed to immerse herself in it. The clothing she wore was encrusted in Gannet's blood. There seemed to be mud and muck ingrained in the fabric of her clothing and her own flesh.

But she never went near the stream without her two followers, Angus and Geoffrey.

She was coming to know them so well.

Angus was a huge burly fellow with long red hair and brilliant blue eyes. His beard was as long as his hair, and he might have been a mad, mythical god in an ancient tale. He was pleasant, courteous—and big. If he chose to make a wall of himself, no man could pass by.

He carried a sword that seemed larger than a lightning bolt. He hailed from the highlands of Scotland, and there, each chieftain was a small king unto himself, and his clan. He had grown up near the north isles still ruled by Norsemen, and had known Eric and many of his kin for years. Listening to them speak, she knew that Eric had often lived among Angus's family, and that his own kin stayed there often, though they hailed from the lowlands. The highlands were most often distant from the battles and dangers that had raged for well over a decade now.

Geoffrey was a far slimmer man, but like all the warriors who had been taken prisoner before they turned the tide, he was deceptively well muscled. Once, when she would have gone down the little path to the stream alone, he caught her arm, and she knew that his grip was as sure as any metal vise. His hair was brown and shaggy, but where once the prisoners had been as filthy, bloody and muddied as she now felt herself, he appeared none the worse for wear. The mail the men had been wearing had surely come from the arms storage at Langley. The colors they wore were their own, and their clothing had been cleaned; their hair had been washed and trimmed. At times, she had heard the men in the stream. They were delighted by the cold stream, and of course, could count on their privacy, since she and Merry were now the only women in the group. Merry would never intrude.

And she would surely die before she would do so.

And so, it seemed that the rest of the little world around her was doing well enough while she lay awake at night, feeling encrusted and caked with blood and debris, while the others took pleasure in the abundance of their surroundings.

There were times when she told herself that nothing about her person mattered in the least. Afton was dead.

Then there were times when she realized that she was alive herself. And while living, she craved air to breathe, water to drink—and a stream in which to bathe.

And unbelievably, it seemed that a time not so long ago was yet already far away. She was alarmed at times to waken and know before her eyes opened that Afton was gone, and had been gone. The day when her husband had breathed his last was beginning to feel like a different lifetime. Afton had been dead no more than a month and a half. Yet the world had changed. She hated herself for the feeling. She didn't ever want to forget him. She had sworn to herself at his death that she would be true to his memory all her life. And already . . .

She knew in her heart at every waking moment that he was dead, and no longer a part of her life, and there was nothing at all she could do about it.

Nothing.

Except despise and mock herself at her own misery for being so terribly filthy.

Eric's wife and child had now been dead more than a month as well. But he hadn't forgotten a single emotion, she knew. His love stayed with him.

As well as his hatred, and his bitterness.

She knew it every time his eyes touched hers.

But at least, that was it. Every once in a while, their eyes would meet. He didn't come near her, but rather left her to his men.

And they were like flies. Always upon her. So near . . . giving her only seconds to slip behind a tree when absolutely necessary.

And that was it.

She was smothering. Desperate.

On the sixth day in the forest, she could bear it no longer. She awoke feeling as if she were becoming a part of the forest floor herself. She lay quietly for a moment, then looked to the right, and to the left.

Both her guardians seemed to be sleeping. Looking across the copse, she could see that Thayer, Timothy, and Brandon still slept as well. And taking a glance around, she could see no one else near them. Eric had left the encampment with Raymond Campbell, as he was prone to do by day, hunting for meat.

She stole away as silently as she could, hesitated, then tiptoed into the trees that led to the stream.

She walked to the water, yet hesitated again, listening. She urged herself to hurry—to strip quickly, jump in the water, jump out. Ah, but then, how could she put back on the loathsome clothing that still carried the dry remnants of Gannet's blood?

She had an extra shift and gown, packed for the long journey to England, but she had left them back at the camp.

And if she went back to the camp, she might wake someone.

And, she told herself ruefully, if she jumped in right there, they could also too easily waken and come rushing down to the stream.

So thinking, she began to walk downstream.

When she reached a point where she felt safe, she slipped her overgown from her shoulders, yet even as she did so, she suddenly heard a cry in the forest.

"Gone!" Geoffrey shouted.

"Gone, she can't be gone!" Angus bellowed in reply.

"The horses, get the horses."

"Nae, lad, she didn't leave by the road, we'll try the stream!"

She quickly slipped back into the trees, trying to get her gown back on. A thrashing in the forest warned her that the men were near.

Instinctively, she ran, deeper into the trees, farther downstream.

"Lady, stop!" Geoffrey cried.

"Go away! Damn it, leave me be for five minutes!" she cried in return.

"She's running, aye, she's trying to run!" Geoffrey called.

"Run her down then!" Angus roared in return. "We cannot lose her!"

"No!" she shouted, ready to explain that they didn't begin to understand.

She was halfway tangled in her own clothing. Far from dignified. She stumbled through the brush by the water, trying to adjust her dress as she went.

A second later, she felt the trembling of the damp earth as one of them hurried after her.

"No!" she shouted again. "Wait!"

But it was Angus.

Huge, his red hair flowing behind him, like the wrath of God.

She couldn't help herself. She ran farther.

She was fast, and she sprinted from the water through the trees, finding a forest path. She felt a moment's wild burst of elation—she actually could run if she chose to do so. The freedom that suddenly pounded in her heart was a sweet feeling.

Her pace quickened instinctively. Logic filled her mind. *She could run, yes. Run, because she could outmaneuver them. Run, because Eric bluffed when he threatened murder. She wasn't worth the lives of others to him. She wasn't worth anything at all to him, she was nothing but a valuable chess piece in the game of war, a token to be delivered to his king . . .*

And what that king would do with her, she didn't know.

She hadn't meant to run, but now there seemed no turning back. The thrashing in the forest seemed far behind her. She had an incredible head start. She couldn't move far without a horse, but she could stay hidden within the trees. Alone, she could travel almost invisibly. If she crossed the border and reached the north of England, she could buy her way south. She had learned, from the treacherous Anne and company, to trust no one.

She was moving with such speed, her feet seemed to fly. And again, the sense of elation that filled her with each step seemed to give her the power to fly. She wasn't winded, she wasn't sore, she was simply soaring . . .

She was stunned therefore when a towering block suddenly invaded her path, stepping from the trees.

She couldn't stop herself from running.

She plowed into the block.

Teeth, nose, chin, hands, crashed into his chest.

She tried to steady herself and fingers wound into her

hair. The thrashing behind her came to a halt. She hadn't been so terribly far ahead.

Angus and Geoffrey were now standing behind her in the path. She could see them because she was in a death lock, and the strands of her hair that weren't tied into Eric's fingers were falling over her face, blinding her.

"Lads, it seems as if you've misplaced something," Eric said, his tone one of dry mockery.

Some*thing.*

Infuriated, tears threatened to spill from her eyes, and in sudden sheer frustration, clenched her muscles to deliver a damaging kick.

But she found herself twisted around, her back to his chest, her wrist now in the vise of his grip, her arm twisted so that she couldn't possibly fight.

"You were right!" Geoffrey said defensively. "She is dangerous, that one."

"Aye, she tried to elude us!" Angus said.

"She'd not have gotten far," Geoffrey said calmly.

"No. She won't get far," Eric said with a deadly calm. "I will see to the lady myself." Her arm was suddenly free. But as she started to step away, she found herself caught up again as his hand landed on her shoulder. "Come, madam. It's time we had a talk."

"No!"

"Yes."

"I've nothing to say."

"That's amazing, but no matter. I shall do the talking."

And she found herself propelled forward.

Deeper into the trees.

And away from all others.

CHAPTER 7

Each time she attempted to halt and turn around, she found herself prodded forward.

"Wait, damnit!" she insisted trying to turn.

"Move!"

"No! You don't understand. I wasn't trying to run—"

"Trying? Madam, you were running."

"I wasn't going anywhere, I can't stand your men with me every minute of every day! I woke and needed privacy—"

His hands clamped on her shoulders. She managed not to scream as he twisted her around and pushed her through the forest path. She shook off his touch, walking on her own.

"What? Are you going to drown me now?" she demanded.

"The thought is tempting."

She came to the embankment and halted again, spinning

around. They were far downstream, far from the others. If
he intended murder, this could certainly be the place for the
crime.

She squared her shoulders and stared at him furiously.

"You!" she said heatedly. "You listen to me. I—"

She was unable to go further because he suddenly seemed
to explode with searing aggravation.

"No. You listen to me and heed me well. You are the
greatest annoyance I've known in years! You don't like
being among my men? I didn't like chasing over the country
after you, but I have done so, and here we are. So let me
explain the situation to you once again. You are in our
custody. A prisoner, a hostage, a pawn. What you like and
what you don't like doesn't apply."

After all the events that had occurred, it didn't seem to
matter terribly what happened anymore. The dream of escape
had died as quickly as it had risen. Standing there, before
him, when he had obviously enjoyed the stream and fresh
clothing himself, suddenly made her feel all the more horrible. And as she stared at him, the driving passion in her life
was simply to remove the blood and mud that seemed to
cake her body. "I am a prisoner, not your subject, not
someone who owes you anything at all, not loyalty, not
courtesy, and by God, what is it that you don't understand?
What on earth can you expect? A prisoner certainly isn't
going to offer blind obedience! And you have not . . . you
have not provided me with the least required for any hostage.
Even Edward gave his caged prisoners a privy! I cannot,
will not, abide like this, I will not accept your ridiculous
dictates willingly, I will not remain willingly; I will not do
anything asked of me. I am an annoyance? I shall be more
so! If that's so disturbing, then let me go, and I will darken
your life no further! Or simply be done with it and take off

my head, or put your sword through my heart, but I will not go on like this! I—''

Her stream of words came to a halt as she suddenly saw the ice in his eyes.

''My apologies, I cannot end your life for you,'' he informed her coldly. ''You are worth more alive than dead, my lady.''

''Then I will be as *annoying* as possible and you will not have a minute's peace from me until you begin to extend not kindness or compassion but some simple necessities— such as privacy and the opportunity for cleanliness!''

''The stream has been here all along.''

''And so have your men!''

''There is no way that you will ever be left entirely alone.''

''I cannot bathe in front of your men.''

''Cannot?''

She should have been forewarned by the slow arch of his brow and the set of his jaw.

''Cannot—will not!'' she spat out.

He moved with such lightning speed that she was taken entirely unaware. His hands were on her shoulders; she thought he meant to shake her, to offer some violence. She realized before a scream could tear from her throat that he was finding the clasp to her cloak. The garment dropped to her feet while she stood in stunned silence.

''What—''

He was going for the filthy, muddied hem of her gown. She tried to move back. ''Stop it, what in God's name are you doing—''

''You want the mud off; so be it!'' he told her, tugging at fabric.

''Wait, stop, no—''

She tried fleeing again, a situation that merely made her trip over her own feet, and caused her to fall flat on her rump. The air rushed from her. He caught her by the arm, his hands filled with linen as well. It began coming over her head. The ties caught around her breasts, the garment was over her face. She couldn't see, could barely breathe and she could feel his hands everywhere, trying to loosen the ties.

"You wretched creature!" she swore, yet she was certain he had no idea of what she was saying, her words were so muffled by the fabric. "Vermin, scum, despicable . . . vile . . . loathsome . . . hideous pretense of a human being!" She struggled as she swore, trying to strike out, to fight, certain that she was in for terrible violence from him, the horror of rape, of a vicious subjugation, no matter his abhorrence for her. Yet no matter how she tried to strike, no matter her words, she could accomplish nothing, she was fighting with the tangle of her own clothing.

"Stop!" she cried, and the word was clear, because she was suddenly sitting in the mud alone, bereft of all the clothing that had been cutting off her words.

She curled her arms around her chest, staring at him in desperation and fury, and humiliatingly close to tears. "You will pay for this. I should have let you die, you ungrateful monster! I will kill you for this one day. Perhaps it's good that I didn't let you die because you should really meet your maker in the most gruesome fashion. And when my brother and the king find out how you have treated me, what you— what you have done to me, you will die the death of a traitor, they will cut you up slowly, rip out your organs . . . castrate you—"

She broke off with a scream because he was reaching for her again. The shock of the powerful feel of his calloused hands against her bare flesh was staggering. His face, so close to her own as he lifted her, was set and grim. She was suddenly afraid that he meant to drag her back to the center of the camp, and see that each and every one of his men violated and humiliated her.

"You will die for this!" she promised, and then, the fury that had so assailed her turned to fear. His hold upon her was like a death grip. He was built like the wall of the castle, with a sudden anger in him that seemed as hot as molten steel. He wasn't a man to be begged or with whom one could barter, but she was suddenly so afraid of what could be done to her that she almost rued her words of fury. "Wait!" she breathed, ready to swear that she'd behave decently if he'd just let her go. "Don't do this! Listen. Let me go, you must let me go. Don't take me back to the encampment. Listen to me! Wait—"

He didn't wait.

He simply released her.

She hadn't realized where he had walked, hadn't heard the sound of the stream around his feet as he moved.

But that's where they were.

In the stream.

And as she fell crashing into the water, it wrapped around her like a blanket of shocking cold ice.

She screamed as she hit the surface, then choked as she slipped beneath it, sinking into three or four feet of briskly chill water. The sting against her flesh was breathtaking, then numbing, stunning her completely. The words she might have spoken as a humble plea were choked against the rush of water that filled her mouth. For seconds, she couldn't move, just feel the rush of the frigid stream sweep around her.

Then she found the sense and instinct to surface, her head only, her torso and limbs kept beneath the surface. Water streamed down her face and sluiced through her hair. Her heart beat in a frantic pulse of fear as she braced for what might be coming next.

She had to be wary, on guard, ready to fight his next onslaught.

But even as her head emerged from the water, he stepped back, a good foot away from her. He towered there, his blond hair shining in the sun, looking down at her. She hated the way he looked down.

She wasn't about to rise. She was still afraid. Of physical violence. Of his anger.

But only his eyes touched her. They seemed a strange blade of heat against the cold engulfing her, a heat that touched her with an uncanny sensation that raced along her spine, and into the center of her being.

She kept crouched down, shivering, teeth chattering, so stunned and shattered that she forgot how much she hated him, and for a moment, no words came to her lips, and it was even difficult to assemble a coherent thought.

He, however, had no difficulty talking.

"I wouldn't dream of denying you a bath, madam. But you'll not be left alone, and so, there you are. Dear God, can it be true? Is she suddenly silent? Amazing, but good, because you need to listen. Your privacy is nonexistent, and your freedom only goes so far. If you decide to take a swim to the other side and streak naked through the forest, I warn you now, I will send every man I have after you, and I will not bother myself with concern regarding what befalls you."

What would befall her . . .

Fear snaked into her again, pushing aside knowledge and leaving only wariness, her own vulnerability, the ease in which he could manipulate her, move her, do whatever he chose to do. Words suddenly spilled from her lips before she could stop then, words that betrayed every sense of her own weakness, and handed him the knowledge that she was indeed a captive of his slightest whim.

"You . . . *you* . . . you wouldn't . . . you're not . . . you didn't intend . . . you're not . . . you weren't . . ."

"You thought, Igrainia, that I intended to rape you?" There was an incredible disdain in his tone. "Oh, madam, that is far too intimate a violence, and nothing but violence, and one that holds no appeal for me. Bathe to your heart's content. Rid yourself of the dirt and the blood—if you can. I assure you, blood is hard to wash away. I'll be on the bank. Again, understand this. You are a prisoner, and one I intend to keep. But nothing more than that. Your ultimate fate lies in the hands of Robert Bruce, not in mine. This is the most privacy that you will get. You will never be left alone, and since you seem able to escape my men, then you are a task I will have to take on myself. You wanted the stream; you have it. Enjoy it."

He turned then, leaving her in the icy water, and walking to the embankment.

Igrainia remained where she was, watching him, afraid to move. He stood on the embankment for a moment, water pouring from his boots, breeches and tunic. His back was to her. Her heart began to thud. Now would be the time to swim away . . .

Except that there was nowhere to go.

He turned again, facing her, then sliding against the trunk of an old oak and sitting at its foot.

"You'll congeal to ice if you don't move," he warned her.

That much was true, she realized. Her teeth were chattering. Her limbs had no feeling.

"It's ridiculous for you to sit there," she told him.

"Ah, but here I am."

"Where could I possibly go?"

"Nowhere. But it doesn't seem that you accept that fact."

"I didn't mean to run anywhere this morning."

"You didn't mean to, but you did."

"I haven't any clothing."

"You might not consider that a problem."

"You are obnoxious."

"You are a pain in the ass."

"How crude, ill-mannered and rude. But to be expected."

"Aye, of course, there is little we learn of chivalry and manners in the barbaric north."

"I can't stand this!" she erupted, then breathed deeply, thinking to change her tactic. "Please . . . can't you just go away—just a little away, for just a few minutes?"

"Unfortunately, my lady, you seem to be an idiot, and therefore, I cannot."

"Sir, there is no insult that you can inflict upon me that means a thing, but, if you don't mind, explain your words. I'm actually extremely well educated," she informed him pleasantly, trying very hard to hold on to her temper.

"You fled the castle, thinking that you could make it to England alone."

"I wasn't alone."

"Aye, then, you had a pair of gentle, naïve rabbits at your side."

"Many pilgrims travel in the countryside."

"And many of them do not make their destinations. Your 'friends' upon the road have most probably been practicing their trade of murder in the woods for some time. It's a nice, fairly easy way to make a living—for those who are not squeamish about shedding blood. Kill a man or woman, steal everything he or she carries, dump the body, and make off with the goods. Do it along one of our poor, rutted roads to the south, surrounded by forest, and the crime might go undetected for decades."

"Had I been killed, I'd not have been a problem for you."

"Ah, but I've told you, you are worth much more alive

than dead." He leaned forward suddenly, his features set in a scowl. "And I don't imagine that man meant to kill you, not right away at least. Most likely, you would have suffered repeated assault, until he tired of you, and then he would have killed you—unless he could have been convinced that you'd still be worth something—though tarnished and abused—to your brother, a very wealthy man."

She stared at him, wanting to dispute him, and feeling colder than ever. She remembered Thayer's comments before the attack, when he told her that Gannet had watched her all the way.

"They were the least likely group to suspect of such evil," she defended herself.

"You may be educated beyond all reason, my lady," he told her. "But you haven't the common sense of a horse. Evil comes in far more ways than the visible encroachment of an enemy army—or a man who openly wears a pair of devil horns."

"I haven't the common sense of a horse—"

He waved a hand impatiently in the air. "You're young, madam, and I assume, palatable enough to some men, especially a filthy outlaw riding in the company of his family, fellow murderers and thieves. Such a man would be desperate."

Such a man would be desperate?

She might *be palatable?*

She was outraged. So much so that she started to emerge from the water, itching to slap him. She remembered where she was, who he was, and her own bare situation, and sank back down, wondering how it was possible to feel such absolute hatred for someone without simply exploding.

"There is nothing," she managed to say smoothly, "that could befall me that could be worse than being your prisoner."

He let out a disdainful grunt. "Let's hope you are never put to the test on those words, my lady."

"If you don't leave, this will be worthless."

"That's your choice."

"I can stay here a very long time."

"The bank is more comfortable."

He leaned back against the tree and closed his eyes, appearing more bored than tired.

He was far more stubborn than a mule, Igrainia decided. But she could be equally determined.

She remained still in the water. He didn't move. She wondered even, after a time, if he had fallen asleep.

The whole of her body seemed to be locking and freezing. As time passed slowly, she began to realize that he might be stubborn, but she was stupid.

She moved at last, at first doing her best to swim through the shallow water just to make sure that she could still move all her extremities. Then, down the way, she saw an outcrop of rock in the water and moved to it, and was pleased to find a fine sand surrounding the rocks that she could scoop up and rub against her flesh, cleansing it. The sand was rough but invigorating and made her feel fresh, and as if she had really washed away the blood and the muck she had worn so long. She almost forgot her silent watcher in the woods, then remembered he was there, looked back, and saw him still against the tree, his eyes closed.

She moved through the water again, thoroughly rinsing her hair. It was better, much better, when she was moving. But after a while, and despite the rays of sun that slipped through the break in the trees that hovered over the water, she was freezing again.

Which led to another difficulty.

How to get out.

She rose slightly, shaking back her hair, trying to smooth

it so that she wouldn't emerge to a head full of mats and tangles. She glanced to the bank again, and was startled to see that he had gone.

She went dead still, carefully looking through the trees, but he seemed to be nowhere about. Anxiously, she looked to the pile where her clothing had been flung. If she hurried . . .

She made haste, thrashing through the water, then flying once her bare feet touched the solid ground. She reached the pile of her discarded belongings and quickly dug for her under gown, only to discover it was entangled in the tunic and inside out. She began to struggle with the entwined linen, fumbling in her haste. She swore as she dropped the garments, both slipping from her numbed fingers. Then she froze, a chill arising from her spine, a sixth sense warning her of danger. She looked slowly in the direction of the encampment. He had returned, carrying a pile of her clothing.

He approached as casually as if she were fully clad from head to toe. His eyes swept over her length, wholly impassive. She might have been a horse—one without impressive stature or coloring or head shape.

"Excuse me. May I . . . ?" she inquired, reaching for the pile of clothing.

He dropped the garments just short of her hands, causing her cheeks to burn before she bent to gather them up. To her dismay, she again had problems, struggling to find the hem of the clean linen undergown he had brought.

A short, choked cry of alarm escaped her as she felt his hands taking the garment from her and slipping it over her head. As she brought her arms through the sleeves, he was waiting with the tunic, and when she had it over her head as well, she found that he was at her side, tightening the strings.

She remained absolutely dead still, not moving. When he

was at a distance, he seemed a far safer man. When he was near, she felt his height. When he touched her, she felt his strength. And the heat that seemed to emanate from him.

The heat was hatred.

And hatred for all she stood for.

She barely dared to breathe, at this nearness.

"Your brush is on the ground. Get it and get back," he said. His tone, little more than irritable and sometimes even amused in their discussions during the day, had suddenly grown harsh.

She plucked up the brush and started walking back to the camp, aware that he followed her all the while.

She managed to forget him in truth when they reached the camp. As she broke through the trees she saw that Thayer was standing up.

She let out a cry of both delight—and fear—and rushed over to him, starting to reach out to him in case he was unsteady, then stopping herself and halting a foot before him.

"You're—you're standing."

He gave her a broad smile. "Aye, Lady. I am standing. Thanks to your very fine care, so I believe."

"You've still got to be careful. You were sorely wounded—"

"Your stitches were excellent. My flesh has mended . . . enough."

"Enough?"

"Aye."

She realized that he was looking at someone who stood past her.

She turned, and of course, Eric was there.

"Tomorrow, we start back for Langley," he said.

She looked at Thayer once more with concern, then back toward Eric, but he had already started across the copse and through the tangle of trees that led to the small patch of shaded grass where they were keeping the horses. She saw that Eric was striding straight toward the great steed he had ridden the day he had first stopped her flight from Langley. She hesitated a split second, then determinedly walked after him.

He had reached the horse. Apparently, he had been out hunting earlier. A pair of pheasants had been tied over the pommel of his saddle and he was untying the cords that bound them there, ignoring her though he was surely aware of her presence.

"It's too soon," she said softly.

"For what?"

"I don't think he should ride yet."

"No one has asked what you think."

"But . . ."

"Go away, Lady of Langley," he said in a low-toned warning.

"Go away! I would gladly go away—"

"Let me clarify," he said sharply, stopping at his task and staring at her pointedly. "Go back to your injured friends. Get away from me."

She felt as if a cold wind lashed against her face. "I'm forced to be with you. Forgive me if I can't make the taking of a hostage an easier affair for you!"

"Don't make me move you."

"Don't make Thayer ride when he isn't ready."

"Igrainia, after a battle, men move while dripping blood from a dozen different injuries, and many survive to tell their tales of valor."

"And many die."

"Thayer is ready to ride. It is his choice. And I must return."

"Then . . . you should go."

She was startled when something that almost resembled a smile curved his lips.

"Where I go, my lady, you will come as well."

"Then . . ." she began, and swallowed hard. "Then we should go, and you should give them some more time here, by the cove."

"We all ride out tomorrow. We'll rest in beds, at Father Padraic's village tomorrow night."

She started. "You know the village?"

"Of course. We followed your every step."

She felt a deep sense of unease. "You didn't . . . you didn't . . ."

"Raze the village, pillage the stores, ravage the maids and behead the men? No, my lady. We refrained—especially since most of the people there do recognize a Scottish king. Now, go back where you belong."

"I belong in London."

He didn't reply right away, but finished untying the birds. "I refuse to play word games with you."

"I don't think of any of it as a game."

She was startled when he suddenly thrust the birds at her. "Pluck these, madam. We want to make sure your gentle injured fellows are well fed before they ride."

"Pluck them?" she repeated.

"Aye, my lady. It means that you should take the feathers out, so that we can cook and eat them. A task with which you're not familiar? Perhaps you should become so."

"I don't know how," she informed him angrily. "I've never plucked a bird, and I don't care to become familiar with the task."

"Such a well-educated, highborn lady! Alas, of course, I forgot. All your life, your birds have been cooked for you, your wine has been poured for you, your clothing washed, your steaming bath brought to you by the backbreaking labor

of others! And you thought that you could run from the
barbarians who rightly claim your castle—and make it on
your own all the way to London! Well, this will help prepare
you for your future dreams of flight. Pluck the birds. The
task is not hard. You'll figure it out.''

She really didn't have anything against plucking pheasants. They were for a meal, and she ate as everyone else
did. He simply had a talent for making her completely and
irrationally furious.

He took the reins to his great warhorse, drew the animal
from the trees, and mounted. Once he was mounted and
staring down at her, she dropped the birds.

"Captives don't pluck pheasants," she said, dusted off
her palms, and turned to walk away.

She never heard him dismount.

In fact, she had no idea that he was directly behind her
until his hands suddenly fell on her shoulders and he spun
her around.

She was startled breathless, yet she wondered ruefully
just what she had expected, instantly angry with herself for
her own action, yet the regret was far too late.

"You *will* pluck the birds."

He reached down for the birds, retrieved them, and caught
her wrist before she could back away. He dragged her to a
fallen log where he sat before forcing her down before him,
first on her knees. But it wasn't where she was intended to
stay. He looped an arm around her waist, pulling her so that
she was forced to sit in the space on the ground between
his legs, against his chest.

A bird landed in front of her.

His arms wrapped around her again.

"This, my lady, is a feather. Not good to eat. These are
fingers. Place them so upon a feather. Pull. Take care not
to break the feather off in the skin—the little stubs do not

taste good at all, and they stick in your teeth. Do it over and over and over again, and then, without too much stress upon thought, expertise, or education, you have a plucked bird.''

She was miserable, stiff, so locked in by his body that she wanted to scream.

''I can pluck the birds!'' she strangled out.

''Indeed, you can.''

But now, even his hands were on hers, his fingers curling with her own, so that he guided them to another feather.

He seemed combustible behind her. Like a caged creature, ready to pounce. She desperately longed to be free from the power of his hold.

''I can do it.''

''I was certain that, with your keen intelligence, you would quickly figure it out.''

''I have done so.''

''Good. Let's keep working then. There are many more feathers here.''

''I can do it alone. You were going somewhere. I didn't mean to stop you.''

''But you must have. Why else throw the birds into the dirt?''

''I dropped them.''

''Dropped them? Really? But then, I must show you that we're not all rude, uncouth, unchivalrous, and so on, by helping you now that they are picked up. Come, another feather, and another.''

His hands were so large, yet his fingers so adept. Covering hers, and gaining feathers all the while. She felt the prison of his heavily muscled thighs, and heard his every breath. She clenched her jaw, praying for restraint.

Then a single word burst from her lips.

''Please!''

"I beg your pardon?"

"Please."

"Once again. I'm hard of hearing. All that clash of steel in the midst of battle and mayhem, you know."

"Damnit—"

"Damnit? Is that what you said?"

"You heard me perfectly."

"I'm afraid I didn't."

"Please!"

He released her hands and straightened on the log, but remained sitting so that she was still imprisoned before him.

"Yes, I imagine you will pluck the fowl just fine. You are expert with a task when you choose to be. Young Thayer fares extremely well."

"Yes."

"You do remarkable stitches."

"Stitches are not difficult."

"You're far too modest. One could say that you indeed saved the lad's life."

He was mocking her, and she bit back at him, far too quickly. "One could say that I saved *your* life."

"But Aileen is dead. And Margot died. In your hands."

Her shoulders stiffened, then, despite her position, she twisted and looked up into his eyes. "You are a bitter fool! Don't you think I would have saved her ten times over rather than you had it been in my power?"

He stared down at her. She heard the lock of his jaw, and for a moment, really feared violence as she saw the blue fire in his eyes.

"Indeed, madam, I suppose you would have."

She quickly turned back to the pheasant, lowering her head. She nearly screamed when she felt his hands at her waist. He rose, lifting her, moving her aside.

He continued to watch her for a long moment. She stood in silence, trying not to shake.

Then he turned and started back toward the horses.

He mounted his war steed, turned the beast and headed hard down the trail.

And she was left alone.

With the log, the pheasant, the feathers . . .

And a strange, disconcerting memory of his heated touch.

CHAPTER 8

There was simply something so aggravating about the woman that Eric was tempted to let her go. Let her be a fool, and run into another group of cutthroats and thieves. If he had waited just one more day to ride after her, or if they had started off just minutes later from Father Padraic's wayside village, she would be dead now. Or in far worse condition, but she would never see that.

Because she was such a thorn in his side, he seemed unable to stop himself from lashing out at the irritation.

One man on a good horse could reach Father Padraic's village in the matter of a few hours. He didn't need to reach the village, only the outskirts where he was due to meet with Allan MacLeod, and receive whatever news there was from Langley, and if any word had been received from Robert Bruce.

He arrived early. The horse he had was exceptionally fine. He had commandeered the animal after a skirmish with a small party of Scotsmen—kinsmen of John Comyn. It had been a battle he hadn't relished, as he knew that the men honored their own dead, and had difficulty accepting the fact that Bruce had claimed the throne.

But no matter what the battle, a man fought for his own life and ideals. And the Comyn men had been supplied by the English, which was why the horses left wandering were so fine.

He had chosen the huge roan despite the horse's initial wide-eyed, rearing reaction to being seized by a different man from the master he had known. A warhorse with a learned loyalty was an invaluable animal, and Eric had been certain he could retrain the mount. He had done so, calling the roan Loki for his Norse ancestor's god of mischief. The horse could run with the agile speed of a purebred Arabian, but his size and strength allowed him to carry a considerable weight and still run for incredible distances.

He was a deeply valued prize of war.

Then there was the other.

The lady of Langley.

She realized nothing. The concept of being a captive seemed to have eluded her. As had that of humility. And simple gratitude.

That they had wasted an incredible amount of time. That he had done so because good men might live and prove to be valuable in his sadly depleted fighting force. They might have ridden today; Thayer Miller was a man who understood the importance of position and movement.

Yet Eric had waited. Given the wounds more time. And he was chafing badly at his inactivity, and the hours in which he'd nothing to do but think. Even here, at this distance, he felt the chafing. He stared up at the sky, knowing that he was early. But it was better waiting here. It was better that he had come early—better, certainly, than seizing his captive and shaking the lady of Langley until he rattled her bones apart.

He heard the sound of a bird's call, listened for a second sound, then returned it and led his horse from the shield of brush where he had waited.

Allan trotted toward him along the trail.

"Eric, I had thought myself early."

"I rode with a fair amount of speed. There was little to keep me, sitting about a forest copse."

"There is much for you to do at Langley."

Eric frowned. "Is there a problem?"

"Not a single traveler has ventured near. I sincerely doubt that many will dare the proximity of the castle for some time, not when it seems that the disease was kept from spreading. But as you had asked, I rode to the inland to the next town, once within Bruce's domain, now under one of Edward's knights, a Sir Ramsey. But men will be men, and whispers will flow. I brought a great deal of ale—thanks to the coffers of the late master of Langley. The people there pray that battle stays away from them, and that there will be a fall harvest. But in their hearts, they remain for Bruce. A deep patriotism burns in every heart, and perhaps, the divide created by Comyn's death will lessen since the Bruce is the one man who can now free the country from English rule. As the ale flowed, I learned that word has reached the Earl of Pembroke that you have seized Langley in Bruce's name, and he is furious. He's heard interesting tales. It seems that the late lord's kinsman, Sir Robert Neville, made his way to the earl, and told how the filthy ragtag band of the worst outlaw betrayers and prisoners brought the castle to destruction with disease, then seized it."

Eric shrugged. "What further is said about us matters little. We all have a death sentence on our heads as it is."

"Pembroke has been ordered to seize Bruce—one way

or the other. He can't afford the men to come to Langley and hold such a castle siege, but this kinsman of the late Lord Afton, Sir Robert Neville, has survived the illness. And he isn't under Edward's command, not in the manner of the Earl of Pembroke, who had been given his orders to find and seize Bruce.''

"Naturally, he will try to raise forces to return to Langley and take the castle back," Eric said. "He planned on being named lord of the fortress after the death of his kinsman, the hereditary lord. If he can take it back, he will naturally be awarded the title and overlordship of the land. Still, we have time. No matter how men may honor a king, they all know that Edward cannot protect them from a plague. And to take such a fortress as Langley, a man needs a large army, bountiful supplies, and a good source of patience. We'll keep our eyes and ears open—there is no way not to know if such an army were on the move. And my intent was never to try to take a castle so positioned and hold it at this time, only to free our families."

"Of course," Allan agreed. "Except . . ."

"Aye?"

"Taking the castle has proven to be a surprisingly pleasant task. The people have been grateful for our steps taken in caring for the sick, in repairing the devastation brought on by the disease. Many of them feel that they were stricken because of the cruelty practiced by imprisoning women and children. God visited the illness upon them for that act, or so some believe. They are a deeply faithful group of people, and follow the words of their priest, who appears to be a uniquely honorable man. They are not nearly as horrified as they might have been to find themselves under the rule of a band of 'savage highlanders'."

"This is still Scotland, after all, no matter how many

Flemish and English may live in the lowlands. And there is a call in most men to be proud of what they are.''

"Which is my point; it will be difficult to abandon these people if the time comes when we are forced to move to the north, or so beset by English forces that we must resort to fleeing back to the highlands.''

"There is nothing we can do but wait and watch.''

"There is another rumor,'' Allan said, "that the king is furious and is ready to lead his own army.''

"The king, the mighty Longshanks, is growing old and infirm, so the rumor goes.''

"His hatred and anger against rebellious Scots keep him strong.''

"But as we have seen, all men succumb to death.''

"He needs to die soon,'' Allan said.

"Aye,'' Eric agreed.

"Do I return to Langley?'' Allan asked.

"Aye. Tell Peter that I intend to make all haste to return myself. And I think that we might have gained three good fighting men on this foray—the lads were not so enthusiastic to serve Edward as they were to find a means of survival. We can provide that for them.''

"How can you travel quickly with injured men, an old couple, and the lady of Langley?'' Allan asked.

"There's nothing wrong with the lady of Langley,'' Eric said. "And she is the only one among the group who is trouble. The others can come at their best speed; she'll travel with me. Also, it's important to find out just where Robert Bruce is now and with what forces—I intend to turn her over into his hands as soon as possible. Perhaps he'll be able to use her in bargaining for the return of his wife, sisters or daughter.''

"Aye, Eric, I'll see what I can learn by the time you've returned.''

*   *   *

Riding back, Eric noted that he did not pass a single traveler along the road, such was the sorry state of the lowlands these days.

As he neared the brush covering the trail through the trees to their streamside encampment, he slowed his pace, searching both the ground and trees for any sign of mounted men on the move. There was none. Still, this area was known to be a far safer place for Englishmen than native Scots, and he wanted to make sure that their dangerously small party was not happened upon by an offshoot English scouting party. The information regarding the whereabouts of the King of Scots now kept him to the north, in lands more friendly to his cause, and so, it was most likely that any strong forces would be hunting him far from here. But just as Robert Bruce had learned that small forces must use intelligence and the art of surprise, attack and running swiftly, so it was likely that his enemies might learn the benefits of scouting out small forces, and picking off the Bruce's loyal men one by one.

When he had assured himself that the grounds near the forced encampment were secure, he rode back down the narrow branch trail to the stream.

As he came close, he could smell the succulent odor of cooking meat. The scent instantly made him hungry, and he kneed Loki, urging the horse forward at a faster clip. Then, nearing the camp, he slowed, letting out the bird call that would inform his men that he was returning, and not an invasion of enemy forces, or even a stranger.

As he reached the clearing he came across Raymond guarding the camp, his sword drawn as he stood blocking the way. At the sight of Eric, he grinned, and sheathed the sword. "I'm a careful man, these days," he explained.

Eric dismounted. "It's always best to be a careful man."

"You've arrived in time for fresh fowl," Raymond said, reaching for Loki's reins. "I'll see to the horse. The old woman has dug into her travel satchel for spices and such. The stringy pheasants we've managed to obtain should be tastier this evening, even if they remain somewhat a challenge for the teeth."

Eric nodded his thanks to Raymond and strode on through the trail. As he broke through the trees, he saw that the fire burning in the center of the camp was bright against the gathering darkness. The others were gathered around it; even Thayer was seated straight among his friends. The birds were taken from the tips of the swords on which they had been set over the fire, and divided among the company. Merry, doing the dividing, was smiling and chatting. There seemed a strange camaraderie about the fire.

"Eric!" Angus said. "You've made it back in good time! Ouch!" He took his finger from the breast of fowl he held, blowing on it. "The birds are hot and savory. We've had a new cook, and she is far better than Raymond or Allan."

"Naturally!" Merry said. "Men think to fill their stomachs, while women know the art of making a meal."

"There are many fine cooks who are men," John chastised his wife. "Why, remember, in the days of Alexander, when we were so young ourselves, Merry, the old lord brought in the fellow from Stirling who could make the toughest mutton seem fine."

"Aye, but he's not here tonight, and I am, so eat your meat, and be glad!" Merry retorted.

Eric took a seat on the ground in the circle, his eyes quickly scanning the area for the lady of Langley, who was conspicuously absent from the group around the fire.

She was by the tree where she slept every night. Her long gray cape was laid out as a blanket upon the ground. Her back was to the group, she rested upon an elbow, and read from a small book. He found himself curious as to whether she had carried the small volume, or if it had been something one of the men had given her.

Was it a book of prayer, or something other?

"Sir, a fine piece of the meat!" Merry said, offering him a hot and greasy piece of the fowl.

"My thanks, madam," he said. The thigh meat in his hand, he indicated the woman under the tree. "Your mistress isn't joining us?"

"She says she has no taste for these birds," Thayer told him.

No taste? So that's all the labor of plucking had taught her—to turn her nose up at their efforts to keep them all well fed.

Let her starve then, Eric thought.

Yet he found that her absence from the group around the fire irritated him as fully as everything else about her.

He bit into his meat. Aye, they were scrawny birds, but Merry had had a way with the seasoning. The meal wasn't just sustenance. He tasted the food, as he realized he hadn't tasted food in quite some time.

Since . . .

Since he had come to Langley.

He took another bite of the meat, then found his gaze fixing on the woman beneath the tree once again. Her hair streamed down her back like the blue-black shade of a moon-touched river at night. There was a great deal of it.

He hadn't noticed how thick and long it was before. Her immersion in the stream for all those hours in the morning had apparently taken away the packing of mud that had kept it mortared closer to her head in the past days. The length of it seemed to carpet the forest floor and become a part of it.

She still had not made a move, or indicated in the least that she was aware she shared the space with anyone or anything other than her book.

"Bless the lord! I have never had such finely plucked fowl in all my day," he stated loudly.

"Why, the Lady Igrainia plucked the birds herself, so she did," Merry said, pleased. "And, as you know, I prepared them, of course, and seared them over the fire."

"And a tasty meal you have created, deep in the wilderness," Eric said politely.

The lady of Langley remained still.

But she had heard him. And he knew it.

"Indeed, Merry, I'm quite in awe of your cooking abilities. But I must say—not a single piece of feather have I hit! Perhaps when we return, the lady of Langley will see that all fowl brought into the castle is so perfectly prepared for the fire."

"But, sir!" Merry said innocently. "The lady of a castle such as Langley does not need to pluck fowl. The castle is filled with servants and kitchen lads and lasses. Well, it was filled, before . . . before the sickness. Still . . ." her voice trailed.

"Still . . . such a talent," Eric murmured. "But then, perhaps she'll not be at Langley long enough to share her skill."

He had finished his piece of meat. Their hunting that morning had not been plentiful, and he did not intend to take more. He rose. "Mistress Merry, that was an excellent meal. If only we had you at all encampments. We ride early. Thayer, you have the strength?"

"Aye, sir!" Thayer said, standing, perhaps to prove that he could do so easily and well.

Eric nodded.

"Before full light, I would be under way."

He walked away from the fire, striding across the copse. He took up his own position at a distant tree, yet he could still see Igrainia.

Darkness had almost fallen.

She still pretended a great interest in her book. She could not possibly see the words.

He unclipped the brooch that held his mantle about his shoulders and rolled the garment to act as his pillow, then lay back in the coming night. He thought of the years gone by, and they seemed endless and futile, and the night seemed like an oppressive, stygian blanket falling around him. He closed his eyes and suddenly longed to be at sea again, but the sea was where they had found the drowning stranger who had brought about so much death. If only he could go back, relive that day, and leave the man to drown. The never ending struggle for freedom had not seemed like an exercise in madness when Margot had lived. It had been a dream, delicate, beautiful, there to pursue for his children, and his children's children ... for Aileen, laughing, smiling ... golden hair waving in the sunlight as she ran to him, calling out his name, making the desperate fight for a future worthwhile.

Sleep eluded him. He heard the others find their places on the pine needles beneath the trees, except for Geoffrey, who was taking the first hours of guard duty, and would remain on the trail. The fire burned low.

He tensed suddenly. There was movement in the camp. He lay still and wary, then realized that Igrainia had risen, and come to where the embers were burning low. She sat before the flames with her head forward, her ebony hair catching bits of light from the dying blaze, seeming to gleam in a blue-black cascade.

She seemed to be as still as he. He almost rose, wary that she had risen for some purpose and was waiting to see if the men would waken and waylay her before she could make any attempt to slip through the woods.

Then he realized that her shoulders shook.

She cried silently in the night.

He did not disturb her.

They received a pleasant welcome from Father Padraic the next day. He remained in horror that he had welcomed such a heinous group as Anne and her family to his bosom, yet talked about the way that Heaven worked in mysterious ways, sending Eric and his men to rescue them when they might well all have died at the hands of the cutthroats.

Igrainia found herself heartened with Rowenna's pleasure at seeing her, and at the joyful way Gregory bobbed and bowed as she dismounted from Skye.

There was a great deal of bustling about when they first arrived, with Father Padraic insisting that Thayer must get straight into a bed. Food would be brought for him, since his injuries were the kind that would take a long time to heal completely, and he would have a long ride back to the castle the following day. While that business was taking place, Igrainia found herself being led into the long hall where the pilgrims ate—where she had first seen Anne and her family band, and Thayer and his companions as well. Rowenna chatted as she served a dish of lamb and vegetables, telling her how very grateful she was to see her alive and well.

"Gregory was right, you see," Rowenna told her. "You must always listen to his wisdom."

She wasn't sure how Gregory had been so right, since she was, albeit alive, still in the custody of her enemy. She arched a brow.

"Well, you were attacked, no?" Rowenna said with a

shiver. "I should have known that the man, Gannet, would prove to be a knave. He watched you as you ate, as you spoke. And the look in his eyes . . . as Father Padraic would say, he was coveting what was not his. Thank God Sir Eric and his party came along when they did."

"You know everything that has happened?"

"Of course. They came through here, looking for you, you must know. And soon after, Allan MacLeod returned, telling us that we must be careful, we had harbored a family of monsters. Can you imagine? There are other such places as this village, churches where pilgrims stop. I wonder how many people they might have killed and robbed . . ." Her voice trailed as she shivered. "But that's it, don't you see? Gregory knew. You fought Gannet for your life, but fought long and hard enough . . . and you were rescued!"

"Yes—rescued."

"The stew is good, isn't it?" Rowenna said.

"Pardon?" Igrainia looked into her bowl. She had eaten as one who had been starving a very long time, though she had only missed one meal, the night before.

The scent of the cooking meat last night had been mouth-watering, and only her fury and her pride had kept her from it. The hunger had stayed with her through the long ride this morning.

"The stew. You are done already. Well, Sir Eric will be pleased."

"He'll be pleased that I have a hearty appetite?" Igrainia said.

"He'll be pleased that you've eaten so quickly. He's eager to get back on the road."

"But we're staying the night."

"The others are. You're not."

"Oh, no, we're all staying, resting here tonight, starting out again in the morning."

As she spoke, she looked uneasily to the door, and as she did so, he appeared. Entering the hall, he stood in the doorway a moment, blocking the sun, yet seeming to shimmer with a golden glow. It was his hair. So very blond. He almost appeared like a hulking god, tall, filling the doorway with the breadth of his shoulders. She remembered when he had come tearing down from the hills like a wild man, hair matted and filthy, face streaked with dirt, clothing so tattered. No more. He had apparently made very good use of the stream whenever he chose. His hair was clean and combed, long and rich. He was clean-shaven. He wore a tunic over his shirt and breeches, and about his shoulders, a mantle in the colors of his clan. The tunic, she knew, had been fashioned from Bruce colors, and she knew that his clothing had been chosen as a declaration—he was not a man to hide his identity or his cause.

His gaze fell upon her, his eyes that cold arctic blue that could appear so remote, that seemed to burn with an ice fire that left no doubt as to the depths of his fury—or his passion, she imagined. She had seen him take on a party of men with twice his own number and arms and armor that were many times superior to his own. She had seen him battle disease, and come through with improbable resilience.

God's will. She thought.

God certainly had a sense of irony.

"So, you've eaten. Then we should leave."

She remained seated. "I confess to being confused, Sir. I was of the understanding that we were all staying, that Thayer should rest here, on a good bed."

"Thayer will rest here."

"I have been tending to his wounds and should ride with him."

"My men have tended to fellows far more grievously wounded, and much farther from any point of healing."

"But—"

"May I remind you, you were the one to suggest that Thayer should stay, and that I should go, and since I am loath to risk any more danger to your noble person, you should come with me."

She stared at him blankly. It had indeed been her suggestion.

"I am eager to reach Langley. I've noted that you're an excellent rider. We should move quickly together."

"But—"

He strode to the table and looked down at her with impatience. "*But* seems to be your favorite word, my lady. It is time to go."

She was absurdly tempted to cling to Rowenna's arm.

He was already talking to the young woman whose near perfect beauty had been marred by the slashing wound across her cheek.

"I thank you," he said softly.

"My lord!" she said, blushing, and dropping a small curtsy.

Igrainia stared at the two, but neither seemed to notice her. She felt a blush sneaking up her own cheeks as she suddenly found herself wondering if Eric had found solace for the loss of his wife with Rowenna.

He took the girl's hand, pressing something into it. Money, of course.

Payment.

Igrainia turned, staring at the empty bowl in front of her.

She jumped when she felt his hands on her shoulders and the rush of his breath against her earlobe as he bent down behind her to speak.

"Are you ready?"

Her throat felt thick and heavy, and she didn't know why. There was no reason to be any more afraid of him now than she had been before. There was less reason. He had stated clearly enough that she was a prize of war he much preferred alive.

She stood quickly, hoping to knock him in the chin with her shoulder. He moved back in time. "Rowenna, my love and blessings to you and Gregory," she said.

Rowenna nodded, smiling. "God bless you, lady, as well."

Igrainia turned and walked from the hall. She saw Eric's huge horse immediately, but the little mare she had been riding was gone. There was a far finer looking horse next to his, a tall, dapple gray with the look of an Arabian.

"Her name is Iona, and I've just purchased her at some expense. But she'll move quickly," she heard from behind her.

"She was expensive? You mean you've had to part with some of the money you surely seized from Langley? I was perfectly fine with the other mount. But then, again, if you wanted this horse, you could have just seized it—as you have seized all else."

"May I suggest that you mount the horse," he said cooly. There was frost in his narrowed gaze once again.

She strode to the horse. For some reason, she was trembling. She had been riding since she was a small child. She had ridden the largest horses in the stable.

But she missed her footing on the stirrup while trying to mount this one.

And there he was, of course, directly behind her, hated hands upon her again as he lifted her and set her upon the mount.

This wasn't his horse. She could slam her knees against the animal's haunches and gallop into the afternoon, and ride hard until twilight, then darkness . . .

"Don't do it."

"Do what?"

"Don't even think about trying to elude me."

"Whatever gave you that idea? I'm delighted to be going home."

"Really?" he mounted beside her. "Even when you won't be staying that long?"

She stared at him too quickly to hide her wary surprise. "Where am I going?"

"I don't know—yet."

"Oh—are you simply going to open the gates and let me run?"

"Hardly likely, my *lady*," he replied, an emphasis on her title. He wasn't watching her then but staring toward the church building. Father Padraic was coming toward them, a thin leather satchel in his hands.

"Meat, cheese, bread and a flask of wine for the journey. A letter as well for my good friend and one time pupil, Father MacKinley," Father Padraic said.

"Thank you, Father," Eric said, reaching for the satchel and securing it to his saddle. "Gifts we will appreciate."

"As we have appreciated yours. Godspeed. And God bless you, Lady Igrainia."

She inclined her head, and managed to say a soft, "Thank you." What she really wanted to do was tell him that Sir Eric Graham was probably no Christian at all, but a heathen still bowing before some ancient Norse gods.

And that his gifts were all stolen goods.

Somehow, she refrained.

Father Padraic walked around to her side, making the sign of the cross. "Sometimes, my child, God sends us on the right path."

"And sometimes he takes good men and innocent children far before their time," she replied, unable to keep her silence then.

"His will be done," Father Padraic said, ever serene despite her words. He smiled at her. "There were murderers among us. God sent salvation."

"A good man still died. Reed."

"But you and the others were saved."

"The world is all perspective, isn't it, Father?" Eric said. He gathered his reins. "You know where we are, Father."

"And you know the road back here."

Father Padraic stepped back. Eric started off at a lope.

This time, Igrainia was tempted to stay behind.

But the dapple gray mare, though not Eric's horse, seemed ready to obey his every command anyway. Before Igrainia could grasp the reins, the mare had taken off after him, and they were on their way.

By late afternoon, she was amazed both by the amount of territory they had covered, and how long it had taken her to cover that same distance when she and John and Merry had come on foot.

Eric rode hard, but never too hard. He had an instinct for when to rest the horses, when to walk them before reaching a stream for water, and when to cross a meadow or plain at full speed. There were so many times as they rode that she thought this was her one great opportunity; she could surely find a time and outdistance him.

But she didn't take the chance. She knew that though he appeared to give her little attention and didn't bother to speak unless it had to do with stopping for water or slowing their pace, she was certain that he knew her every move.

And she didn't want him riding her down, catching her, and either binding her to the mare, or forcing her to ride with him.

It had also occurred to her that somewhere during the journey, he was going to have to sleep. That would be her real opportunity.

They rode into the darkness as the moon remained high in the sky, illuminating the path. She had a feeling, though, that he had covered this ground in his day so many times that he would need no light to know where he was, and where he was going. They kept to the forest paths, and she knew that he was ever wary of others being on the road. But they met no one along the way, other than one old woman hobbling along. Eric did not hide from her, but reined in, paused and spoke to her for a moment. Igrainia was certain that he had given her a coin. And she knew, as well, that it was his way of spreading good will across the land for the king he served, Robert Bruce.

At last he told her that it was time to stop for the night. They were in the middle of the road. She was tired and thirsty and saw no place that looked at all conducive to sleep, but he dismounted and came over to help her down from the gray.

"I can dismount on my own."

"As you wish."

To her great irritation and consternation, her foot caught in the stirrup.

Naturally, the gray mare decided to take a walk.

She hopped along beside the mare, trying to disentangle herself, and cursing the idiocy of trying to dismount so fast.

He caught the horse's bridle, and before she could free her foot, he had lifted it from the stirrup.

"Don't touch me—please!" she snapped out.

He didn't.

And she didn't regain her balance, but fell flat on her rear along the trail. She lowered her head, fighting the sense of self-fury and humiliation. She saw his booted feet before her.

"Shall I assume that you don't want help up, or shall I give you a hand?"

"No, I do not wish your assistance, in any way," she said, scrambling to her feet and dusting the dirt from her hands.

"Try to walk then without tripping over anything else," he replied, leading the way off the road.

He had known the way like the back of his hand. There had been no suggestion at all that there was a trail through the trees and thick brush, much less one that led to another stream with a pleasant copse hemmed in by oak and pine. Here, the needles lay thick and rich, and the branches that rose above them were so dense that hardly a trickle of moonlight flickered down. It was enough, though, to throw a few rays of gem-like glitter upon the dark water. To the far side of the bank, the earth rose in a low sloping hill, making the copse even more private than it might have been. Igrainia was thirsty, and therefore dropped the mare's reins and bent to cool her face in the brisk rush of the spring and drink deeply.

Eric led the horses to the water, then moved across the space to tether them before taking a drink himself. Igrainia ignored him and walked to one of the trees, sinking down. It wasn't something that she would admit, but she was tired and sore. She knew how to ride, she rode well, and she had traveled distances before.

Never like this.

He took the satchel of food Father Padraic had given them from his saddle, then chose a tree himself. He broke the bread, hungrily eating a piece, his eyes, however, never leaving hers.

"You've no interest in eating?"

She stared back at him. "I'm not in a mood to break bread with an enemy."

"I see."

He continued to eat. She closed her eyes, leaning against

the tree. The night felt cool. She pulled the gray cloak around her—the dull gray woolen cloak that had supposedly been her assurance she would pass for a poor pilgrim all the way south to London.

She was hungry and longed to snatch the food from him. She was also tired. More tired than hungry, because she must have dozed. She was startled when she felt his fingers winding around her wrist.

"Not so fast, my lady. My tree is better than yours."

"Enjoy your tree, then, and leave me mine!" she protested as he dragged her to her feet.

"There will be but one tree," he said, and she realized then that he carried a length of rope and had slipped it around her wrist.

"Wait!"

It had been pre-tied in a noose and closed tightly around her arm before the protest left her lips. He tied the other end around his own wrist, using his teeth to secure the knot.

"This is *not* necessary!" she protested.

"I believe it is. I watched your face throughout the day. You thought a dozen times of trying to ride hard and fast across a meadow, and lose me in the next patch of forest ahead. And I saw you bide your time, thinking that I must eventually give way. I've wasted enough time running around the country. You will not cost me any more."

She narrowed her eyes in fury. "I can be more trouble than you can ever imagine. I can cost you time and sleep and thought. I can—"

She broke off with a startled cry as he sat, and the rope pulled taut, drawing her down beside him.

"I could kill you in the middle of the night, you know," she informed him, chin lifted high.

"I doubt that you could, and I know that you would not."

"No, you don't know that."

"You could have killed me before."

"I didn't know just how really, truly wretched a man you were at the time."

"I should have appeared more wretched at the time— you didn't know then that I wouldn't slaughter your people if . . . if Margot died."

"Maybe I'm really desperate now."

"Why would you be so desperate?"

"How do I know your great Robert the Bruce won't decide that I should be executed?"

"Because he doesn't execute women for being the daughters of English earls."

"He merely uses them," she said bitterly.

"He wants his wife back, his child, his sisters. Cheer yourself. You could soon be back in the bosom of your family, having freed some other poor lass as well."

With his free hand, he pulled his mantle from his shoulders and laid it out on the ground. "There's room," he said.

"I prefer the pines."

"Indeed. They can be as sharp as your tongue."

He lay his head down on the cloth, stretched out, and closed his eyes.

She stared at him a moment in anger and consternation. Then she pulled away as far as the rope would allow, and lay down on the pines.

He was right. Beneath a cloak or stretch of fabric, they were soft, making a bed of the earth. Without a cover, they were prickly.

She tried to ease her own cloak up for a pillow. It worked. With a feeling of triumph, she lay her head down. She would never sleep not tied to this man. But she needed whatever rest she could afford.

She lay awake, and the night seemed very dark. It didn't seem to matter if her eyes were opened or closed. She lay very still. Then she realized that whatever the light, he could see, and he was watching her.

"Why were you crying by the fire last night?" he asked.

She tensed. "Why do you care?"

"I hadn't seen you give way to any grief before, that is all."

She hesitated. "Because . . . Afton is gone. And after he died, I had hoped . . ."

"Hoped for what?"

"It doesn't matter. He is dead."

"And gone. You had hoped you would have his child, and you know now that you never will."

"I've known . . . for some time," she murmured.

"I'm sorry."

"You must be very sorry," she murmured bitterly.

He was silent a moment. "If you don't think that I can sympathize with the loss of both husband and a child who might have been, you have less sense, my lady, then I ever thought." His tone was quiet, but had a harsh edge. She bit her lip, remaining silent in the darkness. She closed her eyes again. Her body ached from riding. Her mind seemed as sore. The night was cool, and her cloak was serving as her pillow, and she was afraid to move. She lay there, stiff and cold, until she at last began to drift to sleep.

Dark winds seemed to sweep silently around her. A deep chill settled over the earth, and she dreamed that a permanent ice had come to the land, and it was crawling over her. She longed for the sun. It was near, it was somewhere near, and she was running, trying to find the place where it was fighting through the ice and wind, aching to feel warmth again.

And it was there. She could feel it. She just had to keep running. With every step, there was a greater warmth. It blanketed her. Then the wind died down, and the cold faded, and despite the wonderful warmth of the sun, she slipped into an ever deeper darkness . . .

Her eyes opened on the misty light of dawn.

She felt the man behind her.

Felt him, because they were touching.

And she realized with horror that he had been the sun in the night, the warmth she had sought so desperately.

He had taken his mantle which had been his pillow, wrapped it around her, and drawn her close. His arm lay around her shoulders. His body curved to her back.

She stared at the new day, trying not to scream, keeping still and silent and praying to find a way to inch from his hold . . .

"You're awake. Get up. It's time to ride again."

She didn't need to inch away. He didn't push her, but he moved back himself as if he had been forced to give his warmth to a toad through the night. She was forced to turn back to him as he tugged at the rope, but he didn't even glance at her. He gave his full attention to untying the rope that had bound them together. He stood with an impatient agility and speed.

"Up!" he repeated, staring down at her. Apparently, she didn't move quickly enough because he reached down, catching her hand, drawing her to her feet.

"We can reach Langley tonight."

"Tonight?" she said. "But that's impossible. It took over two weeks to reach Father Padraic's church from Langley."

"You were walking with two old people, my lady. We have good horses, and with them, even riding with you, I can make Langley by some time tonight." He turned from her and started walking toward the horses.

Even with her . . .

She stared at his broad back, feeling a renewed burst

of real warmth within herself. It was the slow simmer of resentment.

"Indeed, let's do hurry. I definitely find the concept of *even* a night in the dungeons preferable to a night like the one I've just spent."

She had the pleasure of seeing his back stiffen before she turned to the water, wanting to wash her face and hands and wishing she dared jump into the rushing stream, clothing and all.

But she didn't intend to be cold again. Ever.

In his presence.

CHAPTER 9

Eric didn't think that he had ever pressed a journey so hard, other than the time, perhaps, when he had last ridden here, determined to re-enter the castle where he had been a prisoner, and retrieve his wife and child and his people.

But then he had not come a great distance, and he had ridden with men, hardened warriors accustomed to nights on the ground, lack of food, lack of sleep and hours in the saddle.

Not a fool to take the chance of killing the horses, he had watched his pace, made stops for water, and even offered the lady of Langley the remnants of their food. She had declined. He had almost insisted, afraid that she'd faint along the way and destroy their chances of making Langley, but then he had decided that if she was so determined to maintain the distance of an enemy relationship, so be it. They had only to reach the castle, and she would be secured within its walls, and he would be freed from the burden of keeping an ever watchful eye upon her.

She had refused sustenance, and hadn't passed out on him, and had kept pace.

They were equally eager to be quit of one another.

And so, they reached Langley just as the sun was fading from the sky.

They were seen riding toward the castle long before they approached the gates.

The great drawbridge was lowered while they were still some distance away. The crimson shades of a dying day were like rays falling upon the earth from a misty pastel palette. It had been a beautiful day, and the colors of the coming night created an impressive picture of the castle's realm; the water in the moat sparkled as it twisted around the castle and headed for the connecting river, the walls gleamed in the strange glow—and the flags of Robert Bruce, king of Scotland, flew from the parapets.

Riders came out to greet them—Peter MacDonald, Allan MacLeod, Raymond Campbell, and Father MacKinley.

"So, you did make a hasty return!" Peter called cheerfully, reining in as they met in the stretch of field before the castle wall. "It's good that you've returned!" He glanced at Igrainia, riding at Eric's side. "Welcome home, my lady."

Igrainia nodded. Eric studied his resistant companion. She was pale and drawn, her face very white against the ebony hue of her hair, her eyes a deep purple in the twilight. He looked away from her. Last night, he had dreamed about spider webs, about fighting to disentangle himself from a black web. He had awakened with her hair in his nose, and noticed then that his captive was quivering convulsively from the cold that had settled down upon them in the depth of the forest after the sun had fallen.

He didn't want her dying of the cold, so he had used his

cloak and body to warm her, and when he had fallen back asleep, the dreams had come again, of being entwined in great, long, shining tangles of blue-black web. Dreams were fickle. From the nightmare, he had drifted into a few moments of haunting recall, and he had cherished the feel of warmth against him, the sweet scent of a woman, and the softness of silky hair, for in those moments he had imagined the hair tangling around him not as a dangerous web, but a cloak of silk, in a gold that rivaled the sun, and when his eyes had opened, he would find he embraced beauty, for she would be there, Margot, and she would smile, and life would again be the most precious gift . . .

He had opened his eyes to a sea of black. And the warmth had been a lie of simple survival, and the beauty he embraced was a bitter enemy, and nothing more than a pawn in the game they played, as dark and dangerous and damning as the color of her hair.

"Igrainia, you must be very tired," Father MacKinley said. "Come, I'll see you straight to your chamber—" He broke off, remembering where the new master of the castle slept. "I'll see you to comfort and rest," he amended.

She tossed back her hair. Those deep violet eyes touched Eric's for a moment. "Father MacKinley, I'm a prisoner here, you know. Prisoners reside in the dungeons."

MacKinley glanced uneasily at Eric. "I'm certain they do not intend—"

"If she chooses the dungeon over other arrangements, Father, so be it," Eric said. "Peter, you will see to the lady, please?"

He spurred his horse, letting Loki race at his full potential to the lowered drawbridge, then slowing him enough to lope the final distance into the courtyard. He was greeted by a young groom who called out his name in a respectful greeting, and when he dismounted he told the boy, "See that he is well fed and well groomed. He has been called upon hard today.''

''Aye, Sir Eric.''

Leaving the horse, Eric approached the main tower keep, walked up the steps, and entered the hall. Old Garth was there, standing with an ornate silver tray that held matching goblets. ''Ale, my Lord,'' the old man said, his face crinkling into a smile. ''Our finest. But I shall be happy to drink first, if you've any doubts.''

Did he still have doubts? Aye, only a fool would not. But Father MacKinley was actually still the real ruler here, and he was an intelligent man, and he knew full well that if these people poisoned him, his men would exact a terrible vengeance.

He drew off his riding gloves and accepted a goblet of ale and drank it down thirstily. Garth was right, it was excellent ale.

''The ale is fine, and these are exceptional goblets,'' he told Garth.

Garth shrugged with a slightly secretive smile. ''They should be, Sir Eric. They were gifts from none other than King Edward himself when the lady married the lord.''

Eric stared at Garth for a moment, his brow arched. Then he burst into laughter. So he was lord over King Edward's own gift of goblets. It struck him as very amusing.

''I believe, if we've others, I may make a gift of them to someone else. Another king. Robert Bruce, will find them fine vessels from which to drink. Then again, he may find that he needs to melt them down for simple silver.''

''They are *my* goblets. You've no right to give them away.''

Igrainia and the others had reached the hall. He turned slowly, eyeing the lady up and down once again, and wondering what it was about her that so inspired him to anger.

"My lady, have you forgotten how eager you are to reach the dungeon?"

Allan made an involuntary gesture, but neither he nor Peter would question Eric's authority in front of others. It was Father MacKinley who spoke.

"Sir, you cannot mean to put the lady in the dungeon."

"It was good enough for our people," he said softly, watching Igrainia.

Her thick black lashes never fell over her violet eyes. She met his gaze coolly. "Prisoners are meant for the dungeons, aren't they?"

"But, in all mercy—" Father MacKinley began

"You are right, Father," Eric said, ready to give a reprieve since he had not intended to incarcerate her in the foul place.

But he never continued.

Igrainia argued against herself.

"I look forward to the dungeon," she said. And she walked past him, heading for the stairway down. No one moved, and she paused. "Am I supposed to lock myself in?"

"Igrainia, you've a chamber above—" Father MacKinley tried to protest again.

"I had a chamber above," she said, and stared at Eric. "And now I prefer the dungeons."

Allan looked at Eric. He shrugged. "By all means, if the lady prefers the dungeons, escort her if you will."

Igrainia turned serenely and continued on her way. Allan looked helpless for a moment, then followed her.

Father MacKinley strode angrily toward Eric. "You, Sir, are blinded by bitterness. Igrainia was no part of the forces who imprisoned your family and your men and their families. And she worked diligently to save lives. It was through the ferocity of the illness that so many were lost, and not through any form of negligence or malice on her part."

Eric leaned against the table, shaking his head. "You heard her, Father. She prefers the dungeons."

That silenced MacKinley for the moment. As the priest looked about for another argument, Eric spoke to Garth. "Perhaps the master chamber is haunted with too many memories of death for the lady. I feel that way myself."

"Lord Afton's kinsman, Sir Robert Neville, had a very fine room across the hall."

"That will suit my purposes while I'm here," Eric said. "I am exhausted, and we'll have a long day tomorrow. Garth, see that supper is brought to me there, please. Allan, Peter, we'll meet here, early, and discuss what we do and where we go from here."

He left the great hall, heading upstairs. His head was throbbing. He was exhausted, and still annoyed beyond all measure.

He didn't like the lady being in the dungeon, and he didn't like the way his own men had looked at him.

She was forcing his hand. And he didn't like that at all.

Before the night was anywhere near over, Igrainia was ruing her pride and her temper.

There were no cobwebs here; indeed, the place was amazingly clean. The sick had gotten well, or they had died, and Eric's men had done an excellent job of clearing and cleaning the cells. There were fresh rushes on the floor, and a clean pallet made a decent enough bed, but she was alone. The crypts seemed far too close, and within the vaults rested her husband, and the lady Margot, and the child, and when the water of the moat lapped against the stones outside and the wind blew in the night and the darkness, she could almost swear that ghosts cried out in the darkness.

And then a rat went racing through the cell.

Father MacKinley brought her supper, and argued that if she were just to say the word, she would be moved.

"I am a prisoner here now. I might as well look at the bars, so that I may remember my position."

"You are guilty of the sin of pride."

"I'm probably guilty of many sins," she said with a sigh. Then she smiled. "You are wasting your breath tonight. I will ask him for nothing. But I thank you for being with me. And I thank you sincerely for the supper. I was very hungry."

MacKinley nodded distractedly. "Igrainia, if you are a prisoner, we are all prisoners, and in truth, people are doing very well. The sickness created a strange bond. They were the outlaws, then the conquerors. It was our castle, now it is theirs, but the difference cannot be so much as noted by those farmers and workers who have buried their dead, and gone back to their lives. Maids sing in the kitchen, most of the men who would have served Afton have readily accepted that a new lord has given the command that life is to be as usual, and everyone is to work to survive. They are aware that he gave the orders that spared many lives. There are many people who come and go with no thought to the fact that the castle has been seized. You do not need to be in here!"

"Yes, I do."

"Igrainia—"

"What have you heard of Robert Neville, Father?" She asked. "He has survived, hasn't he? He must have done so, because he was well enough to escape. He wasn't captured, was he?"

Father MacKinley sat stiffly for a moment. He let out a long breath. "No, Igrainia. Word has it that he reached the Earl of Pembroke's camp. And that, of course, he is in a fury to come back here. But Pembroke has his hands full.

There will be no change here for some time. If you think you can sit in this prison until the English come and rescue you . . . it will be a long wait.''

"I don't know what I'm thinking, Father," she said.

"I must go," he said. "I don't want them to think that we're plotting."

"We have plotted!" she said.

"Before," he murmured. "I wanted you away from here. I feared for you. And there might have been reprisals . . . but there were none. Igrainia, life is going on. War cuts great scars across life, but then it goes on again. Always. Even here. There was a child born today. Catherine, the baker's daughter, and her husband, Thomas, the smith, have had a baby. Neither contracted the sickness, though Catherine's mother died. The girl delivered a hardy, healthy, baby boy this afternoon. There is life again in the castle. I have assured them I will come to their cottage to bless the child tonight."

Igrainia wasn't sure why she felt a sudden sense of being cold again, of being on the outside of something very strange. "You must go then."

He nodded.

"And you must tell them how delighted I am for them."

"Of course."

He stood, hesitating. "I cannot leave you here. Alone."

"You have responsibilities, Father. All the souls in the castle and about. I am fine here alone."

"Please, Igrainia . . ." He broke off suddenly, staring at her. When he spoke, his tone was deep and passionate—he was God's soldier, ready to fight again. "He did not harm you . . . in any way? You're not afraid of him—in any way?"

"Did he molest me, Father? No. I am as hideous as an old crone to him, I assure you."

"Then . . ."

"Goodnight, Father MacKinley," she said very softly.

"Igrainia—you're behaving like a . . . a . . ."

"A prisoner."

He threw up his hands and was gone.

And the night wore on, and on, and on.

In the morning, when she heard footsteps coming through the crypts, she jumped to her feet and came to the bars quickly.

"Father MacKinley?"

"No, my lady, it is I, Eric."

She drew back from the bars. She had just risen. She was certain that twigs from the rushes were in her hair, that she was tousled beyond belief, and looking far more desperate than she cared to be seen.

"What is it that you want?" she asked sharply.

He came into view. He appeared golden, fresh, shaven, smelling delightfully of clean soap, his appearance very fine. His shirt was brilliantly clean, and he was kilted into a long woolen of his family tartan. She hadn't realized before that the contours of his face were strongly positioned but very fine. And his eyes, by day, could be a color that was almost as rich as cobalt.

"I've come to see to your welfare. Remember, you are worth a great deal alive, and nothing at all, I'm afraid, if we don't keep you in good health. How was your night?"

"I slept beautifully, thank you."

"You were brought something to eat last night, I assume?"

"It was delicious."

He nodded. "Well, I'm sure that someone will come along soon now with fresh water and breakfast." He looked her up and down. "The hay in your hair makes quite an interesting contrast to the darkness."

Inadvertently, she drew her hand to her hair.

"Yes, yes, I think you've got it." He moved closer to the bars. "My God, there's mud all over your cheeks."

"You looked far worse when you first arrived here," she told him.

He arched a brow. "I thought you had nothing to do with our arrival."

"You know the man who rounded up your families. Sir Niles Mason. Afton was obliged to open the gates. He argued furiously with Sir Niles. And yet, as far as your being sent to the dungeons, what should he have done? He knew that he was housing dangerous men among his prisoners. And you did prove to be dangerous. Prison and death are the price of your war."

"The price of freedom," he said quietly.

"Have you come down here merely to mock me?" She inquired.

"I told you, I came to see about your well-being. I had an exceptionally good night. I slept deeply, in the comfort of a bed. I awoke to a fine meal of fresh fish and warm bread, and then sank into a bath with steaming water. I met with my men, surveyed the state of our current situation, and was deeply pleased to discover how smoothly the castle is running, how well the people are faring. I even attended the baptism of a newborn baby boy. Our enemies are far away at the moment, afraid that there might be remnants of the plague. The morning has been bountiful. There were so many details in it to be enjoyed, still ... none quite so gratifying as that very long hot bath."

"Do you think, sir, that I would barter my position for a bath?"

"Actually, yes."

"Well, you're mistaken. And I am in good health to be

delivered to your king for his purpose of exchange. So you can go away now and gloat in all your triumph elsewhere.''

''Well, yes, it is a triumph, isn't it? Considering the planned alternative to my life. Do you know everything there is to be found down here, in the bowels of the castle?''

''The prison cells and the crypts are here.''

''I don't suppose you've spent much time down here.''

She hesitated. The secret tunnel was at the end of the long hallway.

He smiled. ''I'm not referring to the tunnel.''

She forced herself not to alter her expression, though it felt as if her heart were sinking. But of course, he would know about the tunnel. He would have insisted on knowing how she had departed without the gates being opened and the drawbridge lowered.

''To what, then, are you referring?''

''There is a door on the opposite side from this cell. A very thick door. Within it is a room filled with interesting objects. All of them are for torturing the poor souls dragged into this prison. You've never been there?''

''Yes, I've been there. The room hasn't been used—''

''Since Afton ruled the castle! Surely, that's what you were about to say.''

She didn't offer a reply.

''The room was intended for use, Igrainia. All manner of interesting and horrific objects had been set out.''

She felt something twisting in her stomach. ''The law . . . there is a fate for traitors.''

''How can a man who has never sworn allegiance to a foreign king be labeled a traitor?''

She walked away from the bars. ''I can only tell you that you are seriously mistaken if you don't understand that the king you don't honor will hunt you down until he finds you, and that he has prescribed death for men judged to be traitors. And that death is the law.''

"Then I must continue to avoid your king's law,'' he said, then asked curtly. "You still prefer to remain here?''

"I do.''

"Have it as you wish.''

He turned and left. She heard his footsteps echoing on the stone. They stopped. She thought that he was coming back, then realized that he had stopped in the crypt, and was standing by the walled tomb where Afton had been laid— and then Eric's wife and child.

She held very still as she listened to the long silence that followed—until his footsteps could be heard against the stone floor again.

Then he was gone.

It was afternoon when Father MacKinley found Eric writing letters at the desk in the chamber he had chosen. There was a map stretched out before him as well. He, Peter and Allan had been estimating the distances to the last known entrenchments of Pembroke's men—numbers, space, geographical advantages, and the time needed to move from one location to another.

MacKinley seemed very much an honorable man, but one who voiced no heated political position. Therefore, after he knocked and entered, Eric carefully folded the map and sat back, waiting for him to speak.

"You can't leave her down there. She might well go mad, locked up not a hundred feet from where her husband lies buried, caught there in the darkness of the night, the wall torches doing nothing but creating shadows upon shadows,'' MacKinley said.

"I have been to see the lady of Langley. She prefers the dungeon."

MacKinley shook his head. "She cannot prefer the dungeon. She is hurting herself to do nothing more than make a point."

"And what is that point?"

"That she is a prisoner."

"Well?"

"Everyone else moves freely here—"

"That she cannot do."

MacKinley sighed deeply. "But if she were to have the run of the castle—"

"She would run right out of it." He leaned forward. "Father, if you can bring her up, do so. I leave it in your hands. The lady's own chamber is vacant and awaiting her. Although . . . it is somewhat changed."

He had left orders that all heraldic plaques and colors were to be removed from the walls—and his own and those of Bruce be set to replace them.

He hadn't been able to bear the sight of the room as it had stood, not after Margot's death. It was not just the master's chambers that had been changed, however. The flags on the parapets had been replaced immediately; those about the hall had taken longer.

"So . . ." MacKinley said. "I have your order to bring her up?"

"You have my permission."

MacKinley left. Eric watched him go, then returned to his letters.

As the day wore on, Igrainia despised herself for her own stupidity. Hours passed like eons. With nothing to fill it, time passed endlessly, and memories haunted her.

She didn't know the time, because it was eternally dim. The torches that sat in sconces high on the walls began to burn low, and she thought that it was late, but then, it might well be only early afternoon. There was no way to tell.

When she heard footsteps again, she jumped up, wary, wondering if Eric had returned. But this time, it was Father MacKinley coming to see her.

He stopped at the bars, gripped them, and stared at her. "Igrainia, God forgive me, but you are stubborn and behaving in a way that is bringing misery to me, and to others. Do you know what you're doing? People are living in peace here, they are managing their lives. But if they believe that you are being cruelly detained here, God knows what they might do. Fight—and wind up slain for their efforts. The innocent could suffer and die, because you are being stubborn. I lay awake most of the night, thinking of all the dire consequences this could bring about. I am telling you, as God guides me, that you must leave this hellish hole and take up residence in your own chamber. There is light there, Igrainia. You have your books in the room, clean clothing, a window to the world."

"My books are in my room, yes, and my belongings are there."

"God does not want you here, I know it. It is unhealthy, this sitting in a cell that is like a tomb, and the dead far too near."

"Father—" she began, ready to tell him that she would come out, but she doubted that her books were available, since it was most likely Eric had chosen the master's chambers.

But she broke off, aware of footsteps once again.

The torches cast a very long shadow on the floor as Eric neared her position.

"She still refuses to come out," Father MacKinley said in dismay.

She opened her mouth to speak, and she wasn't sure whether she meant to protest or not, but it didn't matter because she never had a chance to do so.

"I'm afraid she no longer has a choice," Eric said.

"Why?" Igrainia asked.

"We've come upon some stray English soldiers. We need the torture chamber and all the cells. Not that you'd want to hear the screams from the torture chamber anyway . . . but it's no matter. We can't leave you here to plot with Englishmen."

"Stray English soldiers?" she inquired with alarm. How much time had passed since they had come? Her brother was a young man, but everything she had said about him was true: he had been taught excellently, and he had a great sense of family honor. Since he had been a very young boy, training in the households of other knights, he had known that he would grow up to be an earl, and that he must therefore be responsible, courageous and honorable, and in all things, take care of his family.

Had he ridden here . . . ?

"You've taken English soldiers?" Father MacKinley said, frowning.

She wondered if Eric was bluffing. She feared that he was not.

"It's time for you to leave the cell," Eric said.

"And where will I be going? I don't believe that I can have my chambers. They have been taken. By the new master," she added dryly.

"Actually, they have not," Eric replied. "I am not fond of your rooms. So you are free to claim them once again."

"I am *free* to reclaim them?"

He smiled, a hard smile, filled with impatience. "Are you

aware that you are the most argumentative woman alive? Fine. You will return to your chambers.''

She smiled harshly in return, turned so that her back was to him, and walked to the rear of the cell.

"Igrainia," Father MacKinley murmured softly. "Eric has taken Sir Robert Neville's room. You can be completely comfortable in your own rooms."

"Call the guard," Eric said to Father MacKinley. "He carried the key."

"I'm eagerly awaiting the company of English soldiers," Igrainia said.

"I'm sure you are," Eric replied.

A moment later, she heard the heavy key twist in the lock. She was about to turn and sigh and go willingly— more willingly than they would ever know—but she wasn't given the chance. Hands she was beginning to know far too well descended on her shoulders and she was spun around to face her nemesis.

"I—I won't fight!" she assured him.

She realized then that he wasn't listening. He had stopped walking. They were in front of the large stone monument that sealed Afton, Margot and Aileen into their tomb.

She held her tongue.

A moment later, he started walking again.

And when they reached the great hall, footsteps ceased abruptly behind them. Father MacKinley and another man had been following them from the cell.

She thought that the burly, kilted Scotsman must have been the one with the heavy key—her most recent guard, near her in the dungeons all along, keeping watch, but never being seen.

"See the lady to her room, Jarrett," Eric said and swept past her to the stairs, moving up them quickly.

"Come, my lady!" the man called Jarrett said pleasantly.

He was a very big man, possibly taller than Eric, and heavily muscled, as most of these men seemed to be, but his features were surprisingly fine and he was quick to smile at her. "Thank the Lord, my lady, that you've chosen better ground!" he told her. "The dungeon is no place for a woman." He made a face. "And even the guard's room at the juncture of the crypt and gaol was not a pleasant place to sleep!"

"The bowels of a castle are always damp," she murmured.

"Ah, and the cells are the worst."

"You were—one of the prisoners in the cells," she said, studying his face. These men were so different now. Though many seemed fond of beards and facial hair, they were no longer the pathetic straggle of humanity they had appeared after their capture.

"A long time, so it seemed," he agreed, but continued to offer her a rueful smile. "Still, I had company. I did not have the hours alone here . . . of course, there were the hours when the dead were entangled with the living, but the plague . . . there's not a man alive who does not fear it, and thank God if he survives it."

"Perhaps we should get to the room," Father MacKinley said, looking upward at the top of the stairs, as if he feared Eric would reappear.

"Aye, come along now, my lady, to your fine chamber above the stairs!"

Igrainia knew then that she would have a guard outside her bedroom door as well, but she nodded. This man was courteous. And held no bitterness against her.

And, at least Eric had removed himself from the room she had shared with Afton.

As they passed on through the hall, it was empty. She shuddered at the memory of Eric holding her silver goblets, her wedding gift, and laughing with irony that they should be a gift from one king to another.

It wasn't that she cared so much about belongings. It was that she and Afton had used the goblets, together, the night of their wedding.

She went on up the stairs, followed by MacKinley and the rebel. When she reached the door, the guard took up a position down the hall.

"Jarrett, you are a fine escort. I wish I had known in the night that you were near."

"I'm close, if you need me," he said.

She smiled. She wasn't supposed to have known that he was near. She was supposed to have suffered with the darkness and memories of the death that occurred in the lowest level of Langley.

She pushed open her door, then stopped, talking softly to Father MacKinley.

"Can you arrange a bath?" she asked him.

"I—I believe that I can."

"Will you try for me, now?"

He nodded, pleased to do what he could. He seemed relieved. She was out of the dungeon.

Igrainia stepped into the room and closed the door behind her. And it was then that she saw how the room had been changed.

Every single sign of Afton was gone.

The great shield that had hung over the bed had been replaced by another. A great bird, it seemed, trampling down on another. Latin words were inscribed around it.

The crossed swords Afton had once won at a tournament were gone from the side wall. The tapestries had been changed, and what hung there now depicted the battle of Stirling Bridge, where William Wallace had been victorious.

Another wooden carving of Afton's name and coat of arms had sat on the mantel over the fireplace.

It, too, was gone, replaced by the wretched bird piece.

Infuriated, she didn't think, but turned, bursting back into the hallway. She didn't know where she was going to find Eric and express her rage, but she felt as if she could pummel her way through even a man as large as Jarrett to reach him.

She didn't have to go through such an effort. The door to what had been Sir Robert Neville's room, just down the hall, was ajar. And within the room, standing by the broad oak desk, was the object of her rage.

"My lady!" she heard Jarrett calling after her—but he was too late.

She had entered the room and faced Eric. He had heard her and turned. His expression was nothing more than impatient.

She would change that.

"Usurper!" she charged. She came to a halt just inside the door, staring at him, shaking, burning, her breath coming in great gasps.

"Bastard! Ass!"

"Eric!" Jarrett said in dismay, reaching the door. "She moved so quickly."

"It's all right," Eric said. He stepped past Igrainia, his eyes cold. "It seems the lady wishes to address me personally."

Jarrett nodded and stepped back.

Eric closed the door, turned back, crossed his arms over his chest, and stared at her.

"You were saying?"

She trembled so that it seemed difficult to form words. They came, halted at first, then streamed from her lips without stop. And as she spoke, she found herself walking the few steps between them. "I called you a bastard, an ass and a traitor. How dare you, how dare you touch his things, you low-lying snake in the grass of a traitorous ass! You aren't fit to kneel at his grave, and you have the audacity to take his things, to touch his things!''

There wasn't enough to say. He might be tall and imposing in his stance against the door, but at that moment, his size was no warning, only a further aggravation.

And he was just staring at her impassively.

She raised a hand with the swiftness of a sudden wind and slapped him as hard as she could. And even then, she didn't see the danger in his eyes, but brought both fists up against his chest, and thundered them against him with a strength borne of pure fury.

She was so incensed that she wasn't prepared for retaliation. She gasped, stunned, when his hands suddenly clasped like the bite of wolves around her wrists, and her mad action was halted. She looked into his eyes, and saw the mark on his cheek, and felt the heat of the wrath she seemed to have infused into him. Her jaw locked, and then, no words came at all. She was shoved back, back across the room. Her knees buckled as she came against something . . . the bed. But that she fell back wasn't good enough. He lifted her, threw her further up against the length of the bed, and a second later was straddled over her, long fingers so tightly wound around her wrists, knees so tight against her ribs, that she could scarcely breathe.

For a moment she thought that he would release her wrists and bring his death grip to her throat.

He looked as if he would say so much.

Exact terrible violence against her.

But he didn't speak.

And she couldn't find words.

Then after a moment he said, "Don't ever, ever, lift a hand against me again."

She felt the remnants of anger drain from her as if she were a bird, fallen from the sky, wings completely clipped.

And then, she was startled that she could talk at all.

"I loved him!" she said softly.

And he replied, "I know."

"It was his room."

"But he is gone. And we are here. And for whatever time we hold it, the castle is mine."

She closed her eyes not wanting to look at him again.

He rose, caught her hand, and pulled her to her feet. "Go. Go back to your room."

"It is mine no longer."

"It is where you will live."

"The bars below are truly much better."

"Go now, my lady, because I am trying very hard to remember that you did love your husband, and forget the welt forming on my face."

She shook her head, fighting tears. "It doesn't matter. It doesn't matter what you do."

Yet, as he took a step toward her, she squared her shoulders and turned toward the door. Her fingers faltered as she tried to open it.

He obliged her. She didn't look his way, but walked across the hall, desolate.

And not at all aware of just how dignified.

CHAPTER 10

The first several days, she remained in her room; only Jarrett came to see her, bringing her food, trying to be cheerful, but leaving quickly. Each day, at some point, the monotony was broken as a group of kitchen lads—strangers, rebel Scots—brought the heavy bath, with steaming water, and took it away again.

By the fourth day, she stared at the new coat-of-arms on the wall so long that she couldn't bear it. Despite the strength and effort required to remove the heavy plaque, she got it down.

She slept better that night, only to waken and find that it had been put back. She was alarmed to realize how deeply she had slept—that someone had entered her room when she was sleeping.

She took the plaque down again.

That night, she was stunned when a tap sounded at the

door, and then Jennie entered. She leaped to her feet with joy, racing across the room to embrace her maid.

"Jennie, Jennie! How are you? Tell me, what is going on? I haven't seen Father MacKinley of late. Have Merry and John returned, and the fellows I met along the way? Are the people well, do they fight or protest, or wait in fear?"

Jennie, who had embraced her tightly in return, drew back with a sniff. "The people! They all claim that this is Scotland, and has been Scotland, and it's God's judgment that we accept Robert Bruce. They're fools. The king's troops will come here and butcher us all for such treachery!"

"Aye, that could well happen," Igrainia murmured. "What of John and Merry?"

"They are here, well, and working. And I haven't seen much of the men who returned with them. They train in the courtyard during the day—train with the rebels!"

"What about you, are you all right?"

"I'm well, yes, thank you. But it took Father MacKinley all this time of asking, arguing, and pleading to get our new lord to let me near you. One would think that the two of us could get together and bring down an army."

"Well, you're with me now."

"I'm allowed only a few minutes. To see to your most important needs."

Igrainia hesitated. "I've written a letter. To my brother. I wonder if there is any way at all to get it to him."

"I can try," Jennie said quickly. "I'll have to be very careful."

Igrainia nodded, hurried to her writing desk, and picked up the letter she had written, sealed with wax and imprinted with her family ring. Jennie slid it into the folds of her skirt, looking at the door, which remained closed, as if she expected it would come to life and attack them both.

"Have you heard anything from the outside?"

"Of course, I hear things," Jennie said. She gripped Igrainia's hands. "Other letters have gone out. Apparently, Robert Bruce is to the north, but messengers have been sent back and forth, and then onward ... they're trying to exchange you for none other than Robert Bruce's wife!"

Igrainia felt her heart sink. She might be the daughter of a once great earl, but her father was dead, and not able to put pressure on the king, and her brother had yet to prove himself. Edward would never consider her a possible exchange for the wife of the man who was now his greatest enemy.

"I am lost," she murmured.

"Perhaps not!"

"What else do you know?"

"Sir Robert Neville has not forgotten or abandoned us! He went straight to the Earl of Pembroke, who has his hands full, but from there, he went to Cheffington Castle, where your father's dear friend Lord Danby holds a vast estate. And there, with Danby's assistance he is raising an army of his own. Pembroke will supply him with some troops as well, once he has proven that he can raise men on his own."

Igrainia was silent for a moment. It was not going to be easy for anyone to lay siege here. She feared that her husband's cousin would only manage to get himself killed.

"I believe that he has sent word to your brother as well, who can also raise men."

"He owes his men to the king, and they will be ordered to join Pembroke. Under my brother, I'm afraid."

"What matters is that there is hope. And there is the fact that though this Scottish knight holds Langley, in the lowlands, he is surrounded by enemies." Jennie looked nervously at the door, then back at Igrainia with tremendous sympathy. "They've not harmed you, have they? With everything that has been done . . . what the king has commanded for Robert Bruce's women . . . it's frightening, so frightening!''

"No one has harmed me."

"I've got to go," Jennie said. "That huge guard dog is in the hall. I don't want to be stopped from coming back to you again."

"Of course," Igrainia said quickly.

She hugged Jennie tightly, then her friend departed.

She stared angrily at the plaque she had taken from the wall.

As she did, there was a knock at her door. Afraid that it would open without her assent, she made a dive for the heavy plaque and dragged it behind the trunk at the foot of her bed.

The tap came again. She opened the door. It was Jarrett. "My lady, it's the time you usually summon me and ask for the bath. I've had it brought for you now."

He seemed so pleased with himself for having thought to bring her something that she might desire without having to be asked that she smiled. "You're very kind. Thank you."

He smiled.

She walked over to the mantel and stared into the fire while the parade of people entered, bringing the heavy wooden tub and kettle after kettle of water. At the end, a pretty young woman entered with soap and a linen bath sheet, setting both at the foot of the bed, and then departing with a little bob.

"Is there anything else?" Jarrett asked her.

She shook her head. "No, thank you. What a lovely young girl. I've not seen her before."

"Ah, well, the lass is my daughter. And you have seen her before. She told me that you had nursed her, when her mother, when they were . . . with the sickness. She believes that you kept her alive, and she is pleased to help you when she may."

Igrainia lowered her eyes. "She is lovely, and I'm grateful that she lived. Thank you, Jarrett, and you must thank your daughter again for me as well. And your wife . . . ?"

"She died."

"I'm so sorry."

"Aye, for she was a gentle soul, as sweet as young Amy. If you require anything—"

"You are down the hall. I know."

He started to leave.

"Jarrett," she said, calling him back. "You're a very good man."

He seemed startled. Then he grinned. "Thank you, my lady."

The door closed. She stared into the flames burning in the hearth for a moment, then realized how quickly the water in the bath would grow cold. She disrobed and sank into it, thinking that indeed, this was her one great pleasure in life.

She leaned back, feeling the water surround her.

After a moment, she became aware of a tremendous noise in the courtyard below. She tensed, wondering if the English had returned to take their retaliation against the Scots. Jumping up, she wrapped the linen sheet around her and hurried to the window and looked out. She heard a tremendous clanging of steel, as if a vicious battle ensued. But, she saw quickly, there was no battle, only training. Men had been set in pairs to skirmish with one another, to practice their swordplay.

To the left of the combatants was another group of men. She saw Eric striding among them, shouting instructions. The men were handling long, spiked poles. His voice carried to her as he gave his commands. The men moved forward with great precision, came to a sudden halt, and formed a human arrow of the deadly poles, the "schiltron" the Scots were becoming famed for using against cavalry charges.

Using very efficiently.

She thought about the plaque with his coat-of-arms that so disturbed her and in a frenzy, started looking about the room for a weapon—something she could use to hack the offensive plaque to pieces.

There was nothing in the room that even remotely resembled a weapon. As well as being redecorated, the room had been thoroughly stripped of any item that might be dangerous.

Sounds still came from the window. She wandered back to it, and realized that although she might destroy the coat-of-arms—which seemed to have a will of its own and the ability to return to her wall on its own after it had been removed—she could, indeed, dispose of it. All she had to do was throw it out the window.

But not now.

Not while the men worked in the courtyard.

The training had apparently come to an end while she had been searching the room. As she looked out now, she saw that dusk was falling. There was a lone horseman there, riding hard against a straw dummy with a head that seemed to have been fashioned of cabbage. The horseman slashed with his sword—and brought the cabbage down.

He trotted off, then turned, and came to look at the fruits of his labor. He looked up then, as if aware that he was being watched.

It was Thayer. His face split into a broad smile, and he waved to her. He called out to someone near him, and a moment later two more riders joined him.

Timothy and Brandon.

The three of them waved.

She waved back.

Thayer watched her a moment longer, then leaned over and whispered something to Timothy, who in turn whispered to Brandon. The three rode off in different directions, then came at one another, charging. She gasped, fearful for their lives.

Then she realized that it was a mock charge they had taken. When the three met, they halfway fell from their horses and pretended to rise and fall, rise and fall, rise and fall again, then reach their saddles to manage a sitting position, only to fall over the other way. She laughed out loud, clapping at their antics.

Then, the three of them straightened on their horses, forming a line, serious and not moving. They lifted their hands in a salute and quickly rode away. She frowned, staring at the now empty courtyard, and felt a strange tingling of ice along her spine. She spun around. Eric, in his mail and tunic, his sword still buckled at his side, was so close behind her that it was amazing she hadn't felt his touch.

She clutched the linen sheet more tightly, her breath catching in her throat. But it seemed that he had little interest in her; he had merely been curious regarding her entertainment at the window, and seemed amused himself at the show the men had presented.

But then his eyes touched hers. Blue and direct.

"Where is it?" His tone was curt.

"What?" she whispered.

"The coat-of-arms."

"I have taken it down."

"And it will be put back up."

"And I will take it down again. It's my prison. Where I have dutifully and obediently remained. I've given you no trouble, and therefore, you've no right to enter without warning, without knocking. I have kept my silence and my distance, and—"

"And you are afraid of what the men will think, because I'm standing behind you at the window while you are all but naked?"

"I am not all but naked."

"My lady, you are. And may I suggest strongly that you stay away from windows when you are so undressed?"

"May I suggest you refrain from entering? Especially without knocking."

"Actually, I did knock. You were too involved with the show to hear."

"When no one responds to a knock at a door, it means you should go away."

"When you don't respond, I have to enter, to be certain that you have not drowned."

"I assure you, I will not drown."

"There are those in the kitchen who are afraid that you bathe so often that you will remove your skin, and die. It surely can't be healthful to sit so often in soap and water."

"Please assure them that I am well, will not drown, and do not believe that bathing causes any harm."

"I shall do so. Where's the plaque?"

"I don't know. It's simply disappeared. Perhaps you would be so kind as to do the same."

He turned, and for a moment she believed that he would really leave. He merely unbuckled his sword belt, cast it at the foot of her bed, and sat in the chair by her fire.

She stared at him.

"The plaque, Igrainia."

"The fire will eventually heat that mail, you know. And your flesh will heat and burn, no matter what you're wearing beneath it."

"It will take some time for that to occur. Get the coat-of-arms, Igrainia. I'm in no mood to tear apart the room."

"I'm in no mood to have you in it."

"Produce the plaque, and I will leave."

"Don't you have more pressing battles to fight?"

"Not at this particular moment. By the way, you're losing your towel, my lady."

She flushed, realizing that her hold was slipping.

"Lord, let me help you. I don't mean to be barbaric and uncouth and forget all my manners."

She was amazed to find him instantly before her, reaching for the towel in a pretense of help. His way of helping was to seize the linen sheet. He held it, near enough for her to grab; and stood, near enough to touch. She was alarmed by the trembling that began in her limbs, by the sense of fire that seemed to snake and tease along her spine. The urge to lash out was almost overwhelming, yet she was afraid, very afraid, not of what the violence of his reaction might be, but just that he would touch her in return. And so she stood, several seconds, so very aware of his face, of every line and angle, the breadth of cheekbone, set of jaw, width of fine, piercing eyes. She drew in a deep breath, and that simple act seemed to bring her ever closer to him, but if they touched . . .

The fire in his eyes was deceptive. He was as cold as the steel links that covered his body beneath the tunic.

"Let's see," he said slowly. His tone was deep and quiet, husky. "You're the one who likes to barter, Igrainia. A towel—for a plaque."

Reason returned.

She met his eyes, her own narrowed and sharp, and she held his gaze, remembering just how deeply he disdained her.

"I will only remove it from the wall again."

"And I will put it back—again and again."

"Good, then you may find it."

She turned on her heel, and tried to walk with dignity to

the tub. Once there, she made haste, however, slipping back into the water and sinking down until only her head and neck were visible over the rim.

There was only one serious flaw to her determination—the water had grown quite cold. However, she had started her course. She didn't intend to stray from it.

He walked back to the chair by the fire and sat.

She lowered her eyes, wondering why she was so continually determined to fight battles she couldn't win.

"I will remove it the second you leave!" she said a little desperately.

"You will still give it to me."

"No."

He lifted his hand. "I shouldn't leave too quickly anyway ... it's probably best for the men to believe that I am drowning my grief in the arms of the dead lord's widow."

Her fingers gripped the edge of the tub. "With such a witch as I?"

"You're young, at the least."

She could hear her nails grating against the wood.

"But English."

"Most men are not concerned with nationality, and many may even find a black-haired witch appealing." He sighed with impatience. "After all, in the dark, what does it matter?" There was an emptiness in his tone, a stygian void. She lowered her head, shaking, miserable, very sorry for them both, and yet aware of the deep slashes of war that lay between them, and he remained the triumphant enemy who had never faltered in his quest, no matter the circumstances.

He rose suddenly as she sat in thought, and her head jerked up with alarm. He was at the side of the tub, heedless of the water when he reached in to pull her out. For a moment she was against his form, the water running from her body soaking his tunic, the mail beneath it pressing into her flesh. Her eyes met his with a true rush of alarm, and yet, no sound left her lips, she was so stunned by his action. But he did no more than set her firmly on the soft Persian rug before the fire, seize the towel from the floor, and wrap it around her. "So, you're determined to freeze as well as scrub away your flesh," he muttered. He was at her back, his hands upon her, as he wrapped the large linen bath sheet around her. Then she was standing alone, still silent and stunned.

After a moment, she realized that he must have seen the plaque behind the trunk.

She closed her eyes, listening as he set the plaque back upon the wall, using the butt of the knife he kept sheathed at his calf to force the nails back into the mortar that wedged between the stone in the walls.

She was startled when she suddenly felt him behind her again, his fingers once again upon her shoulders.

"In the end, I should warn you, I win all my battles." He spoke very close to her. She felt the whisper of his breath against the dampness of her shoulders and neck.

She kept her eyes closed, and struggled to reply with indifference rather than malice.

"One day your head may still be axed from your body."

"Until that day, I will win all my battles, great or small. But cheer up. Tomorrow, I'm leaving. And when I return, it will be to arrange an escort south for you."

A moment later, she heard the door close.

He was gone.

And still, it seemed that something of his presence lingered in the room. Perhaps it was the touch of scent that remained, soap and leather, with a hint of steel. Or the memory of his fingers against the bare flesh of her shoulders.

Perhaps it was only the plaque on the wall.

* * *

Peter MacDonald was as dependable a man as Eric had ever known; however, Eric was still relieved in the morning to see the party of men riding to the castle. Unless Allan or one of the other men had ridden out with his letters and personally delivered them to their destinations and returned with a response, he could not be certain if his words were received. He had sent for his young cousin, but had not known if his letter had reached the foot of the highlands, just beyond Stirling.

But as he stood on the parapets at dawn and watched the slope before the castle, he saw the riders, and saw his own family crest and colors, and then Allan MacLeod returning at the side of Jamie Graham.

He called for the bridge to be lowered and rode with Patrick and Geoffrey out to meet the band of men as they neared the bridge.

"What, ho, cousin!" Jamie cried out, grinning. "Now that—that is a castle!"

"A fine pile of stone, aye," Eric agreed.

Patrick reached out to grasp Jamie's hand. "And glad I am you're here. 'Tis said you can hold a mound of dirt from an army with a handful of men. And I'd not like to be responsible for losing Eric's castle in his absence."

"We'll lose it, likely as not, in the end," Eric said, eyeing the stone walls. "If Edward turns his full attention upon Langley, we'll lose it. But that time hasn't come. Dougal!" He called, greeting another clansman, and he loped his horse down the line, pleased to welcome the highlanders who had ridden south to bring a greater force to Langley.

They returned in force to the courtyard where grooms rushed to take the horses and the men dismounted, surveying the courtyard and edifice with curiosity and admiration.

"And you took this place?" Jamie said, shaking his head with amazement.

"In truth? No. The plague took the place, and much more," Eric said.

Jamie set a hand on his arm and told him earnestly, "I'm sorry, Eric. Deeply sorry. Margot was loved deeply, and your babe, and all the others . . ."

Eric nodded, looking at the walls. "Aye," he murmured. "My thanks. All who were among us . . . for some, the entire family was lost. And for those who were here, the farmers, the bricklayers, smiths, maids, masons . . . everyone suffered terrible losses. But there was something so horrible that it created unity once it had passed. I've never slept without my back to a wall, but for the most part, these people don't care about kings or queens or politics. They've seen death, and they are eager for life."

"I'll keep a wary eye as well."

"Always."

"My God!" Jamie breathed suddenly, looking upward.

He followed his cousin's gaze.

Igrainia was at the window again.

"So . . . that is the earl's daughter?"

"Aye."

"No wonder Robert Bruce thinks he has a chance to exchange her for a queen."

Eric studied her. She was frowning slightly as she looked over the new arrivals. He could almost read her thoughts. *More highlanders, clansmen, dirty fellows out of the hills, barbaric, uncivilized, and surely, uneducated.*

"The lady holds a rare beauty," Jamie murmured.

"Does she?" Eric murmured. At that moment, she looked down. Her eyes met his. He saw the color flood her cheeks, but she didn't back from the window nor take her eyes away from his. Perhaps Jamie was right. Her features were delicate and fine, and her strange eyes, so deep a blue as to appear as violet as the summer hills, were large and framed by cleanly arched, fly-away brows. Her skin was the silky shade of a precious pearl, and though he personally disliked the thick black tresses that seemed to cascade far past her shoulders, he had to admit that in the sunlight they seemed to gleam with the shining beauty of a raven's wing. She was excellently shaped, as he'd had good cause to notice, a tiny span of waist, full, beautiful breasts. Her flesh was like silk. He wondered, as Jamie spoke, if he had forced himself to seek fault with her. Because she did create a rage of tumult in him, stirring natural, physical reactions that he doused with a fierce and furious, steel-willed contempt against himself. Touching her, he had wanted to wind his fingers around her, and cast her away.

Precisely because she did feel like silk. She was not a nameless, faceless form to seize for simple release. She was a prize of war, valued for her title.

She was not Margot.

His jaw tightened.

Jamie looked at him sharply. "You've not noticed?" he said, then lowered his eyes, and added softly, "Well, perhaps her appeal is something that you would not notice, not now, not with . . . everything that has occurred . . . not of late. And still . . . well, I had thought myself that Robert Bruce might be seeking too much to trade her for a member of his *royal* family, but then, it's quite possible there are a number of noblemen eager to have her returned to England so that they might put forth their cases in a marriage bid. Her brother, I have heard, inherited his father's title and the main property, but the lady herself has numerous holdings bequeathed from her mother's family. Very rich lands, if my information is at all trustworthy. But . . . the way to the king is treacherous now. And my sources have told me that he must be very careful with his every movement.''

''Indeed, he is careful,'' Eric said. ''But if he can't reach the abbey himself, he will send word, and I'll know what arrangements have been made.''

Jamie nodded. ''What of your prisoner? Is she not to leave the room?''

''Cousin, she may appear as a flower, but I promise you, if so, she is a rose, with long and prickly thorns. We have walled the secret tunnel, and it will stay sealed, unless it is we who need it. There is no other way out, other than the drawbridge. You are welcome to entertain her to your heart's content—if she can be lured down to spend time with the enemy.''

Jamie shrugged. ''Well, we'll see then.'' He said lightly. Then he sobered. ''Eric, through accident and agony, you have accomplished an extraordinary feat. We will hold what you have taken, at cost of our lives.''

''The castle is nothing more than stone, Jamie.'' He inclined his head toward the tower window. ''If you must, abandon it. Just make sure that you bring our bargaining power with you.''

''Ah, then, I will guard the lady with my life.''

''That will be a great service to me, and to the king. Peter will show you around; he is the one with the true knowledge of the castle, and its people. Allan rides like the wind and knows the lay of this land in the pitch of night—he rides out and keeps his eyes and ears opened. Geoffrey, Angus, and Raymond are riding with me.''

''Aye, then. Godspeed.''

''We'll return the moment we're able. This is something I'm desirous to have settled—since I don't believe they'll sit quietly and let us hold this fortress where they're in power for long. And, oh!'' The deaf and mute lad, Gregory, was standing silently by, holding Loki's reins. Eric placed a hand on his shoulders. "This is Gregory. Whatever may come, he is now one of ours. He doesn't hear or speak, but he can read your lips, and can tell you things that you might never imagine. If he does come to talk to you, listen."

Jamie stared at him. "You said that he doesn't talk?"

"He has a friend we've brought back from a journey as well. Rowenna. She speaks for him. You'll find her within the castle, if you need her." He took Loki's reins from Gregory, gave the boy a nod, and called out to Raymond, Angus, and Geoffrey.

They rode out, and the gates were closed and the drawbridge raised in their wake.

When she heard a tap at the door, Igrainia tensed, expecting the newcomer, but it was Father MacKinley who stood at the door.

"Father, come in. I'm delighted to see you."

He cupped her face in his hands. "Igrainia," he said softly, and kissed her forehead. "I have come to lure you from your solitude."

"What?"

"You are not forced to stay within this room."

"I don't believe you."

"You are invited to come down and dine with Sir Jamie Graham, Peter MacDonald, and me."

"I don't think so. I am wary of these strangers, Father."

He shook his head. "I was so eager for you to be free of this place, when I was uncertain myself. But that is your value, my lady, in being returned to London. There is no one who wishes you any harm, since you may bring back loved ones of the rebels."

"Father, thank you, I feel far safer here."

Distressed, he left her at last. That night, though, she paced the room, feeling her confines more closely than ever before.

She had been given a choice.

And still, over the next several days, though he came many times, she stubbornly refused to accept any invitations.

Perhaps she was able to do so because Jennie came many times. They played cards, and chess, and read, and Jennie was able to tell her that she'd gotten her letter beyond the walls through the kind services of a passing tinker. And so, it seemed, time did not weigh so heavily.

When Jennie didn't appear, she received a new visitor—Rowenna. Rowenna was pleased to be with her, and told her that she and Gregory had come to the castle in the company of the healing Thayer and the others after their night at Father Padraic's wayside. She was serving in the kitchen, and Gregory was working with the horses. He had a way with animals, loved them, and tended them well.

Igrainia was glad to see Rowenna, but her enjoyment of the girl was somewhat marred by her memory of her behavior with Eric. Apparently, as bitter and agonized as he might be at the loss of his wife, he did not mind having a sweetheart.

But it seemed that Rowenna was happy and at peace. And it was more evident than ever that she had been beautiful before the scar had slashed her cheek. And of course, in her gentle way, she remained beautiful.

And yet, she was, Igrainia knew, loyal to the man who had brought her here, and loyal to Robert Bruce, and the dream of a free Scotland.

Day after day, Father MacKinley came to entreat her to come down to supper.

On Sunday, she left the room to attend mass at MacKinley's small chapel within the castle walls.

And later, that evening, she assumed that it was Father

MacKinley at her door when she heard a tapping toward nightfall.

It was not. It was the newcomer who had arrived the day that Eric had ridden out.

He stood at her door, bearing an almost uncanny resemblance to Eric, though this man had darker, redder hair, and his eyes were more of a gray than a crystalline blue.

And he smiled, a pleasant smile. His eyes seemed alight with a secret mischief.

"Igrainia of Langley!" he said, and bowed deeply. "I'm Jamie Graham." He offered her a jestingly humble shrug. "I'm known to be an excellent tactician in the art of defensive war, but that's no matter, I'm also articulate, very well educated, and can play a lute. I saw that you were enticed to leave the room for mass this morning. There is no reason for you to be so completely imprisoned here, so far from the world around you! I would deeply appreciate it if you would cast off the shackles of confinement and join us in the hall for supper this evening."

She stared at him.

"Sir, I am but a prisoner in this castle."

"That, my lady, should not let you discard the concept of a pleasant supper among men who are weary of fighting and would find sheer delight in simply having you near. And please," he added hastily, "you mustn't fear for yourself in any way. You're a hostage of the crown, you know. And no man would dare be anything but completely courteous to a—a ward of King Robert."

"Really? I'm afraid that there are those among your number that I'm not so certain I would describe as ... courteous."

"You'll not find them at table tonight."

She watched him, surprised to feel amused—and interested. "Perhaps," she told him.

He bowed to her. "The choice must be yours."

He turned and walked down the hall.

Later, another tap came at the door. It was Father MacKinley, hoping to escort her down to the supper table. He would be at her side throughout the meal, he swore.

She decided to join them. Jarrett greeted her pleasantly in the hall, and downstairs at the great dining table, Jamie and Peter MacDonald were waiting. Jamie Graham greeted her with pleasure, and pulled out a chair that she might sit. As Father MacKinley had said, his place was by her side, and Jamie took the next chair. Another man named Dougal joined them, and though he was far quieter than the outgoing Jamie, he was courteous and pleasant, greeting her with a grave welcome.

Berlinda and Garth served the meal—venison, eel, fowl, and plates of summer vegetables, fresh bread and steaming gravy.

"So, you are Eric's cousin," Igrainia murmured when the food had been served.

"I'm a first cousin, on his father's side, of course, and Dougal is a second cousin to us both. We're from an extensive clan, you see. We've been spreading out across Scotland well over a hundred years now ... close to two hundred years. There are some of us in the lowlands. Some from the highlands, and our particular branch of the family tree is centered not far from Stirling. And, you, my lady, come straight from a fine place not far from London. Your father was supposed to have been quite an impressive horseman, leading the king's troops against the French, I'm glad to say."

She curled her fingers around the chalice in front of her.

"Would it have made a difference to you if he had fought at the head of the king's troops in Scotland? Robert Bruce fought often enough with Edward's men in Scotland."

The table fell silent, except for the sound of Father MacKinley's sigh.

Then Jamie laughed. "Well, you do have an edge about you, Lady Igrainia. Many Scots followed Edward many times. Unfortunately, some of our nobility is entangled deeply with Edward, since English lands have tended to be far richer than those in Scotland, and so many have had holdings in both countries. But the time has come when a man must make a stand."

"Do you truly believe that Robert Bruce can prevail?" she asked. "The English might is overwhelming."

"Ah, but the Scottish spirit is indomitable!" Jamie said. He shrugged, casting his head at an angle, seriously studying her face and then offering a rueful smile. "You see, my lady, we have our forests into which to disappear. There are the highlands, where the terrain has beaten back many a man. And there, in the old lands, the lands where the ancient royalty lie and in death, watch over the clans, there is no rule other than the chieftains, and they choose a man to follow, and will live and die by their choice. Aye, it will be a hard fight. But Robert Bruce will prevail."

She sipped her wine. "I hope he does so before Edward's men swarm over Langley and kill all these good people for being traitors."

Silence fell again. Then Father MacKinley said, "There is nothing stronger, anywhere, than the human spirit—and the power of God. Look at Langley! Just short months ago, it was devastated, a place of disease and death. But those who lived buried their loved ones and the past, and if you look about, you'll see a fine hall, clean and filled with flowers, and the table filled with the bounty of the season."

"Aye, look at Langley," she murmured.

"I believe I will have more meat," Jamie said.

And even he seemed frustrated. But when he had finished eating, he asked her if she was familiar with pipes.

"We may be in the lowlands," she heard herself say, "but this is Scotland."

Jamie grinned slightly. "Dougal can play with a beauty you'll not believe."

"Ah, Jamie! I can barely wheeze out a tune."

"But the lady would love to hear one."

"Aye, Dougal, play!" Jarrett encouraged.

"Because our Jarrett can really dance to the tune, you know. Do you dance, Lady Igrainia."

"No, no, I'm afraid I don't know the dances at all."

"That's because, being the lady you are, you've missed the sheer pleasure of a country fair, my lady! But we shall fix that. Dougal, get the pipes!"

And so Dougal did, and since she demurred determinedly from attempting to dance, Jamie drew up Jarrett as a partner. Dougal really could play, and despite herself, Igrainia found herself laughing over their frolicking on the floor until it grew late, and Father MacKinley took her up to her room.

The next night, she joined them again, and Dougal spoke more, telling her how happy he had been to arrive, and see the old friends who had survived the sickness. To see the family crest and colors on the castle, and the life teeming when the plague had taken so much.

"Yes, actually, I've been quite amazed," said Igrainia. I saw the people when Sir Niles Mason arrived with them and . . . it was really quite terrible and pathetic. Everyone was worn and ragged and dirty, and, of course, so many were suffering from illness. Yet it appeared to be the poorest crowd, and almost magically, men had clean tunics and breeches and tartans, and there were flags everywhere."

"My dear lady!" Peter MacDonald said, shaking his head. "We had been traveling, and then encamped, when the

English burst upon us. Naturally, we traveled with our belongings, our colors, our tartans, our flags, and even much of the mail you've seen was in our trunks. When the English seized us, lady, they seized our goods. A bitter thing at the time, but when we came back to Langley to free our families, many important pieces of our lives were here to be seized back."

"Ah," she murmured.

"We stole back what was stolen from us!" Jarrett said, shrugging.

"Ah, but it's getting far too serious here!" Jamie said. "It's time for the pipes again!"

And so, Dougal played the pipes, and that night, Jamie got her out on the floor, laughing and whirling about as she tried to imitate his movements. And it was Jarrett who was the expert, and soon, he was showing her how to turn about the room as well.

She was so involved in the activity that she didn't notice when another man slipped into the hall, quietly talking to Peter and Jamie.

She didn't see the two leave the hall, and she was dizzy and laughing when he returned.

With company.

She spun as Jarrett had shown her and she came to a dizzying halt, sweeping her hair from her face, then sobering in a horrified instant.

The pipes wheezed to a halt.

Eric had entered the hall.

"Ah, Eric, so you have returned quickly!" Dougal said with pleasure. "And the King, the King is alive and well?" he asked worriedly.

"Aye, Robert Bruce lives, and continues amassing greater troops," Eric said. "Word has it that Edward himself has risen from a sick bed and will lead his own troops, as he is

angry with the failure of the Earl of Pembroke to bring the
Bruce down.''

"King Edward still hasn't measured the mettle of the
Scots," Dougal murmured. "Nor does he understand that
the fight cannot be won in the forests and the highlands and
far to the north!''

Eric stood just feet from Igrainia, towering and gleaming
in mail, tunic, and tartan-weave mantle. He greeted Jarrett,
clapping him on the shoulder, and commenting on the vigor
of his dance, then turned to Igrainia at last.

"Good evening, my lady," he said. He strode to the table
they had all deserted. He drew his gloves from his hands,
casting them on the table, and accepted a chalice of ale from
Garth who had emerged from the shadows to serve him,
thanking the man courteously as he did so. His eyes raised
to Igrainia's once again. "How enchanting, my lady, to find
you in such a pleasant state of mind," he said. "Had we
only realized earlier that we could thaw your anger with
music and dance!''

"I think it's time I retire for the evening," she said.

"I'm so sorry that my arrival must ruin your night," he
told her, and she saw that the hall was beginning to fill as
others entered from the courtyard, Peter, Jamie, returning
from greeting those who had ridden out, and Angus, Raymond, and Geoffrey, who had been with Eric. They were
accompanied by another man, a tall, lean, white-haired and
grim-faced priest. They talked among themselves as they
entered, the riders appearing pale and drawn, and the others
deeply concerned.

A strange fear swept through her like wildfire. They all
looked so grim. Especially the priest. Something had gone
very badly on their mission. She fought a panic rising in
her. The way that they had come . . . and with a priest . . .

could they possibly intend to execute *her* in retaliation for some act of the English?

She stared at Eric, determined not to betray her fear. Because she was afraid she knew what had happened: King Edward had refused to exchange Robert Bruce's wife or his kinswomen for her.

And the king of the Scots was furious. Robert Bruce, too, had his temper. Perhaps he could not be accused of all the atrocities Edward had practiced in Scotland, but he knew how to kill, and he knew how to fight, and there were many innocent victims in war.

The men she had come to know, those who liked her, were looking at her with pitying glances. Geoffrey, Allan . . . Peter.

Geoffrey lifted a hand in greeting, and gave her a weak smile. At his side, Jamie asked him something that drew his attention, but as he spoke to Jamie, he kept glancing at her.

"It would be best if you return upstairs," Eric said softly. Though there was some distance between them, he spoke to her alone, and his tone was very low. "I will be along to speak with you soon. There are a few events which take place tonight and we must prepare here, but I will be up soon to explain what is happening."

She looked around the great hall again. The men had gathered in groups. Berlinda had come from the kitchen to join Garth in serving ale to those who had just returned, tired from their hard ride, and parched.

She saw Jamie speaking again, across the room. He was questioning Geoffrey and Raymond. Father MacKinley was standing there with them as well, a deep frown furrowed into his brow.

It seemed as if they were all casting glances her way. Glances that were filled with consternation and sorrow.

Eric had returned with some news regarding her, obviously, and they were all talking about it.

As she watched, Jamie asked another question of his companions who had ridden out.

She heard Geoffrey murmuring quietly in return. Though he was speaking softly, within the great stone hall, sounds could be picked up and echoed, and heard across the room.

She caught whispered syllables of their words.

With mounting horror, she put them together.

She is to be murdered.

Oh, God, yes, those were the words he was saying!

Murdered. Weakness filled her limbs. Murdered. Her death was to be one of the "events" taking place at Langley tonight. This was a drastic measure. Not even King Edward had executed his female hostages. And now, Eric wanted her to go upstairs so that he could tell her alone, so that she could get some dignity together, compose herself so that her screams wouldn't create an uprising within the castle.

"Igrainia," Eric repeated. "Jarrett will escort you up."

She shook her head, facing him. "No. Find the courage to tell me here and now."

"The courage?" He arched a brow.

"Surely, there is something afoot, and it cannot be a pleasant task for you."

"Not at all," he responded gravely.

"Tell me now," she said, her limbs like ice. "Am I to be killed?"

"Killed?" Eric repeated, frowning and startled. He shook his head, lowering it, a dry, curious smile curving his lips. "No, my lady, I have not returned with any intent to do murder, legal, royal, or other."

"I overheard Jamie's words to Dougal and Jarrett. You don't need to disguise what is happening to me. If I am to be executed, *murdered*, simply say so."

His smile deepened, and once again, he shook his head. "So you hear them speaking, but I'm afraid you didn't hear correctly. You're not to be *murdered*. You are to be *married*."

"Married?" she said incredulously. "Married?" She was stunned, and the absurdity of it was so great that she couldn't begin to think or reason at the moment. She looked then from Eric to the grim priest who had entered with the other men, and back to Eric once again. His ice blue eyes were set upon her hard. "Married?" she echoed a third time.

"Married, my lady. Joined in holy wedlock. I know you're familiar with the contract, having entered into it before."

His impatient sarcasm brought something snapping together within her mind.

"Indeed, I understand the concept. But it is quite impossible. So perhaps you will be so good as to explain why you *think* that I will be married, and to whom."

He set down his chalice with a shrug. "It's not at all impossible, and it will occur—the king has spoken."

"Your king has no power over me."

"I'm afraid he does. This is, after all, Scotland."

"He is an outlaw on the run. He can force me to do nothing."

"But I can," Eric said evenly. "And I am the man to whom you are to be wed."

CHAPTER 11

She didn't believe him, couldn't believe him. But she was suddenly desperate to be away from him, and away from the hall, filled with his people. She was afraid that she would begin to scream or laugh, or go utterly mad in front of all of them.

This had to be an improbable jest. At her expense, surely.

She turned slowly, almost blinded. Jarrett and Dougal stood near her now. She managed to keep her shoulders straight, her knees from quaking, and she inclined her head to them both.. "Thank you for the entertainment, but I must leave now. The hall has become filled with . . . liars and madmen," she finished, and started for the stairs.

She realized then that the hall had grown silent. All eyes were following her.

Behind her, she heard the motion as Jarrett started to move, ready to follow her.

"No," Eric told him. "This is something I might as well begin, as I must see it through myself."

She fled the rest of the way up the stairs, and into her room. And as she reached it, she rued her own flight—it was madness. Eric intended to follow. And then she would be in a confined space with him, alone. If she had remained in the hall, Father MacKinley would have come to her side, he would have explained that it was all preposterous. And still, she thought, this had to be a jest, because Eric himself would never take part in such a farce.

Within the room, she closed the door, and leaned against it.

As if that could stop him from entering.

A moment later, she heard the rapping.

"No!" she said. "No, you can not enter here, go away."

The slam of his shoulder against the door sent her away from it. He entered, closed the door, and leaned against it.

She watched him with narrow, hostile eyes. "Why are you doing this? Why kind of a cruel jest are you playing now? You certainly don't intend to marry me, you can barely stand the sight of me."

"It's a matter of expediency. Marriage among your class, my lady, tends to be a property contract, and little more."

She shook her head. "I am barely widowed! And you . . . for God's sake, why would anyone devise such a ridiculous *joke*?"

"You are about to be married because it seems that King Edward plans a wedding for you next week. By proxy, of course, since he is playing at the bargaining table, refusing to release his own prisoners for your return."

"You're still making no sense," she said, forcing the words.

"Sir Robert Neville has convinced a number of powerful men that he can raise an army and seize the castle in

Edward's name, come up with an amazing military victory while the king continues to pursue Robert Bruce. So, he has let it be known that you will marry Sir Robert in one week's time, as I said, by proxy. I believe it's supposed to be some kind of warning to us—the king really believes that we will deliver you for your wedding. Of course, we won't. We will prevent it. As you can imagine, Robert Bruce is deeply disappointed and furious that there will be no exchange. And so he has ordered this course of action."

"He has ordered it!" she said contemptuously. "And you will follow such an order?"

"It doesn't make the least difference to me."

And it didn't, she realized. He had lost the woman he loved. What was said of his status on a legal contract meant nothing at all to him.

"Surely, you consider yourself an intelligent man. You must realize that this is quite impossible. I am English. The English king has rights over me and my property. And though my father is dead, I have a brother. He must give his permission."

"I can only remind you again that this is Scotland. You are the widow of a man who might have feared and honored the English king, but this land is claimed as Scotland—whether it is bitterly contested now or not."

"Edward will not accept this. It will just be an illegal ceremony."

"It will entangle you in a legal issue that would cast doubt on any of your heirs."

"The pope would annul such a sham! Your king already stands excommunicated for his misdeeds!"

"But there is a strong church in Scotland, lady, and by that church, you will be legally wed, and therefore, any arguments would take years. At which point . . . we can hope that none of it will matter."

He was quite serious about it, she realized, and she could even see what satisfaction of revenge it might create for Robert Bruce, bitter and furious over his own loved ones.

"I will not marry anyone," she said. "And that must be accepted. I remain in mourning."

"You will be married one way or the other by the end of the week. Ah, Igrainia! You deceive yourself with so much pride. To the Scots and the English, you are a prize of property, and your king intends to bestow you upon a man for his prowess in war. Granted, you are worth a great deal to Sir Robert Neville. With your properties and rents in England, and with the castle here, you can make him a very rich man. But then, he was your husband's kinsman. And certainly, you would prefer to be forced into such a situation. But I'm afraid it's not to be."

"You don't understand. I will not agree to *any* marriage. I am in mourning. And my brother will understand. He will not give his permission."

He started to laugh, and it angered her deeply that he could find it all so amusing. It was as if he spoke to a child with no concept whatsoever of the ways of the world. "My lady, you'll excuse me, but your brother is a lad who has yet to prove himself. Do you really think that he can stand up to Edward and tell him no, he will not give his permission to such a marriage?"

"You don't know my brother. He is young but very honorable. Something rare in all men."

"He might be the most honorable man ever to draw breath, but he will not be able to stand up to Edward."

"He knows my will," she murmured, her eyes falling.

"Yes, of course, he does. Such a touching letter you wrote."

Her gaze flew back to his. "You—took my letter?"

"No, actually, I didn't. I allowed it go through. After

making sure that you weren't trying to get the young fool riding out haphazardly to rescue you from the castle.''

Her cheeks flooded with color and she didn't think that it was possible to hate anyone with greater vengeance. Her words, urging Aidan not to think of rescue in any manner, but to have faith—had been filled with tenderness and the assertion that she had married as their father had planned from her birth, and that she would not marry again. She had written that she was well, and not in terrible extremes, as were so many of the enemy hostages, and that no retaliation had been taken against her.

Her fingers curled into her palms. She wished desperately that she could have the letter back—and rewrite it.

"No one can make me marry against my will."

"Igrainia, you are blind. If Edward holds a ceremony with a proxy in your place, you will be married. Unless you are married already."

She still couldn't believe his intent. "I think I might prefer being murdered, sir, to being married to you."

Her words didn't even anger him, and his indifference was chilling.

"You're not being given a choice."

"No? Fine, bring on your wedding. I will shout no firmly to every vow. And Father MacKinley will not perform such an immoral and illegal service!" She spoke determinedly, then gasped, remembering the grim faced priest who had arrived with Eric and his men.

"Father Theobald is from Annandale, my lady, an old, dear, and valued friend of Robert Bruce, and an important man in the Scottish church. He is here for a purpose."

"I—still won't do it."

"But you will."

"And how will you manage? Drag me from the tower to the church? I can cause an uprising here that will shatter your belief that you have turned all these people from their loyalty to an English king to a Scottish one. Try it tomorrow morning, and you will see.''

"My lady, you have a point," he acknowledged. "We could, of course, perform the ceremony here . . . but it should be in the chapel, beneath the eyes of God." He turned away suddenly, opening the door and shouting for Jarrett to come. "Excuse me, my lady," he said politely, and for a moment, the door shut.

Igrainia looked desperately around the room. There was no way out except . . .

She walked to the window and looked to the courtyard far below.

But she knew that she did not intend to jump.

Eric reentered the room, and saw her there.

"I shall jump!" she said.

He leaned against the door, crossing his arms over his chest. "Will you?"

"If you come anywhere near me, I swear, I'll do it."

He moved away from the door, crossing the room slowly to her.

"No closer!" she whispered.

But he was there. And he gave her no time for any further argument or threat, caught her firmly by the waist, and lifted her over his shoulder. She immediately beat and struggled against him, screaming. Then, to her surprise, she found herself cast down upon the bed. He meant to leave her. For a moment, she felt a wild sense of triumph.

Then he came on, grimly. She tried to rise as she saw that she was being wound into the knit cover that had lain upon her bed. The more she struggled, the more wound into it she became. Within minutes, she was as bundled as a sack of grain, and lifted again, like a sack of grain.

She couldn't move enough to offer any force against him.

And when she tried to scream, she sucked in the wool of the bed cover.

He moved quickly. She bounced hard against his shoulders and back with his every step. She wasn't even sure when they crossed the hall, went out into the night, and crossed the courtyard to the small chapel that stood within the castle walls.

A moment later she was standing. She tried to struggle again to free herself from the fabric, but strong arms were around her. There was candlelight in the small chapel, and she heard voices. She started protesting again, her words muffled but furious.

Over the covering, a hand clapped over her mouth.

"Proceed, Father," she heard Eric say. Then she was forced to her knees.

And the priest talked, saying the wedding rites. Eric gave grave vows. She could scarcely kneel, she was suffocating in the maze of fabric and the tightness of his hold upon her. She tried to calm down, to bide her time. She could hear when the priest asked her to give her vows. She opened her mouth to protest and end it all. She wasn't able to speak. His hand was over her mouth, and his fingers had such a grip on her that he forced her to nod her head. Then, though she continued to hear, it all seemed to blur. She was fighting too desperately for breath. If she weren't held so tightly, she would have fallen over.

She was drawn to her feet. And then, suddenly, the covering was drawn from around her. For a moment she was aware of the grim priest standing before her. She saw the people assembled around them. Geoffrey, Angus, Dougal, Allan, Peter, Raymond, Jarrett, Father MacKinley, white and drained, even old Garth . . .

The faces before her began to spin. She started to fall.

She was caught. Lifted.

"She needs air."

Eric's voice.

"She needs to sign the documents," someone said from behind them. The priest.

"No," she breathed.

But there was a quill in her hand. And she was crushed between men, and she still couldn't breathe. She wouldn't sign on her own . . . wouldn't. But strong fingers were around hers. And her fingers were moving. In a blur, she saw her name in ink. She wanted to take the quill and slash it through the document. The quill was taken from her hand.

She was still in a scoop in Eric's arms, and he was walking. The scent of the candles faded away, she was dimly aware of the stars in the sky. Clean night air rushed into her lungs. She looked up into his face. "I should have let you die."

"It's too late now."

They had reached the hall again. He was striding with her through the hall, and up the stairs. "This . . . I saved your life, when I might have thrown you in the river."

"My men would have cut your throat."

"I could have just let you die!" she insisted.

"And if you had, you'd be dead by Gannet's hand now."

"You had no right to do this . . . to me. And . . . I—I will kill you!" she promised as they neared her room. "In the night . . . somewhere, sometime, I will kill you."

His crystalline blue eyes fell upon hers, and the tension in his features was so startling that in fear, she curled her fingers against his shoulders.

"Igrainia, you'll never be near enough to me in the night to manage such a feat." She didn't know what surprise her features might have betrayed, but his next words were both damning and relieving. "You set far too high a price upon your person, my lady. And forget that every time I look at you, I am only reminded of everything that I have lost."

They reached her room. He kicked open the door with a power that might have shattered it. She found herself let loose at the foot of the bed.

She was still too weak to stand.

He never noticed, because he had already departed the room, slamming the door in his wake.

She crumpled to the bed, and lay there shaking, still drawing desperately for air, and wondering why the fact that he was gone had left her feeling suddenly lost.

Time passed slowly.

Igrainia lived in a self-imposed exile, since the only time she was ever invited to leave her room was for the evening meal, and she didn't care to share the hall with the invaders who had usurped her home.

The castle hummed with activity. From her window high in the tower, she could see riders constantly coming and going. Masons worked on the walls; the merchants' stalls, deserted during the past days of sickness, began to bustle once again. Farm animals were herded through the courtyard to the kitchens, the best to be chosen as meals. Flocks of sheep entered into the walled area of the castle town at night, and were herded back out by day.

In the daylight hours, she constantly heard the clash of steel in the courtyard. She often watched as men practiced at arms, with swords, poles, axes, and maces. The smithy was enlarged as work was done to improve, create, and solder damaged mail. Looms wove, fabric was dyed; tinkers ventured near Langley more and more, bringing needles, thread, scissors, knives, and all manner of household objects.

She spent a great deal of time by the window, watching life go by. Every morning, the gates were opened, and the drawbridge was let down. As she studied the world around her, she began to note the patterns of life. Looking far out across the sloping field that led to the walls of Langley, she realized that at least three of the men who rode out each morning did so to guard the roads to the castle—north, east, and south. She became certain that someone would be posted along the long winding river to the west, watching for men who might arrive at a distance on ships, and try to move by night to take the castle by surprise.

She saw that defenses were being strengthened as well. Often, she would see Peter MacDonald in the courtyard with a crew of men, sawing and hammering. Eventually, she saw that he had created a number of small catapults, machines that could be used upon the parapets. His catapults apparently had a tremendous range, and could be used to fire upon whatever war machines might be brought against the castle. If filled with deadly fireballs, they could destroy a larger war machine and create havoc among the men manning it.

She saw Eric every day.

He didn't come near her door, speak to her, or acknowledge her existence in any way at all. She saw him because he worked endlessly in the courtyard. He was with Peter, studying every aspect of the war machines. He was with the men practicing weaponry, and they were well supplied, for Langley had been a rich holding, and before their destruction by disease and warfare with the Scots, the men here had been well armored and armed. Langley was an old fortification. The armory had, from the time the castle had been built, taken the first floor of the entire left wall of the tower itself. Though in general the English were well armed and the troops of Robert Bruce still all but naked, such was not the case here.

She read every book in the room, and there were many—beautiful volumes hand lettered by monks, many religious texts, and many entertaining ones—mythology, the lives of kings, the life of Charlemagne, and many more. She found that she was able to learn a great deal about arms and siege machines herself—Afton had acquired many such manuals, and she found that she had a growing interest in learning about arms.

Jennie came to see her with regularity, bringing clean sheets, wine, water, and news. But though she had always cared deeply about her maid and friend, she wasn't sure that it helped to see her. Jennie's bitterness ran deep, and every time she came, it was with anger. Argyle the smith had died, and there was a highlander working in his place. The kitchens were filled with the strangers. She didn't know any of the laundresses. And then, there was Rowenna, the girl with the terrible scar. She had the run of the castle, and was always about, looking into everything. She seemed to have some special favor with invaders, because not even old Garth questioned her work.

The worst of it was that *he* was there, night after night, lording it over the hall. And the hall was always filled. Someone had brought him three new deerhounds, and there were more and more great dogs in the hall. The men played their wretched pipes, and sometimes there was other entertainment. Jennie hated all of them with a vengeance, but most of all, Eric. She was outraged that they had forced Igrainia into a mock marriage, and though she intended to make Igrainia feel better, she usually managed to make her feel worse.

"Nothing real will come of it—the whole thing was to anger King Edward, and do you know why? He had no intention of exchanging one daughter of an earl for another, especially since the daughter he held was Robert Bruce's wife." As she spoke, Jennie moved to the window. "You're lucky, at least, that he so dislikes you. That you are like a pretty bird in a cage. Every man has his breaking point, but

I don't suppose he'll ever break on that . . . I don't think that he'll need to, not with the scarred girl around.''

"Rowenna is not an evil woman, Jennie. She warned me when I was going to be in danger."

"She didn't warn you very well," Jennie noted, "since you're here."

"My situation is hardly her fault," Igrainia said.

"I do my best to hear everything, and she is always about. 'Will you have more ale, sir, is the meat sufficient, my lord, may I bring you anything . . . anything?' "

"Jennie, you don't need to listen to everything."

"If I didn't listen to everything, I wouldn't have been able to tell you that men had ridden out to make sure that word of the marriage reached Robert Bruce so that he would know his orders would be followed, just as men rode out to make sure that King Edward would hear the news."

"It's my brother, Aidan, I worry about."

Jennie sighed. "I've heard nothing about him, I'm so sorry. But I have told you that Robert Neville is in the company of an old Scottish baron, Lord Danby, a man who holds Cheffington Castle, and with him, he is raising a large troop of men. Sir Robert will rescue you, and then you can be married to him, and he'll hold this castle and it will be as it was before."

"Jennie, I don't wish to marry Robert, and nothing will ever be as it was before."

"You've given up. You mustn't ever give up."

"I haven't given up, Jennie. But Afton is gone, and I don't care to marry again, and my life will never be the same." She didn't bother to say that she did not see what would happen if a bloody battle came to their doorstep, or the death that would ensue if they were besieged.

"But it will. You'll see. Edward is not the 'Hammer of the Scots' without good reason!''

Always, after assuring Igrainia that English troops would come and smash the invaders into the dirt, she would leave.

She never stayed too long, as both women were afraid that her visits would be stopped, if it seemed they might be plotting in any way.

Igrainia did plot, but by herself in the hours that weighed so heavily upon her. She couldn't escape by the tunnel; it had been closed over. There was no other way out of the castle, unless she could scale walls or find a way to depart when the drawbridge was lowered. Unless, of course, she could reach the parapets of the outer walls and risk a death-defying leap into the moat. That was out of the question, of course. Confined to her room, she couldn't even reach the parapets.

Rowenna came often as well, bringing flowers, and trying to be pleasant and sweet. Igrainia found that she had acquired a wariness about the young woman she had liked so much, and though she was pleasant and polite, she was cool, and Rowenna sensed it. Still she came, bearing her tokens to brighten the room, and Igrainia's world.

On Sunday, she left her room to attend mass, escorted by Jarrett and Jamie. Both were charming and pleasant, telling her they wished she would join them in the hall at night.

When they reached the chapel, Eric was already there. Tall, straight, his mantle flowing from his shoulders, his brilliant hair gold and crimson in the light that splashed through a stained glass window, he was the image of the lord of the castle.

Igrainia was dismayed to realize that she was being led to the front pew to take her place beside him. She slowed her walk, managing to come behind Jamie, but at the pew, Jamie slipped back again, bowing to allow her access to walk in. She was wedged between him and Eric as others filed in.

Eric barely acknowledged her presence until they were all on their knees, heads bowed in prayer. As the Latin mass went on, she opened her eyes, and realized that he was watching her. There was a curious expression in his eyes.

She closed her own again, and lowered her head over her folded hands.

"Praying for my quick demise?" he whispered.

"Indeed. Don't interrupt me."

He didn't. But when the service was over and she turned to escape the pew, she found that he had taken her arm.

"Are you interested in a ride, my lady?"

"A ride?"

"A ride. On a horse."

"Where?" she asked warily.

"Across the fields. And back. Nothing more."

"Why?"

"Because I'm assuming you must be ready to go mad."

She hesitated, still cautious. "You will let me go riding?"

"I'm afraid I'll be with you."

"And who else?"

"The two of us," he said impatiently. "I can spare some time. If you'd like to spend some hours in the sunlight, I will accompany you."

She shook her head slowly. "I'm afraid that you could not bear that much time in my presence."

"As you wish."

He started to walk past her. She thought about the feel of the wind in her face and the power of a horse beneath her.

"Wait!"

He turned back.

"What if I were to race away?"

"You would never escape me. And I believe you know it."

"I could still try."

"But you wouldn't like the outcome. You wouldn't like it at all."

There was no threat in his words. Not even a warning. He was simply stating fact.

"I . . . yes."

In the courtyard, she found that Gregory was waiting. He had Loki and the dapple gray mare saddled and waiting.

She greeted Gregory with pleasure, touching his cheek. He offered her his warm, silent smile.

The gates had already been opened, the drawbridge down. She didn't wait for Eric to mount after she had done so, but loped gleefully through the courtyard, and listened to the clopping sound as she rode over the bridge. She knew he was behind her.

Upon the distant hills, she could see the men guarding the approaches to the castle.

She leaned against the mare, wanting to fly.

They rode, and rode. She knew that he was at her side every moment, and she didn't care, it simply felt too good to be out. The wind was sweeter than she had remembered. The sun was brighter, the summer grass greener.

She forgot time, until she heard his voice, calling out to her, "Stop ahead, there's a little brook in the trees. The horses need water."

She reined in. If she didn't, he would urge his great warhorse harder, catch up with her, bring her to the ground, destroy her clothing, and her dignity.

She dismounted, leading the horse to water. He came beside her, leading his own horse.

"Tell me, Eric, when you're in church, do you pray?"

"What a curious question," he said, eyeing her.

"Not at all. You call your horse Loki, in honor of the old Norse gods. You told me yourself you were half berserker. So, when you're on your knees, do you pray? Or is it all for show?''

''Of course I pray.''

''For what?''

''I ask God not to answer your prayers regarding my quick and painful death.''

She was startled to feel a smile curving her lips, and she lowered her head quickly.

''You'll be happy to know, though, that I think He is favoring you.''

She looked at him sharply. ''Oh?''

''I ride out tomorrow. There will be a skirmish, maybe a battle. There are bands of men about the country, joining together, as word has it that the king has left his sick bed to lead the army. It will still take some time for him to have this new enterprise under way, but at every new call to arms, men gather in troops again. Even a king such as Edward has only so much of a standing army. A man's feudal service is prescribed by law, so it is only the high ranking lords, eager for service and the king's favor, who leave their own estates in the hands of others to fight continually. Or men like Thayer, who have nothing, except what they can gain in battle. That is why, no matter how many years it takes, Robert Bruce will eventually win his freedom.''

''What do you mean?''

''Here, the clansman raising his sheep, the farmer whose life is his crops—all will fight, because it is their sheep and their crops they're fighting for, while to many in Edward's service, they are fighting to subjugate a foreign people. We're willing to risk everything, because we've everything at stake. If you were to return to London, my lady, you wouldn't be touched by this war.''

''I wish I'd never seen any of it.''

He studied her curiously. ''Indeed. You seem to have no

really passionate opinion regarding the fight that goes on and on. You're quick to point out King Edward's position and Robert Bruce's different loyalties over the years. But I've never heard you say that in the eyes of God, Edward is right, that the savage, barbaric Scots should kneel down to him in gratitude, and obey.''

"My opinion of war is that it is bloody and cruel and steals the lives of innocents as well as the men determined on combat.''

"Yes, that is a fact of war in general. But what is your opinion regarding this one?''

She hesitated. "I'm English. What opinion would you have me have?''

"A thought of your own.''

"You seem to have known a great deal about my life from the time you first arrived here. I was in Scotland less than a year before your troops were brought in. I grew up in London, where Edward is greatly admired as a strong and powerful king. The country is respected by others because of his power. He is interested in the law, he is brilliant, he has been a good ruler.''

"A man's virtues and his faults are certainly weighed differently when viewed by different eyes. No one denies that he is a powerful king. But does he have the right to rule those who are not his people?''

"We tried very hard to remain outside the fight at Langley—''

"That was your husband's choice. You've still not given me your own thoughts.''

"What do my thoughts matter to you?''

"Perhaps they will matter when I have to make a decision about your future.''

"My opinion is that I hate bloodshed and death,'' she said, exasperated.

She was surprised that her reply brought another smile to his lips.

"Are you laughing at me again? Am I really amusing as well as repulsive?"

"I don't recall saying that you were repulsive—only that you remind me of pain suffered. And I'm not laughing at you. I am amazed at your ability to fool yourself. You won't speak against Edward. But I think that you believe that the Scots should be free, and ruled by their own king. Also, you're mistaken if you think your husband wasn't aware that he couldn't stay out of the fight forever. He had his loyalties, and I don't believe he was a fool."

"What are you talking about now?"

"Afton would have remained loyal to Edward for the same reason many Scottish barons have done so. You were his wife. The estates he gained in England through his marriage to you provided a far greater income than his property here, though Langley might have been his ancestral home. That is why he opened the gates of Langley to Sir Niles Mason, and why, had the disease not brought everyone down or fleeing, he would have allowed every execution Sir Niles commanded to be carried out."

Igrainia pulled on the reins of her horse, walking the mare some distance from the water, and mounting on her own. She knew that he followed her action, and he was mounted on Loki beside her. She turned on him.

"You're saying that riches meant more to my husband than honor."

"I'm saying that your husband was not a stupid man," he replied. "And he wasn't a hothead to behave irrationally, and God knows, enough ill has been done because of treachery and deceit and men's reactions to affronts against their honor. Robert Bruce killed John Comyn in a rage, or else he struck him down and his men finished the act, whichever,

I don't really know, I wasn't there. It has caused him to fight a greater war than that against the English to claim the throne, but perhaps, without Comyn's death, he might not have been able to have himself crowned king when he did. War is bloody and horrible, as you say. But many things are done in the heat and fury of war which men rue in their consciences at later dates. I am not insulting your late husband. I'm trying to make you understand that war can be uglier even than what you've seen so far. And perhaps I'm trying to get it through your stubborn skull that you are more protected here at this moment than you might be were you to gain the freedom you think you want so desperately.''

''What does it matter to you what I feel, think, or understand. You've done an exceptional job at Langley. The walls are a greater defense than they've ever been. Your men are as loyal to you as a group of hounds raised by a man since birth. I spend my life now confined in a room, watching the world go by. There is no escape through your mighty highland guards. The secret tunnel has been walled. You're leaving, and I might as well be chained hand and foot to walls of steel.''

''For one, I don't believe you spend your hours in your room doing nothing—I'm sure you spend the time weighing every possible venue of escape that may become available. And I want you to write a letter.''

''What? A letter? Regarding what?''

''Your brother is in Scotland, madam. And it's my suggestion that you write to him, and let him know that your marriage to me did indeed take place, that it is real and consummate, and you have no desire to be rescued.''

She stared at him incredulously. ''You must be mad! Perhaps you could half-smother me into a ceremony, and force my hand to a piece of paper and create the appearance of my signature, but you can't force me to write such lies to my brother! I knew there was a purpose to this ride, to these hours. Do you think me so desperate that I can be used in this way?''

Loki trotted around so that he was facing her. ''I don't intend to force you to do anything. If you write this letter, it will not be for me.''

''It's for me?'' She demanded.

''You told me that your brother is a young man, and honorable. He will try to come here, against the walls of Langley, to take you. If he does so, I'll be forced to kill him.''

''Perhaps you're mistaken, and he'll bring down the walls.''

''Do you really think that's possible, when he won't have the might of a great army behind him? Perhaps it's rude to remind you of this, but it seems you are not of a great value to King Edward, who is set upon destroying Robert Bruce before wasting time and men on such an effort as the siege of Langley would require. I said that I wanted you to write a letter, that I *suggested* it. The suggestion is because I recognize the fact that I might not have survived myself— if you and your priest weren't endowed with a certain sense of honor and compassion. I believe you love your brother. Therefore, I am trying to preserve his life for your benefit.''

She sucked in her breath, amazed at his confidence and audacity, and yet aware that he was speaking the truth. And it was the closest he had ever come to admitting that she might have saved his life.

''If you believe that Langley is so powerful, why doesn't your king take up residence within it?'' she asked.

''Because he could be trapped. Robert Bruce keeps moving, and therefore, he can keep the English from the advantage of a planned and prepared assault. And from Langley, my lady, I can provide him with something he desperately needs—more men for his fight.''

She watched as the wind teased the golden length of his hair. His eyes were upon her, steady and serious. She was aware suddenly of the shape of his features, well combined to create a face with great strength and handsome lines. He was dressed for the ride in linen shirt, boots, and breeches, his ever-present tartan mantle cast over his shoulders. It occurred to her that in a different time and place, he might have been a man she would have admired.

Then she remembered that he was the captor who had made her life a hell of solitude and taken everything that she had loved.

''I will write the letter,'' she said, and kneed her horse.

When they returned to Langley, she noted that the draw-bridge had remained lowered all that time. As she moved across the bridge and through the entry, she noted the huge vats set over the slatted roof that crossed the parapets at the gate. If invaders were to kill the guard and reach the bridge, the first of their number would die a grisly death; heated oil would be set afire, and cast down upon them.

In the courtyard, she dismounted quickly, ignoring his presence behind her. He didn't follow her. He didn't need to. Jamie had been in the courtyard, discussing his horse with a groom. He finished his conversation, and seemed to wander idly in her wake. When she reached her room, she turned and saw that he had followed her and was leaning against the wall at the landing, watching her.

He waved and smiled.

She liked Jamie. But she didn't respond.

She entered the room and closed the door, and after a moment's sheer frustration, she walked to the desk and began to write to Aidan. She started out slowly, then wrote with greater haste. She loved her younger brother.

Halfway through the letter she paused. He was here to join the king's army. No matter what she said, he could easily fall in battle.

But if he joined with madmen ready to throw themselves against the walls of Langley, it was almost a certainty that he would die.

She dipped her quill into ink again. And wrote with renewed determination.

Eric kept his maps and correspondence in the room he had chosen, well aware that although the castle seemed to move with a cohesive efficiency, there were surely those who kept silently loyal to the English cause.

He was there, studying the map of Galloway, when a knock sounded at the door. He strode to the door and opened it to find that Allan had returned from his scouting mission.

"Eric, I've much to tell you," he said.

"Come in, close the door," Eric said. "I do believe that the halls may sometimes have ears."

Allan nodded and entered the room. "Edward is ranting, but has not quite managed to leave his sickbed. The Earl of Pembroke is once more on the move. He knows that Bruce is encamped at Galston, where you planned to join him."

"Aye, we knew another assault was coming."

"There is more. King Edward remains at Lanercost. In a rage—but he believes that Pembroke will trap Robert Bruce this time, his forces so outweigh the Scots. It seems that he has greeted the news of the marriage of the Lady of Langley with irony. So, although he has put off the proxy marriage, he still intends that it will take place—as ever, assuming he himself is the law. But he is still allowing his clerical advisers time to make that judgment for him, and so satisfy any future question. Word has it that he was completely contemptuous of the claim that a real wedding took place. Any marriage performed in such haste is an illegal show, meant to flout him, and nothing but pretense on paper. And we are nothing but impotent savages, howling in the wind. When he again has the lady in his hands, her words will prove that it is so. Sir Robert Neville will receive the lands and castle of Langley, along with the lady, as soon as he has rid it of the vermin now abiding in it.''

King Edward's reaction was not surprising.

The marriage was nothing but words on paper, easily annulled. Still, for the action to be so dismissed was bruising—along with the scathing remark that they were nothing but impotent savages.

But there were more important issues at hand.

"We leave Peter again in charge of Langley. Jarrett and Angus will remain as well. Any man we've gained and trained ourselves rides with us; we can cut down a traitor in battle, but all of Langley could fall if one man destroys the defenses. The ride will be hard; the town and castle of Ayr are in English hands, and we don't want to be seen riding to join the king at Galston.''

"Aye,'' Jamie said. And they continued to trace the route they would take, and what alternate paths they might take were they to run into English scouting parties as they joined the king.

Then Jamie left. Eric sat in front of the fire, studying the flames, and wondering why he was so irritated with King Edward's dismissal of his marriage to the Lady Igrainia. She meant nothing to him. His wife and child rested in the walls of the castle, far below.

But, perhaps, he realized, she did mean something. He enjoyed his verbal encounters with her; she was a challenge. She had not shied away from tending any illness. He had watched her compassion for injured men and seen her loyalty to those who had intended to help her. He had watched the fury of her fight against the cutthroat on the road as well, and known her instinct for survival as well as her courage and hatred.

And there was more, of course. He had taken Langley. They were engaged in a greater war, and he didn't know if he could hold what he had seized or not. But she was part of what he had taken, and therefore, his.

And then there was the matter of Sir Robert Neville.

She had said that she didn't want to be married to any man, but were she in the hands of King Edward, she would be given to Neville, and there would be no choice in the matter. Igrainia would prefer him to Eric, since he was kin to Afton and loyal to Edward.

But Eric loathed Neville, just as he loathed Sir Niles Mason, the Englishman who had rounded up his family and friends and dragged them to Langley to die. The pompous knight who had so easily seized women and children—and fled at the first sign of sickness.

Since Afton of Langley had been dead when he returned to free the prisoners, Neville had surely been giving the orders. The orders that had kept so many of the dead and dying confined in the wretched cells in the castle's dungeon.

His fingers curled over the arms of the carved wooden chair.

He'd die before he allowed Neville to take anything more from him.

Including the woman Neville coveted.

The prize. The beautiful, black-haired witch of a prize.

Now, his . . .

His wife.

CHAPTER 12

The English army was three thousand strong. They were an incredible sight.

From atop Loudon Hill, a cone-shaped upthrust of rock that dominated the countryside, Eric, mounted on Loki, watched with Robert Bruce, James Douglas, and a few of the king's closest supporters, as the army moved.

The army gleamed. The sun touched upon the burnished basinets, mail and plate armor glimmered and glittered. Shields caught bright rays coming from a blue sky, and reflected light from every angle. Banners flew, pennants waved, and the horses were as well arrayed as the men, caparisoned in a multitude of colors, plumes lofty upon their headgear.

They seemed to come in wave after wave.

Bruce's men numbered in the hundreds.

But they knew the terrain, and they knew Loudon Hill. Below it, a highway stretched across a wide strip of high ground. On either side, the highway was flanked by morasses that were treacherous and deep, spans horses could not pass. They had cut trenches, three of them, in parallel lines from the morasses to the road, closing the gap of the space which they would have to defend.

Closer, closer, closer . . .

"So many," Robert Bruce murmured. "Oddly beautiful, aren't they?"

James Douglas, at his side, spit into the mud. "Aye, like the old man's arse!"

"So many of them," Bruce murmured quietly. In his mid-thirties, he wasn't just a powerful man, but one who had learned to use his wits, strategy, diplomacy, and raw courage.

"We've need of all the arms and armor they will leave when they fall," Eric said.

Robert Bruce slowly smiled, casting him a wry glance. "Aye, and so we do. They've the numbers, but we've the battle cry to best them, as we've done before. It is time!" He raised his sword, and let out a cry as he began the descent to the assembled rank. "For Scotland, and for freedom!"

Eric and the others joined him as they raced down the hill, joining the men prepared to meet the first assault. The king called out orders, and each of his commanders shouted to their own body of men.

Then, the English trumpet of the Earl of Pembroke sounded. The English began the attack.

They came on, the first wave of English horsemen, at full speed. Their colors continued to wave brilliantly in the sun. Their armor glinted . . .

They hit the first rank of defenders, men with long poles forming a wall of lethal steel. And before the steel, the first ditch. Some men charged into it and were unhorsed, and those behind them floundered on the fallen. Those who avoided the ditch came racing at reckless speed, and came upon the wall of men and poles and pointed steel. In the first minutes of the attack, the outcome was decided.

Horse crushed horse. Riders and animals screamed alike. The ranks of the English were thrown into death, confusion, disorder, and more death. In the first few minutes, more than a hundred of their number went down. Then the second wave of Englishmen, sent too tightly upon the first, trampled those in their way, but by then, the order to advance had been called and the Scotsmen leaped from their places with their poles, swords, axes, maces, and sticks, rushing the enemy, picking up the weapons of the fallen, and rushing forward with a vengeance.

Eric slashed his way through the men on the ground. He toppled mounted man after mounted man, and they fell into the mire of blood and dirt and humanity that came to litter the ground. The knights who fell were weighed down with the beauty of their glittering armor, as the Scottish foot soldiers set upon them. The confusion was horrible, the numbers remained great, and in the midst of it, there was no room for anything but the knowledge that a man fought and fought, and moved forward, and trusted in his fellows to watch his back as he watched theirs. His sword swung again and again. The sound of steel against steel was shattering.

And then, it was over. The disorder in the English ranks had become too great. They were called to retreat.

Trumpets sounded, banners waved.

Colors still flooded the horizon, and the English armor glittered and glimmered . . .

In its wake.

A roar went up from the men. They pursued the English, and many more fell as they fled. Caught in the tumult of the pursuit, Eric found himself leaping from his horse to come to a highlander fighting kilted and barefoot, a sword in his hands, but no shield to protect him from the blows of his opponent. When a second helmeted and faceless man came up behind him, Eric accosted the enemy, then found himself fighting on both fronts, worthy opponents. He was being assailed with shattering sword slashes, barely meeting one in time to stem the other, and finding little time for an offensive. His chance came when he saw his opponents raise their swords simultaneously. Deftly stepping back, he let the enemy bring their weapons down upon one another.

Even as they fell, he felt a rush of air at his back. He turned in a fury, catching his opponent in the middle, but causing no mortal injury due to the man's heavy mail. His opponent's sword came down heavily, catching his arm, sliding off the mail, but numbing his limb. In desperation he swiftly cast his sword from one hand to the other, and sliced upward, slashing his enemy in the thigh and groin. The man fell. Prepared for another attack, Eric whirled at the sound of a horseman at his back.

It was Robert Bruce. He dismounted quickly, clapping Eric on the shoulder. ''It's over, over for today. We've a victory that might swell our ranks anew, and bring more men to the cause of Scotland.''

Around Eric, the fighting had ceased.

A cheer went up from the men. A wild, sweet cheer, it grew loud, and echoed over the hill and the highway and even into the morasses. And words began to form amid the echoes.

''To Scotland!''

''To freedom!''

''To Robert Bruce, king of the sovereign nation of Scotland!''

Bruce returned to his horse, mounting to declare the victory loudly, then to thank each man for his love of Scotland over his life, and bid them gather up their wounded, and tend to them well. "The battle for Scotland," he reminded them, "has just begun."

Later that night, with the dead buried, the injured tended, strategy decided, Robert Bruce made a point of speaking to the barons and knights who had joined his forces, and brought men and arms as well.

He had learned from watching William Wallace the value of appreciating every man, and he was, by nature, a compassionate man with an innate charm. After the death of Comyn, he had learned as well the dangers of offending the values of others, and before setting on his crusade to prove himself king, he had done absolution for the act, though it was said he had stabbed Comyn and his companions had been the ones to finish him.

Eric had been consulting with Jamie when Bruce approached him, thanking him and all the men for their part in adding to his ranks, and bringing about the victory. Then he asked Eric to walk with him, and under a canopy of trees he paused and asked him, "Langley remains well in your hands?"

"When I left, all was well."

"Since the earl's army has been here," he murmured wryly, "I imagine it remains so." He hesitated, then added, "My spies tell me, though, that Robert Neville and Niles Mason are gathering troops at Cheffington. And, you know, young Lord Aidan has made his way from England. Now these two men will have a nobleman in their vanguard— they will be able to put out the cry that he has been wronged, that his sister is not your wife but your prisoner, and they will make her a cause to awaken the hearts of my enemies— and those who might be neutral, waiting to see which way the wind will blow, for Scotland and me, or the English king."

"They would still be fools to attack Langley."

Robert Bruce nodded. "That is true, which is why I asked you to help goad the English through this marriage. The lady is a rich prize to any Englishman, to any man at that. I know her. Were you aware of that? At least, I have seen her several times. She was often at the English court, since her father was not just a titled man, but one of illustrious deeds in many of Edward's campaigns in France."

"No, I was not aware that you were acquainted. She hasn't mentioned it."

The king shrugged. "I imagine I am a vacillating traitor in her eyes, and we did not speak more than courtesies, ever, but . . . though Edward has stubbornly refused to exchange the lady, I'm certain that he will support a plan to get her back. He is studying the legalities of her marriage while denying that there can be any. I'm certain that he is plotting for her return. I used to see him watch her. He had an eye for such a beauty, and I could always see him estimating just what such a prize was worth. He bought the loyalty of Langley when he blessed her marriage to Afton, which, of course, had been arranged for years." His tone suddenly changed. "Don't let him get her back. My God, the man imprisons my child! You cannot imagine the service you have done me by this small piece of vengeance. I know that it meant little to you, with Margot . . . gone. Yet I am grateful."

"There was a certain sense of vengeance to my agreement, my lord," Eric assured the king. "I have my reasons to despise those who want her."

"Do whatever you must do," Robert continued, his voice growing harsh and tight again. "In my name. And for Scotland." The king hesitated, his teeth grating. "Edward thinks that he can make a marriage I have sanctioned null and void! That he can crush me as he crushes every man who vowed to free Scotland from his tyranny. He must not get her back.

If he is ever able to seize her, there must be a way that he is prevented from using her in his plays for power, his alliances, his rewards for those who serve him. The bishops have written to Rome, but in the meantime . . .'' He paused again. Then he smiled. ''If there is a God in Heaven, and He loves us at all . . . she will have a child. That would definitely damp the value of the prize when Edward plays his dynastic games of marriage, riches, and barter. He will be forced to recognize Scottish authority. He will be defied at every turn. For the honor of Scotland.''

Robert Bruce placed a hand on Eric's shoulder, then walked on into the night.

A cool breeze whispered over his head.

God, how he had loved his wife. How Margot's unwavering, undemanding love for him had suffused his soul through time until she had been a part of him.

He was human. And battle camps were always attended by women.

But the king had just given him more of an order than a suggestion . . . to do something he had probably been tempted to do from the moment he had first watched Igrainia at the stream.

She had her own grief, and that he had understood as well. And just as well, the anguish they had witnessed with one another had made him hate her at times . . . as much as he had been enticed by innate physical urges, like the need to draw breath, drink water.

A breeze touched him again, and he laughed out loud, a hollow sound in the darkness.

She was, after all, his wife now.

And therein lay the tempest in his soul.

His wife. Beautiful, dark-haired witch, a prize, a pawn. And as tempting as a siren.

Another battle to be waged . . . with her. With himself.

Again he laughed. Another battle . . .

For the honor of Scotland.

Igrainia stood upon the parapets, looking over the field. Word had come that there had been a battle. That the lesser Scots had routed the great army of the Earl of Pembroke. Edward was spitting with fury, raging that he was the only man who could lead his army to victory.

She had found a certain freedom—within the walls of Langley. And she had realized that, with careful planning, she could escape.

But she wasn't certain that she wanted to do so. There was danger in escape. Here, at Langley, the "outlaws" were courteous and respectful. Eric was gone. She had written the letter he had "suggested," and his men had apparently been left with word that she was to have the run of the castle—with a guard in tow at all times, she was certain, but in the past few days it seemed that they had grown lax. There might be many opportunities for escape. Merchants had begun to arrive here with their wares, with carts that rambled back through the gates before dusk. Farmers, milk-maids, servants, others, all came and went.

There was a way.

Jennie urged her on daily.

Rowenna pointed out the courtesies she received, and how she was loved by the people when she walked through the courtyard, how they looked for a word from her, smiled when she smiled, came running to do her slightest bidding.

She had come to love Langley.

But she would have escaped . . . to be free. Except that there really was no escape, because to leave here, she would have to seek help eventually from the English. And go to the king. And he had determined that she would be married to Robert Neville, and . . .

He had been Afton's kin. But it disturbed her that he was so desperate for Langley, so desperate for a quick marriage. He was not like Afton. Afton had loved books and learning, and the art of reason. In all the arguments regarding the prisoners, Robert had been irate, indifferent to the fate of the women and children, as determined as Sir Niles Mason that the men be executed. Most men would have accepted the king's decree that all such traitors should perish, but something about the way Robert Neville seemed to *relish* the judgment disturbed her. Just as his eagerness to claim what had been his kinsman's holding. And wife. Especially since her revenues in England were so great.

She didn't *dislike* Robert Neville. But it had made her uneasy, the way he would touch her at times, a hand on her shoulder, too fervent a kiss in greeting, a chance brush as they passed in the hall. She had never mentioned it to Afton. And at the time of all the illness and death at the castle, she had not thought of anything but the darkness and the pain.

So now . . .

She was certain that she had found a means of escape. She had used the greatest tactic against her enemy—obedience. They were lulled.

Yet her only escape would be to a greater, perhaps more dangerous, imprisonment. If not more dangerous, one that she couldn't help but believe would be even more confining. There were certain facts in life she had to accept. Afton was gone. The idyllic life they had led was over. She did live in a world where birth, property, and position were the guiding factors of life, and it had been nothing less than a small miracle that she and Afton had been friends as children, and then slipped into compatibility and comfort as husband and wife. Perhaps he had even been too fine a man for the position into which he had been born; he had learned all the things the heir to such an estate as Langley must know, but he had preferred books and art, riding in the fields, and such things as a May Day fair to the act of practicing for war. He was eager to listen; her thoughts and words mattered equally in all things. In so many areas of life, men had rights, and women did not, but that had not been a situation she must examine in her own heart and mind, because she had been married to Afton.

With Eric gone and Peter and Jarrett guarding and guiding the daily life at Langley, she found that she preferred being a respected prisoner here to finding herself a different kind of captive—under the dictates of King Edward and the man who had bargained for her, just as he had the lordship of Langley. Allowed her freedom from the confines of her room, she began to live again, and in strange ways, life did become similar to what it had been before. She spent long afternoons in the hall with Father MacKinley and others, and the news they discussed and argued sometimes had little to do with the situation in Scotland. Philip the Fair of France had begun a persecution of the Knights Templar, which horrified Peter, who had befriended many of their number on his journeys to the Holy Land years before. Father Mac-Kinley thought the persecution deplorable as well, yet argued that the highly secretive order of knights had grown rich and powerful since the early days of their existence, when they had lived by a code of chastity and poverty. There was also the matter of the current pope, whom Philip had worked so strenuously to promote into the holy office, and now seemed to be using for his own purposes and gains. The French king had a sadly depleted treasury, and it was true that the Knights Templar had riches across the known world.

All these things they discussed and more, and when she spoke, even when she argued, they listened. When Peter's favorite hound was injured, taking a fall from a crag while chasing a rabbit, he came to her for the balms to heal its wounds. She began to visit the tenants again with Father MacKinley, tending to their sickness, sympathizing with their woes.

She continued to read, finding herself more intrigued with the use and history of mail, armor, and weaponry.

Again, she removed Eric's offensive coat-of-arms. Nothing of Afton's family had been left in the room.

But no one had disturbed any of her sewing or embroidery supplies. She found everything she needed—and she certainly had the time—to create a coat-of-arms of her own. She designed a wall hanging with lions and lilies, the crest of the house of Abelard. She was pleased with the way it looked upon the wall, and found a certain peace and independence upon seeing it each night across the room as she lay down to sleep. She *needed* that sense of herself. Though *he* was gone, it seemed that he remained. He had made his impression here. His judgments were part of daily life. At Langley, the land was Scotland, Robert Bruce was the only king. But life was sacred, and cruelty was not practiced upon the people, and the tenants and servants had not been beaten down. The men did not ravage the homes of those who had survived the illness, nor the homes of those who had died. Men were not slain, women were not raped, and crops and fields and animals were not destroyed. There was, of course, a logic to that. Eric's great determination was to recruit and train more forces for his king. Fighting men needed food and supplies.

But those who knew him best were completely loyal. They waited each day for news of their king, the fighting, Edward's movements, and most important, the fate of their leader. None among them planned for his demise, or coveted his position as their leader. Father MacKinley told her that he often heard the men speaking, and that Eric held such sway because there was no danger he would ask of any man that he would not face himself, nor would he refuse any fight to defend those in his ranks, nor would he put his own welfare ahead of that of any other man. He was a natural strategist, and yet, also a man aware that numbers could be defeated by determination. He had assured his men that they would seize Langley, even when they fought with few weapons and no armor, because they were fighting for those they loved. They would prevail, because they had to.

As the days passed, she was certain that the door to freedom remained open, but she began to question what freedom meant. She should have prayed that Eric fall in battle. She was dismayed to realize that she watched for his return. She needed to believe that she could escape, even if it might not be wise for her to do so.

Her only fear in remaining where she was without attempting to escape was for her brother, and it unnerved her, but as of yet, she'd heard no reply from him. If he had written an acknowledgment of her letter to him, delivered to Peter MacDonald, as steward of Langley in Eric's absence, Peter had refrained from telling her. And she dared not ask in case Aidan was trying to slip word to her through the good graces of a tinker, farmer, or milkmaid.

Messengers did come and go from the castle. At supper in the great hall one night, Peter informed her with pride that the Bruce's men had repelled a heavy English attack on Loudon Hill, and that following that victory, they had gone on to attack a force led by the Earl of Gloucester sent to relieve Pembroke. Gloucester's men had put up a better resistance, but they too had retreated from the battlefield, returning to the safety of Ayr Castle.

She had been surprised to feel her heart quicken. If there had been bad news regarding the man he followed so faithfully, Peter would not have spoken with such pleasure. And still she found herself asking, "And what of the men of Langley?" Despite her promise to personally slay Eric, she realized that she had feared for him after he had gone, an emotion she would certainly not share with him or any of his people. But Peter had been quick to assure her that the men of Langley had performed ably and valiantly in both engagements. They had not lost a man, and the only injury had been a broken arm suffered by one young man-at-arms.

The tide seemed to be turning.

Bruce was prevailing, but King Edward had sent out a summons to all of the leading men of England, all who owed the king feudal service. They were to assemble at Carlisle on July eighth, and be joined by the king's Welsh levies. This time, the king would lead his own troops against Bruce.

She wondered if the Scottish king's strategy, cunning, and pure willpower could still give him victory when King Edward himself took to the field, demanding obedience and solid courage from all the men he could muster under him. She knew the king. He was called Longshanks for his great height, and he was respected as a warrior king with good reason. His personal courage was legendary. He was intelligent, and before the death of his first wife, his beloved Eleanor, he had been compassionate as well at times. Though his policies against Scotland had become merciless and brutal, there had been times when he had shown unusual temperance. Usually, those times came when he knew that diplomacy would serve him better than cruelty.

As she stood upon the parapet, enjoying the gentle kiss of the sun and the soft caress of a pleasant breeze, she heard movement at her side. She turned to see that Peter had come to stand along with her, looking out on the great sloping field to the east.

"Listen!" he said softly.

She arched a brow, and at first heard nothing. But moments later, she heard what Peter had. In the distance, a murmur. A trembling of the earth at first, felt rather than heard, but then she detected the unmistakable sound of the slow beat of horses' hooves against the earth, and a murmur in the wind that was the sound of a troop of men riding hard for the castle.

"Gregory had said that they would return today. He is a remarkable lad."

Gregory was indeed remarkable. She was beginning to learn to read his lips when he spoke. He had told her exactly when a colt would be born, a day when it would rain, and a day when the sun would shine through, even though the morning had dawned dark and ominous.

The sound of a trumpet came along with a cry and the wave of a banner from the guard high atop the eastern ledge, and Peter said with pleasure, "They are returning."

Igrainia felt a curious sensation of both dread and anticipation. In Eric's absence, the days had been good, a time to function again, and to assess her own situation. His men had been as courteous to her as if she were one of their own.

But now . . .

"Well," she said lightly. "I am glad for you that your people have all survived the blades and bludgeons of war. You'll excuse me."

She fled from the parapets, suddenly eager to escape.

Peter was too occupied with the returning troop to follow her, nor did she see Jarrett, or any of the other men, slip silently behind her as she walked.

She meant to return to her room, her retreat, her private space. But when she came back into the tower, she found that the great hall was empty, and she found herself drawn to the steps that led down to the dungeon. Fires lit the stretch of the stone underbelly of the castle, but the long hall of graves and cells was empty. She wondered that it did not make her feel the least uneasy to walk among the tombs and rows of the dead; once it had. Now, Afton rested within the wall, and she knew that if his spirit walked, it would offer nothing but comfort and protection. She paused, touched the stone, and felt now a sweet pain of memory rather than the agony of loss. Then, she found herself turning, curious to know just how they had walled off the secret tunnel.

For a moment, she paused, damning herself for finding this the time to explore the bowels of the castle. But then, the conquering heroes had just returned. They would all be gloating in pride and triumph, toasting one another, Robert Bruce, and Scotland.

No one would be looking for her.

She walked down the long hall, passing by the dungeon cells which remained empty, wood and iron doors ajar. She didn't pause at the room that was a torture chamber, but she felt a prickle of discomfort against her nape. She hurried on, to what appeared to be a dead end, yet slipped around the pillar that appeared to be a part of the wall, and reached the place directly behind it where the tunnel had once begun as a low, barely discernible archway. There had been a gap there, and directly behind it, another walkway that slanted low as it led beneath the moat to the southern side of the river.

She touched the line of the arch in the stone, and realized that what had once appeared to be a wall was now one in truth. Mortar rimmed the stones that had been inset. Still, she thought, Eric wouldn't have made it impossible to use the tunnel for his own purpose. She was certain that the wall had not been built strongly, and that it would fall the moment an axe or pick was brought against it.

Naturally, she quickly noted, no such tool had been left close at hand.

Glad that she had this further knowledge for later use if need be, she turned away from the shadowed end of the long hall and started back toward the cells, the tombs, and the stairway to the hall. Deep in thought, she walked along several feet, her eyes and head lowered, until a strange sensation along her spine and a deeper darkness against the dimly lit hall gave her warning that she was not alone.

She came to a halt, and saw, at first, in the wavering light of the sconces, only what appeared to be a massive obstruction before her. Then the small, flickering wave of flame from the wall gave structure to broad shoulders, the sweep of a mantle, and the glowing gold of a man's hair. Her heart thumped hard in her chest, and she stood very still. There was no sense in going back. And no possibility of going forward. And though his blue eyes were all but black and deeply shadowed in the dimness, she knew that they were fixed upon her with displeasure.

"Ah," she murmured, determining for lack of any option, to still the trembling in her limbs and speak as casually as she might to Peter, Jarrett, or Father MacKinley. "I suppose that all hail and laud are due. The triumphant warriors have returned. You've survived. How . . . pleasant for you."

She hadn't realized that he had held his hands behind his back until he suddenly moved them forward. He held a pick.

"Looking for this?"

She barely glanced at the pick, meeting his dark eyes.

"I came to visit the graves."

"They are at the other end of the hall."

"I had heard that the tunnel was walled in."

"So you came to see for yourself?"

"Naturally. It seemed a foolish idea to me. You never know when you may need such an escape route yourself."

"When I may need it? Or when you choose to use it yourself?"

"You've been gone some time. And I have been the model captive. You may ask your men."

"But you don't mind my men being here. Perhaps life was even pleasant. But now I've returned."

"So you have," she murmured. She decided that further conversation would get her nowhere. Alarmed at the way her heart continued to hammer and her breath to come too quickly, she decided that a dignified escape was in order. She started walking, though the distance between them was short. "I'll return to my cage, the ever dutiful captive, sir, if you will be so good as to let me by."

But he didn't intend to allow her an easy way out.

He caught her arm as she tried to pass. She was forced to halt at his side, wedged between the stone wall and the steel of his frame. She met his eyes with a cool bravado. She glanced at the long fingers cast against the white edge of her sleeve.

"I am here!" she said, afraid that her voice was starting to sound too desperate. "I came to pray . . . and wandered. Curious, no more."

"Ah, so it's not your pick."

"Of course not. Did you think your men would supply me with such a tool?"

"I think that this has been your home for some time and that you are surely aware of where such tools can be found."

He looked all the better for battle, she thought. Noble, powerful, and, as ever, completely confident. She remembered how ragged he had been, how drawn, bedraggled, so much like a wild man, the first time she had seen him. His clothing now was clean, his hair rich and combed, his face shaven, strong, and definitely both interesting and compelling. Still, there remained a tension in his features, perhaps a weariness, and the pain he had not let go.

He had ridden home without mail, apparently certain that the way would be clear. But his sword was belted low on his waist, and the knife he always carried was sheathed at his knee.

"Prisoners are supposed to look for a way out," she said impatiently. He seemed too close, and far too real suddenly. As a man. Flesh and blood, with a pounding heart, eyes that saw too much, and a power that leaped too quickly to the fore. "I am here!" she exclaimed. "When I was not among those fawning at the sight of your triumphant return, did you think that I had, indeed, escaped the *pleasant* life I lead as your prisoner?"

"Oh, no. I knew that you were here. The moment I saw Peter. He would have died to protect what we have seized."

"Stone walls, arms and armor, and a woman, all one and the same."

"All prizes of war," he agreed pleasantly.

"Except that some stay where they are placed."

"Ah, so you do remain eager to escape. Right into the arms and bosom and marital bed of a man who was dreaming of taking your husband's land, title, property, and woman before he had even grown cold in death."

"Listen! I do believe that someone is calling your name in the hall above. Surely, you are needed by your men, after your long absence."

"I don't think that you were a model prisoner at all, Igrainia. I think that you are a rare intelligent woman, and you know that you cannot stand against Edward, if he gets his hands upon you."

"What difference does it make?" She asked desperately.

She could not stand being here a moment longer, so aware of him. She would scream and cry and go running like a madwoman along the corridor at any moment. "My only real escape would be the death of you all! May I please pass by? Surely, sir, you are needed above so that your adoring companions might shower you with laud and praise?"

"It's good that you didn't try to escape."

"Really? What would have happened? Were your men ordered to take a lash to my back? Lop off my head?"

"No," he said evenly. "They would have been forced to lock you within a cell down here again until my return."

"Were they able to stop me."

"I assure you, they would have done so."

It seemed he still didn't intend to release her. He studied her as they spoke, and he seemed to be searching for something in her eyes, or in her words.

"It doesn't matter, does it? You've returned—I am here. Still the bird in the cage, simply given flight in a larger cage."

"This war will be a long one. And I will leave again. And whatever logic moves within your mind and rules your reckless soul, you must be warned. Right now, you feel you rule your cage, and you're now dismayed by the rules within it. That may change. The fact that you are a prize of war will not."

"I haven't the least idea of what you are saying to me!" she exclaimed in dismay. The moment was coming closer and closer when her control would break, when she would become the madwoman, ready to hurl herself against stone to escape him. Her heart hammered; she felt she couldn't breathe at all, and yet each breath was coming far too quickly. "I am not bent on escaping; I am resigned to the confines of my cage and even the smaller space and solitude when you are in residence."

"You may have to *resign* yourself to far more," he said.

"I will resign myself to anything, if you will just let me pass now! You *have* to be wanted and *needed* in the great hall now."

"Alas, I am. And tonight, of course, there will be drinking and feasting, something of a celebration, naturally. You are welcome to attend. I hear that your place at the table has not been left empty for many nights. Don't let my return interfere with your dining habits."

He was still holding her arm. She managed a deep breath and a cool reply. "I don't celebrate death and destruction."

"Not that of your countrymen at the least. I must apologize for the poor manners I have offered you by returning with my head upon my neck."

She tried to break free from his hold then, but his grip was such that she couldn't begin to escape. And so she replied with honesty, glad that her answer would not be one to change his strange mood of insistence to one of anger. "You're mistaken. I was not eager for you to lose your head."

"You'd prefer my heart to be sliced out?"

"I was not willing for your death in the least."

"Take care, I will believe that you were even eager for my return."

She hesitated, wanting to take *extreme* care with what she said. But he suddenly laughed then. "Ah, I see. You weren't particularly eager for my death, but neither were you eager for my return. You did enjoy the time while I was gone, yet believed that my existence meant that you were actually rather *safe* at Langley. And here, in the tunnel now, it's true—you were doing nothing more than assuring yourself that you could find an escape route in the future. If you deemed it necessary. You have decided that I am the lesser of two evils, especially when I'm far from Langley.''

''Please, before God, may I pass?''

''Whether I am here or not, you will find yourself *resigned* to remain at Langley.''

''You may command many things, sir, but never my thoughts or feelings.''

''It doesn't matter what they are—as long as you're not foolish enough to act on them.''

''I am duly threatened and well put in my place. *May I pass now?*''

''Will you be joining us this evening?''

''I will not.''

''You're not wanting to hear music, and enjoy stirring tales of valor and honor?''

''I am afraid that mixing a meal with the boasts of brag-garts would be disturbing to the digestion. Again, I ask you, may I please go?''

To her surprise, he inclined his head in a grave bow and his hand fell from her arm. She fled, trying to walk slowly, her footsteps moving quicker with each step. He didn't follow.

His gaze, she was certain, did.

When she reached the steps, she was running. She didn't feel free from that gaze until she had skimmed the stairs to the hall, slipped quickly through the gathering horde of men there, and nearly flown up the stairs to the second landing and her room.

Her room—her cage. What had been a prison now seemed a haven. She brought her palms to her cheeks, which were burning.

She waited, wondering if he would take his time, then follow her to her room with some new way to challenge her.

But he did not. And she remembered that he had just returned—there were matters that would be of importance to him.

She was not one of them. She was a prize of war, like arms and armor and the walls of a castle.

Time passed, and no one came. When she opened the door to the hall, she could hear voices from below, and she knew that the men were exchanging information about events at the castle, and at the battle site, and perhaps discussing what direction the war would take when the king commenced his march against Bruce.

She was startled, though, to be caught with her head poked out the door. "Igrainia, are you coming down? Is there something that you needed?"

Jamie had brought a stool to the hallway and was whittling at a piece of wood.

"Yes . . . I'd like to send for the kitchen lads, and have the bath brought."

"Of course." He moved to the stairs. She tried to listen to what was being said below without appearing to be eavesdropping. Once Jamie was gone, she could tiptoe to the landing and listen.

But Jamie didn't leave. He called to someone below who went about her bidding. She retreated to her room.

The tub was brought, along with a multitude of kettles, and then one by one, the servants all left, and she was alone again. She bathed, watching the door, ever wary of a rude visitor who might not knock. She took her time, wondering why she risked so much. She washed her hair, and rinsed it clean. And basked some more, always watching the door.

But Eric never appeared. When the water grew cold, she emerged, determined not to leave her room, *not* to attend any celebration for the triumph of the Scots. She dressed for bed in a lace-trimmed, unbleached linen bed gown. She sat before the fire and brushed her hair until it dried.

At last, she curled up with a book. Tonight, tales of the Greek gods would be her company.

No one arrived to urge her to join the group below. Not even Father MacKinley. Jennie didn't come, and neither did Rowenna.

The sun began to fall, twilight came, and then darkness.

Jarrett arrived with a tray bearing her supper. He was cheerful, friendly as ever, but eager to leave. She failed to draw him into a conversation.

Not long after, she heard the sounds of revelry from below.

Feeling an irritation that seemed to fester and swell, she thought that indeed, the conquering heroes had returned.

It was impossible to ignore the music and laughter and shouts that sounded from the great hall. She stared at a single page for long moments before she realized that she had not understood a word.

She could not help but wonder what they were saying, what they were doing. It would be in her best interests to know.

When her curiosity could bear no more, she opened the door. Looking down the hall, she saw no one on guard. She silently trod the length of the hall to the top of the stairs and there looked down on the merriment.

Several men had pipes, and Jamie, who had boasted of his prowess with a lute, was proving it. He and Dougal and other men were standing near the fire. There were a number of women in the hall as well, wives of the many fighting men, who had joined in the meal and entertainment. She had seen some of them about the courtyard, and even spoken to a few.

One woman she recognized from the dire days when so many had been so ill. A survivor from the plague.

And there was Jennie, as she had expected, silently and sullenly serving along with Berlinda, Garth, Gregory, and Rowenna.

At the head of table, naturally, there was Eric.

His chalice was before him and an empty plate. While many others in the room were laughing, chatting, even shouting to one another across the room or urging the musicians on, Eric seemed engaged in serious conversation with Peter MacDonald, seated at his right. Rowenna walked behind the men with a pitcher, bearing more ale. As she poured, Peter absently thanked her. Eric seemed to notice her especially. He smiled, and spoke to her. They exchanged words and both laughed. He was at ease. He had bathed as well, she thought, washed away the dust of the road. He wore a shirt and breeches, and the ever-present mantle, his tartan, his name, evidence of the clan he honored as much as his battle for his sovereign nation.

Rowenna laughed and blushed at whatever he said. Other women apparently found him attractive, strong, virile . . . compelling.

A moment later, as if sensing her presence, Eric looked up.

She froze where she had hunched down by the hard wood banister. It was too late to retreat, though she shrank back against herself. He had seen her.

He stared at her for a long moment. She could not draw her gaze from his.

There was something different about the way he looked at her. His eyes burned with a strange blue fire, and the heat seemed to cross the distance between, and burn deeply inside her.

The feel of fire that touched her flesh spurred her to action.

She rose as gracefully as she could. She didn't give in to

her desire to flee. She continued to meet his gaze. His eyes remained hard upon her.

Then she purposely turned, as if dismissing him cleanly from sight and thought.

She headed back toward her room.

As she walked, her heart began its thunder again.

And this time, he did follow her.

CHAPTER 13

As she heard him on the stairs, she tried to quicken her pace. But he reached the landing and called her name. "Igrainia!"

His tone was pleasant, but hinted at a certain sarcasm or mockery. She stiffened where she stood, not turning to him.

"You're intrigued by the activities in the hall. It's absurd for you to watch from the stairway. Join the company."

"I'm not intrigued. I'm wondering if the noise will ever lessen."

"Not until very late. Or very early," he said, crossing the distance to her. Before he could turn her to face him, she turned herself, back stiff against her door.

"Come down."

"I really have no interest."

"You're lying. You're bored in your little cage, and dying of curiosity. Come down."

"No."

"Yes."

He took her arm, and slipped it through his own in a fluid and determined motion. She could fight to get her arm back, but she wouldn't win.

And he was already walking. She had to move swiftly to keep up with him.

"I am not dressed!" she protested, and he glanced down at the linen gown she wore with its delicate and elaborate lacework. The fabric was thin, but voluminous. In the shadows, it was a concealing and elegant gown.

"You're too modest. That's a lovely garment."

"It's a nightdress. My feet are bare."

"Ah, well, bare feet will keep you from running far," he replied.

"I haven't been running."

"Thus far. We've established that fact, haven't we? You're not the customary captive. I believe my men actually vie with one another for the pleasure of serving you."

She ignored him, for they had reached the hall.

The music stopped. There was a silence as all eyes turned to her.

Then Jamie spoke. "Igrainia! Welcome. Jarrett, lads, surely we've a ballad to welcome the lady?"

They began to play again, a surprisingly beautiful tune that the pipes made haunting, about a maid in a tower, and the young man who watched her night after night.

Eric had maintained his lock on her arm. He moved her through the hall to the head of the table. Peter had vacated his place.

"Sit," Eric said.

"It is Peter's chair."

"Peter no longer requires it."

She wasn't really given a choice. She found herself seated. "Gregory! Ale for the lady!" Eric called. He lifted his chalice. "Indeed, for myself," he said grimly, staring at the chalice. It seemed for a moment that his tone was bitter, yet not against her, but more for himself. Gregory brought the ale, poured it.

"Let's toast, my lady. Lift your glass."

"I won't toast your victories," she told him.

"Fine. Toast life, then, my lady, and the sanctity of it! Hell, drink to old King Edward, may his body rot beneath him!"

She hesitated, her fingers curled around the chalice.

"Toast the memory of your husband then, Igrainia, but lift your cup and drink!"

She had a wild vision of him grabbing her by the jaw and forcing ale down her throat. He wouldn't do such a thing. Or would he? She lifted the chalice. She was feeling the need for a long, long swallow of the hearty ale herself.

He drained his own, set the chalice down with a thump, and stared at her, blue eyes dark and brooding. She drank herself . . . and drank, finishing her own ale, imitating his thud upon the table. "Will that suffice?" she inquired coolly.

He smiled, leaning back then, his eyes never leaving hers. "I don't know. Will it? You were obviously eager to see what was happening. Or else, you were sorely in need of some ale. Or wine—I believe there is wine, if you prefer."

"I prefer not to drink here."

"Why not? Drink enough ale, and we will all become more bearable to you."

"There is not enough ale in all the world," she murmured.

"You'd be surprised what enough ale can do."

Their attention was drawn from one another as a cheerful shout rose in the hall, drowning the murmurs of more intimate conversations.

"Jamie, sing the new song to our good King Robert!" Allan called. He was down the table from where they sat,

his arm around a young woman. Igrainia couldn't recall if
she had seen the woman before or not, but she was pretty
and young, and seemed to be content in Jamie's arms. Her
clothing was fine; she wore a tartan mantle with colors in
blue, green, and red.

"Aye, then!" Jamie cried, and began.

He had a pleasant voice, and a way of telling a story as
he plucked at his instrument. His story was about the Scottish
king, of dark days and sad, of the deaths of those he loved,
and of a night when he was ready to let all be lost, but then
saw a spider, endlessly toiling at a web, beginning anew
each time the rain destroyed what she had worked so hard
to achieve. The sun rose, and the web she then spun was
so beautiful that the king knew he could give no less for
Scotland, because the sun would rise again.

His song was followed by wild applause, and he blushed
and laughed and thanked them all. Igrainia was dismayed
to find that he had caught her eye as he turned around bowing
and called out to her. "Igrainia! Come, please. Eric, you've
not heard her, have you? Neither have I. But Peter tells me
she has the voice of an angel, a lark, and that she played
and sang in the hall at supper while we were away. Igrainia!
You must uphold the honor of Langley. Come!"

She froze in her chair, and felt Eric's eyes again.

He leaned forward. "So . . . you have not just dined with
the enemy during our absence, but entertained as well?"

She moistened her lips. "I really don't think you'd care
to hear any ballad I have to sing."

"Oh, but I would."

"No."

"Yes. I command it."

"I will sing whatever pleases me," she threatened.

"Do go ahead."

She rose suddenly. "As you wish, then. Who am I to deny a conquering hero?"

She swept from the table, walked the length of it, and took the lute from Jamie. He smiled warmly, handing it to her with a deep bow.

Her song was about a love lost, about a knight of infinite wisdom, aware of the power of the written word, the beauty of a field, the wonder of a child. A knight far too gentle for the sword, but born to live and die by it. She was certain that many would know that in the song, the gentle knight was Afton—though he had perished from disease rather than the sword.

Of course, that he was "slain by an enemy, savage and bold," might have surely sent a message into some of their souls. Especially since the enemy was savage, barbaric, from the north, and with a heavy force of arms, but lacking of wisdom, knowledge, and chivalry.

Even as she sang the last of it, only willpower alone kept her from faltering. She was a fool, mocking them all. She meant only to anger Eric. To arouse him to emotion, find a certain vengeance in what power she had herself.

And still, when she had finished, returned the lute to Jamie, and stood, she was astounded by the applause that thundered and echoed about the room. She felt flushed, being near the fire, and parched, and when someone handed her a chalice, she accepted it, and drank, and then demurred when Allan and his lady and then others cried out, asking her for another tale.

"No, really—"

But Jamie, smiling, was at her side, and he asked her if she knew a light and lively tune with no bearing on events other than the argument between a lord and lady, and so he played, and they sang together, and again, the hall seemed warm, and she was applauded and amazed to find so many people beside her, thanking her for the song. The woman with Allan came to her as well, and thanked her for the care she had given her during the plague. Igrainia found herself strangely enjoying the evening, and dancing when Jarrett brought out his pipes again, swirling with the other wives and daughters and lovers, and even laughing when she tripped over Angus's feet when he joined her.

She was enjoying herself. The women did not seem to resent her, and the men were admiring, and complimentary. She felt alive as she hadn't in some time, and she even felt beautiful, their words were so kind.

She forgot she was among the enemy. She smiled and laughed with Jamie, Jarrett, Dougal, Allan and his lady. At times, she noted Eric, talking to one of his men, or perhaps speaking with one of their wives, sisters, mothers, or lovers. She watched the courtesy he showed others. She saw him touch Rowenna's hand again, bow his head close to hear her speak against the talk, laughter, and conversation. Indeed, he could charm.

She turned away from him. For a moment she felt as if she were trying to rage against the wind, to laugh before she could cry, to prove herself a shimmering bird of crystalline colors, strong in flight, untouched by any bars.

She accepted more ale.

She discussed the best poultices for flesh wounds.

She danced again, and again, and listened to the music, smiled radiantly for Jamie, and allowed herself the luxury of accepting his compliments.

She almost made herself forget Eric . . .

Until, in the midst of swirling revelry, she spun straight into his arms, and against his hard chest.

Then, she knew.

No, she had not forgotten him at all. She had performed with a vengeance, knowing he watched, had danced with energy, had laughed with reckless abandon, had teased, charmed and . . .

"It's time for you to return to the cage," he told her.

She felt the supple heat of his body as she was held hard against it. She met his eyes, her own defiant.

"Why? You insisted I come down."

"And now I am insisting you go up."

"Why? Because your men do not find me to be loathsome? Not such a terrible danger? Because there are people here who believe I saved their lives?"

"Because they will come to trust you, and then you will be a really terrible danger. It's time to leave. I'll be pleased to escort you up."

She inclined her head slightly. "I can imagine," she murmured with sweet sarcasm. "But I wish to stay here."

"You are going up."

"Force me rudely, as you are so apt to do, and I will scream."

"And you think my men will then draw swords on me?" he mocked.

"Perhaps they will."

"Perhaps you overestimate your position."

"Perhaps not."

"It's a gamble you're welcome to take."

She stood resentfully silent, tempted, and yet afraid, and praying that she still kept the threat alive in her eyes. But then, it was likely that he really didn't care if she screamed or not, if she walked with dignity, or if he simply threw her over his shoulder and neatly deposited her back in the room, the bird returned to her cage.

"Come along. We have an interesting matter to discuss. It might as well be now."

A deepening sense of alarm and dismay filled her. She didn't want to return to the room, to be shut away. She had disturbed him tonight, she had done it on purpose. She knew it, and she was reveling in it. She was admired in this hall, she managed very well alone with his men, and she wanted him to know it.

She had stoked a fire for warmth, and was burning in its heat instead. She was painfully aware they danced no longer, that she had somehow come against a wall, and she was still within his hold. No weight was borne down against her, but she was still aware of the pressure of his chest and that she was pinned against him as he lowered his head to speak softly to her. They might have been having an intimate conversation. She remembered that afternoon, in the dungeon. How desperate she had felt when he had held her. A new, deep unease stirred, and threatened again to rise to a raging panic. And yet . . .

"My lady?" he leaned lower with the question. His words were a whisper, and his face was close to her own.

The promise of true panic rose within her mind.

She didn't want this . . . closeness.

She didn't want to be feeling what she was feeling, and sensing something frightening that lay in her soul. She felt slightly faint, slightly dizzy, and though she had challenged him by drinking so swiftly, and perhaps too much, it was not the ale. It was not that she longed to slam her fists against him, or that she hated him, and was afraid that he would touch her too long.

It was something worse.

She was trembling, and she was certain that he could feel it. And it seemed like forever since she had felt Afton's fingers moving through her hair, felt a soft whisper against her cheek. Eric was horrible, surely, savage, a foe who had come and changed her life, and yet she didn't want to think about his birth or background or his political passions. She knew, held against him as she was, what she had feared so desperately before. She was drawn to the breadth of his shoulders, the pulsing heat of his chest, the length of his fingers on her arm. She liked the rugged contours of his face, the sound of his voice, the strange adherence to principle he had shown. And most of all, though she had to fight it, she liked the fact that now, he was turned to her, touching her, with her . . .

She liked being held. Breathing the scent of him. And she longed to feel a gentle touch. Not even a gentle touch. A *hungry* touch.

The realization of just *exactly* what she was feeling washed over her like a sweeping wave of deep and shattering heat. He was . . . compelling. He was masculine, sensual. And the restless urge within her to challenge, argue, mock, and anger was because . . .

She wouldn't allow the words to form in her mind. And yet they did. And then the fury she felt with herself, and the horror, and the fear were suddenly overwhelming. And it was true: She had purposely set out to laugh with his men, charm them, shine within the music and dance, and all to make him see that she was not just a prize of war. And now . . .

She wanted only to escape his nearness, and come to terms with herself.

"I . . . yes!" she whispered, and now, the sound of her voice was desperate. Her words were faltering. "I mean no, I'll go, but I need no escort, I require no assistance up the stairs. If we've a matter of interest to discuss, it has to be tomorrow. You mustn't leave your celebration, not when you've proven yourself so perfectly heroic and you're so pleased with the fruits of battle." She saw in his eyes that her words were stirring anger in him. For once, she had *not* meant to do so. "I didn't mean that, exactly. You should stay. You must stay. I can walk just fine. I'm going."

She broke free from his hold, and meant to make all haste to the stairs, and hurry up them, and do as she said—and pray through the night to forget that such feelings had ever swept through her heart and touched her senses.

But as she turned, it was as if she was blinded. She ran past the table. Angus had sat, great legs stretched out before him. And once again that night, she tripped over his feet.

Dangerously so, this time, in her haste. She catapulted up, and nearly fell on her face.

Before she could fall, she was caught. She grasped desperately at the arms steadying her, lifted her face, and met Eric's eyes once again. Before she could speak, she found herself lifted. Angus had risen, rueful, concerned, apologetic.

"The lady is tired, I believe. And then again, perhaps she's really enjoyed our celebration, and had a bit too much ale. She isn't hurt, Angus, and don't worry—I have her."

He strode for the stairs.

And he did not know just how deeply she was hurt, not in the flesh, but in the soul. And now, she could not escape. Either from him . . .

Or from herself.

CHAPTER 14

He wondered just what the hell he had been thinking, insisting she come down.

She'd told him she wasn't dressed.

And that she was barefoot.

But he knew many a man who fought without shoes, and her bare feet seemed no reason not to push the issue. Nor were they.

But the nightdress. Natural linen. Sheer. Caught in the light of the fire. Not while she was seated at his side, but when she stood, when she took the lute, when she defied them all, and they applauded her anyway. When she blushed and laughed and looked so young and delighted, especially dancing with Jamie . . .

He'd wanted to walk up to his own cousin and pummel him. There were things that he shared with his kin, and things he did not. Logic didn't help. They were dancing, doing nothing more than dancing. The lady was learning highland steps, laughing, enjoying the ways of his people. He trusted Jamie with his life. Jamie was doing nothing wrong.

He didn't trust a word that fell from her lips.

She was his captive. Captives weren't to be trusted. She was his wife. Made so while bound and silenced in the confines of a sheet. He hadn't wanted a wife.

But he had always wanted this woman.

And come to terms with it.

He had married her. And what better function did a wife provide than appeasing the hungers that raged in mortal man? She thought herself so safe here. No cruelty in her prison. Just protection against other men, when he was so lost in the torment of his mind that he would reject what any other reasonable man would cajole, demand, seize . . .

He tried to tell himself that the anger that drove him was completely irrational. He had been curt, tense, and determined in their moment together, he had barked out commands, and pushed her as far from him as he could. He had blamed her for what was not her fault.

He was still furious. More tense than ever.

He opened the door to her room with a slam of his foot against it that surely echoed down the hall.

In his arms, she trembled. But when he gazed down, he saw that her eyes were on his, violet, dark, so dark, as dark as the mass of her hair. And they challenged, and hated, and yet . . .

There was something else within them.

"We are here. My cage," she said, her voice tight and breathless. "You can set me down and lock me in and leave."

He set her down on the carpet before the fire. For a moment, her back was to him, her head was lowered. He gripped the mantel, staring at the gleaming dark tresses against the unbleached color of the gown, and felt a burning again, anger so deep that it amazed him he could still be so incensed.

"What did you think you were doing?" His voice sounded deep and harsh to himself, like a roar across a battlefield.

She spun around to face him, eyes wide, pure violet in the firelight. "What was I doing? Obeying every last command of the great, triumphant, warlord! You dragged me down to your celebration, and thus I came. You said I must drink, and so I drank. You ordered me to sing and so I sang."

"About ragged, savage barbarians."

"If you took such words to heart, it was not my intent, and therefore how you see yourself in your own mind— Sir."

She was ever quick, her words some of the sharpest blades he had come to know.

"You posed before the fire in that gown. What were you hoping? That men would come to blows over the perfection of your person?"

"Never!" she denied heatedly, fingers clenched tightly into fists at her sides. "You insisted that I rise!"

"But you knew, my lady, you knew exactly what you were doing. Every man there could see every curve of your body, every intimate detail." He paced from the mantel then, tearing at the brooch that held his tartan at his shoulder, and cast both aside as he strode back. He took the chair at her writing desk, pulling his boots from his feet. "And, madam, the way that you danced!"

"They are your dances."

"Your smiles, your laughter, your tête-à-têtes!"

"I was never ordered to be rude," she challenged, but she had turned again to watch him as he sat, now barefoot, boots and hose cast aside. He nearly ripped his shirt over his head, and threw it with a vengeance on top of his boots.

"Like any little strumpet, you were down there teasing and provoking."

"I was down there, forced to celebrate your prowess at bloodshed," she countered with swift wrath, but then her voice faltered as she at last demanded, "What are you doing? Why aren't you leaving?"

He remained seated, feeling the blaze from the fire radiate over his face, his bare chest and shoulders. "That should be obvious," he said flatly. "I am not leaving tonight."

She remained where she stood, as if frozen, not betraying the least sign of emotion.

He had expected screams of rage, denial, fury. He had been ready to deal with them.

But she just stood, delicate, perfectly cast face pale in the night, eyes unfaltering, the rich ribbons of hair gleaming like ravens' wings over and around her shoulders.

"What?" he inquired. "Is that it? You intend just to stand there."

She took a moment to answer, then lifted her hands in a fatal gesture. "Is there some weapon your men might have missed in this room? A sharply honed knife I could stab into your heart? I am supposed to throw myself from the window?"

"No," he said simply.

And still, he watched her. And still, the fire burned. And it was as he had said. The blaze created light and shadow of her gown. The delicate lace enhanced the hollow of her throat, decorated the fragile structure of her collarbones. Her breasts were full and firm, and if the fire didn't give all away, he already knew the rouge color of her nipples. Deep shadow fell against her tiny waist, and light again found the flare of her hips. Even the ebony secrets at the apex of her thighs were visible in his mind's eye, if not in truth.

"Well?" he murmured quietly to her, still studying the woman before the fire.

And by watching, he saw more and more. She was not so very still. She was trembling like a leaf borne on the wind. The fire, the night, or perhaps his gaze upon her was creating other telltale signs. The peaks of her breast were perfectly, clearly visible, hardened to little pebble-like nubs of temptation. Her nails had curled into her palms, and were all but piercing her own flesh.

"What?" she lashed out. "Am I to come to you? Don't you think, my lord, that would be asking. . . *demanding* . . . far too much?"

The anger fled from him.

"Aye," he said softly. "Aye, it would be."

He rose, and walked to the place where she stood. Her head was bowed slightly, her eyes were fallen, and the ebony spikes of her lashes shadowed her cheeks. He didn't force her to lift her hair, but swept the thick richness from her shoulder and pressed his lips against the silk of her flesh, first there, and then against the length of her throat. His mouth came against the rampant pulse that beat there, and it was then that he caught her chin, and raised her face to his kiss. There was the briefest moment when he touched upon her lips when they were pursed, cold and tight. Then they gave, parted to him. He tasted the sweetness within the recesses of her mouth, delved and pressed and demanded, and as he did so, a pulse, a pounding began within his head and his groin, and he pursued his purpose with a deep, urgent passion. His fingers threaded into the thickness of her hair, cradled her skull. She didn't deny the pressure of his lips, yet neither did she participate as she allowed the liquid sweep and plumbing of his tongue. Yet he felt the drum of the hearbeat within her. Her hands came to rest upon his shoulders, tentatively, then a bit desperately, as if she struggled to stand. He realized in a haze of raw desire that she was aroused, that she wanted, wanted *him*. But he knew her, and knew that a will of steel was keeping her aloof.

He brought his palm against her cheek. Stroked it with his knuckles, and allowed his hand to caress downward until his fingers moved over the ties in the field of lace upon the gown. The thin fabric slid from her shoulders in a slow cascade, and all the perfection to be found was his. If she had lost her last vestige of defense, she didn't seem to know it. She trembled, the touch of her fingers upon his shoulders more desperate, the tips of her nails curving into his flesh.

He lifted his lips from hers. Her eyes remained closed, her mouth parted and damp. His hand curved first around her breast, dark against the paleness of the flesh. He lowered his head, tongue laving around the crest, then mouth affixing upon the fullness of it. A sound escaped her at that, and he fought the raging buildup in the erection straining against his breeches. He tasted the sweetness of each breast, then lowered himself, blond hair brushing against the dampness of tongue-swept flesh as he delved lower and lower.

"Don't . . . don't . . . I will fall," she said in a strangled whisper.

"No, you will not," he told her.

In the end, she did. But not until he had stripped away the last of her pretense. His hand spanned the slender circle of her waist, slipped down to her hips, and his head lowered still. He steadied her, listening to the wracked breathing that escaped her lips, felt the quiver become a deeper tremble. He cupped the round of her buttocks, drawing her tightly against him, drew his fingers in a slow, destined caress from her calf to her upper thighs, and then between. Her scent was intoxicating, her taste an aphrodisiac that raged within the senses, and made a man mad. And still, he fought the hunger that had become a burning anguish, and stroked with touch and tongue through to the most intimate petals of her body, nestled in a sea of tight ebony curls as soft and luxurious and damp as liquid silk.

Her knees did buckle and give and she fell against him, a cry tearing from her lips. When he lifted her in his arms and carried her to the bed, she kept her eyes closed. He paused above her for a moment, despite the now desperate state of need that was like thunder with him, wracking him from head to toe. But then he untied the breeches in silence, allowing her the denial in the lashes swept so thickly over her cheeks. When he slid his weight between her thighs, her arms curled around his neck. A gasp escaped her, and at last, her eyes flew open as he thrust fully into her. She closed them again, tightly, yet her hands remained clutched to his back, her arms around his shoulders, and when he moved, she moved with him, and in moments she was arching and straining to meet him. Her hips hiked suddenly and tightly about his; she writhed, arched, and went still. He heard the breath go out of her lungs, then something like a sob that she was not quite able to catch at the back of her throat. And again, as she drifted downward, he felt a trembling beneath the damp ivory of her flesh. He was free to unleash the tempest. Tension filled his body, every muscle within him taut and constricted. Thunder pounded fiercely, through his head, his groin, and every limb, until it seemed that a lightning strike ripped through the storm, and his climax seemed to rip through him with the power of the wind.

He eased his weight from her, and lay beside her. She curled away from him, and he was left with her back, and her tangled hair, like a cloak of darkness, swamping over his chest.

"Igrainia."

He didn't know himself why his voice sounded so harsh.

"If you've any mercy in you whatsoever, you will not make me talk now!" she whispered.

"Then don't turn away from me."

She stiffened, then turned back. He drew her into his arms, against his chest.

And she did not fight him.

She had a dream in the night. It was warm, seductive, entirely sensual, and sexual to a point where it seemed she would crawl from her own skin. Sheer wonder, ecstasy, and pleasure. She felt kisses against her flesh, her shoulders, spine, buttocks, hips, and her lips . . . and she was kissing back, wildly, unable to get enough of the lips that formed over her own, taste enough, delve . . . fill that mouth, as it filled her own.

And all the while, she knew that the dream was real, and though the fire had burned low, and the darkness was deep, she knew as well the man, the gold of his hair by day, and the breadth of the chest so thickly matted with crisp blond curls. She knew the whisper against her lips, her cheeks, her flesh, yet the words were a blur. And she knew that she responded to every touch with a rampant fever of her own. She had wanted . . . ached . . . needed . . . wanted . . .

And she had gotten.

And still . . .

She was grateful for the darkness.

And the sleep that came to close the door against the gnawing guilt that lay in her heart.

* * *

He lay awake when she opened her eyes, startled by the sunlight. He was on his back, his head rested against his bent arm as he stared across the room.

"What is that?" he demanded, aware that she had wakened, and staring at the crest she had so painstakingly designed. He leaped out of the bed in a sudden surge of energy, going to stand by the wall.

He reached out, as if he would take her handiwork, and throw it in the fire.

"It's mine!" she cried out quickly, and when he turned to her she quickly added, "Mine! The house of Abelard. My family name," she continued softly. And she forced a word from her lips. "Please . . . it is just . . . mine."

"All right," he said after a moment. "Yours stays . . . as does mine."

She bit lightly into her lower lip. This wasn't the conversation she had expected to have this morning.

He strode across the room for his breeches, drew them on, tied them. Igrainia lay back down, drawing the covers around her, turning as if she would sleep again. She felt his weight as he sat on the bed. He caught her shoulder, drawing her back to him.

"I told you there was a matter we have to discuss."

She felt her cheeks burn. "There is nothing to discuss."

He arched a brow, then a small smile curled his lips. "I wasn't referring to the events of last night."

"Oh." If possible, her cheeks burned more brightly.

"Though perhaps it does merit mention first."

Merit *mention*?

"I have not, since we have come here, meant to hurt you. I know what you have suffered, and in truth, there was nothing I, or anyone, could have done that was worse than what the plague wrought upon us all."

She lowered her eyes. "You didn't hurt me."

"I know." Again, that supreme confidence.

Her lashes flew open again, but there was a brooding quality in his eyes that silenced her. Then that was suddenly replaced by a look of amusement.

"You might have mentioned at some earlier point that you were not quite so hostile to me, in particular, as you so often pretended."

"But I am hostile," she assured him.

She tried to keep her eyes on his, aware that he had read everything about her last night, as easily as someone might read the pages of a book.

"All right, then, my lady. My own pride is great; I'll leave you with yours. But nothing will be turned back. Your crest may stay, as will mine. Your "cage" has become shared space."

She didn't respond.

"You understand?"

"Yes."

"You don't seem overly disturbed. But then, neither did you last night."

"Would it have made a difference?"

"We'll never know, will we?"

"There was nothing I could have done. There are no weapons—"

"Um, well, you could have taken a needle to my chest."

"I'll remember that for future reference."

"Remember what you like, admit what you like. Live with whatever dreams make you happy. Close your eyes, and in the dark, imagine that Lord Afton has returned. But don't try to change anything."

He stood up, grabbing his shirt, hose, and boots. The shirt went over his head. He seated himself, pulling on hose and boots, before she spoke in reply.

"Is that what you do?" she asked softly. "In the darkness ... imagine that you are somewhere else, with someone else?"

His right boot was on; he pulled on the left, rose, and walked back to the bed. "I'm afraid that I am forever and completely grounded in reality. I never imagine anything, Igrainia. Even in the dark, I am always aware of what is there. But I do not begrudge anyone else the escape of fancies and dreams. Now, as to the subject we need to discuss ..."

"What?" she asked thickly.

"I have news regarding your brother."

CHAPTER 15

She was so startled that she nearly bolted out of the bed, but she refrained, clutching the covers to her chest.

"What about Aidan?"

"You're aware that he's in Scotland? He is at Cheffington, with the lord of the manor, Ewan Danby. A decent man— a rarity among the minions Edward has sent to Scotland. But he has believed every word he has heard about your mistreatment and abuse at the hands of the Highland rabble who have so viciously seized Langley. Among the knights gathering there are Sir Niles Mason and your own Robert Neville. From what we've learned, they are planning on marching here, within a few weeks time—before answering Edward's call to arms—with a party of nearly three hundred."

She looked down quickly. "That is a large body of men. When you cannot have more than a hundred or so here, if that many." She looked up at him and met his eyes again.

"Since I'm assuming you left a number of the men you had armed and trained in the service of Robert Bruce."

She was right, and she knew it, and startled when it didn't seem that he was the least afraid of the number of men who would come against him.

"Large numbers—but not enough to take Langley."

"They'll come with siege machines."

"Aye, they will."

"Perhaps you should abandon the castle."

"Perhaps I will have to—one day. But not now."

She shook her head. "I don't know what response you want from me. Naturally, the English are going to try to wrest Langley from your hold. And with such a party of armed men, with the money and supplies they will have . . . it's likely you'll be defeated."

"No, I won't."

"Then . . . I still don't understand what you want from me."

"I want you to write to Aidan again."

"Do you think he can stop Niles and Robert from coming?"

"No, I don't."

"Then . . ."

"I'm warning you."

"Warning . . . me?"

"To tell Aidan not to ride with them. He might well be killed."

She stared at him, her eyes widening with incredulity. "You might be killed. The walls could be breeched, and if a flood of men break through . . . the castle could fall."

"It will not," he said.

She shook her head. "I can write to Aidan. I can tell him that it is a foolhardy mission. But . . . it's not likely he'll pay heed to my words. He is in the company of seasoned warriors. He is certain to think that his own honor will be forever in question if he doesn't ride to rescue his own sister.''

"Write to him. I'm sure you'll think of something to put on paper that will warn him, at the very least, that he is taking a grave risk. You might think of finding a way of setting the truth down on paper—that your wedding was performed by a priest, and that your marriage is real in every way.''

"But you said yourself before—it is the king who is . determined that he will do what he wants as regards my future.''

"King Edward is not rising from his bed to ride against Langley—he is too concerned with cornering Robert Bruce. It is your brother you must convince that you have no desire of rescue.''

"You are afraid of that many knights and men-at-arms coming at Langley!'' she accused him.

"Actually, I rather relish the thought of meeting Sir Niles Mason face to face,'' he told her, and in the harshness of his tone, she felt chilled, knowing he spoke the truth. "Believe me when I tell you this, the warning is a courtesy I am extending to you. I owe you that much. Do with it what you will. Good day, my lady.''

With that, he left.

Igrainia stretched out on the bed again, far more weary than she had been the night before, and very afraid for Aidan. He would ride in the front. She knew that the castle could withstand strong efforts, and she knew as well that any fortress could fall.

But Eric was far too confident, so she was certain as well that he would be prepared for the attack, and since he had given her the warning, she knew that Aidan would be in danger. She would write; she would write anything she could think of, any lie and any truth, that might prevent him from coming.

But her prospects of success seemed bleak.

And if he came . . .

And they were successful in their attack?

So many men she had come to know, to care about, would die. And if Robert and Niles seized the castle, they would die horribly; the prescribed death for traitors would be dealt to every last man.

Tears sprang to her eyes and she found herself hating both kings—Edward Plantagenet and Robert Bruce. Men vacillated in this war, and their greed was usually the strongest part of their loyalty. There were many as Aidan had been, sympathetic toward one, yet recognizing the power of the other. Both had turned far too many decent men into butchers.

And they had destroyed her life.

She lay then with her tears drying, her eyes open, as a wave of guilt assailed her. She could write that her marriage was real in every way. She could tell her brother that she was resigned. She could tell him that . . .

She mourned Afton, she would never love another man again. But whereas Robert Neville had the ability to make her uneasy, she was, at the least, shamefully attracted to the enemy who had seized the castle and made her his wife.

She prayed for sleep, to forget the night. To forget the world. To forget that she had set out to enrage and arouse the enemy, and succeeded far too well.

For a long time, the haven of sleep eluded her, and she stared into the dying embers of the fire, and thought again that the Scots were mad, like wolves howling in the wind, and that they would never break the might of the English. They might win skirmishes . . . seize castles . . . but in the end, they would have to give way.

She had betrayed Afton. Here, in the room where they had laughed and read and dreamed like children.

Where he had died.

And now Aidan could die.

And if he prevailed, then others would be hanged until half dead, dragged down, disemboweled, castrated . . . and at last, mercifully, beheaded.

Even the embers began to die in the hearth. Cold, she clutched the covers more tightly around her. She mentally planned her letter to Aidan. And she began to wonder if it wouldn't be better if she were to escape, and ride to Cheffington, and throw herself upon Lord Danby's mercy. If she could prevent so many more deaths . . .

But no one wanted her alone, she thought bitterly.

It was Langley they were coming to seize.

She closed her eyes. For a while, the tempest of her thoughts continued to plague her. Then, at long last, she slept.

Eric spent most of the day with Jamie and Allan, scouring the countryside that surrounded Langley. They followed the route that led to Cheffington for a distance, encircled the castle, and rode into the nearby woods, determining the natural geography of every line of defense.

Late afternoon, he returned to the great hall to find Angus worriedly awaiting him. "Igrainia has not arisen," he said. "One of us has remained at her door during the morning. Breakfast was brought to her, but she has not opened the door . . . she has not asked for the bath and water to be brought."

That seemed the most dire omen of all to Angus, who didn't mind a good washing now and then, but still believed that the lady of Langley was washing away her skin and her life with every long soap and scrubbing. "I have been tempted to burst into the room, but she could not have drowned in the bath, since she has not called for one, and ... I even looked in the moat, so I know that she did not ... did not decide to cast herself into water."

Eric was tempted to laugh, yet Angus was so sincere in his concern, that he placed a hand on his shoulder. "I'll see to her immediately."

As he walked up the stairs, he wondered if he had pushed her over the edge of reason last night. But he didn't really believe that. Time could work mysteriously, or life and instinct itself, but he felt certain that he had not caused her any great hardship. It was almost as if she had been waiting.

She had been a captive at Langley, she had been forced into marriage, but last night she had not been forced, and living with her own desires was surely going to be harder for her than anything he had wrought against her.

And so he found himself taking the stairs two at a time, passing Jarrett quickly in the hall, and opening the door to the master's chambers with a force that nearly took it off the hinges.

He looked around the room and saw a crumpled mass beneath the pile of linen sheets and furs on the bed. His throat constricted, his every muscle tightened, and he quickly strode over the distance to the bed, sitting, pulling the sheets back, and seeking through the tangled blanket of black hair.

She suddenly let out a little cry, trying to disentangle herself from the sheets, her hair, and his touch. Drawing wild, stray tendrils from her eyes, she stared at him in alarm.

"What is it?"

The relief that filled him brought laughter to his lips. He leaned back against the bedpost himself, drained. "Nothing. I'm sorry that I've awakened you."

He rose and left the room. There seemed to be little sense

in letting her know that they had been afraid he might have made her so desperate that she had taken her own life.

He was tempted to stay, because finding her in such a pleasant state of disarray definitely stirred thoughts of shirking duty, but he could not afford to lose the daylight hours.

Night would come.

He rose and left the room, closing the door quietly in his wake.

When she woke, Igrainia found that she was starving, and she was surprised to find that Angus was seated on the floor directly outside her door. He jumped up the moment he saw her, ready and eager to acquire anything she might like, and more than willing to follow her anywhere.

She wasn't eager to go anywhere, just yet, she was just hungry and would like the bath to be brought up as quickly as possible. She noted that in his curious, touching haste to please her he didn't pass the order on to anyone else, but hurried down the stairs himself, moving with an amazing agility for a man his size.

When she had eaten and bathed, she sat down at the writing desk and composed her letter to Aidan, telling him that she was treated with kindness and respect, and that he must not worry that she was in any danger. Knowing that those words wouldn't restrain a young man eager to prove his valor to himself and others, she began to write about the situation as a whole, and spoke about the losses in Scotland and that the best use of his talents would be to obey King Edward's summons, and prove himself with the force that the king was sure to wield.

With the letter written—she didn't bother to seal it, knowing full well that her words would be read and censored—she sat back, and knew then that it was time to visit the tombs. It was Jarrett who waited outside her door then, and as had become the custom of her watchdogs in the days when Eric and his fighting force had been gone, he merely bid her a good morning and followed in her wake.

The great hall was empty except for a few servants sweeping, and a few great hounds resting near the fireplace.

Jarrett followed her down to the tombs, waiting a discreet distance as she knelt in front of the wall where Afton lay in eternal rest. On her knees, she tried to form words of apology. That she had honestly loved him with all her heart was easy to swear, but to pretend that life had not gone on was not. She had loved her husband, with his wonderful ability to see and know life and human nature, but though she still felt torn and in a tempest, there was a strange peace to be had here, even though she had thought that she could not cure herself of the guilt piercing her soul. And as she prayed, head bowed, she wondered if he saw as well that they had spent their time together almost as children, in a life that ran smoothly, with wealth and material beauty, and in a strange union that few people in their position were ever allowed. Theirs had been an arranged marriage of almost uncanny happiness. Perhaps something so sweet had never been meant to last.

Before rising, she again begged his pardon, prayed that he was at peace, and swore that he would remain in her heart always.

Returning to the hall, she discovered that it was late, darkness had fallen, and though the hall was not filled, Eric's immediate advisors were gathering there. Jamie was quick to greet her, as were the others, and their manner was much as if she were one of their own, their courtesy that which they would have extended to the true and honored wife of their leader. Only Eric was missing. She hadn't decided yet if she would come down for the meal that evening, but after she hurried up the stairs with Jarrett watching from below, she found, when she reached the door to her room, that there was noise within. Eric was there.

She quietly left the door, feeling a new frustration. She would be a liar to admit less to herself than the full truth; with whatever fancies had stirred her mind, she had wanted him to return, and had wanted him. And she was more than resigned to the nights that would come, though she refused to allow herself to believe that she was eager for them.

But she didn't want him living in her room. That invasion of privacy was the most distressing.

Still, he was there, and so she returned to the hall, and accepted a cup of ale from Jamie, and took her place at the table. It was startling to realize how many men she had come to admire, and to like, among the Scots. Angus, of course, and Peter, Allan, Jarrett . . . and Jamie, who was genuinely the most interested in her, and always able to draw her into conversation. Seated next to him, with Eric's empty chair at her side, she found that she was smiling at some comment he had made to Allan regarding the finer meat he had provided for the table. His eyes were a fine gray, and his features, very like Eric's, were well formed and handsome. He made a point of including her in the conversation, and asked if she didn't think that they did, at least, manage to bring a fine supply of food to the table.

She agreed, then asked him, "But aren't you weary of being here? Haven't you a home, a wife, children?"

She was surprised to realize that she had touched upon a sore spot within him. For a moment he did not reply, studying his chalice. Then he told her, "A home, yes, just beyond Stirling, and far too close to English power to enjoy. A wife, once. She is gone."

"I'm sorry."

"Langley is fine enough," he told her. "It's true, that

we are all little but outlaws now. There were the very dark days after the defeat at Falkirk . . . and many of us took to the highlands. There, you know, there is little law but what the chieftains say, and they cast the weight of their clans with the man they most admire. Most often, though, they are fiercely independent, and therefore, ready for the call of freedom. Our own clan is such, one that has spread far and wide. Since Robert Bruce has been crowned king . . . for many of us, the fight is reawakened, and we will readily die to follow him, and become one nation where the English are not free to ravage our homes, steal our property, and slay our people. I am a vagabond, madam. There is property which is rightfully mine, but it is laid waste. One day, it will be home.''

She hadn't realized how closely she had lowered her head to hear him, or how softly he had spoken, until he raised his head, and looked past her. ''Eric, we've a great debate going on here tonight, so you will have to decide on which plate of meat you find to be more tender. I contend that I am able to bring down the young and tender bucks, while Allan chases after those old creatures who can barely hobble through the forest!''

''And I am to judge in this contest?'' Eric said. ''Cousin, I haven't the courage!''

Laughter rang around the table. The meal went on. Igrainia didn't look Eric's way, but sat, giving her attention to her plate and the food for which she had little appetite. She was alarmed to find that she was so keenly aware of his physical presence at her side.

And disheartened to realize that now she was remembering his touch.

And anxious for it once again.

Eventually, he spoke to her. ''Your letter is an excellent example of diplomacy, Igrainia. You could be writing missives for kings, and perhaps avoiding much of the bloodshed spilled in our times.''

"I see. You have read it already.''

"You knew that I would.''

"I still don't believe that it will stop anything.''

"Perhaps not.''

He was watching her, she knew. She still refused to look his way, giving her attention to the hounds by the fire.

"It's strange that you've suddenly grown so quiet,'' he said.

"Perhaps I've nothing to say.''

"I don't believe that, madam, you've always a great deal to say. When I entered, you were deep in conversation, fascinated with whatever information you and Jamie shared.''

"He is an intelligent man.''

"I agree.''

Garth came behind Igrainia, clearing plates. Then Rowenna was behind them, pouring more ale. Igrainia murmured a thank you, and felt a strange chill, aware of the gentleness in Eric's tone when he thanked the woman as well.

Someone, at the end of the table, was strumming a lute. A soft, quiet song. Igrainia suddenly longed to escape.

When she would have risen, she felt his hand on hers.

"You're departing so quickly?'' he inquired.

"Yes. If I may.''

"What if I were to say that you may not?''

"Then, I would be forced to sit here.''

"I would give a great deal to know your thoughts.''

She turned to him at last, wondering why she was feeling such a sudden urgency to depart. "You can force many things, Eric. But I told you before, my thoughts and my emotions are my own, and something that you can't touch. And though . . .'' she began, and faltered. "And though I am resigned to many things, including you, it does not mean that I have to like them. And I am well aware of what your feelings are towards me.''

''Interesting, that you detest me so,'' he said, and his tone indicated that it didn't matter in the least.

''Why? I find it rather amazing that you have discovered that you can touch me without appearing to have the need to push me as far away as possible.''

He shrugged. ''You're mistaken. I do not dislike you.''

She didn't know why the comment seemed worse than an avowal of hatred. Perhaps because that would have meant some kind of a real emotion.

''Then would you be so merciful as to please allow me to leave this hall?''

He released her hand. ''Go.''

She rose, and departed. She bid Jamie a goodnight, and smiled to the others as she left, shoulders squared, head high.

She didn't think that any of her guards followed her up the stairs. She knew, however, that Eric watched her as she went.

It was late when he came to the room. The fire had burned down to embers. She heard him disrobe, and join her in the bed. The covers shifted. For a moment, he was still, and she knew that he had paused, perhaps surprised that she had gone to bed as bare as he.

Then she felt the brush of his fingers. A touch so light, and yet like lightning. His caress, almost like a whisper, moved with an excruciating slowness, up and down her spine. She felt the hot moist pressure of his lips against her nape, and following the path his fingers had taken. His arm moved around her waist, and his hand cupped her breast, and his thumb moved with the same, almost tortuous lightness of caress around her nipple and aureole before sliding down her midriff, abdomen, and between her thighs. And there they stroked with an enticing practice of rhythm, knowledge, and purpose that brought a spasm racing through her, and when he turned her to him, she was glad of the darkness that would at the least cloak the mindless thirst that had seized her for more of his touch. She met the deep passion of his kiss with a rage of need, and allowed her hands to fall upon him. Her fingers delved through the thick mat of hair on his chest, curled to his shoulders, dared to stroke along the length of his back, and feel the hard muscle structure of his buttocks. She moved her hand low against his abdomen, and, still consumed by the overwhelming force and seduction of his lips against her own, did what came naturally, curling her fingers around the shaft of his sex. The pulse and power of his erection only stirred the coil of desire within her, and by the time he had entered her, she was desperate, aware of nothing but the need to be filled, and the essence of the man who would see that she was sated. She was near frenzy when climax seized her, and then it seemed that there was fire in a hearth where the embers had burned low, that stars filled the darkness where there was nothing but ceiling, and . . .

She had never felt like this before . . . never.

Sleep, Eric decided, was the greatest healing balm God had ever granted to man. Sleep provided dreams, swept away the inhibitions of day, defied thought and emotions. He awoke in the morning to find that she was against him, head curled into his shoulder, delicate fingers splayed across his chest, a long, slender limb cast over his hip.

The temptation to stay was almost overwhelming. But

time was closing in on the forces at Langley. Every daylight hour mattered.

He disentangled himself gently from the woman at his side, and rose.

The days continued much as they had been, though with an urgency in the air. Every afternoon, Igrainia heard the clang of metal in the courtyard as hours and hours went into training. She could look out the window at almost any time and see that the parapets were being filled with arms, small war machines, and more.

Igrainia's day fell into a pattern.

She never woke before Eric, and was glad of it. She didn't want to talk by morning's light. She was sometimes vaguely aware when he left. And how she slept, against him. In the night there were times when she knew that she was cherishing different moments of the darkness. There was something in the heat of his body, the expanse of his chest, that offered a bizarre contentment and security as well. That she could be passionately, wildly aroused by him was one thing. That she could take such pleasure and comfort in simply sleeping beside him was another.

She bathed early, and spent at least an hour every day on her knees before the tombs. Sometimes, she would ride, though these days, it was never Eric who came as her escort. He was consumed during every hour of daylight with the training of the men, and the defense of the castle.

She took her place at the table every night. And partly because she knew it irritated Eric, she was animated when she spoke with Jamie, laughed at times, listened intently to others. She came to realize after a while that it was her form of a subtle revenge.

One night, she and Jamie tried to teach Angus to play the

lute. He was terrible, his large hands fumbling as they moved over the strings. She knew that Eric, deep in conversation with Peter then, watched them. She made a point of enthusiastically discussing music with Jamie, and joining him when he asked her if she knew different songs.

The next morning dawned badly. Which was strange. She had slept exceptionally well. Though she pushed her friendliness to Eric's men as far as she dared in the hall, she always came upstairs long before Eric. And she always waited for him. Even if she drifted off to sleep, she waited. And wakened at his lightest touch.

When she woke that day, however, it was to a tapping at her door. It was Jennie who had come, to collect laundry, to straighten the room. She bid Igrainia a cool good morning as she entered, and started moving about the room.

"Jennie, are you all right?" Igrainia asked her.

Jennie dropped the pile of clothing she held and stared at Igrainia, her eyes full of fury. "Am I all right? What does that matter, my lady, to you? You've embraced the enemy. You've welcomed the men who killed Afton. You have become like an eager bawd night after night for the man who usurped everything and you flout the memory of a good and decent man with wanton shame, in his own bed, where you slept with him, where he died!"

Igrainia was taken aback. She was tempted to slap Jennie, and she might have been in the right, but she held her temper. "What is your suggestion, Jennie?" she asked coldly. "They are here, they do rule the castle. Against my will, I was married to him. And if you've not noticed, he is far more powerful than I."

Tears suddenly stung Jennie's eyes. "You could hate him!" she whispered. "At the very least, you could hate him."

"I—I do," she said, but her words faltered. She was lying.

Jennie turned away from her in disgust. She suddenly felt ill.

Then her maid spun on her. "You are so convinced that they have all the power! Well, my lady, they do not. For the fields and farms to function, men and women come and go from these gates every day. And there is secret word to be had—for those who are willing to hear it. If you ever remember who you are, what you are—if you ever need or care for your own kind again . . . tell me!"

With that, Jennie fled.

Igrainia spent hours pacing the room, wondering just what Jennie meant, determined to corner her and find out just what she knew, and with whom she had been in contact. She wondered if Jennie had somehow managed to get letters out now without them being seized, and if so, if she had corresponded with Aidan.

Jennie's accusations rang true, and the guilt she had willed to the back of her heart for a long time seemed to come painfully to the fore.

Somehow, she had to find the time to talk with Jennie. They had become strangers, but it was imperative that they talk soon.

Feeling a deep sense of tempest and guilt, she bathed, ate, and headed for the tombs. She didn't so much pray to God as she tried to put everything that had happened in order for Afton, as if she could speak to him with her thoughts.

But he couldn't give her any answers.

Still, that day, she spent more than an hour on her knees, but neither time nor sore knees seemed to do anything to still the inner tumult that had swept over her with Jennie's words. At last, she returned to her room.

As always these days, she could hear the clang of steel from below as men trained and practiced in the art of war with a great urgency daily. Compelled by the sounds from the courtyard, she walked to the window and looked out, expecting to see the men, divided into pairs, learning sword techniques.

What she saw filled her with horror.

The men had been practicing with swords, a large group of them. They were still there, still bearing their weapons, and their defenses, but practice seemed to have taken a twist.

Only two men were actually brandishing their weapons.

They were not among the newly gathered men, raw recruits who had worked in the fields or practiced a trade and been won over to the cause of Robert Bruce.

The two combatants who fought in a cleared circle, surrounded by the others, were seasoned warriors.

She recognized them for the colors they wore. The distinct shapes of their conical helmets. The design of their visors.

For the family crest that was the same on both tunics.

Eric and Jamie.

They were both well clad in mail and plate. Both worked with swords, and carried shields, likewise designed with crest and colors.

And they both maneuvered their lethal weapons with skill and vengeance, their fight fast and furious, as vicious and determined a battle as she had ever seen.

For a moment, her heart caught in her throat, and beat like thunder in her mind. They would kill one another.

And her heart sank again, and she was filled with remorse.

She had caused this. It was her fault. She knew that she goaded Eric when she purposely sought out his cousin, when she teased him, laughed with him. And she had thought that he hadn't noticed, or if he had, that he hadn't cared. She was the prize he had married on order of a king, and the prize that he slept with at night. A woman that he didn't dislike, *yet for whom he felt no real emotion.*

Suddenly, Jamie was backing away as Eric came on with blow after blow after blow which it seemed that Jamie was barely defending.

Eric seemed to move like lightning, bringing on such an assault that Jamie was sent down to his knee, his shield jerking with the heavy fall of Eric's sword.

Jamie would die! She thought.

And his blood would be on her hands.

CHAPTER 16

Igrainia turned from the window and raced across the room. She didn't notice who was in the hall, if anyone. She tore along the hall, down the stairs, through the great hall, and the entry, and out to the courtyard. A group of men were circled around the combatants; she had to push her way through them. As she burst through, Jamie raised his shield just in time for Eric's sword to pound against it with a ringing that rent the air. Both men fell back. And as they did, she raced the last few steps to where Eric stood, throwing herself against him as he prepared to raise the massive weapon once again.

"Stop!" she cried. "Please, stop!"

She couldn't see his face for the visor. Beneath mail and plate, she felt the tension of muscle in his body, and for a wild moment, thought that he would hurl her aside and continue his assault.

"Stop, you idiot! He's your kinsman, and you're going to kill him!"

Eric's sword and shield fell into the dirt. He raised the visor on his helmet. She saw his eyes, and would have backed away, except that his gloved fingers curled into the hair at her nape. "You little fool! You might have been killed."

By then, Jamie, too, had dropped his sword and shield, and raised his visor. He strode closer to where the two of them stood, a smile on his lips. "Igrainia, what is this?"

"Evidently, Jamie," Eric said, and the fingers in her hair tightened, "she feared for your life," he said lightly. "Igrainia, I believe, was of the opinion that you and I were trying to do one another in."

She was aware that they had an audience, all of Eric's men around them, all of those who were entering into training as men-at-arms. And aware that she had made a serious mistake.

Eric never released his hold on her, but turned to the gathered men. "And there you have it, good fellows. Knowing your opponent's move, and using your shield to deflect a blow while planning your next strike. It's a pity, of course, that most often on a battlefield, there will be no gentle lady to come flying between you and the promise of death, if you don't learn both offensive and defensive moves. Part of the battle is in practice and strength, and a great deal in the mind, and in intuition. We'll end here for the evening."

A cheer went up suddenly, as if they had been performing some entertainment. Jamie dramatically took a bow. And then the men began to disperse.

Eric's hold hadn't lessened a bit.

"I apologize for the interruption in your quest to teach men to bash one another to pieces," she murmured, wanting nothing more than to be away at that moment. She winced, feeling the tension in him increase. "I saw you from above. It appeared . . ."

"As if we were at one another's throats?" Jamie asked. "Of course, you realize now, we were teaching defensive techniques," he said very softly. He caught her hand, drew it to his lips, kissed it. "I thank you for the rush you made down here to save my life."

Embarrassed, unnerved, she withdrew her hand quickly.

"Amazing, she didn't in the least fear for *my* life," Eric informed Jamie.

"Indeed," Jamie said, mock affront added to his tone, "apparently, she doesn't believe that I'd be the victor in this fight."

"Nor does she realize that kinsmen such as we never take up arms against one another," Eric reasoned, his voice casual. She thought that there was so much more to that statement. *We do not take up arms against one another . . . and never, never, would, over you.*

"Never, we fight but one enemy," Jamie told her gravely.

"Of course," she said, only a trace of sarcasm in her voice. "Again, I beg pardon for the interruption. I'll leave you alone to return to your play-acting and mock battle."

"It's never play-acting, Igrainia. Learning is life or death," Jamie said.

"Then you must excuse me, and resume," Igrainia said. Dear God, did she want Eric to let her go! She wanted to crawl into the ground. At best, be alone. Anywhere. Away from the laughter that Eric was surely feeling, along with his anger, that she should begin to presume that they might have fought over her.

"The light is dying, the session is over," Eric said curtly. "We're done here now." *Because of you.*

She was released at last as he stooped to retrieve his sword and shield. She glanced at Jamie, who seemed touched and amused and sympathetic, then quickly took advantage of her freedom. "Again, I apologize."

She turned to start briskly for the hall.

"Igrainia," Eric said, and she halted, turning back slowly.

"You speak so scathingly of this training. Perhaps, were you to see some of these people under attack on a battlefield, you would not be so contemptuous. The time will come when they will need these techniques against men more than willing to hack them to pieces."

"Once more, I beg your pardon," she managed to say, and she turned and walked swiftly with all the dignity she could muster. Men still lingered about the courtyard, removing bits of their accouterments, stopping at the well for water, or simply dipping their faces in the trough, for though the day was pleasant, they were dusty and sweaty with exertion.

Thayer hailed her; she hadn't seen him in some time, and as he walked to her with an eager smile, she was forced to stop and acknowledge him.

"Thayer! Healed and at practice, I see. Are you well?"

"Very well, my lady. In fact, I wanted to say how grateful I am to you."

She was startled. "Grateful?"

"First, I'm not sure if I ever really thanked you for my life, after that vicious attack we all suffered upon the road. Thank you for all you did to heal wounds that might well have become infected and killed me, as the cutthroats came so close to doing. And second, for speaking on behalf of me and of Timothy and Brandon. Seeing that we were brought to Langley. These great fellows here might as well have cut us down on the road where we lay—after all, we were heading for England. I've never been happier. Learning so much. And being here. And believing that we can fight for Scotland, and honor our rightful king."

"I really did nothing; you proved your own value and mettle here," she murmured, aware that Eric was not far behind her.

"You gave the three of us life—and a chance at a future," he insisted.

"I'm pleased if I've done anything for you," she murmured, wishing to be away.

"And you were quite beautiful, you know, flying into the midst of battle like that."

"She was quite stupid," Eric said, approaching them from behind. "She might have been killed. Had either of us swung with her between us, it would have impossible to stop the weight of the sword. Thayer, get rest this evening, the time is coming closer when you'll need all you've learned. My lady, come, you can help me with the buckles on the plate, and to shed this coat of mail."

He didn't touch her, but proceeded toward the hall.

"God bless you, lady," Thayer said, and bowed, and turned away, expecting that she would be pleased to follow Eric. "We would all die for you, you know."

"That is kind, Thayer. I pray you are never called upon for such a sacrifice," she said, hoping that Eric had not heard the last.

But he must have. He turned back impatiently, "Igrainia!"

With little choice, and enormous dread, she followed him.

She didn't think that he really needed her help; his helmet and visor were cast aside when she reached the room, just seconds behind him. But he took a seat in the chair before the fire and beckoned to her as she came into the room. "Come. You're so taken with swords and mail. Help with the shoulder plates."

"I don't believe you really require my assistance."

"But I would so like you to render it."

She walked across the room, determined that she was going to stay in cool control. The shoulder plates he wore were attached over the mail with heavy leather straps and metal buckles. She undid the first buckle, and was startled by the weight of the plate that fell into her hands. She managed not to drop it, and placed it on the floor by his side. He didn't speak, and neither did she, though she was aware of the brooding look in his eyes as he watched her.

The second plate lay by the first. She started to remove the chest plate. His hand caught hers, and he spoke softly. "You had best thank God, Igrainia, that your words, when you plowed into me, were not heard by the men."

"My words? That you should not kill your kin?"

"No, madam. Those words in which you referred to me as an idiot."

"And if they had been heard? What would you have done?"

"Beat you, of course," he said gravely. "It would be required, for me to keep my dignity among my men. I can never lose their respect."

Her fingers froze where they lay against plate. He had spoken matter-of-factly, and with a full explanation. And still, she wasn't at all certain that she believed him. She had never seen him be anything but gentle with any woman in his contact. Except, of course, with her. It was an admirable quality she could grudgingly accord him. He was aware of his great strength, and because of it, was well able to afford to offer mercy. A virtue she had seen over time.

"I acted as I felt I must at the time," she said. And pretending not to be affected by his words, she continued with the task, trying to keep her fingers from trembling.

"Take care with the level of confidence and power you are feeling," he warned.

"I don't know what you mean."

"I'm sure you do. Since it seems there are those who are more than willing to die for you."

"I hadn't even spoken with Thayer in a very long time."

"Thayer has reason to be grateful to you, and he is young and idealistic. And I'm not referring to Thayer."

"Then . . . what?"

"First, my lady, you should be aware that Jamie and I are cousins, with the honor of a name between us, and a deep friendship formed through years that were often filled with hardship and battle. He would never betray me, in any way, and it would be amusing that you might believe that you could bring us to blows, if it were not such a serious matter. Second, I'm well aware of your determination to charm every one of my men—especially Jamie. I'm not blind, nor am I deaf, and I have noted your antics in the hall. The men, however, are not aware that you are not equally charming in the time we talk alone, and therefore, you've appeared to be no more than gracious. I've let you play your game, since it's caused no harm, and it has seemed to give you a twisted pleasure. But you must be aware—not a man here will ever defy me in any matter regarding you, no matter how many you believe would lie down and die for you, and no matter what you have set out to do."

She drew away from him, feeling a rush of blood to her face, and turned to the fire. "I have not set out to do anything. Thayer and his friends were good, decent men, which you discovered yourself. He meant to protect me, and I was in his debt when I did my best to keep his wounds from infection. And as to your cousin . . . I speak with Jamie because I like him."

"That was evident this afternoon. But you needn't fear for him—he's one of the finest swordsmen I have ever known."

"So, could he have taken you down?" she inquired politely, turning back to meet his eyes.

"Are you hopeful?" he inquired.

"Curious, no more."

He walked away from her, removing the heavy chest plate, and then the mail, without faltering beneath the weight. As he laid out the heavy coat of mail, she started across the room again, afraid that he was far more angry than his manner and words betrayed.

"I'll leave you to your privacy, and go on down to the hall," she murmured.

"No. I'm covered in sweat and mud. Summon Jarrett for me, and ask that the bath be brought."

She hesitated at the door, her back to him. "Certainly. I will ask him on my way down."

"No."

She turned uneasily, watching him.

He stripped off the coat of padding he wore beneath the mail. The linen shirt he wore beneath was nearly plastered to his chest. "No," he said. "You will not go down, not as yet."

He was some distance from her, still by the fire. Maybe a sense of resentment, and maybe the tone of his voice brought about her challenging query.

"Why not? I am certainly not going to rise and try to go running from a room filled with your trustworthy men. And nothing that I do influences anyone, so you need have no fear of my behaving in any way to upset you or bring on battle."

"You won't go down just yet . . . simply because I would like you to remain here."

"You would like me to remain here? Or you order me to remain here? If I walk out of this room now, will someone drag me back at your command?"

"If you want to find out, take your chances."

He strode to the door where she stood, hands on hips, a half-smile that offered no real amusement curled into his lips.

"Well?" he said softly.

"If I walk out the door, someone is going to drag me back," she murmured.

"Possibly, and if so, it will likely be me. So?"

She allowed her gaze to fall from the top of his damp hair to his feet, the grime of battle practice heavy on him.

"So?" he repeated softly.

She raised her chin in an expression of distaste.

"You would ruin my clothing with the least touch," she murmured. Back against the door, she slid a distance from her stance before him, then brushed by and walked back to the fire, taking the chair between it and the bed.

"You didn't call Jarrett and ask that the bath be sent," he reminded her.

"You're by the door."

"So I am, but so were you. And I asked you, politely, I believe, to summon him."

"I can only repeat what I have said several times before. I am a prisoner here. Prisoners are not expected to be charming lackeys who obey a master's commands."

His smile deepened. It was a dangerous one, she thought. And she remembered that she had first been eager to escape the room because she wasn't certain just how angry he had really been when they had arrived here.

He took a step toward her.

She rose. "I'll see that the bath is brought."

She slipped around him, opened the door, and saw Jarrett in the hall. She called to him, telling him that Eric required water and the bath.

She was deeply tempted to run after him.

A hand on her shoulder kept her from doing so.

"Why, thank you, my lady, how kind."

She stared at his hand where it lay then on her upper arm. "Must you?"

"Indeed, I believe I must, since I wouldn't dream of allowing you to give in to temptation, run down the hall, and find yourself in the degrading position of being thrown over my shoulder, and dragged back."

"How very polite of you to worry now about the humiliation such a thing might cause. It's truly a pity you didn't think of it on the night of our mock marriage."

"A legal ceremony, no matter how you arrived for it."

"And never so much as opened my mouth!" she reminded him.

He shrugged. "Come farther into the cage, little bird."

Her eyes narrowed, and she wished that it didn't seem he could read her every thought. His touch propelled her back into the room. She strode to the fire again, feeling the confines of a chamber that was really more than generous in size.

"Fine," she murmured. "I will stay here, and we will cast cruel and miserable words at one another while you bathe."

"I'm actually trying to understand why you feel the need to cast barbs, Igrainia. You're a prisoner. One allowed to keep every stitch of rich and valuable clothing. Your prison is a room that has been your home. You tease, talk, laugh, and sing in the hall. You eat well. You admit to liking some of your evil captors."

"They are still my captors. And I am a prisoner while you train men to fight against those to whom I owe my loyalty. Those I love."

"Good King Edward!" he scoffed.

She hesitated. "I grew up in England. And in England,

he is considered a great and glorious king. Tall and golden, a Plantagenet with the power to rule, to make laws, and govern well.'' Her voice faltered slightly. ''I have seen him at court, and I have seen him be kind and generous, as befitting a king.''

''Ah, yes. The earl's daughter, knowing about royalty in the great and glorious halls. So, you have seen him, and know him. And you know Robert Bruce as well. And surely, Edward finds you as grand and beautiful a pawn as Robert Bruce. Except that he refused to rescue you. There is your kind and generous king. *He* betrayed you. And you know as well that he has often ordered wholesale slaughter.''

''I know that men from both sides have been vicious and brutal when invading one another's land,'' she said.

''We had no fight with England. Edward is fighting a war here of pure aggression. We fight hard in our defense. And we will continue to do so. I train men to fight for the freedom of their land, against the aggression of a tyrant.''

''Your war against me is a battle of aggression! Haven't I the right to fight back against a tyrant?'' she asked him sharply.

''Your war has long been lost, the fight is over, and you are the conquered territory. And I am far from a tyrant.''

''You certainly are a tyrant!'' she protested, ''and like Scotland, I will keep fighting.''

A tap sounded on the door. Igrainia bit her lip, swallowing back her denial. She didn't want to fight in front of the servants.

Especially since it did seem she had lost long ago.

Even the battles within her soul.

Eric opened the door. Garth had come, leading the party of servants with the endless kettles of water. At length, they finished.

The door closed behind the last of the servants. Eric

stripped off his soaked shirt, boots, hose and breeches, and settled into the water, as if she were not present.

She remained in the chair, her fingernails digging into the wooden arms. His head disappeared below the surface of the water as he soaked his hair.

He emerged a moment later, and seemed to bask comfortably in the steam while she felt the tension increase in her limbs moment by moment. She nearly jumped when he moved, taking soap and cloth to scrub, then rinsing the cloth, placing it over his face, and sinking back into the heat.

Finally, she could stand it no more. She rose and walked to the tub. His distrust of her was apparent as he quickly drew the cloth from his face, eyes narrowing as he watched her.

"What? You're eager to scrub my back?" he inquired.

"Don't be ridiculous, I am not Margot," she replied, then felt her limbs grow cold as she saw the frost that entered his eyes.

She couldn't believe what words had escaped her lips in her haste to retort.

"No, you're not," he said, and leaned back again. "You are not Margot at all." His tone certainly implied that she lost in the comparison.

She should leave it be, walk away. She shouldn't have spoken those words.

"But," he said suddenly, "you are what I have now."

She should still walk away! she warned herself.

She had begun what she shouldn't have, but his last words were like salt in a wound, and she found herself unwilling to let it lie.

He had actually given her the opportunity to walk away. She could not take it.

"I am what you have now . . . not the perfect wife, adoring from the moment she became your bride, willing to cast aside her own loyalties and thoughts and feelings for any passion you had in your mind. No, I am not that woman!''

He rose, water running from his body, now gleaming with soap and steam. She jumped back, turned and fled, headed for the door, certain that he wouldn't follow her dripping and naked into the hallway.

But she didn't reach the door before he caught her. Heedless of his dripping state, he held her shoulders and backed her against it. ''Are you so curious? Let me tell you about her then. Margot was no blushing bride when I married her. She was my companion for years before we wed. I defied my father and family when I did so, since it was assumed that I would marry a woman of means. She brought nothing to me in the way of lands, estates, or riches. But she did bring an unwavering loyalty. She ignored the disdain of others to follow where I led. And I don't think I knew myself just what she endured, and what she gave without question or demand, until we had been married. She was educated, intelligent, and beautiful, and cast away what promised prospects she had herself when she chose to follow me.''

Igrainia found that she was shaking, though she wasn't certain exactly why. She knew that he wouldn't hurt her. Except for the pressure of his hands, gripped hard into her flesh. But there was a blue fire in his eyes that seemed to burn her, and the wet pressure of his body, against hers in anger, somehow brought a greater misery than a slap across the face might have done.

''I can't be Margot!'' she whispered.

''And I cannot be your precious, idealistic Afton, living in the clouds.''

''When she spoke, you probably listened!'' Igrainia murmured.

''Since you never care to really speak to me, except to inflict a wicked barb with your words, it would be difficult to listen. You are what I have now. And I am, Igrainia, what you have as well. You are not held in chains of steel, starved, or beaten. Perhaps upon occasion you would consider giving in just a bit.''

She lowered her head. ''I am already an outcast among my people for what I have given in on.''

He caught her chin, lifting it. ''What people, Igrainia? Who? Those who lived at Langley and survived the plague and my people, imprisoned here, were treated just the same. This is Scotland. People have bowed to Edward out of fear. They are more than willing to embrace a king who might lead them to a real freedom. Do you see anyone here walking about in chains? The gates open daily. Men and women are free to leave.''

''Except for me,'' she murmured.

''And where would you go?''

She held silent, exhaling. He shook his head, serious as he studied her eyes. ''You know as well as I that both Niles Mason and Robert Neville are butchers. And unless you manage to escape to a nunnery on the continent, far from Edward's power, you will be a prize for Neville, a trophy, wrapped in the ribbons of your lands and riches.''

She knew that she was trapped in her own argument. He was awaiting a reply. ''At the least, you are not a butcher,'' she murmured. ''I'm not at all sure what you gain. What can my lands in England mean to you?''

''Nothing,'' he said. ''Absolutely nothing.''

''You have Langley,'' she said.

''Aye.''

''So what can my value be to you?''

''Interesting question,'' he murmured, without replying to it. ''But I am grateful for your admission that I, at the least, am not a butcher. I take that as a great concession, coming from you,'' he said, with a small curve of his lips

but a somber tone. "What is your value? The point is that
I do have you, and I am not displeased with what I have
now."

"You are not *dis*pleased. Because you don't *dis*like me."

"You do know your own power, and your assets, Igrainia," he said dryly. "You've the face of an angel and the
form of a goddess."

She was startled by such a compliment from him. Even
if it was spoken impatiently.

She moistened her lips, watching him, still wishing she
could escape.

"Of course, you have the fighting spirit of a fire-breathing
dragon," he continued.

"You think that you are made of steel," she countered.

He shrugged. "Perhaps. And perhaps it is an illusion that
keeps me alive."

His shoulders were nicked with scars. She touched one
without thought, following the jagged line with her finger.
"But you are flesh and blood. You've been wounded."

"But I have always survived. My opponents have not."

She started to draw her hand away from his flesh. He
caught it, drawing the palm against the heat of his chest
once again, fingers locking around her hand, keeping it there.
"What do you want from me, Igrainia? Your freedom? I
cannot give it to you. An assessment? You are, indeed,
stunning. Young, perfect, intelligent, compassionate. I
deeply grieve for Margot, and will, I imagine, for a long
time to come, just as you grieve for someone who was
articulate, noble, and fine, and adored you beyond life itself.
And you cannot imagine what it is to lose a child. But they
are gone, and I cannot change that. And we are alive, and
I am sorry for the bitterness I have felt, and sometimes held
against you. I am glad that you like Jamie, and glad that
you have found a certain affection for many of my men.

Just don't try to use it against me. I swear to you that I don't intend any harm to you; we are caught in a war, and that is the way it is, and there is little I can do to ease that tempest for you. By the laws of Scotland, and our church, you are my wife. I would rather have a wife than a prisoner. A black-haired witch, or violet-eyed enchantress, I'm not at all certain which, but I must admit to being stunned at the pleasure I have discovered in the fact that prisoner, wife, witch, seductress, you have become mine.''

She held very still, breathing deeply, painfully aware of him, and his nakedness.

"I am sorry that I brought up Margot's name," she whispered.

He was silent for a moment and nodded. Then a slow smile curled his lips. "I believe it's time for a few small regrets," he murmured.

"You're sorry because . . . ?"

"I'm about to ruin your dress," he said.

"My dress?" she breathed.

But she understood completely. She closed her eyes when his body pressed her more tightly against the door. She felt the ripple of muscle and sinew, and the conspicuous state of his arousal. Amazingly, instantly, intoxicating. Sensual, sexual, but no more evocative than the sudden touch of his hand against her cheek, and the way that his lips formed over hers, with a touch so light at first . . . then molding with force, and the swiftly rising burn of passion . . .

His lips broke from hers. He murmured against her forehead. "I do believe that I've acknowledged there are absolute perfections about you."

"Scarred, but decently formed," she returned, her fingers playing over his shoulders. She leaned her head against his chest. The dampness still there beckoned. She pressed her lips to his flesh, teased each little drop of water with the tip of her tongue, and relished the spasms that seemed to wrack each detailed flex of hardness and sinew upon him. She drifted downward against his body, finding that the water had not all left him, that he was damp from head to toe . . . everywhere, between. Physically, he fascinated her. A wall of muscle and sinew, perfectly honed, with a raw sensuality that she could not deny. There was a dangerous magnificence to the very power of his height and the breadth of his shoulders and . . .

And the sexuality he exuded. She was compelled.

He spoke, words of desire, passion, encouragement, yet she had no idea of what he said to her. The sound of his voice alone drove her on. The breath seemed to wrack from him, the length of him knotted in tautness. His fingers moved into her hair. He gave a low groan, awaking and arousing her as just being near him could do, as this . . .

She did wield tremendous power, and she relished it.

Savored it. And succumbed to it. In nurturing such wild desire, she discovered herself falling beneath the spell of urgency as well.

He raised her up against him, found her lips once more, his kisses hot, wet, fervent, invasive, reckless, pillaging. She was able to stand only because of the door at her back, bracing her. It didn't matter. He swept her into his arms, and onto the bed. She had been clothed. She felt his lips and fingertips against bare flesh. He touched where she hungered, created sensations that swept away the world. And yet in the mindless fury of fire that engulfed her, she was aware of one thing.

She had adored Afton . . .

But he had never, ever made her feel like this. As if the earth itself was engulfed. As if she would almost die, as if the sky, day and night, were filled with flames. He had never made her so very weak, or so very strong.

Later, she reflected somewhat ruefully that her clothing was indeed ruined.

Shredded, nearly.

She could not be sorry for the loss.

CHAPTER 17

Every day, the scouts rode out.

They waited. Knowing that forces were coming. Not certain when, or how.

Despite the tension, it was a strange time for Igrainia. She found that the guards did not follow her everywhere.

There was always someone in the great hall, always someone in the hallway up the stairs. If she needed something, there was always someone about.

She took greater care in the great hall, enjoying Jamie's conversation, his gentle, sympathetic way with her, and his music. But she spoke to others as well . . . and learned that she could talk with Eric without their words falling into an instant argument.

Two weeks had passed since Eric and the men had returned.

The enemy forces did not come, though the fortress remained on extreme guard, and in readiness.

On a morning when Igrainia had slept late, she woke to find Jennie staring down at her on the bed. She clutched her covers and sat up, staring at the maid.

"They will come, you know!" she told Igrainia, then looked over her shoulder to see that the door to the room was closed. Then she sat excitedly at the foot of the bed. "I get word out, Igrainia. There is a girl who comes in to sell small wares to the soldiers ... she carries my letters out. I have informed your brother, Lord Aidan, that you have no choice here, that they have completely seized all and everyone. But you needn't fear, I've never told them the truth. They will be here soon, and I've warned them how the men have worked in the courtyard, and that they are setting various traps. I wish I knew more about what they were doing ... I received this yesterday."

From her bodice, she triumphantly produced a letter tied in silver blue ribbon.

"For me? From Aidan?" Igrainia's fingers trembled as she reached for it.

Jennie handed her the letter. She knew that it was from Aidan instantly; she recognized his bold scrawl across the page.

Dearest Sister,
   I have not forgotten or deserted you. I have read your letters, and between the lines, and I know that you are under great duress. I know your fears, and I know how you suffer. Please don't fear. You will be free. Wait for me. For the love of our late father and mother, I will not let you down.
                                                            Aidan

Igrainia stared at Jennie, shaking her head. "Jennie, you don't know how strong the defenses here are! I didn't want Aidan coming for me, I'm so afraid that he'll be killed!"

"They know—they know all about the Scots, I have seen to it that they do. They will not be killed, they will ride in triumph. Igrainia, I don't know what these people have done to you, but I love you, and I will see that Aidan does come, and that you are rescued."

"Jennie, Jennie! I love you, too, but you mustn't take such grave chances, and you are so sorely mistaken. The king will hand me over to Robert Neville, and I am more afraid of him than of any of these men."

"They have poisoned you," Jennie said sadly, reaching for the letter and hugging it to her chest like a lover's gift. "But your brother loves you, as you see. I cannot thank God enough! I have gotten through, and Aidan has written back!"

"Jennie, now I'm afraid for you as well. Promise me that you'll practice no more treachery, carry no more notes!"

Jennie stood, glancing at the door again. "I will look after you," she promised Igrainia. "I will swear to your safety, though you may have lost your mind."

"Jennie, leave the letter. I'll burn it!" Igrainia told her. But Jennie was heading toward the door, the letter clutched to her bosom. Igrainia leaped up to follow her, paused to grab a cover from the bed, and threw open the door to the hall.

Jennie was gone. Jarrett was there.

"Good morning, my lady. How may I serve you?"

"Um . . . breakfast, Jarrett, thank you so much."

She slipped back into the room, and dressed quickly, determined to find Jennie.

She couldn't find her in the castle, not in the rooms above, the great hall, or even in the crypts. She walked to the chapel, wanting to tell Father MacKinley what had happened, swear him to secrecy, and enlist his aid in talking to Jennie.

But Father MacKinley was out riding with Eric, she learned. She could get no help from him, not then.

She walked to the stables, thinking that for some reason she might find Jennie among the horses. But she did not. Gregory was there, smiling broadly as he saw her, and she walked over to him, placing a gentle hand on his shoulder.

"How are you? Well, I pray?"

He nodded strenuously.

As he looked at her, his lips formed words that didn't leave his mouth. She studied the movements of his mouth, since she was getting better at understanding him every time she saw him.

He said something about a baby, and looked at her abdomen.

She shook her head. "No, Gregory. I am well, but I am not having a child."

"He says that you will, and that it will be a boy."

Igrainia spun around and saw that Rowenna had come into the stables. She carried a basket of carrots, Gregory's treats for the animals he tended so well.

In all this time, she had not come to love Rowenna again as she once had, and in her heart, she knew that she was jealous. She was certain that Rowenna had been sleeping with Eric, and in the past days, she had not dared to wonder if it might still be true.

Because he was pleased with what he had did not mean that he offered her any real affection or loyalty. And liking what he had did not mean that he didn't want more.

She had suffered many humiliations. She was not sure that she could reasonably deal with more.

She shook her head again at Rowenna. "I am not having a child."

Rowenna smiled, walking up to her. "Well, it's not at all strange that you wouldn't know it yet . . . but Gregory has known for several days. He says that you will have a very handsome boy, born with pitch black hair and brilliantly blue eyes. A handsome lad, robust, and healthy.''

Looking at Rowenna, Igrainia found herself illogically angry, and determined that although there were many things Gregory might be able to "see," this wasn't one of them.

"I am not having a child," she said firmly. Then she remembered her purpose in the stables. "Have you seen my maid, Jennie?''

Rowenna frowned, shaking her head. She looked around Igrainia at Gregory, and after a moment nodded. "He's very worried about her. She pretends to work, but hovers where the men are talking. She listens too much.''

"Does he know anything more?" Igrainia asked carefully.

"He's sorry, no," Rowenna said.

"Well, thank you," Igrainia said, and started to leave.

"Gregory, it doesn't matter," she heard Rowenna say behind her.

She turned. "What doesn't matter?''

Gregory was grinning ear to ear again.

"What?" Igrainia persisted.

Rowenna sighed and told her, "He is very excited for you. He says that Sir Eric and King Robert the Bruce will both be very pleased.''

"King Robert?" she persisted.

"The Scottish king was naturally concerned that you should have a child as an absolute proof of your marriage," Rowenna said. She shrugged. "I'm afraid that I heard Jamie and Peter speaking on the parapets the other day. King Robert was infuriated that Edward of England would dismiss his power, and that of the Catholic Church, to sanction such a marriage. And naturally, well I know your husband, and I know he will be pleased. He will have a son, a legitimate heir. Any man would be pleased.''

Igrainia felt her temper simmering as if coals had been lit beneath her feet. For a moment, she was so angry she couldn't get her breath to reply. Then she said, "I'm afraid, Gregory, that there is no child. This time, you are wrong."

She turned, fighting to stay in control as she left the stables.

Peter called to her as she walked through the hall to the stairs. She heard him, but did not reply.

Jarrett was in the hallway.

She ignored him as well. In her room, she paced before the fire, her cheeks burning. She wasn't even sure why she was so upset. Yes, she was.

She had been married to a man because his king had ordered her. Just to slip her away from others, to anger another king. That was bad enough.

That she had slept with Eric might have occurred eventually no matter how unwilling she might have been. Men had been known to force unwilling wives, and for that matter, invaders on both sides of the deadly issue had been known to rape any lone female, from the tender ages to the ancient, when they had torn apart an enemy's village.

But she hadn't been forced. She had come to him willingly . . . eagerly. She had wanted him. And—God forgive her pride, or her sense of self-importance, as Eric might have termed it—she had, at the least, assumed that he had wanted her as well.

But he had been *ordered* to sleep with her. She was being bred like prize livestock.

She paced herself to exhaustion, growing ever more furious. The hours passed. She was aware of sounds in the courtyard, of the never-ending work with swords and weapons. She knew as the sun lowered and pink light filled the sky.

She didn't go down to the hall for dinner that evening.

She summoned Garth from the kitchen, and had food and her customary bath brought.

That day, she waited purposely for the water to cool, hoping it would calm her spirit. It did nothing, except chill her flesh.

When Eric returned, late at night, she sat in the chair before the fire, clad neck to toe in her plainest, heaviest linen gown. She didn't turn when she heard him come into the room. She knew that his eyes were hard upon her, though, that he had noted her absence at dinner, and it was more than possible that someone had told him she was behaving strangely.

He walked around behind her, and leaned against the mantel.

"What is your dark mood this evening, Igrainia? You sent for a meal, shunning the great hall and the company of your enemy. And now I find you . . . so."

She stood, because he was too close, because her illogical rage had been building to a point she could scarcely control. She walked a short distance and turned to stare at him. Her fingers knotted into her palms. She had never been more aware of the arresting strength in his face, or the perfection of his tightly muscled form, and it added fuel to her fury. She hated herself because she could not remember the time now when he had seemed like nothing but a barbaric heathen destroying her world. And she hated the cool way that his eyes assessed her in return. He didn't *dislike* her. No matter what words he had said since, that casual, indifferent comment seemed to burn in her mind.

"You slept with me," she said, her voice low yet filled with venom and rising, "because the king commanded it?"

He arched a brow slowly, surveying her, regarding her anger, and not in the least concerned with it. "What difference does it make to you as to *why*?" He demanded.

She didn't directly answer the question. "I will never, never have your child!" She swore to him. "I will not let you *and your king* use me as a small but annoying point of power in your wretched war."

"You're being ridiculous," he said.

"Ridiculous!"

"First of all, Igrainia, the king could not have ordered me to do anything that I was not more than willing to do."

"For the honor and glory of Scotland!"

"And," he continued, as if she had not mocked him so vehemently, "you did not seem at all averse to the arrangement."

"I did not seem averse!" she whispered, then lied with tears of fury stinging her eyes. "I did not seem averse! Surely, you knew that every single night here I survived by closing my eyes and seeing another man, by pretending with all my heart that you had never come here, that I slept with Afton, lay with Afton . . . and I . . . I tell you again, I will never have your child."

"I believe that you already carry a son."

So, Rowenna had spoken to him. Naturally.

Yes, *Rowenna had come to know him well.*

She shook her head furiously. "Because a poor, deaf-mute boy has said so? I tell you, it's not the truth, not the truth at all, and it will never be!"

"Gregory has yet to say anything which I have not discovered to be true," he informed her with a shrug.

"Even if it is true now, it will never happen!" she assured him.

For a moment she thought that he would move from the mantel and offer her some violence. Then he spoke coolly and smoothly once again. "I don't believe that you would intentionally destroy a child you carried, any more than I believe you would be such a coward as to throw yourself out a window,'' he said flatly.

''He is wrong!'' she insisted passionately. ''And you may tell Rowenna that I am certain he is wrong, very wrong. Insist to her that he is wrong.''

''I should insist to Rowenna that he is wrong?''

''It seems that you talk with her constantly, she is your very dear friend and confidant, and she is his mouthpiece, so yes.''

''You're disturbed that Rowenna is . . . my friend?''

''No. Never mind,'' she told him. ''Say what you want to whom you want. Perhaps Gregory is right, of course he is right, he 'sees'. So, your duty here is done. You've obeyed your king's orders!''

He walked to where she stood and she backed away a step, facing him like a cat with hackles raised, knowing she had nowhere to go.

He reached for her, drawing her to him. ''You're a little fool, Igrainia. If I hadn't wanted you, God himself could not have *ordered* me to touch you.''

''Really? But then I'm not at all sure that you believe in God, so that doesn't really mean much of anything does it?''

''This is an absolutely ridiculous argument!'' he exploded.

''Let go of me,'' she said stubbornly. ''You've served king and country.''

''You are my wife.''

''No. Your wife lies in the crypts below. I'm just part of the great cause for freedom, and I don't care to be a part of it anymore.''

''You are a part, whether you care to be, or not.''

''Do you intend to force me to be with you?''

''Madam, I've never needed or desired force in my life.''

''Then let me go!''

Before he could respond, there was a hard tapping on the door. His eyes, hard on hers for a moment, promised that they were not finished. He released her, and walked to the door.

Jamie was just outside. As he started speaking in a hushed tone, Eric stepped into the hall, and closed the door. Igrainia nervously waited.

A moment later, Eric stepped back in, his hands behind his back.

"A very curious correspondence has just come to light," he said.

"Oh?"

Her heart seemed to cease its beat. She had been in such a state over Rowenna's words that she had forgotten the importance of finding Jennie.

And seeing that Aidan's letter to her had been burned.

When he strode across the room then, she knew that her anger had cost her dearly. The letter had not been burned. It had been found.

He drew his hands from behind his back. He held the letter.

"Where did this come from?" he demanded harshly.

"What is it?" she bluffed.

But he knew her too well. Knew that she was lying.

"You haven't even glanced down, Igrainia. You know full well what it is."

"I—don't."

"How have you been getting secret letters to your brother out of the castle?"

"I haven't been. I swear it."

"But you have this. And someone is bringing word to the enemy about our movements, and our defenses."

"Well, this may be Scotland, and the people may be

happy, as you insist, but you must remember that Langley was held by a man loyal to Edward before your arrival.''

He watched her for a long while, then turned, heading for the door. In the hall, he shouted to Jarrett. ''Watch her—see that she doesn't move!''

She heard his footsteps in the hall, down the stairs.

More footsteps . . .

And voices from the hall. He had gathered his men; they would be discussing the letter, creating new strategy . . .

Searching for the one who had betrayed them.

She began to pace the confines of the bedroom again, wondering what would come next. He didn't believe her, she thought. Didn't believe that she wasn't the one writing to Aidan. And he knew that there was someone else involved, someone who was a traitor among them.

Jennie had to be stopped, of course.

But she didn't dare give her away!

What would Eric do? It was imperative that they stop the flow of information. She felt chilled, then hot as fire. Through the ages, men—and women—had been tortured to force them to give information.

She had to warn Jennie. Warn her that they knew someone was sending information. And that way, Jennie could get away.

And then, when they asked her, she could tell the truth, that she had thought that Jennie was just rambling with resentment, but that she was gone, and she had been the one giving away every little bit of information she could glean.

She ran to the door, threw it open, and found Jarrett across the hall, leaning against the wall, arms over his chest. His gaze now was hooded and mistrustful. And he didn't speak to her. He just stared at her, as if he were warily keeping his eyes upon a caged but rabid dog.

She backed into the room and closed the door.

Hours later, she had worn herself out walking around the room. She finally lay down, exhausted.

But sleep eluded her. Hours passed. Finally, she closed her eyes.

She woke with a start.

Morning had come. Yellow shafts of daylight poured into the room. She glanced around, seeking for signs that Eric had come, and slept beside her.

He had not.

When she rose and stepped into the hall, Angus had taken Jarrett's place. He stared at her not with anger, but with sorrow.

"You're not to leave the room, my lady," he told her, his tone apologetic and softly accusing.

"May I see Father MacKinley?" She asked.

"The priest is not here."

"Where is he?"

"Gone."

She inhaled a deep breath, praying that Father MacKinley had not paid the price for someone else's action.

"Will you tell Eric that I need to talk to him, please," she said.

"I cannot, my lady. He is gone as well."

"Where?"

"I am not to say."

"Angus, please, I need to speak with him."

"It's impossible now."

"But when will he be back?"

"I don't know."

Aggravated, she slammed the door. Then she opened it again. "For your information, I didn't write letters and have them spirited out of the castle. Though if I had, it would have been right. This was my castle, and you have taken it over!"

He just stared at her.

Again, she slammed the door.

"There . . . there!" Allan exclaimed.

"Where?" Eric demanded.

"East, northeast, in that break of the trees . . . you can see them."

From the height of an old gnarled oak, Eric peered in the direction Allan indicated. And he could see them. Hundreds of them. Canvas tents stretched out, arms and armor rested around them, and men moved about, settling into their camp for the night. As the light began to fade, the blaze from their cooking fires and the smoke rising above them became apparent.

Eric remained in the tree, studying the layout of the camp, and every trail that led to and from it. A twisted little spit of stream ran behind it, making it a sound location for troops to rest the day before an assault.

Eric nodded at Allan, and they both skimmed down the tree, jumping down the last few feet and landing softly on the earth beneath them. Jamie waited with their horses, and the men he had chosen to ride with him were gathered in a nearby copse.

"They're settling in. We'll strike at midnight. Jamie, you, Allan, Raymond, and I will go in first," he said, hunkering down to draw a diagram of the camp and the trails leading from it. "Allan, you'll take the stream, Jamie, you're here, Raymond here . . . and I'll be here. They'll have guards out. We'll have to take the guards first. We'll leave the horses here . . . bring the men this far, and after we've silenced the guards, we meet here . . . so . . . then give the signal to the men. What we have to work with is speed and surprise. I'm certain they were expecting to find men at the posts we planned guarding Langley when they reached it, but they can't be in the least afraid of an attack at their camp. This is important—we scatter their horses. If we have to make a hasty retreat, we don't want them following.''

Grim nods assured him of their understanding. He and Allan mounted their horses, and rode back to the others, troops silent except for the occasional soft sound of a restless hoof moving or the brush and clink of riding accouterments. He outlined the plan. The force of fifty he had brought against the hundreds in the camp was well aware of their odds, and all that stood in their favor as well.

''Father MacKinley,'' he said, addressing the priest. ''Will you say a prayer for us?'' he asked, watching the man all the while. He didn't think that MacKinley had been guilty. He hoped that he was not, because he had come to like and admire the priest.

''I will gladly say a prayer for the souls of all men,'' he said.

The company dismounted, and went down on their knees. MacKinley invoked the Most Holy Father. He prayed for the souls of all men, and at the end, he prayed for the lives of those down on their knees before them.

MacKinley had either been fully conscripted to their side of the fight, or he was a priest in need of defrocking.

Eric hoped it was the first.

They rode as close as they dared to the camp, dismounted, left Father MacKinley and two men with the horses, and slipped through the high summer grasses and trees toward the camp. They waited, low in the grass, watching the movement they could see through the trees and brush. By midnight, all the horses had been tethered. The men slept on the ground, or in the tents.

Eric gave a signal and he, Raymond, Allan, and Jamie started out, splitting off in the darkness. Each followed his prescribed course, taking care every step of the way, knowing that there must be guards set out, whether the enemy expected an attack or not.

His own trail brought him straight toward the center.

He saw the posted guard and held back, watching. The man slumped against a tree, and yawned, bored with his duty. Eric silently trod the few steps to the tree, and attacked in a swift, fluid motion from behind. The guard's head slumped down. He looked as if he slept, except for the pool of blood that trailed from his throat.

Eric listened sharply all the while, heard the call of a night owl, and knew that Jamie had found another posted guard. He circled around carefully. Allan, hunched low, was padding around the outer circumference of the camp. Jamie came from his left, Allan from his right.

He stood, waving his hand in the night.

A flurry of movement was borne on the breeze.

But it wasn't heard by the men sleeping so peacefully on the earth until it was far too late.

Many of them died before ever waking.

Some lived to fight.

A few were trampled by the horses, sent into a commotion as Eric's men forced them to run from torches they had seized from the dying campfires.

Though the raid was a stunning success, creating far more havoc than Eric had even imagined they could achieve, he dared not make a real battlefield of the campground. When too many of the living began to rise and seize weapons, he shouted the order to retreat. His men seized what arms they could easily carry while running on foot, and departed.

MacKinley, his men, and the horses waited. They mounted with all speed, and galloped into a darkness barely illuminated by a pale moon.

He put distance between his men and the camp. When

they halted at last, he and Jamie made a count of the men,
asking about injuries and losses. None dead.

Four wounded.

"They won't follow until daylight!" he announced, when
they were gathered in the woods. "They won't be able to
hunt down enough horses until then. We can take a few
hours' rest, but be on guard. Peter, you and I will take the
first watch, Jamie, you and Allan the next."

He thought he would have no difficulty staying awake.
His mind was restless, churning. But he'd had no sleep in
hours now, and he jerked himself awake several times.

Finally, the watch changed.

He lay beneath the trees, and his eyes closed. He thought
that he was still planning further strategy, but he was suddenly aware of someone walking through the trees. It seemed
that it was a long time ago. He had been younger. He had
come from the sea, his real love. The earth seemed to rock,
as it was prone to do, after so many days in a boat. The
rocking gave a sweet comfort. Hair as gold as the sun
streamed down the woman's back. He knew her face. So
pale, eyes so blue. Smile so quick. She came straight to
where he lay, gathered the folds of her shimmering white
dress in his fingers, and straddled him. She whispered to
him, bending low to brush his lips.

The kiss was sweet. She drew away. He opened his eyes
lazily, ready for whatever sensual pleasure she had in mind.

With a start he saw that it was not Margot at all, and time
had passed, and wild, tempest-torn violet eyes were staring
down at him. She had a knife gripped in both hands, and
she was ready to slam it into his heart.

He rolled . . .

And smacked his head into a tree. Wincing with the pain,
he woke. He rubbed his forehead, then came to his feet.

Across the clearing, awake and on guard, Jamie watched him, frowning.

He looked up, and saw that Allan had found the tallest tree.

"Are they in sight?" He asked.

"Aye, but only a small party, searching for our trail."

"Where?"

"Due north."

"How many in the party."

"Thirty-five, forty."

"Aye, then, come down." He strode across the clearing, booting awake those men who hadn't already begun to rise. "Come on then, what—would you have them come across us in like fashion?" he inquired. He reached Jamie, who was now standing, waiting for him.

"We split. I'll double back with twenty-five, you move forward. We'll catch up. There will still be a sizable force, but if we can foray back and cause a greater loss, we should be able to test their mettle. When we arrive, lower the gates. Then we wait until they are full upon us, and come out after them. It is the last thing they will expect."

"And maybe the most foolhardy we can do," Jamie commented.

"You came up with half the idea."

Jamie shrugged. "We've been foolhardy for years. Why change things now?"

Eric called out the names of the men who were to follow him. They mounted first, and he explained their purpose. All were eager.

Jamie waved as he rode north, then called to the others to mount.

Eric and his force rode until it was time to dismount. He gauged his distance ahead of the riders coming their way.

Half of them climbed into the branches of the trees. Then they waited, in silence.

Allan, sent ahead, let out a soft whistle of warning.

A few moments later, the mounted riders were beneath them.

They burst from the bushes, dropped from the trees. The English had the advantage then of their armor. The Scots wore only padded breast coats, the only protection they could have used with such tactics. And still, they struck with such surprise that their enemy were toppled heavily from their horses, and cut down before they could gain positions from which to fight.

The combat was hand to hand, man on man. Someone among the English shouted for rank and order, but the command was ignored. Men began to split into trails and copses; many tried to escape.

Eric found himself off the trail, not in pursuit, but battling the crafty swings of a man in full, expensively crafted armor. He had the disadvantage of finding the place to strike his enemy that could bring him down, while his opponent could injure him with a glancing blow. And still, though the man was able and courageous, he was far more slender, and Eric came at him with persistence and stamina, striking forward again and again until at last he struck with such a deadly blow that his foe's sword slipped out of his hand. The force sent him slamming back against a tree as well, then sliding down the length of it. Eric grasped his sword in both hands to thrust down through his enemy's throat.

Then he stopped. There was something on the man's tunic that gave him pause. A coat-of-arms.

A family coat-of-arms. One he had seen before. It had hung on the wall before him; he had been waking to it every morning.

The crest of the house of Abelard.

He heard a roar from the road. Allan raced into the clearing. "Most of the men are coming, it's time to retreat to the castle."

Eric turned back to his disarmed enemy.

"Do it, by God! Kill me if you will!" the man against the tree shouted.

His fingers tightened around the hilt of his sword.

CHAPTER 18

From her room, Igrainia could hear the thunder of hoof-beats and the cries of the men. She couldn't see the gated entry to the castle.

When she heard the sounds of the men returning, she leaped up and raced to the door, throwing it open. Jarrett was there, seated in a chair, whittling.

"How can you just sit there? What is happening?" she demanded.

"It's only the first of the troops returning," he told her.

"How do you know?"

"The lookouts announced their arrival."

He still looked at her as if she were the greatest traitor alive. She returned to the room. In time, from her window, she could see the riders gathering in the courtyard. She saw Jamie and others she knew, but no sign of Eric. Something was happening, though. Men were taking positions upon the parapets. There were always guards there, watching, but there were more now.

She remained at the window, seeing the quivers full of arrows that men were carrying up the steep steps to the walls. She could see longbows and Peter's war machines being dragged into place. There was a tap at her door. She strode to the door and opened it.

Rowenna was there, carrying linen sheets and a broom. "I'll take them," she said stiffly.

But Rowenna glanced over her shoulder at Jarrett. "There's work to do in the room."

Igrainia turned her back on the girl and returned to the window. But a moment later, she realized that Rowenna had followed her.

"She's gone," Rowenna said hastily. "You have nothing to fear. Jennie is gone."

"Gone where?"

Rowenna shook her head. "I don't know. But they were questioning everyone. And she could not be found. And Gregory has said that she is gone." Rowenna made an impatient sound. "You can tell them now, without fear for your friend."

"How can Gregory be so certain? There are places to hide in the castle, places where she might not be found for days."

"Gregory has a gift."

"Then why didn't he see before that it was Jennie, not I?" she asked bitterly.

"He has a gift, he is not omnipotent."

Rowenna was certain, absolutely certain, Igrainia realized. She walked back to the window. "Thank you," she said briefly.

She listened as Rowenna went about her work. She

couldn't bring herself to speak to the girl further. Finally, she heard the door close.

Far below, she could see that Jamie was shouting orders, and that the activity was increasing. Animals that had been out in the fields grazing were beginning to fill the courtyard, and herders urged them into the stables and loft in the lower levels of the inner tower walls. There was still no sign of Eric.

She flew back to the door, throwing it open.

Jarrett was still whittling.

"Jarrett . . ."

He looked up at her. His eyes did not conceal his mistrust.

"Jamie is down there. Eric is not."

Jarrett stared at her. "No, he has not returned as yet."

She returned his stare. She wanted to exclaim that she had done nothing, but she heard shouting then, and went back to the window. She leaned out and craned her neck, trying to look in the direction of the great gates. Again, men began to pour into the courtyard.

She was halfway out the window when hands were upon her waist. She screamed with instinctive fear, not certain if she was about to be tossed to the courtyard below, or dragged back in. But a second later she was standing on solid ground, and Eric was before her.

She hadn't realized how afraid she had been for his life until she saw him. He wasn't in mail or any plate armor, but the padding beneath his shirt and tunic made his shoulders and chest immense. Dried blood spattered most of his clothing. His face was lined with dirt.

She wanted to throw herself at him and begin to laugh and cry hysterically. He was alive. The worse for wear, but alive.

Somehow, she managed to stay still, looking at him, awaiting what would come next.

"Two more inches, and you'd be a pile of broken bones below," he told her.

"I know how far I can go," she said. "You're covered in blood." The temptation to reach out and touch him was almost overwhelming.

"Not much of it is mine. It's time for you to go."

"To go?" she repeated, trying not to betray the dismay that seemed to hit her like a physical blow. What had happened? Had an arrangement been made at last and she was to be exchanged for a prisoner dear to the Scots?

He reached out his hand to her.

Like the rest of him, it was streaked with dirt, specks of blood. He noted it before he touched her. Stared at it, turned it palm side up. Then he said, "Come on."

She didn't accept his touch. A tightness formed in her throat. "I didn't write letters to my brother to be slipped out the castle walls," she said.

"It doesn't matter now."

Perhaps he didn't want to touch her, so heavily encrusted with the blood of battle. But he was going to.

She backed away a step. "Where are you taking me?"

"Below."

"To the dungeon?"

"To the tunnel," he said impatiently. "If things go badly ... there will be someone to take you out, and north. To the highlands."

She thought she was going to fall, she was so relieved. She stumbled forward, and he had to catch her with both hands, holding her against his chest.

"What is it?" he asked.

"Nothing. I just ... tripped."

She didn't care about the remnants of battle that so stained his clothing and person. She was glad to be next to him.

He caught her chin gently, lifting her face.

"You've seriously wronged me, you know," she told him.

"Maybe . . . and maybe in many ways," he said softly, the tip of his thumb moving over her cheek as he studied her eyes.

"I'm glad you're alive," she told him.

"I'm grateful. And I will do my best to preserve myself, since I don't want to distress you further in any way." There was a slight mischief in his eyes. She smiled, and laid her head against his chest. She felt his fingers in her hair, cradling her there. "We have to move," he said softly, and with a regretful sigh, she thought. He cupped her face in his hands, standing back. "I'm not locking you away. You've got to understand, if this does go badly . . . Jarrett will be with you. He'll see to it that you escape, and he'll take you so far into the hills that the English will never find you . . . unless you choose, one day, to be found."

"Don't—" she began.

"Let's go."

He took her hand then, leading her from the room, and down the stairs. Jarrett was at the table, busy with Garth. She saw that he was in process of securing supplies in a satchel, should they be needed. Igrainia felt a tremor of fear in her heart, seeing how they were preparing for any contingency.

Before Eric could approach Jarrett, the great door to the courtyard burst open and Jamie came striding through.

"The men reached their positions, and just barely in time. The English are coming on us now. Hard."

"Go with Jarrett, Igrainia," Eric said, and went out with long, determined footsteps, Jamie at his side.

Igrainia glanced back. Jarrett was still absorbed in his task. She skimmed lightly across the floor, reached the door, and slipped out.

She didn't understand the battle plan. There were men mounted in the courtyard, which made little sense. The drawbridge was up, but the inner gates had not been closed. Men were rushing around her in all directions, some in heavy armor and mail, and some in the simple clothing of their everyday life. She saw some of the men ushering the women and children into the comparative safety of the stables, storerooms, and armories along the base of the tower walls.

One of the steep flights of stone steps to the parapets lay directly across from her position. She sprinted across the distance and ran up the steps. If the men in their haste to follow orders knew that she was not supposed to be about, they were too concerned at their tasks to waylay her.

And maybe Eric had never let it be known, except to his intimate circle, that he had ever suspected her of corresponding with her brother, his enemy.

She reached the top of the steps without being waylaid. She stood, watching, and as she did so, she saw the English troops coming. She knew Ewan Danby, Lord of Cheffington, knew his colors and his crest, and she knew that he rode at the head of the troops. She saw Robert Neville's colors as well, and the ostentatious mail of Sir Niles Mason.

Trumpets sounded as they came, dragging war wagons and a huge catapult at the end of their ranks. She watched as they crossed the trail to the north and began to descend the slope that led to the moated castle at the base of the hill.

"Igrainia! Good Lord! What are you doing here?"

It was Peter, Peter with miniature catapult, dragged to a position where his burning missiles might be hurled at the point just beyond the bridge. Other men were rushing to him. In the narrow confines of the parapet, they were bringing huge vats of heated pitch.

"I had to see!" she told him, eyes in torment. "Peter . . . you must believe . . ."

"Get down!" he commanded. "They are forming their archers!"

She ducked as he commanded her, but couldn't force herself low enough so that she could not see. She realized that Eric was not far from her, across the rise and machinery of the drawbridge. As she watched, he dropped an arm, signaling someone or something that she couldn't see.

As the English came forward, dragging their equipment, there was suddenly a wild, savage cry from the forest. She understood then, some of the battle tactic.

The Scotsmen seemed to pour from the forest, trapping the English invaders between the dense growth of trees and the stone walls of the castle. At the same time, the men at the parapets began to fire, and Peter's small war machines went into action. Huge balls of stone, metal and peat were set into the catapults and sent flying down on the English forced to the walls.

The invaders fought back valiantly. Their massive catapult was being drawn into position. From the walls, she could see that the archers, with burning arrows, were aiming for the machine.

She looked around wildly. Eric was gone from his position.

Below her, she saw that men were streaming into the moat, ladders were being rushed forward to be drawn up against the walls.

An arrow whizzed by. She heard a cry from the man beside Peter. She turned to help, but saw that the weapon had pierced the man's heart. He died as he struck the floor of the parapet.

She saw that his job had been to light the missiles placed in the catapult. She scrambled over the fallen body, and picked up the torch he had used. Peter stared at her.

She lit the missile in the machine. Peter used his great

strength to let it fly. Again, he turned, creating another burning ball to fly.

She rose slightly and saw that there were men climbing up a ladder that had been wedged in the mud next to the wall. Peter's head was bowed over his work. She rose quickly, catching the rungs of the ladder, pushing with all her might. One of the Englishmen was nearly at the parapet.

"Peter!" she cried.

He rose instantly, and added his strength to hers. The man crawled with desperate vigor to reach the parapet before the ladder could crash back to earth. She saw his hand grasp the stone, saw the knife caught in his teeth. He was nearly over the stone while Peter still shoved againt the rungs of the wedged ladder.

Against the stone lay Peter's sword. She dived for it, and gritted her teeth against the weight of the weapon. She drew it up in time, and tried to remember everything she had read about weapons and war in Afton's books. Weight, counterweight, balance . . .they could mean everything. She watched until the man teetered on the brink, ready to throw his leg over the stone. She swung, catching him right against the steel of his helmet. For terrible seconds, he wobbled there, almost on the stone, not quite.

He lost his balance. She watched in horror as he went crashing down, hitting the ground at the base of the stone first, then falling into the water.

Peter at last heaved the ladder over. It crashed into the moat. They heard the screams of the men upon it as it went down. They both stared into the water. Then Peter stared at Igrainia, as if amazed.

"He would have killed me, had he come over," Peter said.

She just stared at him, white-faced, knowing that she hated battle more than ever, now that she had killed a man.

Another arrow whizzed overhead. Peter caught her shoulders, pulling her down. They both rose again as shouts rang in the air, and another wave of battle cries sounded.

The archers had managed to set a fire on the huge catapult on the slope; it was burning with a vengeance. The drawbridge was lowering, and as it did, armed men went riding out of the castle, joining in the hand-to-hand combat that ensued when the Scots had attacked from the their ambush in the forest. Eric was leading the men from the castle, immediately entering into battle, his great sword swinging again and again from his perch atop the mighty Loki.

"Peter!"

This time, a ladder had reached the parapets at their side. A man was about to step cleanly upon the stone edge.

She grabbed one of the peat balls and threw it with all her might. The man, taken by surprise, offset by the weight of his mail, instantly went falling over. Peter thrust the ladder from the walls. Igrainia raced down the parapet and watched as the battle continued. It had been reduced to pockets of men, recognizable by their colors, and the crests on their armor banners. She saw that Eric was still horsed, and heavily engaged near the drawbridge. At a distance, she could see Lord Danby, on the ground, fighting valiantly. She didn't see Niles Mason or Robert Neville, but the fighting was so tight and fierce in many places, they might well be in the midst of any number of groups.

Eric, surrounded by other men, was forcing the enemy outward, away from the gates. Her eyes were suddenly attracted by a glint in the sun and she looked forward, outward from the gates. And there was Aidan, her own family crest etched into the plate of his chest, and in beautiful color on his mantle. He was valiantly pushing forward.

Her hand went to her throat, terrified. He was surrounded by so many Scots!

A sword sent a harsh blow against his chest. She was certain that she heard the clamor of it all the way to the parapets, over the deafening din of the battle itself.

"Aidan!" she breathed.

The Scots moved on. They were forcing the English back to the north.

She spun around. Peter was busy setting the machine again. There were no ladders drawn to the walls; the English had given up that form of entry.

She raced down from the parapets. A few horses, animals that had lost their riders just beyond the gates, had wandered back in, and stood as if lost about the courtyard. Men were still rushing about. The cries she was hearing were of victory. The military tactics of the defenders, executed with craft, cunning, and brash courage, were proving effective.

But she could feel little jubilation. Aidan lay in the dirt, perhaps dead already, perhaps bleeding to death.

"Igrainia!" She heard her name bellowed. Near the great doors to the tower, she saw that Jarrett had by now realized that she was not within the castle. He was stopping men as they rushed by, demanding to know if they had seen her.

Her brother lay in the dirt.

She ran swiftly, her decision made that she must be the first to reach Aidan. She caught the reins of one of the riderless warhorses, and swung into the saddle.

Even as she did so, Jarrett came rushing to her and grabbed the reins of her horse. "Igrainia, have you gone mad?"

"My brother is out there; let me go."

"Someone will see to your brother."

"Someone will put a sword through his heart!" she cried.

Jarrett didn't intend to let her go. He was close enough so that she could kick out at him with all her might.

The stirrup caught the side of his head. He staggered away and fell.

She winced inwardly, praying she had not hurt him too badly. But Aidan might be dying. Her brother, her flesh and blood, lying in the dirt in his pursuit to free her.

She kneed the animal with a vengeance, low against its neck as she raced over the bridge, her heart pounding along with the thunder of its hooves. Within a few minutes, she had reached the spot where Aidan lay, a prone, sprawling pile now of shimmering armor in the sun.

She swung off the horse at his side. He lay facedown. She caught his arm, struggling to roll him over, looking over his form for blood and injury. She got him onto his back, and saw the great dent on the plate that covered his chest.

She struggled with his helmet, drawing it from his head, then struggling with the circlet of mail at his throat.

"Aidan! Aidan, are you breathing?" she whispered, not aware of the riders around her, barely hearing the constant clash of steel, the screams, the commands. "Aidan!" She leaned low against her brother's face, and felt the stir of his breath against her cheek. He was alive. She had to get him up, and on the horse, and into the courtyard, where she could tend to him. Black hair lay matted over his forehead. She touched it, praying that it was damp with sweat and not blood. "Aidan . . ."

He groaned. His eyes closed again. "Aidan!" she said more desperately, seeking the straps and buckles to the plate upon his chest. His eyes opened again. "Igrainia . . . not . . . cut. Just . . . winded . . . breathing . . ."

He tried to rise to a sitting position, and nearly crashed down again. She caught him, and he shook his head, and smiled at her. "Black . . . stars . . ." He blinked then, and it seemed that his senses had returned. And suddenly, he was yelling at her. "What are you doing on a battlefield! Foolish girl!"

She drew back. "You may be the earl," she informed

him. "But I am your older sister, and I am trying to save your fool life!"

She screamed then suddenly, because someone had come behind her. There were arms around her, hands on her midriff, drawing her up.

"We've got you!"

She twisted about to see the visored image of Robert Neville.

"Let me go!" she demanded. "Aidan's hurt. I'll see to him; your battle is lost, you must retreat!"

Robert Neville ignored her entirely; she might as well have not spoken. "Aye, the battle is lost, but the prize is gained. You are rescued, Igrainia!"

"No, Aidan is down, I don't know if he has broken bones! Let me be—"

But he ignored her. He grabbed her with a rough strength, spinning around, and throwing her on top of his horse. He mounted behind her. She twisted and turned, furiously trying to push him from the horse, to break his grip upon her, to make him understand. She wasn't even aware of the depths of her own peril at that moment; she only knew that her brother was on the ground.

"Aidan is injured!" she screamed. She slammed a fist against him. Hit mail and plate armor. Agony burned through her hand. "Robert! Aidan is down, let me go!"

"Niles has Aidan," he said curtly. "And we are in full retreat."

His horse reared suddenly as he spurred it with a vengeance. She grasped the animal's neck, but it was an unnecessary gesture. Robert Neville had hold of her with his left arm that would have defied a full forward flip by the animal. The horse pawed the air, then leaped forward as if flying into a breakneck gallop.

Her hair whipped into her eyes.

She could see nothing.

She could hear the trumpets sounding retreat.

The Scottish cries of triumph were deafening.

Eric was pulled from Loki by his men, and lifted high among them as their shouts of elation filled the air. He caught the hands of his men as they moved him through the throng of victors at his side. Jamie, who had led much of the action, was picked up as well, nearly thrown into the air, and, as if they were going to meet for some great mock play battle, they were brought together in the middle of the field. Eric grasped his cousin's hand in a tight clasp, the thrill of the total rout they had given the English deep in his own heart as well.

Then he shouted, "Men, you've done it! By God, today we have proved that Scotland is a sovereign nation, and that we honor our own king, Robert the Bruce!" A roar of approval went up, a great salute to the king. "He knows that he will win his country, not just through the nobles of his realm, but through the spirit of every man among his people. Because we are a free people. And we will continue to prove it to the English!"

Cries went up again, and then he knew that they could afford no more time basking in their glory. "We've injured on the ground, men. Our friends, who have fought as we have!"

He was lowered to the ground, and as one, the men began to move, covering the field of battle once again.

Clearing the ground would take until nightfall, and they would still be finding the dead and injured of their own, as well as the English, tomorrow.

Set down upon the ground himself, he charged Allan and Raymond with the task of moving into the forest, and following like silent wraiths in the wake of the English. Angus was left in charge of seeing that parties were formed to bring in the wounded, and to see that the dead were delivered to biers at the small chapel, that the proper rites and all honor might be bestowed upon them.

Only when his orders had been given did he mount Loki again and ride back over the drawbridge.

Peter came rushing up to him, white-faced and tense.

"Igrainia is gone."

"Gone?" He didn't believe it at first. "She is not gone; I ordered Jarrett to take her to the dungeons, to break the seal on the tunnel should they need to escape."

"She is gone," Peter persisted. "Come into the hall; Jarrett can tell you what happened."

Tense as a strung bow, Eric slipped down from Loki and strode in fury for the great hall. He was immediately ready to go for Jarrett's throat, until he saw the man, and the gash and bruise against his forehead.

"What happened?" Eric demanded.

"She saw her brother—"

"How did she see her brother from the dungeons?"

"We did not make the dungeons," Jarrett said, shaking his head. "I was packing what meager supplies we dared take, as you had told me. You were out of the hall and she was in the courtyard before I ever knew you had brought her down."

The sickness and the fury that seized him were so great he was still ready to fly at Jarrett, and pummel him into the ground, if only to ease his anguish. He felt a hand on his shoulder. Jamie. He fought for control.

"Then what?"

"I found she was not in her room. I searched for her; Garth said that he had seen her in the hall, with you. I came out."

"I found her on the parapets," Peter explained. "But I couldn't force her down because the battle had commenced. Then she was gone—"

"And I found her. On a horse."

"And you didn't stop her."

"Oh, aye! I went to stop her. But she screamed something about her brother and all but put her foot through my head. I've not received such a blow from the enemy in many a match!" Jarrett said, shaking his head. "She kicked me!" he repeated, and he was indignant, but looked as sick as Eric felt. "I fell on the ground, blacked out entirely, woke . . . and saw that it had ended, and the lady was gone."

Eric stood very still, a tempest racing through him. His fingers flexed in his palms, his head felt as if it would burst.

"So she was ready to betray us," he murmured.

"Eric," Peter said, "Don't be so hasty."

His eyes flashed like ice on his old friend.

"Hear me out!" Peter said. "On the parapets . . . she grabbed my sword and dislodged a fellow about to scale the wall. She saved me from his knife, and helped me topple a few of the ladders. She was fighting *with* us Eric."

"You let her fight?" he demanded.

"Well, now, I did not command her to risk life and limb in the fury of battle, but neither did I forbid her to lay that sword against a man about to take my heart. Jonas MacFadden, at my side, caught one of the first arrows. The lady was a formidable warrior, taking his place."

"But then she seized a horse and rode from the castle," Eric said.

"It might well be true that her brother was in grave danger."

Eric turned, striding for the door. "Peter, come with me. We've got to see the bodies of the dead and injured English. I've got to know if Aidan is among them . . . and Niles

Mason and Robert Neville. After, Peter, you'll begin what repair is needed. Jamie, form a party of our fleetest men, those most capable of moving in silence, attacking in stealth. We'll need pack animals to carry arms and armor . . . there are abandoned wagons in the field, we will need them.''

"Eric," Jamie said, stopping him. "They'll take her to Cheffington. It's their base, and Ewan Danby is a decent man, and an honorable one. He has never come into a town or village and slain the innocent.''

Eric nodded. "I know."

"Cheffington is a walled fortress, just as Langley. "To attack with a small party would be suicide.''

"There is always a way into a fortress,'' Eric said. "Always.''

And he strode out, praying that he would find the slain bodies of Robert Neville and Niles Mason on the field.

By nightfall, it was evident that the men were not among the dead. Nor was the body of Aidan—dead, injured, or moving—to be found. But among his own were those who had seen the English retreat, and at last, a man who had seen the Lady Igrainia ride to the field and fall to the side of an English lord.

And he had seen, as well, that one of the mounted knights had taken her with him upon his warhorse before following the thunder of the retreat.

"Did you know the man's colors?''

"Aye, Sir.'' And the man spat in the dirt. "He was in mail and plate, but I know his coat-of-arms well. She was taken by Sir Robert Neville, while her brother's body was lifted from the field by the butcher who began this all, Sir Niles Mason.''

Jamie was with him when he learned for a fact what he had so dreaded in suspicion.

"What is your plan?'' Jamie demanded.

"To get her back."

"How?"

"That we'll decide as we ride," Eric said.

"Against a horde!" Jamie murmured. But he shrugged. "Ah, well, it's not as if we're ever favored by the gods! I had always said that if I were to go down, I would want it to be in a blaze of glory!"

"My intention is not to die in a blaze of glory, but to live by it," Eric informed him. "Time is everything now, Jamie. We must ride."

"Aye, we must ride."

"Peter will stay and hold Langley," Eric said. "We need everyone but a skeleton crew here." He hesitated a moment. "The priest comes with us again. And Gregory."

"Gregory?"

"Aye, I want the boy with us. And Rowenna, as well."

During the long ride to Cheffington, Igrainia was in a fury.

Lord Danby recognized that they traveled with many injured. He was the supposed true leader of the forces, but he was aging now, a man of sixty-plus years, and he had given a great deal of control to the two young knights who commanded the men under him.

He was a handsome aging fellow, with clear green, thoughtful eyes, and snow white hair and beard. He would not allow Igrainia's tumult over Aidan and the other injured to slow them down, but he rode at her side, and they both rode behind the litters carrying those who could not walk.

There would be no stopping. Every heavy piece of equipment had been abandoned. The charred hulk of the once mighty catapult had been drawn, at the end, across a trail, there to waylay the Scots, should they come in pursuit.

Though Robert Neville had insisted to Lord Danby that she must not have her own mount but should ride with him, Lord Danby had scoffed at his fears regarding her loyalty, and assured him that there was no way the lady was leaving her brother, certainly not after she had dared the swords, arrows, and trampling horses on the battlefield to come to his side.

And so, at first, she had ridden with Danby, and near Aidan. But by the second day of their continuing march, Niles Mason had convinced Danby that they might soon be ambushed from behind, and Lord Danby himself had given the order that Robert Neville and a small party of men should ride ahead, and thus bring Igrainia to the safety of Cheffington as quickly as possible. Igrainia protested that she would not leave her brother, but by then, Aidan had risen from the litter himself, and insisted that he had been winged, and was ready to ride hard. He didn't want his sister exposed to the danger of the road any longer. She had been a prisoner of the Scots for long months, and he wasn't about to let her out of his sight.

And so, with Robert Neville and her brother forever dogging her every movement, she reached Cheffington.

When they arrived, she begged exhaustion, and was brought to a handsome chamber in Lord Danby's fine fortified castle. Servants were quick to bring her water, food, a bath, fresh clothing, anything that she might require. What she wanted was time. She didn't want to be around Robert Neville until Danby arrived. She believed that Aidan would support her in her desires, but she couldn't be certain. Danby, a devout Christian, would be deeply concerned about the marriage vows she had already taken. He would defend her and stand between her and Robert Neville until . . . .

Eric had already suspected her of trying to reach Aidan

with secret letters. Rowenna would tell him the truth, of course . . . and Rowenna was his dear friend, but . . .

She had deserted the castle and ridden out to the battlefield herself. She wondered if he would ever understand that she could not leave her brother in the dirt, abandon him to death.

The Scots hadn't the power to seize a place as grand and fortified as Cheffington, not even if they would have the desire to do so, if even a prize of war such as she would be worth the risk. Especially if Eric believed, even in the smallest way, that she had been willing to leave.

She was in a desperate situation. And probably on her own. But as yet, she didn't want Robert Neville to know that his bid to marry her had become more repugnant than ever, and that she would never consent to being his wife. She had never imagined that she would actually be afraid of him.

But then, when she had known him day by day before, Afton had been alive.

When she was at last alone in the chamber that had been given to her, she ate, bathed, and dressed, knowing that she had to keep her wits about her at all times. She sat by the fire in her close quarters, and thought carefully of every word she would say to Aidan, and then she rose and walked to her door, ready to discuss everything with him.

But when she reached the door, she found that it would not give. She pulled harder, and jerked at it, and still, she could not open it.

The door was bolted from the outside.

She had indeed left one prison for another.

Tomorrow, Lord Danby would arrive. And she would be indignant and furious, and demand to know how Robert Neville dared to lock her in, and keep her from the young earl, her brother.

She tried to still her growing sense of fear with the reassurance that Danby could, and would, protect her.

Until the time, at least, when she might be given over to the King of England.

There would be a way out before then, she assured herself. Edward would be very busy right now; the day was drawing near when all the men he had summoned to serve their feudal duty would arrive at the chosen meeting ground, and his great march to smash Robert Bruce would begin.

She was physically exhausted, and at last, with at least the illusion of assurance in her mind, she lay down to try to sleep. At last, she dozed, and then her sleep became deeper.

She didn't know what had wakened her, but her eyes flew open suddenly with a true sense of alarm.

"Igrainia."

She bolted up. Robert Neville was in her room. Clean and shaven, elegant in an embroidered tunic. He was a handsome man with rich sable hair and smooth features, and he had apparently determined to look his best. He sat by the side of the bed, and was ready to set a hand upon her.

She skimmed back against the headboard, staring at him.

"What are you doing in here?" she demanded sharply.

"Igrainia, I've just come to see to your welfare. We are to be married, you know. You must be hurt, afraid, feeling very lost. I've just come . . . to be with you."

"I was sleeping. Therefore, not hurt, afraid, or lost."

"You have been in the hands of the barbaric enemy far too long. Forgive me if I want to put my arms around you, and comfort you."

"Robert, you have to understand this—I wasn't hurt. And I can't marry you—I cannot marry anyone. I am already married."

"Not by law!"

"By the Church, and the law of Scotland."

"There is no sovereign Scottish law!"

She was on dangerous ground. If there truly was a God, he knew all about the evil in men. He would certainly understand any half-truth she gave in her desperation to ward off a man she was beginning to believe might be just as evil as any other. "There is the law of God, and I don't care to imperil my immortal soul." She spoke both sincerely, and passionately.

And, at first, she thought that he had taken her words to heart.

He rose, walked to the fire as if thoughtfully, then turned on her. "You whore!" he said very softly. "You barely buried my cousin before entertaining the most wretched and evil of the men who killed him in the very bed where he died."

The gentle compassion and pretense of care he had given was swept away with the fury of his tone.

She fought to keep her temper. "Get out, Robert."

He came back to the bed, sitting at her side again, and taking her hand. "I'm sorry. They terrified and abused you. You were a victim of force and rape. I will try to remember that, though it may be hard at times to forget that the filthy hands of such a brutal wild man were on your flesh."

She snatched her hand away. "Robert, understand this. I was not abused or harmed in any way. Nor was I raped. I cannot, will not, marry anyone until my case has been thoroughly studied by the most learned men in the Church."

She saw his knuckles grow white against the sheets. "Who do you think you're talking to?" he suddenly demanded. "And who do you think you are? The king has said that I will have you, and Langley, and so I will."

"It doesn't seem to me, after today, that you will have Langley," she couldn't help but reply.

It was a mistake. He lunged at her, seizing her shoulders so quickly that she was given no chance to fly or fight back.

"I will take back what is mine by right!"

"Yours by right! Langley was Afton's, as I was Afton's wife. Afton is dead, and no thing of his is yours by right. Certainly, not I!!"

"And you would spurn me, but accept a highland savage in my stead!" She remained dead still, jaw clenched, staring at him. "Maybe I've not been forceful enough. I've not simply seen what I want, and gone for it."

His fingers fell to the lacing at the top of her borrowed nightdress.

She screamed, as loudly as she could, shoving away his hand, using all her strength against him. To her amazement, she managed to push him down to the floor. He fell with a plunking sound, and sprawled there. For a moment, he stayed flat, then he pushed himself up to where he sat, and stared up at her, still stunned at her force of power, rage contorting his handsome features.

She had pushed him off a bed. That didn't mean that she could fight him and win if he was determined on force.

Retreat, and finding help, seemed her only salvation.

Robert Neville was starting to rise.

She turned and fled for the door, screaming again, shouting her brother's name.

She reached the door.

Robert Neville's fingers threaded into her hair, jerking her back with such brute force that long strands tore away in his fingers . . .

And yet he held her firmly, still.

She shouted for her brother again. Screamed.

Neville's hand clamped over her mouth so tightly that, in a matter of minutes . . .

The room began to spin to black.

CHAPTER 19

It was late at night when the defenders of Langley caught up with the remnants of the English invaders on the road.

Eric was deeply disappointed. He had assumed that the party would stay together, keeping their force and numbers full in anticipation of an attack from the rear.

But they had not. They had chosen the best tactic for eluding capture. They had deserted anything heavy that they carried, they had left their wagons behind.

As they had left behind their own people, those who could not keep up.

Eric and his men had caught up with the injured, deserted on the road save for three women and two priests. The priests were reluctant to give information, and acted the part of men ready to become martyrs to their cause. There was no reason to press for information from them—one of the women was eager to talk. She was contemptuous of the great lord and imperious knights who had so easily left the injured and dying on the road.

They had sacrificed those who could not ride, and those who could not so much as walk or stand, those with broken bones, those bleeding to death. They did so, according to the sharp-faced, sharp-tongued Sir Niles Mason, in honor of their king, Edward of England, the rightful lord of this domain. The woman called herself a laundress, and was obviously a camp follower, but in her disdain for men who would leave their fellows to die, she was noble in her anger.

Eric could ill afford the men to remain with their injured enemy. But he had discovered that men, abused by those they had served loyally, had a tendency to become avid followers of a different man, and, in their bitterness to one, find a lasting loyalty to the other. It was decided that Jarrett, with a group of five able men-at-arms, would take on the slow and tedious task of returning with the injured to Langley.

"They deserted them to slow us down," Jamie told Eric, as they sat on their horses, having divided their numbers.

"Partially," Eric agreed. "And partially to get themselves off the road before we could catch them. They were hampered by the litters they bore, and they knew that we would be riding unencumbered."

"They will have reached Cheffington long before we are able to do so," Angus said. He looked at Eric, sympathy in his eyes. "And once they are behind the walls . . ."

"Once they are behind the walls," Eric said. "We are ever more challenged to use our wits against them."

"Cheffington is built of stone, and the walls are ten to twenty feet thick," Angus reminded him.

"Angus, we can't ride through stone, no matter how thick," Eric said. "There is only one way to make a fortress like Cheffington fall, and it's a tactic with which we should all be familiar.''

"And that is?" Jamie inquired, but looking at Eric he said softly, "When Nigel Bruce held Kildrummy castle, he had the strength and supplies to withstand a very long siege. But they were betrayed from within by the blacksmith who set fire to the stores of corn, and created an inferno, allowing the invaders in, and forcing the surrender.''

"Aye," Eric said.

"We bring them down from within.''

Angus watched them both. "So . . . we must find a traitor among their ranks," Angus mused. Then he grinned. "A traitor, or a host of loyal Scotsmen, afraid of Edward's power, but ready to cast their lot with a victorious force of their own countrymen. And . . . there may be many of them.''

"Exactly, Angus," Eric said. "Exactly.''

Jamie was still watching him. "It is an ambitious undertaking," he said. "Many men might see pure futility in it. And others might see certain death.''

"No man needs ride with me, if he fears I ask too much," Eric said.

Jamie shrugged. "I have little else to do, except fight for country, in whatever fool way we find. But I am glad that you intend to force no man on such an errand. Especially when Edward's troops will soon amass, and our duty by right will be to find Robert Bruce's position, and defend him to the last.''

"I know that time is crucial," Eric said. "In many ways.''

"Crucial, but still, you're going to have to give the men rest somewhere soon along the way," Jamie pointed out. "And as eager as you are to reach Igrainia, we can't walk through stone walls. We must come to a halt until we've figured out how we're going to get the castle to crumble from within.''

He read the tempest in Eric's eyes.

"You must remember, Igrainia is with her brother, and he is young, and unproven—but he is an earl," Jamie said.

"He was injured."

"But not so severely—he was not among the wounded. Therefore, he can ride. Which surely means that he is fully conscious, and able to speak his mind regarding his sister. He is a peer of England, Eric, and can protect her."

"It is just that I have been a prisoner of Sir Niles Mason, and I know how he treats those he despises—those he considers traitors. And I have come face to face with Robert Neville, a man eager for the butchery of "prescribed" execution. I have seldom seem a man so eager for power and glory."

"It still remains that Igrainia is the daughter of a respected earl, though he may be deceased. And once again, she is in her brother's care."

Eric nodded, and turned Loki. Angus and Jamie followed as they trotted back to the main body of men, waiting for their next command.

Eric announced that no man was obliged to follow him further, and he waited. No one left the ranks. Then he said, "We'll ride another hour tonight, make camp, and continue in the morning."

"If any man can get us into Cheffington, Eric, it is you!" Timothy shouted. "And I will follow you to hell and back, if you ask it of me."

A round of agreement rose.

"Let us hope we will not have to go so far," Eric said dryly.

He saw that Gregory was watching him in silence. As he returned the boy's grave stare, Gregory lifted his hand, and pointed northward.

Eric turned his warhorse, and led the way in the darkness.

* * *

The door burst open. Despite his youth, Aidan made an imposing appearance. He was already very tall. Still slender, but well muscled. His eyes were the deep blue, almost violet color of her own, and as he burst into her room, they appeared almost black with indignation.

Robert Neville had disentangled himself from Igrainia the instant he had heard the door moving.

"She is so deeply distraught!" he said, as if greatly pained and hurt.

"Distraught! Robert Neville came into this room while I was sleeping, and intended rape!" she said furiously.

"Igrainia! Never would I lift a hand in force or violence to you!" Robert protested. But his tone changed slightly as he looked at Aidan. "Though she is to be my wife, and will be so, by the will and *power* of King Edward, she has been among those highland wild men far too long. I'm afraid she is suffering from it . . . in her mind."

She had never known, or even suspected, that Robert Neville could be such an excellent actor. He stood behind her straight and dignified, and spoke as if he cared for her with the greatest tenderness in all the world.

She saw a flicker in Aidan's eyes, as if he doubted her word, and believed that under the circumstances, Robert could certainly be right.

"She may be in need of constant care and . . . observance," Robert said.

"I am not in need of anything, except a night's sleep!" she snapped. She stared at Aidan. "I was married by a priest, Aidan. And I swear to you, this man risks his immortal soul and mine. I beg you, as my brother and head of my family, to protect me."

"There is nothing she needs protection from!" Robert

said, as if he were offended to the core that she could even imply any wrongdoing on his part.

Aidan spoke slowly and carefully. "Robert, I believe my sister is upset tonight; it has been a long and trying ride. Have patience. There are matters which must be brought before King Edward and the Church. As she may well be extremely distraught, I will watch over my sister tonight."

"Naturally, as you say, Lord Abelard."

He walked by Aidan, accepting his logic, but Igrainia saw his face as he passed her. She turned after him, ready to close the door as soon as she could after his departure.

He caught the door before she could press it closed against him and spoke softly, for her alone to hear. "Take great care, Igrainia. You will be my wife, and then you can scream until your throat closes, and there will be no one to help you. I will not forget your betrayal of Afton, or me."

She forced the door closed and turned, leaning against it, meeting her brother's troubled stare.

"Sir Robert surely came to talk to you, and ease your mind after all that has happened," he told her. "Igrainia, you know that the king has promised you to him. You will be his wife."

"Aidan, I screamed for you because he was attacking me!"

"Are you certain that he wasn't just trying to com—"

"Yes, I'm certain!"

He turned and walked toward the hearth near the bed. "I had thought that it would be the most natural thing in the world for you. He is Afton's kinsman. He would regain Langley for the king, and for you. The home you had come to know would still be your own."

"He was Afton's kinsman, yes, and as such, I cared for him. I did not realize until this occurred just how covetous he was of Afton, and all that was his."

"You're against the marriage?"

"Aidan, I am married!" she insisted quietly.

"But King Edward can and will see such a marriage annulled."

She wasn't sure that she wanted her brother to know just yet that she didn't want her marriage annulled.

"Aidan, I don't want to marry Robert Neville."

He lifted a hand in a gesture of futility. "Igrainia, you're well aware of the working of the world. It was arranged that you should marry Afton."

"Once again, I am already married."

"You were forced into an unholy alliance."

"Aidan, we may have been on opposite sides, but you're mistaken if you believe that I was cruelly used in any way. Eric is not a heathen, a wild man, or a barbarian. I have seen him be far more just than any of the English invaders in Scotland."

Aidan turned away from her, studying the flames. She walked up behind him, placing a hand on his shoulder. "Aidan—"

He turned and studied her eyes, still troubled. "I wish that Father were still alive."

"But he isn't, Aidan. You are the earl now."

"An earl . . . and yet too often, these men think they can treat me as a boy. And the king thinks that I am his to mold. Igrainia, I don't know what to believe, or even what to say to you. King Edward considers you his ward to bestow as he sees fit. He has said that he will act as a father for you, since your own dear parent is dead and gone. I don't think that Edward even imagines that you might protest Robert Neville as a choice; and, as I did, he probably assumes that Robert Neville is already your friend, and would fill the void of the lord of Langley and husband to you better than any other man. But frankly, I don't think he'll care what your feelings are about the matter. Perhaps you had better reconcile yourself to Neville.''

''All right, Aidan, all I ask is this—until the matter is solved, I beg of you, and this you can demand as my brother—keep him out of my bedroom.''

He smiled at her, a slightly wicked smile that reminded her both of his youth, and of the wisdom he was rapidly gaining. ''I'm here, aren't I? And Neville is out.''

''Yes. Thank you, Aidan.''

He was taller than she by several inches, and already, his physical stature demanded a certain respect. He placed his hands lightly on her shoulders and kissed her forehead. ''Get some sleep. I won't leave you. I'll be in the chair through the night.''

''Bless you, brother!'' she told him. He took the chair by the fire, watching the flames. Igrainia crawled back into the bed, grateful to feel so safe.

But before she could drift into sleep, she said, ''Aidan, I swear to you. Eric is a uniquely honorable man. He has never hurt me, and would not do so.''

She thought that Aidan hadn't heard her, or that he simply didn't have a reply, but after a moment he turned to her. ''I suppose that I must believe that.''

''Why?'' she asked, his tone causing her to lift her head from the pillow.

''We met, in the woods.''

''What?''

''We had a glorious assault planned. We even had word that there would be men staked out to ambush us, and we knew where they were supposed to be waiting. They found out that the information had slipped, and they ambushed us before we even neared Langley. We were fighting . . . and I wound up in combat with him. My sword was broken. He could have taken my head, then and there. But he recognized the Abelard crest and knew I was your brother. And he walked away.''

Igrainia lay her head back on her pillow. She was in incredible danger here, and it appeared that there was little help for her. Even if Aidan understood her feelings and sympathized with them, even though Eric had spared him on the battlefield, he had just admitted he didn't have the power to stop the king from commanding what would and would not happen in her life.

At this moment, she refused to let fear and desolation grip her heart. Eric had met Aidan in hand-to-hand combat. He could have killed him.

He had not done so. He had walked away.

She closed her eyes. She was desperate for sleep, and she would sleep. And there was a way out of every prison.

She would find the way out of this one.

Cheffington had been a fortress in the days of Roman rule when, in conquering Britain, the Romans had decided that they conquered far enough. There was little beyond but hills, rugged mountains, and savages. They had contended that such fierce and murderous men were not really worthy of Roman effort, and so in coming north, they had built walls against the dangerous hordes to the north and forts built of wood on high mounds to protect the men they sent to the outreaches of their domain. When the Normans had conquered England, they had begun to build in stone, and when King David, raised at the English court, had come to claim Scotland, he had seen such natural defenses, and turned them into high fortresses of stone.

But whereas Langley was surrounded by the additional protection of a moat, Cheffington had none. The inner yard, the land between the defense walls and the tower, was far larger; and the castle was more of a sprawling center of commerce, with wagons going in and out on a frequent basis. The outer walls, if attacked by an army with heavy equipment and many men, were not so well constructed for a lasting defense.

But Eric hadn't a large force of men, and no siege machines.

They camped in the surrounding forest, and spent a day watching the comings and goings, and the activity within the courtyard. They watched the positioning and the rounds taken by the guards, and they watched the common men and women, working in the fields beyond the walls, carrying in supplies, going about the daily business in the castle. Masons worked to repair places in the stone and structure where time had taken a toll.

They purchased a wagon from a farmer, and Jamie and Jarrett, never having been seen by any of Niles Mason's men or at Langley, drove through the open gates on the pretense of trying to sell hay. They spent the day circling the public areas of Cheffington, hawking their hay, and watching. They returned and reported what they had seen— the many people engaged in business within the walls, the blacksmiths, weavers, laundresses, dyers, and more as they moved about in the courtyard. Eric found himself most interested in Jamie's information regarding a group of players who came, setting up a stage and a puppet show in the courtyard. As far as Jamie and Thayer could tell, the poor band of entertainers certainly appeared to come and go at will. They spoke with the guards, teased and mocked them, did cartwheels and other acrobatics until they could gain a few coins from those men as well as what they were able to receive from those who watched their shows.

Thayer went back the following day with Timothy and

Brandon. They wore rough wool cloaks and again, hawked hay throughout the afternoon.

The guards were on the lookout, but they were watching for armed outlaws, ready to descend upon them. No one gave a second glance to poor farmers selling their excess hay for whatever they could earn.

They spoke long that night, drawing diagrams in the dirt with the layout of the inner castle and walled town. Jamie talked earnestly about the people with whom he had talked. He was convinced that most of them, terrified of the English rulers, would turn their backs and offer no resistance if "outlaw" troops descended upon the English guard.

Gregory and Rowenna sat in on the discussions. Later, at night, when Eric lay alone, his mind still working in a constant flow of strategy, Rowenna came to him, sitting by his side.

He glanced her way.

"What does Gregory 'see'?" he asked her.

"Images do not come to his mind at will; only God really knows the future, and there are those who would debate that, since He has given man free will," Rowenna said.

"Ah."

"But he believes in the Lady Igrainia," she told him. "He wants you to know that she is strong, and clever, and that she can fight her own battles very well."

"Um. Well, I believe that," he murmured. Then he asked her, "And what of the fact that she is with the English? She is, after all, one of them."

Rowenna nodded. "Yes, she is English. But Gregory doesn't believe that she deserted Langley, rather that she loved her brother."

"I'm trying to believe that as well," he told Rowenna.

She sat silent for a moment. Then quietly, she left him.

When morning came, Eric determined that it was time

for him to enter Cheffington as well, hidden in the hay in the back of the wagon. He had to be careful, since both Niles Mason and Robert Neville knew his face. The robes of a friar stood him well, and he took his own assessment of the strength within the castle.

He watched the entertainers, spoke with the acrobats, and seamstresses.

Throughout the day, he noted the guards—where they met, where they stored their weapons, where they slept, how many were on patrol.

He saw Igrainia.

She was at some distance from him, on the arm of an older, silver-haired knight. Lord Danby, certainly, as the fellow was, deferred to by every man and woman who came close to him. Igrainia was dressed in fine garments, and she talked earnestly with him, smiled frequently, and seemed content and at ease.

He watched her with both relief and anger. Had she been forced to flee? Or was it that she perhaps considered herself free at last, among her people, the English?

He longed to run across the courtyard, seize her, and shake her. He fought the temptation.

A sudden flurry of activity behind the drape drawn by the entertainers caught Eric's attention. He hurried there, drawing the curtain, to find that one of the guards had seized upon Jamie, and was making demands regarding his business at the castle.

He held Jamie by the cloth of his shirt at his throat. Against the pulsing blue vein that ticked just above the man's hold, the guard pressed the blade of his knife. That Jamie could defend himself, Eric knew.

That he could do so now without creating a commotion, he wasn't at all certain.

Eric walked quickly behind the man and seized him

around the neck from behind. The fellow struggled; he tightened his hold. Eventually, he fell.

Jamie stared at Eric, and exhaled. "Very good timing, Eric," he said. "But we can't leave the body here."

"No," Eric said thoughtfully, "we can't."

"Fine sword he has at his side."

"Indeed. We can make use of it."

"Eric, I have befriended one of the seamstresses here. The lass came to me, talking, perhaps saying more than she should. She introduced me to her father the tall, big-necked fellow there. He is the leader of the entertainers. We can cover the body here, for now, and set it in the wagon when they're breaking down."

"How do you know we can trust him?"

"He was at Berwick, and barely escaped."

"You believe him?"

"I saw some of his scars."

"So what are they doing here?"

"Relieving the English of all the coins they can. And watching, of course. Always watching."

That night, Eric, Jamie, and the others rode through the gates with a full wagon. When they reached the forest, they had the bodies of a number of the guards.

And the tall, thick-necked man who led the troupe of players.

Igrainia thanked God that she had been born the daughter of an earl. And though her father was gone, her brother now held his title. She knew that Robert Neville was frustrated to near fury. He dared not insist on any matter since he was only *Sir* Neville and Aidan was *Lord* Abelard.

Lord Danby also provided her with a strange margin of safety. He had arrived soon after she had herself, early in the morning the day after. She was summoned that afternoon to dine with him and the others in his great hall. He was filled with concern for her, and quick to assure her that she was now among her people, and safe.

"I am distressed to hear, of course, that you consider yourself really married to that outlaw," he told her, pacing the hall.

"I am really married to him," she said.

"It's a matter the king will deal with for you," he said, his tone dismissive. "Robert Neville is a fierce warrior in the king's godly fight here, and he is dismayed that you are so against the prospect of becoming his wife. Igrainia . . . the king has said that it will be so, and therefore, you must resign yourself." He came to where she sat at the table, taking both her hands, and looking at her earnestly. "Spend time with him. You'll begin to remember him as your husband's kinsman and good friend."

"I'm afraid, Lord Danby, that spending time with him only makes me realize how he resented the fact that Afton was the lord of Langley."

Danby sighed with frustration. At that point, Robert Neville entered the hall with Sir Niles Mason.

Mason, she thought, looked like a fox. His features were fine, he gave the appearance of an aesthetic man. He was anything but.

He was in the prime of life, a proven knight, hailed for his victories against the bands of Scots who often seemed to arise everywhere. Niles was one of those men who quickly put a subjugated people in their place. Those of little importance, Afton had told her, usually died on the battlefield, but Niles enjoyed the entertainment of a good execution. He delighted in hunting down the men the king most despised, and with the law behind him, creating a show of butchery.

"Ah, Lord Danby, trying gently to talk sense into our ungrateful beauty."

"The lady is deeply concerned with the legality of her situation, and, of course, her immortal soul," Danby said.

"Do you think so?" Robert Neville inquired, following Mason to the table to help himself to Lord Danby's ale. "I think that she has become bewitched, indeed, that she may even be an enemy of the king."

"Bewitched?" Niles Mason inquired. "I think that the lady has fallen where many of the most gracious of our fair and noble women may—to the nightly talents of such an animal as the outlaw. Don't forget, I know this man, Lord Danby. He is a like a wolf in the forest, hungry, matted, dirty, and probably desperate. Not so grand as he would have us believe. He brought down Langley through sickness, not prowess."

Robert looked at Niles sharply. "And he attacked and slew a party of well-trained knights to get back into the castle when he had escaped from it," he reminded him. "He's a dangerous man."

Niles Mason stood by Igrainia, smiling down at her. "Perhaps, when he came into the castle, filthy and diseased as he was, the lady had already decided that she was longing to be rid of her husband, and willing to take up with a wolf."

She started to rise, furious, then afraid. Aidan had come into the room. "Sir, you are speaking about my sister!" he stated.

"Aidan, he speaks because fools are incapable of keeping their mouths shut, and you are above an argument with such a man."

"This will stop immediately!" Lord Danby thundered. "Sir Niles! Igrainia has suffered a great deal and you will not torment her with such discourtesy. And you do, indeed, owe her brother an apology. Where is your sense of chivalry?

There is no need for any of this. The king will soon know
that she is in our care; his churchmen are already debating
the legal issue. In time it will be settled, and Robert, you
and the lady will come to peace with the situation.''

Igrainia was tempted to stare at Robert and tell him that
she would rather die. She managed to refrain. With Danby
here now she was eager to be a guest at the castle, rather
than a prisoner.

''There is one thing that will certainly solve it all,'' Niles
said. His dark eyes, as sharp as his face, turned on her. ''He
was my prisoner. Due to die. And because of the plague he
brought upon good men and women, he escaped.''

''He escaped! You fled with the first sign that the illness
was real!'' Igrainia accused him.

''My life is valuable to the king. If I die, it will be at
arms, defending the realm,'' he told her. ''But that outlaw
was my prisoner, and I swear, he will be so again, and once
his head and limbs and extremities are severed from his
body, the legal state of your marriage will not matter in the
least, Igrainia, because he will be dead. Excuse me, Lord
Danby. Since it seems that I do distress the fair and innocent
Igrainia, I will dine with my men this evening.''

Robert Neville had come to the chair at Igrainia's side.

''Aren't you going to follow your dear companion at
arms—and butchery?'' she inquired.

''No, my dear betrothed. I am going to suffer through
your hatred, with kindness of course, until such time as . . .
as you are legally my wife, bound to honor and obey.''

Igrainia looked across the room and saw that Aidan was
watching Robert. ''Sir Robert!'' he said suddenly. ''On
another matter of importance, I was talking to the head of
the guard. He says that he's greatly distressed. Men have
been disappearing. Can it be that they are deserting, going
over to the enemy?''

Robert scowled.

"Lord Danby, were you aware that a number of men had disappeared?" Aidan asked politely.

"What's this?" Danby said sharply.

"We are looking into the disappearance of a few of the men."

"Why have I not been informed?"

"We were hoping to learn what had become of them," Robert admitted.

"Do so!" Lord Danby ordered.

"Of course, my Lord Danby," Robert said.

Igrainia wondered if he stared with as much venom at Aidan as he did at her. She was grateful for her brother.

She was also worried.

Jamie pretended to be drunk. He weaved as he walked along the alley between the smithy and a grain storage bin.

At the end of the narrow throughway, two guards watched the lower courtyard. They talked, mindless of the drunken peasant staggering his way alone.

"Aye, I was a young man at Berwick. Now, there was a way to make war! Some say that it's the shame of King Edward, and I say it's a way to put a nation of upstarts in their place. We killed them all, men, women, children. There was such an outcry about the children. But I say, kill a Scot when he's a mite, and he'll not become a tick of an outlaw, drinking the blood of his betters!"

"Ride with Neville and Mason," the other boasted, "and you'll see men who know how to best the outlaws. Slay them all. And do it with style. Neville likes to see a man dragged for miles at a horse's arse, then dragged up by rope, dropped, dragged up again . . . and then, if he's not yet dead, Neville sees that water is tossed on him until he wakes up

enough to know that his entrails are about to be burned
before him.''

Looking down the alley, he saw that Angus was coming
toward him from the other direction, weaving as well. Angus
called out to him, calling him a name. He went forward,
calling Angus a bloody asshole.

''What, ho! What's the problem here?'' the first guard
demanded, coming toward them.

''Well, it's like this,'' Jamie said, and beckoned the man
closer to hear his whisper.

He locked an arm around the man's neck.

And slit his throat.

''What is going on there now?'' the second demanded
with exasperation, walking toward Jamie and the man now
slumped on his shoulder.

Before he could make a cry of alarm, Angus stepped
forward. He didn't carry a knife, but he had the mighty
power of his arms.

The man's neck broke with a sharp snap.

''Down the grain hatch,'' Jamie said quickly. ''They'll
start to smell in time, but . . . well, time is what we don't
have anyway.''

Igrainia spent each day with the hours passing slowly and
tensely. She tried to believe that the men who had once
been her captors would ride to release her from this new
imprisonment.

Then she would mock herself. Even should Eric really
care enough to expend the effort, he could not throw his
small number of men against a walled town such as Cheffington. They would also soon be expected to ride to the defense
of Robert Bruce, since her captors would soon be required
to ride hard to obliterate the Scottish King.

If she were to escape, she was going to have to do so on her own. And she was going to have to study her every option with care, since it was unlikely she would get a second chance. She had to watch and learn the habits of those in the castle itself, and in the walled town. She was going to have to leave at a time when no one would be expecting to see her for hours, as they did each night in the great hall. On her own, she was going to have to find a way to travel far from the castle before her absence was noted.

Igrainia knew that she was proving herself to be something of a fair actor. She sought out time with Lord Danby, and talked to him about friends she had not seen since coming to Scotland. They discussed the king's ailing health, and she sympathized with concern. He walked with her around the grounds of Cheffington, and she admired the work of his smiths, and enjoyed the antics of a troupe of entertainers who had taken up residence in the courtyard. They juggled, performed acrobatics, and played out silly little sketches about everyday life. There were a number of women in their group, but they sewed clothing, collected what coins they could gain from whatever crowd would take pause from daily labor. They did not take part in the performances, except for the young woman who sang sometimes while they were setting up. They could be very funny, since the parts of wives, daughters, lovers, and even princesses in distress were played by the men, some of them small and lean, a few big fellows with girth and shoulders. Igrainia enjoyed their good humored jesting about daily life, and some of the wonderful stunts they could do.

She did not so much enjoy the puppet show they performed, in which outlaws were cornered, and a sword battle ensued. An English lord engaged in a sword battle with a Scottish lord, and the latter's arms and legs were torn off. Then in a bawdy twist of play, he was castrated as well, and still, upon the stump of his bloody torso, he continued to challenge the Englishman.

Lord Danby saw to it that she was provided with every comfort, down to rearranging the sleeping quarters of his guests—she was given a new room with a connecting door to Aidan's. She learned that Danby was fond of her brother, and believed that he would grow to be not just an exceptional military man, but that in England, he could prove to be a fine statesman as well. His wife and his only son had died of a fever a few years back, and she realized that to Danby, Aidan had become the son he had lost.

She was sincerely grateful for his devotion to her family, though he argued with her continually, insisting that she would eventually realize that she had been imprisoned, coerced, and so set upon by the outlaw that she didn't know her own mind. She would return to England once Edward had led his own great army against the Scots, and subdued the outlaws. And once there, she would remember a better life.

She was careful not to argue too strenuously with Lord Danby. She knew that messengers had gone out to inform the king that she was now in his care, and to ask the king's pleasure regarding the current state of affairs. But it would be some time until word came back, since the king was so involved in his plan to lead his men himself and crush Robert Bruce once and for all. Danby was sorry—he had liked and admired Robert Bruce.

She spent time with Aidan, trying to explain to him that it was not disloyalty against Edward that had risen in her soul, but rather a chance to judge the ethics of individual men that had made her appear to be a traitor.

She had been in the castle for several days. She, Niles Mason, and Robert Neville had come to a silent truce, since

Danby would have none of the arguments. What barbs were cast between them were subtle.

At night, her door remained bolted from the outside. When she mentioned this, Lord Danby assured her it was for her safety. He didn't try to explain why she was safe being locked in, and she realized that he was telling her as kindly as he could that he understood Robert Neville's determination that she not leave the "protection" of Cheffington.

If she were going to try to disappear, she was going to have to do so by daylight. And probably soon.

Sarah, daughter of Thomas Quinn, head of the players, put the last touches of ash beneath Eric's eyes, and pulled the cloak hood low over his forehead. Eric looked at Jamie. "Well?"

"You're the ugliest woman I've ever seen."

"I've done the best I could," Sarah said. She was a pretty girl with warm brown hair and eyes, somewhat shy and serious, despite the fact that she traveled with actors, loud, boisterous, ever seeking the laughter of those they would entertain. She sang sometimes, luring their audience, and she was excellent in creating new faces upon the men in the troupe for their new roles.

"Sarah!" Jamie said. "You've done excellently. There is, of course, only so much you can do."

"Do I pass? What will the guards think?" Eric asked.

"That you're the ugliest women *they've* ever seen."

"Very amusing." He rose from the log on which he had been seated. "Let's see how you fare. Sarah, if you will transform Jamie, please."

"Me? I was doing fine as a farmer!" Jamie protested.

"Don't make him too pretty, Sarah. Make sure he's at least the second ugliest man the guards have ever seen."

When she was done, Eric surveyed his kinsman. "Why, Jamie, you're almost pretty."

"I always said I was the more handsome," Jamie replied with mock humility.

Rowenna, who had watched Sarah's work upon the men's faces, clapped her hands with delight. "Jamie, you are a beauty!"

Jamie groaned.

"Aye, I'm sorry to say, Jamie Graham, you do make a fair lass!" Angus told him.

"Well, he is a handsome man!" Rowenna said. "Ah, but Angus, not half so grand as you!" she told him.

Angus shrugged. "'Tis more of me to be grand," he teased. "Ah, but I'll never have those gray eyes like Jamie. And with your hair, lad—you'd best be watching out for those English warriors!"

Around them, many of the men roared with laughter.

"Ah, now, I'll be taking my sword to the lot of you!" Jamie warned. But he spoke with good humor, until he walked away and joined Eric, speaking to him gravely.

"This is, by far, the most outrageous thing you've done yet."

"We are doing amazingly well," Eric reminded him.

"Aye, your strategy has worked well. Divide, and conquer—and destroy the number of the enemy by picking them off one by one . . . but do we dare move in so closely as we plan tonight?"

"You were right, Jamie. Most of the people there will gladly turn away, even if they actually know what is happening. We have a great deal in play already."

"Aye, but is it enough?"

"I have to know what is going on in the castle itself. I have to know what has been done to her . . . and just exactly where her true loyalty lies."

"You are risking life and limb—and other body parts."

"Each time we ride against Edward, we do so."

"Aye, but Eric, this is for a woman. Is any woman worth this?

"I'll not lose her to the English, Jamie. I'll not lose to them again."

"What does Gregory have to say about this venture?"

"Apparently, he has seen nothing."

"Um. He's not seen much of late at all," Jamie noted.

"I still believe that there is something about the boy. And I am glad to have him with us."

"If disaster were awaiting, he would have some insight."

"Aye, well, perhaps. Whatever the risk, Jamie, I must go in. Now. I have a sense that time is closing in, when we must see how well our preparations have served us. Aye, the English, I'm certain, are receiving the rumors we have spread. And . . . again, I swear, Neville and Mason will not triumph this time, I swear it. Were we to make a pact with the devil himself, I would gladly do it."

"Careful, Father MacKinley will hear you."

"Ah, well. We'll let him say a prayer for us. In lieu of a pact with the devil, I am willing to accept the ardent words of one of God's holy men. Are you ready?"

"Aye." Jamie shook his head, staring at Eric. "Do you think he'll manage to pray without laughing?"

"Jamie, you'll not be such a lovely maid if I put my fist across your face."

Jamie laughed again, then sobered.

They joined the others.

MacKinley prayed.

That night, Igrainia was seated at the table in the great hall when Niles Mason came in, pulling his gloves from his fingers, and tossing them by his seat with a strange show of pleasure and elation. "Lord Danby, I believe we are earning our keep!" he announced. "There has been word that there are parties of outlaw Scots ranging the nearby woods. No great armies, just bands of men, living off the earth. Some say that Eric Graham is among them. We have spies out there, naturally. I am expecting word regarding greater detail as to their location. As soon as I have it . . ." he turned and smiled at Igrainia. "Well, as soon as I have it, we will see that Igrainia's moral dilemma is solved with all due speed of the law."

Igrainia smiled at him in return, though it felt as if her heart had grown cold. "Are you so certain that you can catch him?" she inquired.

Robert Neville had apparently entered the hall when she had been paying heed to Niles. He walked across the room to the table, giving her the answer as he came. "We are so very certain, that we've started the builders working on the scaffold for his execution," he said. He took his place at the table. He grabbed a leg of fowl from a massive tray being brought in by one of the kitchen servants. "We'll see that you have a front row seat, Igrainia, and therefore, cannot be left to doubt in any way that you are entirely free . . . to marry again." As he spoke, the tray held by the servant, a big woman in loose clothing, tottered. Juice spilled on his sleeve. "Inept old witch!" he cried. For a moment, it looked as if he would beat the servant for the stain upon his clothing. Then, he apparently remembered that he was Lord Danby's guest here, and Danby never lifted a hand against his servants. "Get back to the kitchen, you are fit for lifting and hauling and nothing more."

With a head bob, the ungainly woman started for the kitchen.

"Perhaps your scaffold will remain empty," Igrainia said evenly.

"Perhaps, but I don't think so," he said, scowling at his soiled sleeve.

"I would prefer a more jovial subject for conversation during the meal," Lord Danby said firmly.

A moment later, Aidan joined them. Igrainia felt her brother watching her, and she was afraid. Eric was out there in the woods somewhere, and these men knew it.

She fled the great hall as soon as she could. In her room, she sat before the fire, studying the flames, debating her best course of action. She had to find the Scots, and warn them.

A soft rapping came at the inner door. She threw it open, certain that Aidan had come to talk to her. She was dismayed to see Robert Neville.

"What?" she asked sharply.

"I have come only to talk—with the blessing of Lord Danby and Aidan, of course," he told her.

"Talk about what?" she asked.

He sighed. "Igrainia! I am dismayed that you have suddenly become so hostile toward me! What evil did I ever do to you? I was Afton's right hand at Langley, always. We were close. Our grandfathers were cousins, did you know? Had my grandfather been born before his, I would have been the man you'd been promised to since your childhood."

"But your grandfather was not born before Afton's, and I was his wife, and now he is gone."

She had remained at the door, keeping him to the other side of it. He pushed hard against the wood, forcing her back.

"What can I do to reconcile you to what is to come? I have been cruel with my words, perhaps, with . . . my sense of urgency to be with you. Will you think of me any more kindly if I promise not to make you witness the spectacle of your outlaw's death?''

''Those are fine words, since you do not hold him as yet.''

''Igrainia, it is a matter of time. And whether he is dead or not, the king will soon order that our marriage take place. And it will be binding in the eyes of Rome, since the wretched Scottish king stands under Papal excommunication.''

''Robert, you are a fool to want me. What if I am carrying this man's child now? Will you want your first son to be another man's?''

His face grew mottled with a swift and impotent rage. The look he gave her assured her instantly that he had never considered such a possibility. ''Such matters can be dealt with, Igrainia. The date of a child's birth can tell the father. And it is sad but true that far too often, babes perish soon after birth.''

''You would murder a child?'' she demanded.

''Infants die,'' he repeated.

She stared at him, afraid to exhale. ''Get away from me,'' she said quietly at last. ''Get out of this room.''

''Igrainia—''

''My brother is surely next door by now. And we are in Lord Danby's castle, and word has not come from the king. Get out.''

His face grew darker. ''One day, my lady, you will rue your discourtesy to me. The time will come when you beg me on bended knee for mercy . . . and I will remember every single time you looked at me with disdain.''

''Get out,'' she told him.

He slammed his way out of the room. She sank to the bed shaking. Almost immediately, there was a tapping at the outer door. She gazed across the room at it. What now?

Niles Mason to tell her just how he intended to torture his captive—once he reached the scaffold?

"Yes?" she called.

"The tub, my lady," a soft voice called in return.

"Enter, please," she said distractedly. The door opened, and she saw the servants who had come, bearing the tub and the kettles and the water. She thanked them as they began to stream in, then stood, and went to the connecting door. She tapped, and waited for her brother to answer, then slipped in to see him. Aidan was seated at a writing desk near the fire, quill in hand.

She sank to her knees at his side, shaking, then covering her hands with her face. "Aidan, I cannot bear him!" she whispered.

He instantly set down the quill, took both her hands, and drew her up and over to the side of the bed to sit with him. "Igrainia, please don't be so distraught. I have watched Robert Neville these many days . . . him and Niles. They are the kind of men who have made the hatreds here so very bitter. But, of course . . . King Edward's anger caused the first butchery, at Berwick, and it seems that in this war, there is no brutality beyond the abilities of men. They are within the law—the most cruel executions are ordered for such men. In Scotland, men wept. But in England, crowds cheered as William Wallace went to the scaffold, was hanged until half dead, then . . . well, never mind, you understand what I am saying. I can't protest Niles and Robert when they are doing the king's will. But I've been looking into legal and ecclesiastical books, and I've been busy, writing my own letter to King Edward. I've questioned the validity of a marriage when Robert's relationship to Afton was so close . . . and I've written that your affairs are incredibly important since, were I to die without issue, my inheritance would fall to your male heirs, should you produce them."

Studying him, she smiled slowly, then threw her arms around him. "Aidan, you are a wonderful brother. A truly wonderful brother."

He smiled back. "Aye, well, I'm doing my best. Especially since you were fond, at times, of referring to me as your *little* brother when we were younger. In fact, you did so far too often!"

"That was before . . . when we were at home. And I was very mature, and about to be a bride, and you were being sent away to learn the ways of a knight."

"There were good years, when we were young. In those days, the knights I saw were the great men who rode in the tournaments. I didn't know the truth about war. I remember when King Edward was such a gallant and stately figure on horseback, a golden, glowing giant, truly royal, and a gentle man to his wife, at the court . . . ah, well, that ended when his first queen died. Now . . . now he is a king who will have his way, so it seems that the best I can do is persuade him that he must make this marriage wait."

"Bless you, Aidan." She kissed his forehead. "Thank you." She rose. "Aidan, I truly love you, and thank you for everything you have done, and . . ."

"And?"

"And I pray that you forgive me."

"You were taken captive, Igrainia. There is nothing to forgive."

She lowered her head and bid him goodnight. Perhaps he had nothing to forgive her for now. Soon, he would. She was grateful to him for using his wits, letters, the law, and the church, to try to help her.

It gave her a new hope.

And yet, she dared not think that it would be enough.

When she entered her room, she disrobed thoughtfully for her bath, still contemplating the various ways and means she might attempt to escape. She heard something, and thought that it seemed a furtive sound. Glancing to the door, she saw that the hall door remained tightly closed. Still . . .

She glanced up at the arms and plaques covering Lord Danby's walls. Before slipping into the tub, she intended to arm herself.

The water remained hot. Soothing. It seemed to seep into her muscles, and ease some of the strain of the day. Then . . . she heard a noise.

And she stiffened, her fingers tightening around the hilt of the knife in her hand.

CHAPTER 20

He waited until he was certain that she had closed the connecting door to her brother's room tightly and securely. Then he waited again, dead still behind the tapestry, listening intently until he could determine that she was alone. He heard the slight splashing as she got into the tub, and at last, he dared to slip from behind the wall covering, and tread lightly across the room. He had to reach her quickly.

Silence her.

Make sure that she didn't scream.

But just as he reached the rear edge of the tub, she rose and spun around. Water came sluicing down the length of her sleek, bare, perfectly curved and angled form. Her right arm was raised, and there was a lethal looking knife in it. With instinctive speed he reached out in time, and caught her wrist.

She stared at him, her mouth opening for the scream he

had feared. He stepped closer, bringing her soaked body against his as he clamped his free hand over her mouth.

The knife fell into the water with a plop. She struggled furiously in his arms.

"Igrainia! Stop! It's me, Eric."

She went dead still in his arms. Violet eyes widened to glimmering moons. He eased his hand from her mouth, but continued to hold her wet and trembling form next to his own.

"Eric?" she repeated, and stared at him with incredulity. With what she saw, she was doubting what she had heard. He pulled the hood from his head, and the wig, hastily constructed from dark horsehair. His face, he knew, was still lined and distorted with the fleshy paste Sarah had made, and he hadn't muscles, but breasts, created from a folded chest padding.

"Eric!" She blinked, and stared again. Then she realized that it was, indeed, he, and she gasped in horror, trying to struggle from his hold again. "You're mad! What are you doing here? They mean to hack you to pieces, they are all but drooling with relish just from the idea of seeing you finished in the most torturous way. You must get out of here as quickly as possible—"

"Igrainia, hush!" he said sternly, searching her features thoroughly for any sign of harm. "I know exactly what they are planning. In fact, I watched them start to build the scaffold today."

She gasped again. Then she spoke in a heated whisper. "You are a fool! Eric, please! They are lethal, like a pit of vipers. You are in an English stronghold. Eric, this door is not bolted from the inside, but from the outside. My brother is in the next room."

"I'll go, I'll go!" he assured her. "Not just yet. I hadn't expected this opportunity, to come so close, to speak with you. It was easy to find work in the lord's kitchen—they need strapping maids like me," he said wryly. "But then I proved to be too clumsy for the lord's dining hall . . ."

"Oh, my God, Eric! You should be locked away—you were in the great hall tonight? For your own good, someone should lock you in a dungeon!"

"But being so severely reprimanded in the kitchen brought me here. Again, such a well-fed countrywoman as I can really haul heavy kettles of water."

"Eric, you are mad!"

"I had to know . . . about you."

"About me?" she breathed, studying his eyes. Her own narrowed. "You thought that I had chosen to come here? You—"

"I have seen you about the grounds with Lord Danby."

"Lord Danby is one of the most decent men I have ever known. He is loyal to King Edward, because he is a noble Englishman born to give him allegiance. You have come in the middle of the night to accost me and accuse me . . . I should scream, call every guard in the castle, and let them teach you a sense of humility. I should—"

"Igrainia!" He pressed his hand against her mouth once again. "I have seen more," he said softly. "And I know Niles Mason and Robert Neville. I had to make sure for myself that you were safe." He stared at her a long moment before removing his hand from her mouth.

"Far safer than you at the moment!" she assured him, still indignant.

"And I thank God," he murmured.

She was shaking. He lifted her from the tub, and no amount of ridiculous padding he wore could keep him from feeling the rise of his own body at the sweet wet contact of hers. He groaned, cradling her against him, lifting her chin, finding her lips, forgetting that seconds and life ticked by as he tasted and savored the depths of her mouth. He felt the beat of her heart, the fullness of her breast, and before he knew his intent, he had taken her to the edge of the bed before the fire, fingers stroking over her length, assuring himself that every inch of silken flesh remained unmarred.

She pushed away from him then, looking at him with her eyes still as large as twin violet moons. "Eric, *please*, I'm begging you, you've got to get out of here! Your nose is already twisted. Wait . . . I'll fix it." She made an adjustment. "Eric, for the moment, believe me, I am in no danger. Lord Danby is a good and decent man. But you are in the greatest peril."

"I can't go so quickly. Not now . . . now that I am here."

"You must."

"Igrainia, you can hardly send a *woman* away like this!" he protested, catching her slender hand to show her the extent of the problem. She snatched her hand away quickly, but couldn't seem to restrain a soft laugh.

"Eric, you are the *ugliest* woman I have ever seen. For that alone, a man such as Niles Mason or Robert might see you hanged and beheaded! Listen to me, please, they know that you are here, and that your men are in the woods—"

"I know that, Igrainia, I heard them talking in the great hall. I have heard even more," he told her, his voice growing deep with anger.

"Eric, they are only trying to get their spies to tell them exactly where to find you and your men in the forest, don't you understand, and then they will come after you."

"I know what they're doing."

"When they have their 'details', they will hunt you down. And they have men and arms and tremendous strength here. So you understand, you must leave!"

"I will," he said huskily. "Soon. But I did risk much to breach your door."

"You risked a great deal," she accused him, "to see if Robert Neville had breached it first."

"If he had, he would lie dead already," Eric said curtly.

"Did you come to kill a man because of your pride?"

"It is not my pride for which I will one day kill Mason and Neville. It will be for all the agony they have brought."

She studied his eyes carefully, and lowered her head, and he knew that she was wondering what had really brought him to her that night.

"Igrainia," he began.

But she lifted her eyes to his once more, perhaps not wanting to know if he had dared come here for hatred and vengeance or for care and concern.

At this moment, he only knew that he had come so far. And that she was alive and real, damp and naked, and in his arms. His wife, and a woman of vitality, and passion, with a tempest in her soul to match his own.

"Eric," she whispered urgently. "My brother is just beyond that door! Please, you've got to leave."

"I can't. Not yet."

"You must."

"Is your brother in the habit of breaking in on you?"

"Of course not."

"Then . . ."

She fully understood his intent. He felt it in the trembling of her body against his own. The sparks of flame seemed to dance in the air from the heat within her.

"You must be gone, Eric! I'll scream," she protested, though her pulse beat like thunder at her throat.

"Not tonight," he whispered softly against her ear. "Tonight, you must be the quietest lover."

"Eric, you've got to get out of here."

"I will. But as I have pointed out, I cannot go like this. You have led me to the edge of madness, certainly. If you wish me to leave with any haste . . . then you must hasten to be with me.''

''You fool, you could die if you stay.''

''I think I will die if I leave now.''

She let out a soft cry of impatience and threw her arms around him. The kiss she molded upon his lips definitely reshaped his nose. He rolled with her upon the bed, aware that her urgency was half borne of fear, yet ignited by that frenzy. She was wet and sweet from the bath, hot and trembling, and more sensually afire than he had ever remembered. He could not help but long to touch each inch of her, the swell of her breasts, indent of her belly, the damp ebony thatch between her legs. His padded ''breasts'' were quickly lopsided, but he was glad of his woman's dress, making access to bare legs, hips, and groin an easy affair. She bit into his shoulder, strangling back sound as they came together, and locked her long legs around him with a determination for speed that became a thunder of arousal. He had never been so incensed, so afire, driven into frenzy. And the way that she arched and strained . . . rubbed against him. It was fear, it was urgency, it was sheer wonder at stolen moments . . . life or death . . . and there were moments when he'd have gladly died, rather than desert such a volatile, desperate bliss.

Climax burst upon him with a violence that nearly brought a groan from his lips. He felt her teeth sinking through cloth into his shoulder as she locked against him in a final spasm of ecstasy. Then, almost instantly, she was pushing him away, and there were tears in her eyes. ''Please!'' she whispered. ''Please! You must get out of here.''

He looked down into the beauty of her face and wondered why he had not seen it from the day he had met her. He smiled. She wasn't aware that, aye, he was in danger.

But not quite so gravely as she might think.

It wasn't time to tell her yet what might be dangerous for her to know.

"Eric, please, I am so afraid—"

"Igrainia!" they heard, and there was a tapping at the connecting door. Aidan, from the next room. "Igrainia, is all well?"

Their eyes locked. "It is only the woman with the bath, and she is leaving!" she called.

"She is leaving now!" she whispered vehemently to Eric. "You must get out of here, and away, and you cannot worry about me, I am safe, with Lord Danby here. Do you understand? You must be forewarned; they will hunt you down in the forest and kill you. They'll be gone in a few days time, riding to join Edward's great army. Where . . . I'm certain you must be as well to join Robert Bruce."

"Bide your time carefully!" he told her in return. "We will be coming for you."

"No! You must get away, and leave me to my devices. Don't let them catch you in the forest. And, dear Lord, Eric, please leave now. I could not bear it if you and Aidan were to meet here, if you . . . you and he were cast in a battle of arms where one had to kill the other. *Please!*"

Her eyes were shining again with a hint of tears.

"I'm going," he assured her softly. "As soon as I fix my nose."

A moment later, he held her in his arms a brief second, then started for the door.

"Wait!" she cried, running after him. "How will you leave? There are guards in the halls."

He pulled the horsehair wig down over his head. "Don't worry. The guards let me walk on by. I'm the ugliest woman they've ever seen."

He touched her lips again. Then, scooping up two of the water kettles, he knocked on the hallway door. A moment later, it was opened. The guard, looking at him, shuddered. "They do breed some fine lasses in Scotland, and some damned ugly ones as well!" the man said crudely. "Get back to the kitchen, woman, and for the love of God—stay there!"

Eric started down the hall, feeling the man watch him as he went. He heard the footsteps as the fellow came in his wake.

"Wait! You, there!"

He paused, as directed. Turned slowly.

The man had unsheathed the long sword at his side as he approached. Eric waited, making no move. The man had to be closer to him. He didn't want him crying out an alarm, or calling others to assist him.

He waited, waited . . .

The guard came close enough. Eric took one of the heavy kettles and swung. The thud of the metal against the man's skull seemed very loud in the darkened hall.

The guard fell to the floor, making no more sound than an expulsion of breath. Eric bent quickly to retrieve the body, and hurried down the hall to dispose of it. He was tempted to go back to Igrainia at that moment.

There might still be too great a risk tonight.

Soon. Neville and Mason needed 'details' to hunt him down?

By morning, he determined, they would have their details.

With the light of dawn, there was a great flurry of activity about the castle. Igrainia came down quickly, anxious, terrified that she would discover it was all because Eric had been caught on the castle grounds in the middle of the night.

She was greatly relieved to discover that was not the case.

She was pleased at first to discover that both Robert and Niles were gone, riding with a party of armed men.

But then Lord Danby informed her, and not without a gentle empathy, that they had discovered the hideout of the rebellious Scottish outlaws, and had gone to corner them in their forest lair.

Fear filled her heart, and she knew that she could wait no longer.

She lowered her head before Lord Danby, and prayed that he would forgive her, but she felt that she must be alone, and would spend the day in her room.

She did return there. But only to procure the plainest brown wool cloak that she could find among the belongings of the late Lady Danby which had been so generously bestowed upon her. She took the knife as well that had graced a plaque on the wall, the one she would have used against Robert Neville had it been he attacking her in the bath—the one she had raised against Eric, and nearly driven into him

In her days of constant watching, she had learned that the troupe of players came and went, but they departed the walls of Cheffington at dusk, and she could not wait that long.

There was, however, a wagon that left the stables mid-morning, filled with the rushes that were swept from the great hall each dawn when they were replaced with new. They were usually filthy, what with the hounds that lay within them and the mud from the boots of the men who came and went so constantly from the hall.

But only one man drove the wagon out of the gates to discard the old rushes in the distant fields, and she didn't think that anyone would think to search through dirty rushes for a woman they did not expect to find trying to escape.

She left her room quickly, certain that were she to come across any of the guards, she would sweep by them, and if she was stopped, she would merely say that she was looking for Lord Danby. But the halls were empty, and she easily made her escape from the inner castle walls, and started a brisk walk through the walled city.

It occurred to her as she walked that she did not know if Aidan had accompanied Robert and Niles and their men-at-arms to the forest. She felt a terrible quickening in her stomach as she worried about her brother. She couldn't go back. Nor could she change her course of action.

She walked quickly to the stables, hesitating at the stall of a silversmith as she watched the wagonmaster come and go with his sacks of rushes. During one of his trips outside the stables, she slipped in, and when he came back almost immediately, she dived into a fresh pile of hay that lay stacked deep against the walls. She waited. When the man departed again, she crawled quickly from the hay and headed for the wagon.

Before she had quite figured out how to reach it and crawl beneath the filthy rushes, she felt a hand on her shoulder. She spun around in instant fear.

"Aidan!" she gasped, seeing her brother there, his eyes grave as he surveyed her.

"Where are you going?" he asked quietly.

"I . . ."

"To warn the Scots," he told her.

"Aidan, I have to leave here!" she told him desperately. "The king will rule in Robert Neville's favor . . . please, God, Aidan! You have to let me escape a life with such a man."

"Igrainia, you have no faith in me."

"You have admitted that you cannot fight King Edward!"

"I am an English peer. I cannot allow you to betray the King of England."

"I am not trying to betray the King of England, I am only fighting for my own life."

Her brother stared at her with eyes too much like her own. "Your life has never been threatened, Igrainia."

"Aidan! As you have said, you have watched them, come to know them ... my life might as well be ended, were it to be at the mercy of such a man as Robert Neville."

"I cannot let you go to the enemy."

"Aidan, please! Aidan ... Aidan, I am married to him. I'm going to have his child. Neville has said that he will kill it if a child is born. And he will do so, don't you understand? I must leave here!"

"Will you use that knife you have stolen against me if I refuse to let you go?" he asked.

"Aidan! My God, you're my brother, and I love you, but I must leave!"

She suddenly realized that he wasn't listening to her. There were sounds coming from the alley and courtyard beyond the stables.

There was a hint of smoke in the air.

"By God, what has happened!" he exclaimed suddenly. Turning from her, he rushed to the stable doors. Igrainia ran after him in time to see that armed horsemen and sword-swinging foot soldiers were running everywhere. Buildings were on fire; people were screaming, rushing about.

"Sweet Jesus!" Aidan breathed, and drew his sword, stepping out into the melée.

"No!" she shouted.

He had gone after a man fighting one of the men in Lord Danby's guard. The fellow turned on him, and Aidan gave a good accounting of himself pressing forward.

But another man in mail and armor joined in the fight. And then another. Aidan's sword went flying from his hands.

"No!" Igrainia shrieked, rushing forward. She picked up

the sword, and rushed forward, putting herself between the men and her brother, wielding the sword from side to side before the two attackers.

"Igrainia, give me my weapon, I'll not hide behind your skirts!" Aidan cried. He reached around her, grabbing for the sword, then pushed her aside, ready to leap forward. His sword clashed with that of one of the attackers. She stood in stunned amazement for a moment; the smell of smoke was stronger now. Buildings in the walled town were burning.

Aidan was fighting for his life. He fought hard, but again, his sword flew. And again, Igrainia dived to retrieve it, coming between Aidan and the man he faced.

"Please . . . !" she gasped.

"Igrainia!" Aidan roared. "Give me my sword!"

But the attacking swordsman lowered his weapon, then he lifted the visor of his helmet.

"Jamie!" she gasped.

"Get out of the battle, Igrainia!" Jamie told her furiously.

"No, no, you cannot . . ."

She broke off. A mounted man in full armor appeared in the doorway of the stables. The sun, casting strange rays in the smoky air, hid his visage. His horse pawed the ground for a moment, then he ducked his head and rode in.

CHAPTER 21

The glittering knight on the great warhorse lifted his helmet and visor from his head, casting them to one of the foot soldiers who ran in closely in his wake.

Eric. Magnificent upon the horse. The knight triumphant.

He stared down at her.

"My lady, you are covered in hay. And throwing yourself before sword blades once again, casting yourself into the middle of the fight to protect another man. Who also appears to be wearing a fair amount of hay. What is this man doing, hiding behind your skirts, my lady?"

Aidan stepped forward indignantly. "I do not hide behind my sister's skirts, and I am more than willing to fight and die for the honor of the king!"

"This is your brother?" Jamie demanded.

"The earl?" Eric inquired.

"I'd thought that you had met," Igrainia said.

Eric's eyes fell on Aidan's. "Metal to metal, but never face to face," Eric said.

"I will still fight and die, sir, for the honor of England!" Aidan said with great dignity.

Eric's horse pawed the earth again, nervous at the smoke. Eric reined him in and spoke to Aidan. "England's honor has never been at stake, Lord Abelard. Only Scotland's freedom. Jamie, will you see to it that the earl and his sister are conducted back to the great hall? I will be along at all speed, as soon as I have seen to it that the fires are put out and the gates and prisoners are secured."

He started to turn his horse, now visible through the haze as Loki. Igrainia ran after him, causing him to pause.

"Secure the gates . . . ?"

"Cheffington has fallen," he told her.

She stared at him, not believing it was possible. "Any power can be destroyed from within," he added softly.

"And . . . Lord Danby?" she asked.

"Ah, he is well. He was accosted at the castle, and was never able to draw a weapon, nor was one used against him." He kneed Loki, and was gone.

Dead men lay in the alleys where commerce had so recently taken place. Igrainia could not look down, choking as she stepped over them on her return to the great hall. She wanted to talk to Jamie; she wanted to know how the Scots had managed to slip in and take Cheffington with such uncanny speed. She felt the tension between her brother and her outlaw, and she felt as well that Jamie seemed no more certain of her than of her brother, and so she walked in silence.

The great hall was empty when they reached it.

But there were spatters of blood upon the walls and floor. She lowered her head, sorry that unknown men had died. Unknown men, bred to a different loyalty, cruel men who rose high in the ranks when wars were fought. They rose for their ability to kill with blind determination. And as well, there were decent men in every war, those who fought as they believed their duty demanded. She felt ill.

They died as well as the others. And she was sorry. And sick.

Aidan took Lord Danby's chair at the head of the table.

"And what now?" he asked Jamie.

"We wait. Sir, Igrainia, please." He waited until she had taken a chair, then chose one at the end of the table himself, easing his long booted legs upon it as he watched the two of them. Igrainia stared at him, then her attention was drawn as two women entered from the direction of the kitchen, bearing a large flask of ale and goblets.

At first, Igrainia barely noticed the two. Then she stared at the one woman and nearly gasped aloud. It was Rowenna.

She set the ale before Jamie, pouring him a cup, which he accepted with thanks. The other young woman was pouring ale for Aidan as Rowenna brought a cup to Igrainia. Igrainia bit her lip, longing to strike out and send the cup flying. She restrained herself, refusing the cup, which Rowenna set before her. She had been certain that the woman had been about to speak to her; whatever she had to say, Igrainia did not want to hear.

She had been rescued from a life with Robert Neville.

She didn't think that she liked any man at all. Her brother somehow added to her sudden sense of fury when he spoke to the young woman serving him, catching her wrist. "You are the singer, are you not? With the players that Lord Danby so welcomed here."

She flushed and pulled her hand away. "I am a singer, aye. But Scottish," she said proudly, and quickly walked away. Rowenna paused to exchange low words with Jamie, then both women retreated to the kitchen.

She, Jamie, and Aidan sat. Jamie seemed completely at ease. Igrainia felt a growing tension. Time passed, then at last, Eric came striding into the hall. He smelled of smoke, as if he had been engaged in dousing the fires. He had cast off his mail and defenses, but his sword was sheathed in the belt around his hips.

"Lord Abelard," he said, addressing Aidan, "you are a prisoner of Robert Bruce, King of Scotland. Soon, you'll be escorted north, until such time as either your exchange, or your fate, shall be decided. For the time being, you are welcome to your quarters here, and every possible courtesy will be granted to you."

Aidan sat in silence for a moment. "Perhaps, as one of your courtesies, you'll be so good as to explain why you think you will hold this castle."

Eric shrugged. "I'm not certain I intend to hold this castle. But as to the difficulty . . . the one element in this war the English continue to forget is that the land, castles, and towns they hold are Scottish. Our war is not just fought by men-at-arms, but by every man and woman with a yearning to be free. We came in here because the people were willing. We didn't break down the gates, they lay open to us. We've been in for days now . . . just waiting for half the forces to ride out, seeking to find us and slaughter us."

Igrainia listened to him incredulously. Then she knew why he had dared so much last night. His men had been in Cheffington—to what extent, she couldn't know—for days. They were the reason for the disappearance of so many men. They had been befriending the people who lived and worked in the walled village.

She felt her cheeks grow hot, wondering if the only danger he had faced last night was the fact that her brother slept in the next room. He hadn't been afraid of the English forces riding after him—he had been waiting for their number to be gone so that he could come in with full force and arms when the odds were more in his favor.

"So," Aidan murmured. "I am courteously confined to my quarters. What about my sister?"

"Your sister, *my* wife, will be with me."

"You do realize that I am the earl, and the head of Igrainia's family, and since she was widowed at the death of Lord Afton, she can legally be no man's wife without my blessing," Aidan said coolly. "The King of England has made other arrangements for her."

Igrainia stared at her brother in astonishment. "Aidan!" She glanced nervously at Eric, who appeared tired and irate. Despite her own simmering anger with him at the moment, she rose and walked to Aidan's chair. "You know that I loathe Robert Neville."

"Perhaps there are better things than to choose between a Scottish wolf and an English viper," her brother told her.

"And perhaps there are not other options, and therefore, I would have the wolf over the snake!" she said.

Aidan stood abruptly then, staring at Eric. "Well, then. She has chosen a wolf. You have my blessing."

"Thank you," Eric said politely, then glanced at Jamie. "I've a few more matters to attend to. If you would escort Lord Abelard—and his sister—we'll meet back here."

Jamie led the way up the stairs, bowing as Aidan entered his room.

"Igrainia can enter through here as well," Aidan said.

"Igrainia will be staying elsewhere."

Aidan looked as if he would disagree.

"Aidan, I will be all right," she said.

"Yes, of course. You chose the wolf yourself," he said, and she bit her lip against the strange look he gave her. His door closed sharply.

"You're down the hall," Jamie said.

"Why? Why am I being sent up here at all? Why am I being separated from my brother?"

"It's just for the time being," Jamie said pleasantly. Then he reached a door and opened it for her. She still stared at him accusingly. "Igrainia, your brother is an English nobleman. And he is your brother. Eric will be along shortly. There is a lot to be considered and planned now, Igrainia. Be patient."

She would have liked to be patient, but she was too distressed. She was rescued once again . . .

And once again a prisoner.

By the time he arrived up the stairs, she had worked herself into a long simmering anger.

Rowenna had been to see her, bearing food, talking excitedly about the ride through the forest in her wake, the injured men they had come upon, and the careful and cunning way they had watched Cheffington, day after day. She left the room without ever knowing that Igrainia was disturbed.

He had traveled many miles, hours, and nights, with his men, of course. And with Rowenna.

She sat stiffly in a chair in the strange room, all but locked into place, there had been so much tension in her limbs for so long before he arrived. When he came in and closed the door, she didn't move. He walked around the chair slowly, meeting her eyes, then crossing his arms over his chest.

"What is the matter with you, Igrainia?" he demanded.

"What is the matter with me? Why nothing. I am a prisoner again. The faces of the captors change, and that is all."

"You're not a prisoner. You're here for your safety and protection. And because you're my wife, and it's the room I've chosen."

"You will pardon me if I am not weeping with ecstasy."

She couldn't sit any longer. She rose, putting the chair between the two of them. "You made a fool out of me," she told him. "Last night . . . I was nearly dying with fear that you should be discovered. You already had men in the castle. It was all but yours. If you had been caught in here, you would have shouted out an alarm, and, I imagine, men would have poured from the woodwork and the kitchen servants would have taken up arms."

"We had men in the castle, yes. But if I'd been caught here last night, many more lives would have been lost. The bloodshed would have been terrible, with the number of English troops who were in residence then."

"But you could have told me—"

"I couldn't have told you anything. You could have inadvertently given us away to Lord Danby or your brother."

"I was desperate to warn you about them when you were eager that they leave!" she exclaimed.

"I did what I had to do," he told her flatly.

"Yes, you always do, don't you? Seize the castle, for your king. Capture the lady, for your king. Marry her, for your king. Sleep with her, for your king. And now . . . let her shake through a night with fear. You don't dare trust her. She's English. She might do something—that would be against the honor and glory of Scotland!"

"For the honor and glory of Scotland!" he repeated, a note of anger entering his tone. "Aye, for that a man risks his life again and again. Do you know how many men willingly risked their lives to come here?"

"Oh, aye! They followed you once—and Langley fell to them. They followed you again, and they have taken Cheffington. The men—and women—who have followed you. It is amazing, Eric. You have the ability to take everything. Including people. Those who rode with me and were injured . . . Now they are your most loyal followers. And even a poor girl and deaf-mute I befriended . . . they are yours as well.'' She paused for air.

''Ah, you're speaking mainly of Gregory and Rowenna, aren't you? How curious. And correct. We've gained a great deal through you. I was most determined that I would not come here without Gregory—and, of course, Rowenna.''

''Ah, Gregory! You—the great warrior! Always so willing to trust in his 'sight'! Aren't you ever just a little afraid that his vision may be hazy?''

''Actually, Igrainia, I do believe in God. And it seems that the boy has an affinity with his maker. I've yet to see him proven wrong. So I do listen to his words, then follow what judgment I have made on a situation. And he is a fine young fellow. I am always glad to have him in my company.''

''Him, and Rowenna. Well, then, surely they are free to celebrate with you on this newest victory. You should return to them.''

''I don't believe it,'' he murmured.

''Just what is it that you don't believe?''

''That you, the noble beauty, beloved and admired by all those she touches, can be jealous of a poor scarred girl.''

She braced herself and spoke as coolly as she could manage. ''I am not jealous. How could I be jealous? I am simply the prize that you were ordered to take. A pawn, passed from player to player in the game of war.''

''Ah.'' he said, not protesting her words. ''Well, she will accompany you on your journey north.''

She started at that. ''She will accompany me . . . north.''

''My king—and the honor and glory of Scotland—call. We have to join with Robert Bruce, and prepare for Edward's advance. Sirs Neville and Mason are surely fuming and in a rage out in the forest somewhere, and they remain a danger.

I'm sending you north, to the safety of my family in the highlands.''

She felt ill, suddenly riddled with fear again. He would be leaving soon. To join the king. And he proved himself to be almost a magician, his strategy against odds was so calculated and cunning.

But King Edward himself was riding against the Bruce now.

And when Edward led the might of the English army, victory was almost assured.

She managed to remain standing, but couldn't voice a reply.

He walked over to her. She realized that she wanted him to take her into his arms. She wanted him to tell her that she was wrong, that she wasn't just a possession important in a tug of war of power. That he wanted no one else when he had her. That he had ridden for her because he had discovered that she was as important to him as his beloved Margot had been, that . . .

He loved her.

But he didn't pull her into his arms. He plucked at something in her hair.

''Hay,'' he said. And he turned away from her. ''Of course, like your brother, you'll be treated with all the respect due your position. I know how you love your bath . . . one will be sent immediately, because it's growing late, and, of course, you will be at the celebration we're planning tonight . . . and of course, my men will all be grateful for this new great glory we've achieved in our pursuit of you.''

''I—will not celebrate any more slaughter with you!'' she countered.

''Oh, but you will. You'll come down tonight, on my arm—or dragged along by it.''

To her great dismay, he turned and left her.

* * *

There were a number of pressing matters that had to be settled.

He was grateful that Jamie was with him, since his cousin could deal with statistics and defense as efficiently as he could.

But there were certain details he had to deal with himself.

The first was Lord Danby.

He found the dignified old lord where he was being held, in his own chambers. He stiffened by the fire as Eric entered, as proud and noble a warrior as Eric had ever seen.

"So," he said. "Cheffington has fallen. And I was incarcerated in my own room as it happened, without even raising a sword."

"Cheffington, my lord, is Scottish," Eric said simply.

"And you believe you will hold it?"

"I believe that the Scots will hold it, and that, sir, were you to decide to honor Robert Bruce, it might remain your holding."

"I am not one of those men seeking only grandeur, comfort, and riches, Sir. I do not bend and bow to the wind, but do my duty, whatever that may bring."

"I see. And it brought you Robert Neville and Niles Mason."

White lashes fell briefly over Lord Danby's eyes, but he gave little other sign that Eric's words had disturbed him.

"Sir, you had the daughter of an English earl in your holding. It was the correct and chivalrous thing to bring her back."

"And would it have been the right and chivalrous thing to hand her over to Neville?"

"Had the king given an absolute order, it would have been so."

Eric smiled. "But the King's *absolute* order did not reach you, and so you did not."

Danby nodded.

"The lady is my wife, and will remain so," Eric said. "And though it was certainly not done for my accord, I am grateful that you chose to protect her. And though I swear, if it is ever in my power, by God, both Neville and Mason will die. But it has not been our policy to show brutality or cruelty to men for proving that they are loyal to their King, yet obedient as well to the dictates of their conscience. We intend you no harm. You will be taken north, where the King of the Scots has greater allegiance, and if and when arrangements are made, you will be returned, in the best of health, if not spirits, to Edward."

Danby bowed his head. "I am grateful for the honor and chivalry you have proven in battle, sir," he said stiffly.

"And, I, my Lord, remain grateful to you," Eric told him.

He left Danby's quarters then, wishing that the man were on their side.

His next stop was Aidan's room.

He found the young Lord Abelard busy at his writing desk.

Aidan looked up as he entered, set down his quill, and rose.

"My sister, sir?"

"Your sister is well, I assure you."

Aidan nodded, watching him. "In the woods that day . . . you would have killed me, if you hadn't realized who I was."

"When engaged in a sword battle with a man who intends to kill me, I am most usually called upon to fight him unto death," Eric said dryly.

"In truth, I do not hide behind my sister's skirts."

"In truth—I did not mean to accuse you of doing so."
Aidan inclined his head.

"I came to give you my thanks."

"For?"

"You were here when Igrainia needed you."

"She is my sister."

"Ah, but many men might have seen only the white or black of war, the right or wrong of his own side."

"I assure you, I did nothing to aid outlaws."

"Of course. But . . . you are welcome to come to the hall tonight."

Aidan squared his shoulders. "I'm a prisoner, and therefore, not interested in communication with the enemy. Sir, you may be as decent as my sister says. But I am an Englishman. I may acknowledge certain virtues in such a man as you, but I will not turn my back on my country."

"I understand," Eric told him. "But I must say as well . . ."

"Yes?"

"I'm glad that I didn't kill you."

He left Aidan then. There was still a great deal do to before the evening.

The first was to plan for tomorrow.

CHAPTER 22

At first, Igrainia ignored the bath that was sent. She was nearly beside herself with misery. It had been one thing to accuse him of regarding her a prize of war, a wife as ordered by the king—and another to reconcile herself to the fact that it was true.

And though he enjoyed his time with her, it was a pleasant interval, but not one that would disturb any other desires he might find upon a long ride in her absence.

Without her absence, perhaps . . .

Now he wanted her at a celebration.

She intended to walk down without him touching her. To walk down with the "nobility" he had granted her.

And so, she bathed and was ready when he returned for her, apparently braced and ready for a fight, a very determined look on his face.

She shot through the door before he could speak, or touch her.

When she came down to the hall, she felt her temper melt somewhat. Even as she walked down the last of the steps, men were coming to meet her. Jamie first, who bowed over her hand and kissed it. Angus, Brandon, Thayer, Timothy, Allan . . . and finally, Father MacKinley, whom she had least expected to see.

"You've taken to arms, Father?" she asked him.

"Many a priest travels with troops, Igrainia. And many a man of the cloth has picked up a sword."

"So you pray for these men now?"

"Aye, that I do. And, of course, I have other functions," he said with a wink. But he didn't explain what functions he meant. He smiled at Eric as he came behind Igrainia, then went on to speak with Angus.

"Your place at the table awaits, my lady. Ah, in fact, we've arranged the meal so that you many take your customary chair."

She couldn't shake his firm touch upon her arm as he led her to the table. There were new faces in the hall, now, mingling with those she had come to know. She recognized the players who had presented the shows in the courtyard, the pretty young singer, and others. There were smiths she had seen at work with the horses and repairing armor, and there were the masons she had seen working during the day.

The hall was filled.

It was not Rowenna who served ale to them, though, but another girl who had been among Lord Danby's kitchen maids.

Eric was to her left, in Lord Danby's chair, and Jamie was to her right. Beside him, handsomely dressed in a clean tunic of Eric's colors, was Gregory. His silent smile for her was so warm that she could not help but return it.

Then she noted Rowenna, not seated, but standing at the end of the table, talking earnestly to Father MacKinley. And she, too, was differently attired. She was truly beautiful, and the scar could not touch the glow and magic that seemed to have come to her face. She was wearing a soft white linen gown, and a circlet of flowers in her hair.

As if aware that Igrainia was watching her, she turned to her. Her face seemed to beam anew as she offered Igrainia a radiant smile.

"She is such a graceful, natural beauty, is she not?" Eric whispered to Igrainia, his head low, so close to hers.

"Indeed," Igrainia agreed stiffly.

Eric rose suddenly, tapping his knife on the table, and drawing the attention of those in the hall. When they were silent, he spoke.

"We've much to celebrate here tonight. Another victory against our oppressors, and in it, the safe return to our fold of my wife, the Lady Igrainia. With each such step we take, we come closer to the goal of our people, a free and united country."

Cheers greeted his words.

"We have endured years of battle; it's likely that we will endure more long years of hardship until we have truly evicted the foreign powers from our lands. William Wallace sacrificed his life in the pursuit of a dream for his country, not for power, for glory, or for gain. Few men have ever been so willing to sacrifice everything for a cause. But now a man who is aware that his loyalty was often misspent has been crowned king of Scotland, and has taken to the field, and in the brutal deaths of so many of his family members, in the imprisonment of the women he loves, he has learned the agony of sacrifice as well, yet casts his life and his crown against a mighty strength. That Robert Bruce is king, and will prove himself king, marks a new beginning for us, one proven in this victory we have wrested today. We feast at the hope and prayer of a new, free Scotland. Our land. And what better way to toast the future than to celebrate the hopes and dreams of the future of a man and woman Scottish to the core. Angus, Rowenna, may the wedding you celebrate tonight bring you the love and loyalty to strengthen your hearts always, in the good and bad days that lie ahead, and may the unity of your hearts and souls be constant, and may your children be blessed to grow and prosper in a country we will call our own.''

He raised his cup. Around the room, other cups rose as well. More words of cheer and congratulations were called out, and as Igrainia watched, still astonished, Angus walked over to Rowenna and gripped her hands. The two of them stared at one another with radiant adoration.

Then Father MacKinley raised his hands in prayer, and those seated stood, and first he praised God for their lives and their victories and the food they would eat. And then he announced that the wedding would begin.

It was simple and beautiful, Father MacKinley's words spoken with strong, fluid tones, and the bride's and groom's vows given with certainty and assurance. When they were pronounced man and wife before God, there were more cheers, and the happy couple were swept up and kissed and congratulated all around in good cheer.

Igrainia hadn't dared to look at Eric through it all. But as the cheers rose and the feasting began, she felt his hand on her arm. ''Aren't you wishing to congratulate the happy pair, my lady?''

''Of course,'' she murmured awkwardly. He drew them up. They approached, and she had to force a smile, she was still so stunned. But Angus took her in a bear hug, thanking her for being the great lady she had proven herself to be, and swearing his loyalty to her as well as to Eric. Then Rowenna embraced her as well, and thanked her. ''My life ... my life was nothing until I met you. I'd have never known Angus, a man so great and so gentle, and so unaware that this scar mars my face.''

Shame filled Igrainia. She hugged Rowenna in return. ''You owe me nothing; it is Eric who brought you to Langley. And you have been deeply and sincerely appreciated there, and you are beautiful, and it is only the truly blind who do see the scar you wear, and . . . forgive me, for ever doubting you.''

Rowenna drew back, perplexed. ''Doubting me?''

''Never mind, it doesn't matter. I pray for your every happiness.''

''We will be together, you know. Traveling north to safety. Eric and Angus have both insisted,'' she said.

Igrainia nodded. ''It will be wonderful to have such a good friend on the journey.''

The pipes had begun to play. As Rowenna smiled at her, innocent of any evil thoughts Igrainia might have had, Angus claimed his bride.

Igrainia found herself swept into the steps she had learned from Jamie at Langley. Then she was dancing with Thayer . . . Timothy . . . Allan, and Father MacKinley. Great trays of food filled the tables, ale flowed freely, and the night passed in a whirl. She saw Eric, with the players, dancing with the girl, whose name was Sarah, with the wrinkled old woman who cooked the meat in the kitchen.

But he didn't talk to her until it was very late, and the newlyweds had left the hall, and the men were beginning to leave, or to find a place upon the table, or on the floor in the rushes, to sleep for the night.

Only then did he take her arm.

And she found herself hurrying before him up the steps, head lowered as they entered the room he had chosen. She heard him close the door, and she knew that he leaned against it, and that he watched her.

"Well?" he said softly.

She couldn't find the words she should have spoken quickly.

He walked to her, not touching her yet, just the sound of his voice brushed her ear.

"Aren't you feeling just a wee bit ashamed?"

"Yes," she said simply.

Then he did touch her, pulling her into his arms. She looked into his eyes, and admitted, "Very ashamed." Then she was free, she knew, to throw her arms around him. To press her lips to his with a wet, open-mouthed hunger, and die a little in the rough plunder of his tongue, the force of his hands upon her. She felt that she melted against him, into him, like snow on the mountains, or steam rising into the cool air of a summer morning from a stream that had been warmed by the sun the day before. Their clothing was shed, and she lay with him, in a tempest of triumph, in the tenderness of time, and in a strange, sweet and savage ecstasy of belonging. And when at last they lay together, spent, sated, and exhausted, she was newly thrilled when he suddenly rolled over her, pinning her fiercely, and saying, "What a little fool you are! In truth. We bested an impregnable castle for you! Do you think that I would lead such a force if I were so easily entertained elsewhere?"

"I am the wife you have now!" she reminded him.

He looked down for a long moment. Blond hair fell over his forehead, somewhat shielding his eyes from her view.

"You are the wife I cherish now," he said simply, and lay beside her again, pulling her against him.

After a while she told him, "Gregory is right. We are going to have a child."

"I never doubted his word," he said, his voice slow and heavy, as he was falling asleep.

And yet, she added, "It's not going to be a daughter, Eric. Not a girl with hair like wheat in the sun."

"You will have my son," he told her. And she could not read the emotion in his voice, but his arms were around her, and so she chose to rest in them.

"You must sleep," he told her. "Tomorrow, we will ride hard, in different directions."

"Tomorrow?" she said in dismay.

"We dare not risk the time. Edward's troops have assembled. The men and I must reach Robert Bruce, and you must be far away from here."

"Tomorrow!" she repeated with dismay, turning in his arms.

"Igrainia!" he said, as she rose against him, her eyes damp. He let out a soft moan, and cradled her into his arms, giving way to a new rise of passion. "We can sleep along the way," he decided.

Allan would lead Igrainia and her party north, Eric had decided. He was most familiar with the trails to the highlands, and with Eric's family who resided there.

There were still a few last minute details to be settled before they rode. But while Allan and several of the men were already mounted, as well as Aidan Abelard, the women had yet to leave the castle and mount their horses.

Seated atop Loki, Eric gazed down at the bodies that had been gathered in the courtyard. Those which they had hidden in their secret war against the castle by night had been removed from their hiding places, since Eric did not mean to leave Cheffington riddled with any form of disease that the rotting corpses might bring about.

But along with those of the men who had been killed was

that of a woman. Beginning to rot and bloat, it was a horrible sight. And yet recognizable.

"Jennie," Father MacKinley said, mounted by Eric's side. "She must be buried quickly. I don't want Igrainia to see her."

He was startled when young Aidan brought his horse around to view the pile of the dead. He looked at Eric. "Who killed her?"

"I don't know," Eric said evenly. "She was the one sending you information from Langley. And she left Langley. Apparently, she came here."

Aidan looked down again. "Her throat is cut."

"Aye, so it appears."

Aidan stared at Eric again. "Lord Danby would never order such a vicious and senseless murder."

"I sincerely doubt that Danby ordered it." Eric waited for Aidan to accuse the Scots—since they were the ones she had betrayed.

"Neville," he said softly. "Or Mason."

"So it must have been," Eric agreed.

Aidan looked at him strangely. After a while he said, "I remain your prisoner—or a prisoner of your king. But you can rest assured that I will guard my sister as passionately from certain Englishmen as any of your outlawed men."

Eric smiled, but sobered, nodding solemnly. "Thank you, Lord Abelard." Then he looked at Father MacKinley again. "See that the bodies are quickly removed; I will go in and hurry along the women."

Igrainia stood in the hall, far more prepared for the journey north than she had been for the abrupt ride here.

But she was loath to go.

Once they had reached a certain distance, Eric would turn,

and ride away to join with his king. A great battle was about to commence.

And she might never see him again.

He came striding with purpose and determination into the hall, looking for her, she knew. And he saw her, standing before the great fire, still and pale.

"What is it?" he asked her.

Her heart seemed to quicken. It was so strange. It was as if she couldn't remember a time when his towering gold presence was not the looming factor in her life—and in her heart.

She threw her arms around him. She shook, trying to hold back sobs.

He held her, smoothing back her hair. "We must go now."

After a moment, she nodded. The waiting was always the misery for women. Whereas . . . Well, he had come for her. He had found her, seized her from the hands of his enemy. She was his wife. She was cherished. Wanted, certainly.

And yet . . .

He'd never said that he loved her.

War awaited. He had done what he had to do. She was moving on to safety, to the heart of his family, where she knew, just as she knew the clan bond between him and Jamie, that she would be protected every day of her life, no matter what his fate in battle for the honor of his king.

He paused, and kissed her deeply, cupping her chin, and studying her eyes as he was prone to do. Then he said at length, "Come, we must really go."

He caught her hand, led her out, and helped her to mount. He leaped atop Loki, and in a mass, they rode through the gates of Cheffington.

For two hours they rode together, north. Then it was time to split. Allan, in charge of the men escorting her, Rowenna, a few of the players and other men and women from Cheffington, Lord Danby, and Aidan. Gregory would be riding with the men to battle.

There was little time and no privacy when they parted ways. Eric rode Loki to a point next to her own horse, reached across the bit of space, and pulled her into his arms. His lips touched hers with both tenderness and passion. And he told her, "Guard our child."

She nodded.

Tears blurred her eyes.

And he was gone.

CHAPTER 23

It was Igrainia's love of water that warned her, the following morning, of the presence of the horsemen so very near to where they had stopped for the night.

On waking, she had seen Allan, awake and aware, at the edge of the path leading to their encampment. Near her, Rowenna still slept, while her brother and Lord Danby were sleeping nearby, guarded by Brandon and Timothy.

She could hear the trickle of the stream. She had slept on a bed of soft earth and grass, and had thought that she would awake cool and cramped since they had not lit a fire. Allan had said that they must not. She had realized then that Eric and his men were going after Neville and Mason before joining the king, and that Allan had been warned to take the most extreme care until they had traveled far to the north.

She understood. None in their party had questioned the absence of a fire.

And she had not wakened stiff and cramped. The woods were cool, but not cold; summer had even allowed for some beautiful sunshine this year, and the day dawning through the trees promised to be beautiful.

Sitting up, stretching, she could look over the brush between her and the stream, and see that a light mist was rising from the water. She rose, and stretched, careful not to wake those around her.

She trod softly through the grass, weeds, and wild flowers, and moved down a distance, determined not to wake those who had not risen as yet. She cast off her shoes and hose, and waded in. The water rushed over her toes, as pleasant as she had imagined. She hunched down, heedless that she dampened her gown, since it would surely dry in the day's promised sunlight. The water splashing over her face felt wonderful. It tasted cool and delicious.

But as she smoothed back her dampened hair, she heard sounds that didn't belong in the forest. The jangle of a horse's bridle . . . the sounds of men speaking. She held completely still, and strained to hear. She began to catch pieces of conversation. Snatches of sentences, phrases, words . . .

". . . and the tracks to the east are well laid."

"And . . . certain that we are on them."

"Aye, we'll pick up the trail this . . ."

". . . close, I know that we're close."

"Aye, and the moment we've got them . . ."

". . . they'll not all survive the first onslaught."

"Any man who survives . . ."

". . . the woods will be alive with the smell of burning outlaw entrails."

". . . need only follow . . ."

As she sat entirely still in absolute horror, she realized

that she knew the voices of their speakers. Robert Neville had spoken first.

And Niles Mason was the second speaker. The one enthusiastic to smell the burning entrails.

She rose very slowly. The pleasant water at her feet suddenly felt as cold as ice. She swallowed, barely able to breathe. Seconds swept by her as she realized in desolation that something had to be done to waylay the Englishmen, or else every man among the Scots would be captured, and immediately cut to ribbons.

Neville and Mason were leading a body of armed men. Those who had set out to cut down a large party of outlaws in the forest.

Allan was leading a group of prisoners and refugees, with perhaps ten able men to wage battle if necessary.

She knew that the Scots were famed for their lightning attacks, and the defense maneuvers that allowed them to beat back huge forces that offered incredible odds.

But these odds were overwhelming.

They would be overcome, and the men would be slain, and she would be captured again. And the hint of what life might have been if she had been free—even to wait in fear for each battle of this war that was waged—had been so sweet that even this moment in the stream was charged with agony.

"Igrainia!"

She turned. Rowenna, smiling tentatively, had come to the stream. On the bank, she was stripping off her shoes and hose.

Igrainia paused just a split second longer, feeling the beautiful breeze in the air, the soft warm kiss of the rising sun on her cheeks.

One way or another, she was going to wind up back in the custody of the man she loathed.

She sprang to life then, racing to the place where Rowenna stood, clamping her hand over the other girl's mouth. Rowenna struggled for a moment in surprise, then seemed to acknowledge Igrainia's whispered, "Shsh!"

She drew her back from the stream, whispering quickly then. "They're there, Neville, Mason, and their men. They're on to us. I'm going to take a horse and split the trail—"

"No! My God, they'll seize you. You can't—"

"Rowenna! Understand this. They will attack and slaughter the entire party and I will be seized, one way or the other."

"I can't let you do it. I will scream, I swear it. Allan will stop you. We can get away." Her voice quavered. She knew that they could not get away.

"Rowenna, you know as well as I do that we cannot! You've got to help me, because Allan will allow himself to be captured and slaughtered like a boar in order to keep us safe. And Neville will have me anyway. Don't you understand? Please, God, don't let me wind up back with them, and have the deaths of these men to live with, day by day, as well!"

Rowenna breathed slowly.

"I can go." she said. "Neville doesn't want me."

"Niles Mason is a murderer. I am the only one with a chance. If I go, Rowenna, Allan may know how to reach Eric's forces. Rowenna!" She shook the girl. "Neville wants my lands in England, and he wants to be lord of Langley. He can't be those things without me. He wants to marry me . . . to . . . own me. Please, you have to help me. You have to keep Allan occupied while I get a horse . . . and get away. Rowenna, I am begging you, for the love of God, if we chance much more time, they'll find us right where we are now, and everyone will die. I am an excellent rider, I've spent much of my life on horses, and I'm riding a well-fed mount that had belonged to a rich man. Now. I must go now!''

Rowenna's wide-eyed look of desolate horror assured Igrainia that she understood the peril. She understood that Neville could not have Langley or English riches without Igrainia.

"Go to Allan. Keep him talking, while I take my horse. He'll want to know where I am. Tell him that I'm bathing in the spring, and that I need a little time, and privacy. He will not have trouble believing that,'' Igrainia said firmly. She didn't wait for Rowenna's reply, but grabbed her hose and shoes and stumbled into them as quietly and quickly as she could. She started back, following the water's edge to the camp, treading in determined silence past the others who were still sleeping, or just beginning to wake. She found the graceful, beautifully bred mare she had been riding. There was no time for a saddle. She slipped the mare's bridle from the line where the animal was tethered, urged her from the group of horses and into the clearing. She walked her through a nonexistent path, winding through the trees, to avoid having to pass any point in Allan's vision, and once she had made her way back to the main road, she mounted at last.

She retraced the steps they had taken the night before, then began riding hard along a path that took her far from the little party in the woods. She crossed the streambed, passing by the point where Neville and Mason had been camped. So close . . . yet through the night, neither party had known of the other's presence.

She doubled up on the track where she had run, making certain that there were plenty of hoofprints in the dirt along the trail, and that she had broken limbs from the trees and bushes along the way. Even if she hadn't been missed at first, if Rowenna had explained that she was bathing in private, Allan would soon begin to worry about her.

Riding near the enemy camp, she judged her distance. She needed to come close enough to ensure that someone heard a commotion along the trail.

And she needed to stay far enough ahead to force them out to follow her . . .

Follow her long enough so that they were led far, far away from the others.

They had just woken from the night's encampment and were preparing to start out on the day's ride when Eric saw Gregory—who had been about to mount his horse—suffer a strange spasm as he stood there. For a moment, he shook, violently.

He dropped his horse's reins, and doubled over.

Eric strode to him instantly, afraid that the boy was having a seizure.

But Gregory rose, still looking as if an unendurable agony tore into his flesh.

"What's wrong? Father MacKinley! Come, quickly!" Eric commanded.

MacKinley came running over. Gregory was mouthing words.

"He says that we must double back instantly," Father MacKinley began.

"I can read that . . . I can read his lips fairly well . . . but what is that last word he is trying to say?"

MacKinley stared at him.

"Igrainia. He is afraid for Igrainia. He is saying her name."

Igrainia knew that the men were behind her.

She hadn't waited for them to mount their horses and

start out in a breakneck pursuit, but rode ahead at a ground-eating gallop herself. Neither Niles nor Robert would feel the need to do so, since they believed they were following behind a somewhat hampered party of prisoners and women.

But when she had put some distance between herself and the campsite, she slipped from her horse and knelt down, setting her ear to the ground. At first, there was nothing. Then, she could feel the vibrations, and she knew that they were following behind. As she rose and mounted again, she once more had reason to be thankful for the time she had spent reading Afton's books on the art and skills of warfare when she had been a prisoner in her own chambers at Langley.

She could only pray that Allan would have the sense to gather help before making any attempt to come after her.

Nudging her horse firmly, she started to ride again.

Eric and his men doubled back, returning along the trail they had followed, trying to catch up with Neville and Mason and their men. As he rode, he knew that they had laid the trail, knowing that he would send Igrainia to safety before joining with Robert Bruce.

He damned himself for his stupidity as he rode.

They found the English encampment by the stream. And they saw the broken brush and branches leading to the northwest. The trail had been covered by a number of horses.

As he prepared to mount and ride again, Jamie told him, "Listen!"

He did. He heard the hoot of a night owl, soft on the breeze.

It was day.

Jamie returned the call.

A moment later, Allan came bursting through the trees on his horse. He was white-faced and grim.

"Igrainia?" Eric said.

"She tricked me," he admitted, his white features betraying his dread for the words he had to say. "She sent word that she was bathing . . . and created a trail for them to follow."

"She tricked us all," Aidan said, riding up behind Allan. "She knew . . . she knew that they would slay your entire party. And possibly me and Lord Danby as well. After all, we stand in the way of what he wants."

Despite the sick, choking rage that grew in Eric, he knew that there was nothing he could say to them. He knew Igrainia.

And in his heart, he knew that she had made the only move she could. His head spun with a cold, sick fury, yet it was against himself.

He had misjudged his enemy.

"We ride after them," he said simply.

And he spurred Loki forward, racing against the wind.

As the day wore on, Igrainia was in pain. She hadn't come upon a stream again in hours. She had ridden so long and so hard that her thighs ached. She was hungry, and yet her stomach seemed to be roiling. At last, she nearly fell from her horse.

She had to stop, and had to find water.

For herself, and for her horse.

She dismounted. For a moment, she was so dizzy that she had to pause, bend over, and wait until the dark cloud over her vision passed by. She straightened. Her stomach rebelled. She stumbled into the bushes and then emerged, more desperate than ever for water.

She tried to mount again, and realized that she hadn't the strength then to leap onto the back of her mount. She led the mare to a fallen log, and managed to drag herself back on. She spoke to the horse, telling her that she was an animal, she was supposed to instinctively know how to find water. At last, by standing still on the road, she could hear a bubbling sound, and she followed it through the trees at the side of the road, crashing through branches and limbs, until she came to the water. She drank too fast, and found that she was sick again. She drank more slowly. Cooled her face with the water. The horse drank its fill. Finally, Igrainia led it from the trees, then, before mounting again, she dropped to the ground and placed her ear against the earth.

She heard the vibrations instantly.

They were close.

So much closer than they had been before.

She stumbled up, and onto the horse.

Rowenna rode hard to make her way to Eric at the lead. Her cheeks were tear-stained. "It's my fault. I knew, but she knew . . . and she said that he would get her one way or the other, and that she couldn't bear it, being his captive, and knowing that so many had died because of her."

Eric glanced at Rowenna.

"It is no man's fault, except my own," he said.

And he pushed harder, riding ahead.

She didn't need to drop to the ground to hear the horses.

They were right behind her. She leaned against her horse's neck, urging her, pleading with her, begging her onward.

She knew that she couldn't outrace the many riders.

She slipped from the horse, swatting the mare on the rear so that she would keep running.

Then she ran herself, into the woods. She dodged through the trees, trying to put distance between herself and the road. If she were lucky, the road still ran by a stream. If she could reach the stream, run through the water, they might lose her trail.

She ran so fast that she missed a root tangled between two trees. She reached for the trunk of one, trying to keep herself from stumbling over it.

She grasped only a thin ribbon of leaves. They ripped from the stem as she tried to hold on. She went down hard, striking her head on more roots pushing through the edge of the soil. For a moment, the earth spun. She lay stunned and winded. The world blackened. She kept her eyes closed, trying to stop even the blackness from spinning. She blinked furiously, opened her eyes, and saw stars. She blinked again, opened her eyes, and saw Robert Neville.

She blinked. He did not disappear.

"Well, well, my lady!" he said.

He reached down for her. She wanted to scream. She hadn't the breath to do so. Nor to cry and rant and sob, and damn the heavens.

He pulled her to her feet. She wavered there . . .

Then the blackness spun before her eyes again, and what he did then didn't matter.

"Whoa, Eric! Hold up."

It was Jamie who called to him. He reined in. Loki pawed the ground, protesting. Eric had sensed that they were close. Even the animal seemed to know it.

Jamie caught up with him.

"It's Gregory. He nearly fell from his horse."

Eric dismounted, leading Loki back. Gregory was on the ground. Sweat created a sheen on his face. His lips were moving. MacKinley was on the ground beside him.

"He says that . . ."

"What?"

"He says that they have her."

Eric stood in paralyzing, impotent rage and pain. Then he started to turn, ready to race again, desperate just to reach her.

"Wait!" MacKinley called.

He forced himself to pause. MacKinley didn't need to decipher Gregory's next words. Jamie was speaking to him, and they were words of reason.

"Eric, we need a strategy. We can't go running in like madmen. They'll kill us all, and she'll be no better off. She knew that this morning."

He paused in an agony of indecision, torn to run, but knowing that Jamie was right. Once, he had told Margot that he must escape the castle at Langley, that he had to leave her to come back with the men to rescue them all. He had known that he had been right then. He had not known that in the time needed, the consequences would be deadly.

But now, equally, he had to make the right moves.

"They have her," Jamie said. "And they'll be setting a trap, knowing that you'll find out, and that you'll come after her."

Jamie was speaking the simple truth.

Silence seemed as loud as thunder.

Then he heard himself speaking, and his voice was unbelievably calm and rational. "They want me as well," he mused. "Well, they can't have us both."

"What do you mean to do?" Jamie asked him.

"Offer them a trade."

"A trade?"

"I'm going to offer to surrender to them."

"Jesus, Eric! You know what they'll do—"

"I know what they'll *try* to do." He managed a rueful smile. "I run with some of the finest rebels in all Scotland. Excellent swordsmen, uncanny marksmen."

"Whatever you're planning," Jamie said softly, "it could fail."

"Then I will pay the price," he said simply.

She heard the voices before she opened her eyes, and hearing them, she determined not to let them know that she was conscious.

"We have Igrainia. The sensible move is to run," Robert was saying.

"Igrainia! I want the outlaw," Neville said.

She barely opened her eyes, leaving her lashes low. At a distance, she could see that though the men had dismounted, they were in full armor and had their weapons at the ready. Robert and Niles Mason were closer to where they had laid her at the foot of a giant elm.

"We should ride on as hard as we can, to meet with King Edward," Robert persisted. "The outlaw will have to join up with the Bruce—all Scotland knows that the King is nearly ready to rise and lead his army. And when Edward leads this battle, the rebel Scots will fall like flies. This man, like the others, will most probably die."

"Is it that easy for you? He's the man she's supposedly wed, and while there is a question as to her marital status, none of her riches become yours. And if he is dead . . ."

"So what is your plan? We were supposed to ambush him and his outlaws in the forest. Fall upon them as they slept. Now, they are well armed, and dangerous."

"If we threaten to kill Igrainia—" Neville suggested.

"Threaten to kill her! Danby and young Lord Abelard are probably with them!"

"If we threaten to kill her as a traitor to the crown."

"If the King finds out, which he will, with Abelard and Danby among them, I will receive nothing but a pool of mud in some desolate hole!" Robert said.

"What if Abelard and Danby die in the melée?"

"Good Lord, Niles, you've lost your mind! The men will never stand for it."

"Oh, I think they will. Most of these fellows are my own, hand-picked, hand-trained, and accustomed to what must be done to win a war. And, of course, not only do I have finely trained Englishmen in my crew, but Scotsmen. Aye, yes, good Scotsmen—kin and followers of the murdered John Comyn, and they will not mind in the least if they are obliged to kill a few Englishmen who are standing in the way of justice."

"But the murder of two peers!"

"Not the murder. The battle loss. The sacrifice. They'll both die heroes."

Igrainia could bear no more. She struggled to her feet and accosted the two. "If you kill my brother, you had best kill me," she said.

"My lady, I would like nothing more than to oblige you," Niles said.

Robert looked at her with equal distaste, but stared at Niles. "There must be another way. I would just as soon lock the Lady Igrainia eternally into a tower myself, which may certainly be the way to endure marriage now, as it stands. But I must be legally wed to her, if I am ever to have Langley and her English properties and rents."

"Don't worry, my dear," Niles told her, smiling pleasantly. "We will think of another way to kill the outlaw."

* * *

"It's dangerous for us to send in any man," Eric said, pacing a groove in the earth in the center of the copse where they had gathered to talk. "They may simply seize him, and we'll lose a man and solve nothing."

"I'll go in," Father MacKinley said.

They all paused and stared at him.

He shrugged. "I'll be safe. Even King Edward himself has yet to order the execution of an ordained priest."

"These men do not have to answer to the powerful peers, and the Church," Eric reminded him.

Aidan Abelard stepped forward. "I'll go with him."

The group grew silent again.

"How can we trust an Englishman?" Angus demanded, spitting in the grass.

"They are holding my sister," Aidan reminded them.

Eric studied Aidan. "They might not pause at killing one of their own either, Aidan."

"They can't kill us at first, they won't get what they want. If I ride with MacKinley, they'll be more likely to believe that you're making an honest offer."

Aidan had a point. And if he meant to go over to the English, this was the time for him to do it.

He and MacKinley started riding again. Their horses were rested, and they galloped forward on the path.

"You and I are going to take a walk," Robert Neville told Igrainia, taking her arm.

She balked, looking at where Niles Mason stood, at the center of the large clearing where they had paused, staring back up the path. He was giving a messenger last-minute instructions. The man was to ride back and warn them that the Lady Igrainia could be killed in the action if they were to attempt an attack.

Their men were now ringed in an arc, ready to meet a party of armed riders, should they come on.

Dusk was coming.

"I don't care to walk anywhere with you."

"No? Well, you will be walking with me. Actually, you will be doing anything that I say. And I'm not waiting any longer. We're going to get to know one another intimately, now."

"You're about to engage in battle! You can't take the time."

"I can be amazingly quick."

"I'm not going with you," she said, straining against the arm that held her.

"That will suit me, my lady. I don't think I'll be particularly bothered by an audience. I had thought that you might mind, but then again, you're accustomed to mating with animals, so what will a few eager eyes looking on mean to you."

She was afraid that he meant it.

"You don't want to do this."

"Oh, but I do."

She shook her head. "You don't want to do this now, because then you'll never know. If you manage to kill Eric and King Edward forces our marriage, and I do produce a child, you'll never know if it's yours—or his. And will you murder your own child? Or spend your life wondering if the son you're raising is your own?"

He stared at her with a mottled fury. "I believe you've hinted that you're with child. So if your firstborn dies, it will simply be a pity, one of those sad things that happen in life."

"Am I truly having a child? Or have I used that as an argument against you?"

Before he could reply, Niles Mason shouted out to him. "Riders coming!"

Robert had her wrist and he dragged her after him, meeting Niles on the road. Igrainia saw Father MacKinley and her brother trotting toward them.

Aidan's eyes were instantly for her. "Igrainia," he said. "You're unharmed?"

"Aidan!" Robert said in mock distress. "Why would I hurt the woman I love and long to marry?"

MacKinley had dismounted from his horse. "Sir Niles Mason, Sir Robert Neville, I have a message for you from the Scotsman, Sir Eric Graham."

"Give it," Niles commanded.

"Sir Eric is willing to give himself over to you on the condition that you immediately give his wife over to my care, and that of Lord Ewan Danby. She is then to be allowed to travel northward to a clan seat of his family, until the time when her child is born. Then, if it is still the order of the English king, she will return to Langley, and meet her obligations to her overlord."

Igrainia stared at MacKinley in disbelief. Eric couldn't allow himself to be captured again. He didn't understand that these men would not take him to a place of execution. They would perform their vengeful murder here and now.

"No!" she said. "He can't do it. I won't be a part of this! I won't—"

"You are not involved in this, Igrainia," Aidan said softly.

"Not involved! But—"

"Tell Sir Eric that his proposal is an amazingly generous offer," Niles Mason interrupted, "but . . . he must understand. His execution will take place here—and now. Aidan, you and Lord Danby may accompany him, but not his men.

If I see a single one of his Scottish outlaws with him, the Lady Igrainia will forfeit her life as well. Is that understood?"

"He will ride in alone, except for Lords Danby and Abelard," Father MacKinley said.

"No!" Igrainia protested. "No, tell him not to do this! They'll kill all of you, any of you—"

"This is an agreement between knights, Igrainia," Aidan interrupted.

"And one last thing," Robert Neville said fiercely. "The Lady Igrainia watches."

"No, this isn't going to happen!" Igrainia protested furiously. "Aidan, I'm telling you, I've heard them—"

"We need to discuss the exchange," Father MacKinley said firmly.

"Once the outlaw has arrived, he comes to me, and we allow Igrainia into your care, Father. And yours, of course, Aidan, and that of Lord Danby. She watches the event, and then she is free—until the birth of her child."

"What guarantee do we have that she'll return as promised?" Robert demanded.

"I am her brother, and an English peer," Aidan reminded them. "She will do as I say, and as her king commands."

Robert started to protest again. Niles set a hand on his arm. "We are agreed. Bring the outlaw in. And we will hand over the lady."

"Well, of course, he is going to make Robert shut up!" Igrainia exploded, trying to jerk free from Robert's hold. "They don't mean to honor a thing they say—"

Robert pulled her back, hard. "We are all men of honor!"

"Honor!"

"In a minute, you'll be gagged, my lady!" Niles Mason warned.

"Lord Abelard, I believe you can now return with the terms," Father MacKinley said, addressing Aidan. He came to Igrainia's side, and reached out, ready to take her hand from Robert's hold.

"What is this?" Robert demanded. "What are you doing? You must ride back with the terms as well."

"For the moment, Robert Neville, you will take your hands off my sister," Aidan said sharply from atop his mount.

"Igrainia will wait with me—under the eyes of your armed men, of course," Father MacKinley said. "It is what the outlaw has demanded. He wants to be sure that she is unharmed when he gives himself over in exchange."

Aidan saw that she was in MacKinley's grasp, rather than Robert Neville's, then turned his horse, and was on his way. Igrainia started shaking uncontrollably, unable to believe what was happening.

Aidan returned, and gave them detailed information on the ground the English had chosen, and repeated every word that the men had said.

"It's a trap, of course," Jamie said. "They mean to kill you, and then seize Igrainia again."

"Of course, it's a trap," Eric said.

"They're liars. They don't mean a word of their agreement."

"We don't mean any of ours, except, of course, that I must hand myself over." He was silent for a moment. "We're asking a lot of Father MacKinley. He is a man of God."

Jamie was very grave, heedless of the fact that Aidan was present as he said, "MacKinley will do well enough. But you must think this out. She is a woman, Eric. A beautiful woman, but no matter what our plans, they may fail. If one of us falters, you're a dead man. Worse, you'll be praying for death. Weigh this carefully. *Is she worth it? Is she really worth it?''*

Eric managed a grin for Jamie. He offered no explanations, or excuses.

"Yes," he said simply.

"Well, good then," Jamie said. "If you're going to take such a risk, it's good to know why."

"Yes, she is worth it," Eric said impatiently.

"Then, if you're ready, it's time to begin."

"There is no other way," Eric said. Then he hesitated, turned back, and looked at the grim faces around him, at those who had ridden with him, so long, and so well.

"Remember, not one of you is to be seen. They will kill her. I know them, and no matter how much Robert Neville wants his riches, Niles Mason wants his vengeance more. And remember this as well, no matter what happens, you must see that she gets away," he charged them. He mounted Loki, and Lord Danby and Aidan, too, swung onto their mounts.

Eric looked at Aidan. "You must see that she is pulled away, quickly."

Aidan sighed. "You keep forgetting that she is my sister."

Eric turned then to Lord Danby. Danby had been taken from the back of the ranks; he wasn't aware of the full plan.

"Lord Danby, I can only warn you that these are *not* men of honor."

Danby replied, "I will demand that the lady be respected."

Eric turned to his men one last time.

"No one, no one, is to be seen," he repeated.

"Aye, Eric," Jamie vowed.

It was time. More than time. Eric spurred Loki, and the fine horse broke into a gallop. It occurred to Eric that he could be racing to his own date with death.

CHAPTER 24

As they waited, Igrainia was forced to watch the arrangements.

She wondered if it wouldn't have been better to have Robert drag her into the woods.

The scaffolding was makeshift, thrown together with whatever logs they could find. They arranged them under a tree to suffice for the height they needed to cast the rope over so that they could hang their prisoner until he was choking and half dead.

Water buckets were brought so that his head could be wetted if he passed out and became unconscious in the middle of the proceedings. The crucial point of such an execution, Niles pointed out, was that a condemned man suffer for the wrongs he had done. A sword ended a man's life, but . . . it also made his atonement far too short. Traitors could pray while they were in their agony, and perhaps win redemption before God. Niles was irritated not to have proper execution tools at his disposal. He needed a sharp, hooked blade to properly reach into the body and extract the organs correctly, to keep the prisoner alive while he was ripped apart.

Father MacKinley grew quite pale, but he was quick to point out to Niles that God was the final judge for all men, and perhaps he preferred to mete out his own brand of atonement, once a man had passed from this life to the other.

"Won't matter any, Father, this outlaw will be cast from the pain of the blade to the fires of hell," Niles said.

Father MacKinley looked sternly at Robert Neville. "I personally watched over you, Sir Robert, when you were at death's door. I helped see to it that you escaped Langley before any retribution fell upon you."

"You helped me out of the castle. And I've not yet managed to return to it!" Robert reminded him. "Mind your prayers, Father. We will, of course, allow you to say them over the condemned. And Igrainia! I had thought that you'd be on your knees already!"

"If I were to say a prayer that was needed now, Robert, it would be for your soul. However, since I hope you burn in hell forever, I will not bother."

She thought that he would have struck her, had Father MacKinley not stood so staunchly at her side. Yet as she spoke, they became aware of hoofbeats on the earth. She bit hard into her lip as she saw that Eric was coming. He rode between her brother and Lord Danby, just as had been agreed. With a sinking heart, she saw that he had meant his agreement.

He had come with no help, with no sign of hope.

Niles walked forward with pleasure. "Igrainia is there, with Father MacKinley. Aidan, Lord Danby, you may join her. Igrainia is placed there, right by the trail, and may take

your horse and ride the moment your head is severed from
your body, *Sir* Eric,'' he said.

Eric nodded. He didn't look at Igrainia. She started to
rush forward. MacKinley held her back. Aidan and Lord
Danby dismounted, standing on either side of her and Father
MacKinley.

Niles had a rope which he had fashioned into a noose,
and with deadly accurate aim, now threw it over Eric's head.
The noose tightened around his neck, and he was dragged
from his horse. Instinctively, his hands flew to the rope to
still the tightening around his throat. Niles called to one of
his mounted men, and the fellow came forward, spurred his
horse, and began to race through the clearing, dragging Eric
over the ground.

Igrainia screamed. She tried to rush forward, to stop what
was happening. She looked in dismay to Aidan and Lord
Danby who were emotionless as they watched.

''My God, no!'' she breathed, struggling with MacKinley.

His hands bit into her shoulders. ''Stay, you must stay!''
he begged her.

''I cannot!'' she said. ''My God, I thought this had to be
a trick, that Eric would ride in with his men, that . . .''

''He couldn't do that. Don't you see? He couldn't let
them do . . . what they might have done to you.''

''It could be no worse!''

She watched as Eric's body thumped over rocks and earth,
and she tried to turn against MacKinley's chest. Robert
strode to where they stood, wrenching her around.

''You are required to watch, Igrainia.''

The horseman had come to a halt. Eric lay still. She feared
that he was already dead.

Niles walked to where he had stood. As he was about to
reach down, Eric came to his feet. Blood trickled from his
forehead, and his lip. His face was covered in dirt, and

marred with red scratches. His rich blond hair was matted, near brown from the dirt through which he had been dragged. His clothing was torn and ragged.

As he stood, another of Niles Mason's men walked swiftly behind him, grabbing his wrists, pulling them behind his back, tying them tightly together. Eric didn't move a muscle in protest. He stared at Niles all the while.

Niles caught the rope around his neck and tossed it to the man at his back. The rope jerked, causing Eric to stumble momentarily. He regained his balance, and walked, shoulders squared, back straight, head high.

She couldn't bear it. She started to run to him.

She escaped MacKinley, but not Robert Neville, who stepped forward, catching her by the shoulders, jerking her back and forcing her to look again. "There is your warrior husband, Igrainia. A beaten animal, ready for the final slaughter."

Aidan stepped forward. "Robert, you will leave my sister to me. It is part of the agreement we made."

Robert released her far too easily, and with far too charming a smile.

But it was good that she was with Aidan then, because Niles called out that MacKinley was welcome to come forward and open his prayer book. Father MacKinley did as he was bidden, walking to the tree trunk scaffolding and slipping his prayer book from his cassock.

The rope around Eric's neck was thrown over the tree. Another man joined the first to lend his weight to the rope so that they could lift Eric from the ground.

Igrainia watched Eric's face turn to crimson as he struggled and gasped for breath.

She began to scream.

He fell, dropped to the logs by his executioners.

Niles stepped behind the logs, ordering that Eric be spread

out properly atop them. He took his knife and ripped open Eric's tunic and shirt.

"And the Lord bless you and forgive you, and welcome you into the bosom of his arms!" MacKinley said, bending over Eric to make the sign of the cross on his forehead.

Igrainia could bear no more. Her screams filled the air as she wrenched free from her brother's hold.

"Igrainia!" Aidan shouted in dismay.

She started to rush forward. But before she could reach the scaffold, and before Niles Mason could dig into Eric's flesh with his raised knife, Father MacKinley made a stunning move. He dropped his prayer book.

Beneath it, he carried his own knife. It was a small weapon, but a weapon, nonetheless.

And with an awkward upthrust, he speared it into Niles Mason's belly.

He didn't kill Mason, but he hurt him bad enough to send him staggering backward.

And in that time, Eric rolled from the logs, and struggled to his feet.

"It's a trick, a trap! Kill them! Kill them all, the traitors!" Robert Neville cried. He was rushing forward himself, sword drawn, eager to reach Eric as he rose with his hands still tied behind his back. His preoccupation to reach Eric in all haste caused him to push past Igrainia, ignoring her.

"No!" she raged, and her scream turned into a cry of fury and hatred. "No!"

She leaped on his back. She beat him in a frenzy as he tried to dislodge her.

She heard a whizzing sound. Arrows flew through the air. The two men who had wielded Eric on the rope fell dead.

The party of Mason's and Neville's men, off-guard in their fascination with the execution and taken by complete surprise at the sudden turn of events, seemed to come to life suddenly in a mass movement. They surged from their arc around the site of execution, but even then, they were unprepared for the Scotsmen. A hail of arrows suddenly seemed to fly, and in their wake, men were falling from the trees like ripe fruit. The arrows had taken down many a man, but others came forward. A great clash of swords began, and everywhere Igrainia turned, which was dizzying as Robert spun about madly in his efforts to dislodge her, she saw more men engaged in combat.

At last, Robert managed to disentangle himself from her fierce hold upon him. It didn't matter. As she flew from his back, she saw that Father MacKinley had used his knife to free Eric's bound wrists. Jamie, sprinting by Eric in the midst of deadly hand-to-hand combat, tossed Eric the sword he had carried in his left hand.

Filthy, bloody, bruised, and scratched, Eric turned on the first man coming forward to do battle with him.

That was the last Igrainia saw. She landed with her back hard against a tree, and fell to the base of it, stunned. She blinked, scrambling to rise. As she did so, she saw that she had Robert Neville's full attention now. He was walking toward her. He had apparently forgotten that she was the key to the riches he had so coveted. His sword was raised.

She braced herself against the tree. There was no weapon to grab. And there was nowhere to run.

Yet, even as he came within reach of her, something strange touched his eyes. He opened his mouth as if he would speak.

Then he crashed down before her. Behind him stood Aidan, Robert Neville's blood dripping from his sword.

"Igrainia, I was charged with getting you on a horse and out of here!" he chastised irritably. "You made me fail at my one important task."

"Aidan! Behind you!" she shouted, and he turned, whipping his sword around, just in time to fell the man who had been rushing to him.

Aidan was instantly engaged anew. Igrainia saw a man scrambling over the body of one of his fallen fellows, and heading toward her with a lethal fury in his eyes. She dropped to her knees, straining in her efforts to retrieve Robert Neville's sword. Neville's dead weight was upon it.

Someone stepped past her, engaging the enemy bent on her demise. She pulled the sword free, clutched it fiercely. She saw Lord Danby cut down the man who had meant to take her life.

"Lord Danby!" she breathed. "You fought ... an Englishman."

"No," he said. "I fought for the honor of the English—which does exist," he said firmly.

She smiled. "I know," she told him.

Then she was grateful she held a weapon, for the fighting had become desperate, with no mercy or consideration for a woman. She hadn't the power or the expertise of the men. She was able to defend herself until one of the armed men surrounding her came to her defense. She became posessed with the desperation of defense, turning, swinging the sword in an arc to keep any enemy at bay. The men at her side were all engaged when a shattering blow fell against her blade.

She looked up. Niles Mason, grinning from ear to ear, had forced her weapon to the ground.

She struggled to free it. Smiling, he moved his blade. She raised her own, and met with the same shattering force. He began to swing again and again, methodically. She was forced back. She didn't think she could hold the blade any longer.

Someone thrust by her, pushing her back.

Eric. He and Niles engaged. She gasped for breath, then

swirled, stunned as she saw another man rushing to accost her. She spun in a wide arc as he came, catching the man in the middle. He staggered away, scraped, but newly infuriated.

Jamie stepped in.

She swung around, hearing someone at her rear.

''Igrainia!''

She knew her brother's voice. She went still.

He came to her, taking the weapon. She realized then that the clearing had suddenly gone still.

And in the center of it, Eric was still face to face with Sir Niles Mason. Theirs was a contest that seemed to go on and on.

Eric was scratched and torn, covered with grime, and appeared ready to fall. There was blood coating Mason's tunic.

And he must have seen that his men lay fallen, like piles of castoff metal.

Eric's men stayed back, creating a circle around the two. As Igrainia watched, Eric took a step and stumbled. A choked sound escaped her. She started to rush forward.

She was caught around the waist by Jamie.

''Help him! He's half—he's half dead!'' she said. ''Niles has suffered a flesh wound, MacKinley is no warrior. Niles may know he is about to die, but he is so maddened for blood that he will die with pleasure if he is able to take Eric with him. Jamie, you must go in, kill him, get him away from Eric!''

''No,'' Jamie said softly, holding her.

''But—''

''This is a fight Eric has to win himself.''

She opened her mouth to protest again, then drew her hand to her mouth, biting down on it to keep from crying out as Niles lifted his sword in a heavy swing. The clang it made as it slammed down on Eric's weapon seemed to shatter the air. She nearly rushed forward again, ready to do battle against Niles herself.

But Jamie held her firmly back.

Eric found the strength to wield his weapon. Once, again, and again. Niles was sent in scurried steps back across the clearing. But then he took the offense again, coming so hard and fast and swinging with such fury that at the end, she thought he would slice off Eric's legs at the knees. But Eric had found the power and agility to jump above the swing, and land upon the logs where it had been intended he should die. He jumped down from them then, and once more, it was he on the offensive, shattering the air as he drove forward again, and again, and again.

Niles took a swing that caught Eric's upper arm. Igrainia choked back a sob as she saw a trickle of blood appear. As Eric clutched the new wound, Niles moved forward, faster, harder, pushing Eric back. Eric stumbled, and went down. Niles took his sword in both hands, ready to thrust hard into Eric's heart.

But even as she screamed, Eric rolled. He came to his feet with a vengeance and a will, and he whirled with a mighty strength and fury.

Igrainia watched as his sword ripped across Niles Mason's midsection.

For a moment, the man remained still, poised there, as if pausing in the middle of a dance.

Then, he fell forward.

For a moment, Eric was still. Then something dark touched his face, and he took his sword in his hands, and in a fit like madness, he brought the weapon down again, and again.

"Jamie, let me go, please!" she begged, and struggled to push from him.

He released her.

"Eric!" she cried his name, and his sword stilled. She rushed behind him, closing her eyes against the sight of Niles Mason.

She circled her arms around Eric from the back, laying her head against him.

"It's over!" she breathed. "It's over."

He remained taut above the body. "The first," he said quietly, "was for Margot. For my child . . ." His voice faded. He turned, and she looked up as he stared down into her eyes. "And then . . . for you."

"It's over!" she whispered again. And she thought that something in him had cracked, that he had suffered more grievous wounds than she could see. Then he stiffened, and his arms around her tightened.

"What in God's name are you doing here? Aidan was to have you on a horse and out of here before this all began."

"Aidan tried, but . . . how was I to know that you did have a plan?" she countered.

He caught her chin with bloodstained fingers. "You should be beaten, you know. Locked away somewhere safe. You . . ."

His fingers fell from her chin. He collapsed against her. She didn't have the size, strength, or power to hold him up.

They fell to the earth together.

Streambeds were an excellent place to heal. They lay against crystal clear bubbling waters. They provided a multitude of healing mosses and herbs for poultices and salves.

Eric was sorely wounded, yet most of what he sustained was superficial. Some of the slashes on his body ran deep, and would add to the scars he had already sustained. His throat was roughly scratched and bruised from the rope. The cut on his arm needed stitches, as did one gaping slash in his thigh.

The first few days, he was so sore and weak that he was a good patient, lying on the bed she arranged, barely aware of the tender care she gave.

There were many wounded. Thayer again sustained serious wounds, but they didn't seem to bother him. Each one, he assured her, taught him something new about defending himself.

One the afternoon of the second day, while Eric lay sleeping and others tended to the rest of the wounded, Igrainia sat on the bank, her toes in the water, with Jamie beside her.

Jamie chewed on a blade of grass. "You'll be far safer now, you know," he told her. And turned to her. "But when he rises, Eric will join Robert Bruce."

"Has Edward risen then to lead his great force to battle?"

"I don't know. Allan and some of the others have ridden out to find out what is happening," Jamie said. "You gave a fine accounting of yourself, you know."

She flushed. "It was the worst time I have ever spent in my life. And there have been many awful times of late. I had no idea that you all were coming . . . I couldn't believe that Eric would just allow them to . . . to . . ."

"It's over," Jamie said softly.

"But it's not. You all will ride off to battle again, soon enough."

Jamie didn't dispute her. With a shrug he said, "There are quite a number of us; the clan has grown and covers many areas of the country. In fact, we've bred a few very black sheep, but for the most part . . . we've kin who followed Wallace each step of the way, and they will be with Robert Bruce when Scotland is really free, and he is king in truth of a sovereign nation. Eric's loyalty will never be questioned.

But, yes, we will ride off to battle again. Eric will do so. You can't stop a man from fighting for something that has become more than a dream,'' he said. ''But . . .''

''But?''

''You can take pleasure in the knowledge that you have brought him back from a nightmare of torment worse than death.'' His gray eyes were on her again, both sparkling and grave. ''He loves you, you know.''

She hesitated, biting her lip. ''I'm his wife. And . . . I am going to have his child. I am . . . what is his.''

Jamie laughed, drawing her sharp gaze.

He shook his head. ''Igrainia, when he planned on giving himself up, we knew that we were taking a grave chance. He knew it. And I asked him, *is she worth it*? He said yes, Igrainia. No man offers himself up for possibly taking that kind of torture for a woman he doesn't love. He wasn't just willing to give his life. It was more, far more.''

''I've seen him being noble for many people, on many occasions. He has never said that he loves me.''

Jamie smiled. ''Facing the possibility of disembowelment, castration, and beheading goes a wee bit above the call of being noble,'' he said.

''Yes, you're right.''

''Don't let Margot's ghost stand in the way of what happiness you two will have the time to seize,'' he told her. ''Remember this, they were together for years. Before Margot . . . well, he was a seafaring man. He was a roamer. But when he loved her, she was everything in his life. Margot's benison is something wonderful for you. He is a man who loves a woman with every ounce of devotion and loyalty in his soul. Don't worry about words. Know what he has done, and that it was done for you, and let it suffice.''

Impulsively, she kissed him on his cheek. ''He is going to want to ride to the side of Robert Bruce,'' she said. ''As are you, I'm certain. But . . . he shouldn't ride too quickly, Jamie. He does need time to heal.''

''If the great battle is about to take place, no force on earth will stop him.''

That night, she slept beside Eric, listening to his even breathing, grateful that he was doing so well. The next morning, she went down to the stream. She walked in wearing her shift, eager for the waters. She had begun to feel that she would never rid her own flesh of all the blood that had spilled.

She cast her head back into the water, letting it rush through her hair. She smoothed it back with her hands, and looked up.

Eric was standing. Battered and bruised, but apparently stronger in muscle and mind, he watched her from the bank. She rose quickly, and rushed to him, afraid that he would falter and fall. But as she came forward, he caught her in his arms, and pulled her against his chest. He didn't kiss her, and he didn't even speak for the longest time, but held her there. And she felt the strong, unwavering beat of his heart, and she was glad.

He eased himself down to sit upon the bank, and she came down with him, searching his eyes to assure herself that he was well enough to be up and moving. ''Whatever am I going to do about you?'' he asked softly. She was on her back, her head in his lap. He smoothed a lock of wet hair from her forehead. ''You are always in the midst of things, just when you should be away and safe.'' He wasn't really looking for an answer; he had the one he wanted. ''You've still got to ride north, you know.''

''I know.''

''What, no argument? You're quite certain? Niles and Robert may both be dead, but the south isn't safe. Even if

Langley has thus far stood firm. But . . . at least, there are really beautiful bodies of water in the highland country.''

"That will be lovely.''

"You're far too agreeable. Am I more gravely injured than I knew?''

She shook her head. "I simply can't change what is. And I know that you will ride to join Robert Bruce. And that I will die a little bit every time you're gone, and . . . live for those moments when you will return.''

His hand, which had moved lightly on her hand, fell still. "Will you?'' he said, but again, he didn't really want an answer. "I've told both your brother and Lord Danby that they are free. They may ride to join Edward's army, or go wherever they like. They proved themselves truly gallant and honorable men in the past days, and as I can't change what is a passion in my heart, I don't expect them to forget that they are Englishmen. Since Aidan is your brother, I'm assuming you'd just as soon that I did lock him up and keep him safe. But I can't do that. He is young, but very much a man, and worthy of being Lord Abelard.''

"I am glad that you have left the decision to them.''

He nodded. "And what about you, Igrainia? You are English as well. With me, you're the wife of an outlaw. And in the future, I can't promise any rich castles, fine clothing . . . actually, as of late, I can't even promise a bed on which to sleep.''

She almost laughed. "I have been prized for who I am and what I possess. You are the one receiving nothing. My estates in England will certainly be confiscated, and Langley . . . Langley belongs to the man who holds it.''

He was silent for a moment, then he said huskily. "Neither lands nor riches are the prize, Igrainia. You are the prize.''

She trembled where she lay. "I, alone? King Edward

would never believe that. Nor, I imagine, would Robert Bruce.''

''Robert Bruce did point out how very beautiful you were.''

She arched a brow. ''He told you that? When he was ordering you to sleep with me, I believe.''

He offered her a subtle smile, taking no offense. ''Actually, it was a day by a stream, much like this one, when I first realized just how completely beautiful you were.'' His smile faded then and his words were as serious as the sudden, dark depths of his eyes. ''Igrainia, forgive me whatever cruelties I offered when we first met. I was in an agony such as could never be bestowed on the flesh. I know that you suffered as well. It wasn't you that I loathed with such fury, it was death, and each time I looked at you, and thought that you were beautiful, I was angry at myself. That you were actually admirable was something I refused to accept. And when I was forced to accept the fact that you were so very desirable, it was more than painful. But then . . . when it seemed that I was losing you time and again, despite my best efforts and what I've always considered a sound military mind, I was forced to realize that . . .''

''That . . .'' she said hopefully.

But he never had a chance to reply. There was a sudden shouting and cheering by the stream bank. Igrainia sat up quickly. Eric rose, helping her to her feet. Anxiously, they started walking back together. In a few minutes' time, they were running.

The injured, the care-givers, and those just passing the time by the stream were all risen, all together, and gathered around Allan, who had returned on a sweaty horse, and remained atop it, flushed and windblown, but grinning ear to ear.

''What has happened?'' Eric demanded.

"He's dead! Edward I of England is dead!" Allan shouted. "He rose from his sickbed, mounted his horse, rode but six miles in four days, had to stop—and died! Dear God, the king is dead, long live the king!"

"Allan, details! So what is happening now?" Eric demanded. Allan at last dismounted, approaching Eric where he stood, where the others had gathered around him. "He died, telling his son that his heart was to be brought to Jerusalem, and that his bones should be stripped of their flesh and carried with him into battle against the Scots— and that they should remain unburied until the Scots are at last wholly subjugated and subdued."

"Those bones will stay atop the ground forever then!" Angus called out.

"Aye, for it seems that Edward II has stopped all the action. He's not done what his father asked, but has made arrangements to inter the body at Waltham Abbey, and has called back favorites whom his father had banished. In short, he sits with his assembled army."

Allan saw that Igrainia was staring at him blankly. He spoke softly for her benefit. "Edward was merciless here in Scotland. But he was a warrior king. A true Plantagenet. While his son . . . Igrainia, the great battle will not come now. Robert Bruce has been given time, precious time. He can travel north through the country, subdue his enemies within it, gain a solid foothold in Scotland, and then . . . then make his stand against the English."

She smiled slowly at Allan. Again, cheers went up.

Sad, perhaps, that so many could celebrate the death of a man, a king.

And she had known him. Known him in better days when he had been, to his own people, a great king. Handsome, gallant, powerful, a force to create a strong England.

And yet . . .

She had to be glad.

Eric had her hand. While the throng around Allan continued to shout and cheer, he led her down the stream, a long way down the stream. He released her hand and walked into the water. He turned back to her, beckoning. She joined him.

"He was your king. I'm sorry."

"I'm sorry as well. Once, in his way, he was a great king. But . . ."

"Aye?"

"If his death means that you'll not ride to battle so quickly, then . . ."

"Aye?"

"Then there is something to be grateful in it."

He reached out, touching her face, smiling. "Do you remember how I told you that the first day I really knew how completely beautiful you were was that long ago day at a different stream?"

She nodded. "So you say."

"I was really furious with myself . . . for what I wanted."

"And that was . . ."

"Well, here we are in the water again." He pulled her into his arms. His hands were on her shoulders. The damp shift slipped from them. "Since we're here, I can just show you."

"You're injured!" she reminded him.

"Oh, no. I think that I am healed. I believe I can prove it. And the way that you love the water so much . . . well, there's more to love about it."

Later, when they lay on the bank, he spoke. "You said that you had no riches left, Igrainia. Do you know that you are still holding the greatest treasure on earth?"

"And what is that?"

"My son," he said. He rolled over and kissed her softly on the lips. "My God. He'll be half English!" he mused.

"There are many, *many*, good English people, you know."

"Indeed, Igrainia. I have always known that. And had I not, well I have seen how valiant your brother and Lord Danby have proven themselves to be. Never traitors to their beliefs, but strong men with a passion for right. And then, of course, Robert Bruce's wife is English . . . and then there is you." He said the last words very softly. But before she had time to muse on them, he rose, and reached down for her. "Come, my love. It's growing late. We need to get back. There is a twist in the future; new plans to be made."

She came to her feet but stood perfectly still. She hadn't heard anything more than the words *my love*.

She remembered all that Jamie had said to her. She had so much. His actions, far more telling than any words . . .

And yet she savored them.

"Igrainia."

"What? I'm sorry."

"I said, come, my love, we've a future to plan."

"You'll still ride to battle," she said.

"Oh, aye."

"For the honor and glory of Scotland!"

"Do you mind so much?"

She shook her head. "No. I want our son to be born in this land where freedom is so highly prized, and where it has been gained at last."

"That day is coming. But until I do ride again . . . I'm sorry for Edward's death if it brings any pain to you. But I can't be sorry that it's given us a special boon. Time."

She looked into his eyes, and nodded. "Aye," she said, and paused, carefully testing the words herself, "aye, my love."

"The fight may be long. So we must take what we can."

"It doesn't matter how long the fight will be. I will always be there—well, wherever you would have me. And I will wait, forever."

He laughed. "For the honor and glory of Scotland?"

"Since that is what it will take."

He laughed, elated. He pulled her quickly into his arms, holding her there for a moment. He kissed the top of her head.

"My love," he murmured.

Then he caught her hand, and together they hurried back to the others.

To plan for the days, and the years, that lay ahead.

Chronology

c6000BC:
Earliest peoples arrive from Europe (Stone Age): Some used stone axes to clear land.

c4500BC:
Second wave of immigrants arrive (New Stone Age or Neolithic). "Grooved ware," simple forms of pottery found. They left behind important remains, perhaps most notably, their tombs and cairns.

c3500BC:
Approximate date of the remarkable chambered tombs at Maes Howe, Orkney.

c3000BC:
Carbon dating of the village at Skara Brae, also Orkney, showing houses built of stone, built-in beds, straw mattresses, skin spreads, kitchen utensils of bone and wood, and other more sophisticated tools.

c2500BC:
"Beaker" people arrive, Neolithic people who will eventually move into the Bronze Age. Bronze Age to last until approximately 700BC.

c700BC:
Iron Age begins—iron believed to have been brought by Hallstadt peoples from central Europe. Terms "Celts" now applied to these people, from the Greek *Keltoi;* they were considered by the Greeks and Romans to be barbarians. Two types of Celtic language, P-Celtic, and Q-Celtic.

c600–100BC: The earliest Celtic fortifications, including the broch, or large stone tower. Some offered fireplaces and freshwater wells. Crannogs, or island forts, were also built; these were structures often surrounded by spikes or walls of stakes. Souterrains were homes built into the earth, utilizing stone, some up to eighty feet long. The Celts become known for their warlike qualities as well as for their beautiful jewelry and colorful clothing; "trousers" are introduced by the Celts, perhaps learned from Middle Eastern societies. A rich variety of colors are used (perhaps forerunner to tartan designs) as well as long tunics, skirts, and cloaks to be held by the artistically wrought brooches.

55BC: Julius Caesar invades southern Britain.

56BC: Julius Caesar attacks again, but again, the assault does not reach Scotland.

AD43: The Roman Plautius attacks; by the late 70s AD, the Romans have come to Scottish land.

AD78–84: The Roman Agricola, newly appointed governor, born a Gaul, plans to attack the Celts. Beginning in AD80, he launches a two-pronged full-scale attack. There are no roads and he doesn't have time to build them as the Romans have done elsewhere in Britain. 30,000 Romans marched; they will be met by a like number of Caledonians. (Later to be called Picts for their custom of painting or tattooing their faces and bodies.) After the battle of Mons Graupius, the Roman historian Tacitus (son-in-law of Agricola) related that 10,000 Caledonians were killed, that they were defeated. However, the Romans retreat southward after orders to withdraw.

AD122: Hadrian arrives in Britain and orders the construction of his famous wall.

AD142: Antoninus Pius arrives with fresh troops due to continual trouble in Scotland. The Antonine Wall is built, and garrisoned for the following twenty years.

AD150–200: The Romans suffer setbacks. An epidemic kills much of the population, and Marcus Aurelius dies, to be followed by a succession of poor rulers.

ADc208: Severus comes to Britain and attacks in Scotland, dealing some cruel blows, but his will be the last major Roman invasion. He dies in York in AD211, and the Caledonians are then free from Roman intervention, though they will occasionally venture south to Roman holdings on raids.

AD350–400: Saxon pirates raid from northwest Europe, forcing the Picts southward over the wall. Fierce invaders arrive from Ireland: the Scotti, a word meaning raiders. Eventually, the country will take its name from these people.

ADc400: St. Ninian, a British Celtic bishop, builds a monastery church at Whithorn. It is known as Candida Casa. His missionaries might have pushed north as far as the Orkney islands; they were certainly responsible for bringing Christianity to much of the country.

ADc450:   The Romans abandon Britain altogether. Powerful Picts invade lower Britain, and the Romanized people ask for help from Jutes, Angles, and Saxons. Scotland then basically divided among four peoples: Picts, Britons, Angles, and the Scotti of Dalriada. "Clan" life begins—the word *clann* meaning "children" in Gaelic. Family groups are kin with the most important, possibly strongest, man becoming chief of his family and extended family. As generations go by, the clans grow larger, and more powerful.

AD500–700:   The Angles settle and form two kingdoms, Deira and Bernicia. Aethelfrith, king from AD593–617, wins a victory against the Scotia at Degsastan and severely crushes the Britons—who are left in a tight position between the Picts and Angles. He seizes the throne of King Edwin of Deira as well, causing bloodshed between the two kingdoms for the next fifty years, keeping the Angles busy and preventing warfare between them and their Pictish and Scottish neighbors. Fergus MacErc and his brothers, Angus and Lorne, c500, bring a fresh migration of Scotia from Ireland to Dalriada, and though the communities had been close (between Ireland and Scotland), they soon after begin to pull away. By the late 500s, St. Columba comes to Iona, creating a strong kingship there, and spreading Christianity even farther than St. Ninian. In AD685 at Nechtansmere, the Angles are severely defeated by the Picts; their king Ecgfrith is slain, and his army is half slaughtered. This prevents Scotland from becoming part of England at an early date.

AD787: The first Viking raid, according to the Anglo-Saxon chronicle. In 797, Lindisfarne is viciously attacked, and the monastery is destroyed. ''From the Fury of the Northmen, deliver us, oh, Lord!'' becomes a well-known cry.

AD843: Kenneth MacAlpian, son of a Scots king, who is also a descendant from Pictish kings through his maternal lineage, claims and wins the Pictish throne as well as his own. It is not an easy task as he sets forth to combine his two peoples into the country of Scotland. Soon after becoming king of the Picts and the Scotia, he moves his capital from Dunadd to Scone, and has the ''Stone of Destiny'' brought there, now known as the Stone of Scone. (And recently returned to Scotland.)

The savage Viking raids become one focus that will help to unite the Picts and the Scots. Despite the raids and the battles, by the tenth century, many of the Vikings are settling in Scotland. The Norse kings rule the Orkneys through powerful jarls, and they maintain various other holdings in the country, many in the Hebrides. The Vikings will become a fifth main people to make up the Scottish whole. Kenneth is followed by a number of kings that are his descendants, but not necessarily immediate heirs, nor is the Pictish system of accepting the maternal line utilized. It appears that a powerful member of the family, supported by other powerful members, comes to the throne.

AD878: Alfred (the Great) of Wessex defeats the Danes. (They will take up residence in East Anglia and at times, rule various parts of England.)

AD1018: Kenneth's descendent, Malcolm II, finally wins a victory over the Angles at Carham, bringing Lothian under Scottish rule. In this same year, the king of the Britons of Strathclyde dies without an heir. Duncan, Malcolm's heir, has a claim to the throne through his maternal ancestry.

AD1034: Malcolm dies, and Duncan, his grandson, succeeds him as king of a Scotland that now includes the Pictish, Scottish, Anglo, and Briton lands, and pushes into English lands.

AD1040: Duncan is killed by MacBeth, the Mormaer (or high official) of Moray, who claims the throne through his own ancestry, and that of his wife. Despite Shakespeare's version, he is suspected of having been a good king, and a good Christian—going on pilgrimage to Rome in AD1050.

AD1057: MacBeth is killed by Malcolm III, Duncan's son. (Malcolm had been raised in England.) Malcolm is known as Malcolm Canmore, or Ceann Mor, or Big Head.

AD1059: Malcolm marries Ingibjorg, a Norse noblewoman, probably the daughter of Thorfinn the Mighty.

AD1066: Harold, king of England, rushes to the north of his country to battle an invading Norse army. Harold wins the battle, only to rush back south, to Hastings, to meet another invading force.

AD1066: William the Conqueror invades England and slays Harold, the Saxon King.

AD1069: Malcolm III marries (as his second wife) Princess Margaret, sister to the deposed Edgar Atheling, the Saxon heir to the English throne. Soon after, he launches a series of raids into England, feeling justified in that his brother-in-law has a very real claim to the English throne. England retaliates.

1071AD: Malcolm is forced to pay homage to William the Conqueror at Abernathy. Despite the battles between them, Malcolm remains popular among the English.

AD1093: While attacking Northumberland (some say to circumvent a Norman invasion), Malcolm is killed in ambush. Queen Margaret dies three days later. Scotland falls into turmoil. Malcolm's brother Donald Ban, raised in the Hebrides under Norse influence, seizes the throne and overthrows Norman policy for Viking.

AD1094:	William Rufus, son of William the Conqueror, sends Malcolm's oldest son, Duncan, who has been a hostage in England, to overthrow his uncle, Donald. Duncan overthrows Donald, but is murdered himself, and Donald returns to the throne.
AD1097:	Edgar, Duncan's half-brother, is sent to Scotland with an Anglo-Norman army, and Donald is chased out once again. He brings in many Norman knights and families, and makes peace with Magnus Barelegs, the King of Norway, formally ceding to him lands in the Hebrides which has already been a holding for a very long time.
AD1107:	Edgar dies; his brother, Alexander, succeeds him, but rules only the land between Forth and Spey; his younger brother, David, rules south of the Forth. Alexander's sister, Maud, had become the wife of Henry I of England, and Alexander has married Henry's daughter by a previous marriage, Sibylla. These matrimonial alliances make a very strong bond between the Scottish and English royal houses.
AD1124:	Alexander dies. David (also raised in England) inherits the throne for all Scotland. He is destined to rule for nearly thirty years, to be a powerful king who will create burghs, a stronger church, a number of towns, and introduce a sound system of justice. He will be a patron of arts and learning. Having married an heiress, he is also an English noble, being Earl of

Northampton and Huntington, and Prince of Cumbria. He brings feudalism to Scotland, and many friends, including de Brus, whose descendants will include Robert Bruce, fitzAllen, who will become High Steward—and, of course, a man named Sir William Graham.

AD1153: Death of David I. Malcolm IV, known as Malcolm the Maiden, becomes king. He is a boy of eleven.

AD1154: Henry Plantagenet (Henry II) becomes king in England. Forces Malcolm to return Northumbria to England.

AD1165: Malcolm dies and is succeeded by his brother, William the Lion. William forms what will be known as the Auld Alliance with France.

AD1174: William invades England. The Scots are heavily defeated; William is taken prisoner and must sign the Treaty of Falaise. Scotland falls under feudal subjugation to England.

AD1189: Richard Coeur de Lion (Plantagenet, Henry's son) now king of England, renounces his feudal superiority over Scotland for 10,000 marks.

AD1192: The Scottish Church is released from English supremacy by Pope Celestine III. More than a hundred years peace between England and Scotland begins.

AD1214: William the Lion dies. Succeeded by Alexander II, his son.

AD1238: As Alexander is currently without a son, a parliament allegedly declares Robert

Bruce (grandfather of the future king) nearest male relative and heir to the throne. The king, however, fathers a son. (Sets a legal precedent for the Bruces to claim the throne at the death of the Maid of Norway.)

AD1249: Death of Alexander II. Ascension of Alexander III, age seven, to the throne. (He will eventually marry Margaret, sister of the king of England, and during his lifetime, there will be peaceful relations with England.)

AD1263: Alexander III continues his father's pursuit of the Northern Isles, whose leaders give their loyalty to Norway. King Haakon raises a fleet against him. Alexander buys him off until October, when the fierce weather causes their fleet to fall apart at the Battle of Largs. Haakon's successor, Magnus, signs a treaty wherein the isles fall under the dominion of the Scottish king. The Orkneys and Shetlands remain under Norse rule for the time being.

ADc1270: William Wallace born.

AD1272: Edward I (Plantagenet) becomes king of England.

AD1277–1284: Edward pummels Wales. Prince Llewelyn is killed; his brother Dafyd is taken prisoner and suffers the fate of traitors. In 1284, the Statute of Wales is issued, transferring the principality to "our proper dominion," united and annexed to England.

AD1283:   Alexander's daughter, Margaret, marries the King of Norway.

AD1284:   Alexander obtains from his magnates an agreement to accept his granddaughter, Margaret the Maid of Norway as his heiress.

AD1286:   Death of Alexander III. The Maid of Norway, a small child, is accepted as his heiress. Soon after the king's death, Edward of England suggests a marriage treaty between the Maid and his son, Edward.

AD1290:   The Maid of Norway dies. With the number of Scottish claimants to the thorne, the Bishop of St. Andrews writes to Edward, suggesting he help arbitrate among the contenders.

AD1291:   Edward tells his council he has it in his mind to "bring under his dominion the king and the realm of Scotland."

AD1292:   November. Edward chooses John Balliol as king of Scotland in the great hall at Berwick. Edward loses no time in making Scotland a vassal of England; King John, he claims, owes fealty to him.

AD1294:   The Welsh, led by Madog ap Llywelyn, rise for a final time against Edward.

AD1295:   Edward has put down the Welsh, and the principality is his.

AD1296:   Not even King John can tolerate the English king's demands that Scotland help him finance his war against France (ancient ally of the Scots). John rises against Northern England; Edward retaliates with brutal savagery at Berwick. King John is forced to abdicate and is taken prisoner. The king of England demands that the barons and landowners of Scotland sign an oath of fealty to him; this becomes known as the Ragman Roll. Among those who sign are the Bruces, who, at this time, give their loyalty to the king of England.

AD1297: September 11. Wallace and de Moray command the Battle of Stirling Bridge, a spectacular victory against far more powerful forces. De Moray will soon die from the mortal wounds he receives during the battle. But for the moment, freedom is won. Wallace is guardian of Scotland.

AD1297–1298: Wallace is knighted. England is invaded, the country of Northumberland is raided of food and supplies for Scotland's population. For ten months Wallace governs his country, his spies informing him of the massive English army being formed by King Edward.

AD1298: July 22. The Battle of Falkirk. It is later argued that the battle might have been won if Comyn hadn't taken his troops from the field. The Scots suffer a brutal loss: Sir John Graham, longtime close friend and supporter of Wallace, is slain. The eight remaining years of Wallace's life, as later recorded by the historian Blind Harry, are full of both legend and myth. Knowing that he hasn't the army he needs to defeat the English, Wallace turns his talent in other directions, seeking foreign recogni-

tion and aid. In this time period, he definitely travels to France (probably twice),
receives the king's friendship. The French
king's favor of Wallace is documented
when later, before he is executed, letters
from the French king commanding that
Wallace be given safe passage to Italy to
put his case before the Pope are found on
him. More than one historian relates the
tale that he did indeed come upon the
pirate Thomas de Longueville and find
pardon for him. During this period, the
vacillation in Scotland continues, with certain barons bowing to Edward, while others desperately cling to their dream of
freedom. Violence continues during Wallace's lifetime and though he has no army,
he is believed to have participated in skirmishes after his return. During the winter
of 1303–1304, Edward again invades
Scotland, receiving little opposition. At
that time, Wallace is in the area; and many
men are charged with the job of appre-
hending him. Relatives urge he submit,
but he refuses. King Edward, however,
means to give no quarter. Robert Bruce,
for one, was ordered to capture Wallace,
yet there is speculation that later, when
the king's men were close on Wallace, it
was Robert Bruce who sent him a warning
to flee. Robert Bruce has learned something important from Wallace: the loyalty
of the common man is one of the greatest
powers in the country.

AD1304:   Many men, including Comyn and Lamberton, come to the king's peace at Strathord. The king's terms are easy, probably because he intends to besiege Stirling Castle. The king offers terms to many men as a bribe to demand the capitulation of Wallace; to his credit, Comyn, sometimes accused of being a traitor at Falkirk, scorns such a demand.

AD1305:   March. King Edward suffers a seizure. More men rally around Wallace, but, according to Harry, Robert Bruce, in England at the time, arranges to leave London and meet with Wallace on Glasgow Moor on the first night of July. Bruce does not appear. On the eighth night, Wallace is betrayed by Sir John de Menteith and his nephew, Jack Short. His faithful friend, Kerby, is killed immediately. Wallace fights with his bare hands until he is told they are completely surrounded by English troops. He is taken, and only when his hands are tied does he find out that they are not English troops, and he has been betrayed by Menteith. He is turned over to King Edward's men. He is bound on his horse for the long trip to London, surely knowing he is doomed.

AD1305:   August 22. Wallace arrives in London.
August 23. Wallace is tried at Westminster. He denies to the end that he is a traitor, for he has never sworn an oath to the king of England. He is brutally executed at Smithfield, being hanged, cut

down, disemboweled, castrated, and finally, beheaded and quartered. His head was placed on a spike and carried to London Bridge. The death of this great patriot creates a legend of mammoth proportions, and in the years to come, many brave men will rally to battle, shouting his name.

AD1306: February 10. Robert Bruce and John Comyn meet at Greyfriars Church. Comyn is murdered. Controversy remains as to whether Bruce did the deed, or if he wounded Comyn and his men completed the task of killing him. As well as fighting the English, Bruce will now have the relatives of Comyn as his enemies.

March 25. Bruce is crowned King of Scots at the Abbey of Scone. Palm Sunday, forty-eight hours after his first coronation, he is crowned again so that the ancient rites of tradition may be carried out—Isabella, sister of the Earl of Fife, married to the Earl of Buchan, Edward's ally, has arrived. To assure his succession, Bruce goes through the ceremony again, in which the golden circlet was placed upon him by Isabella, representative of the family.

May 22. King Edward knights his son, and in turn, three hundred young men eligible for the honor are knighted by their future king.

June 18. Bruce, with the men he can muster, draws up before Perth, where the Earl of Pembroke has brought his forces. Unable to take the castle by traditional means,

Bruce challenges Pembroke to an old form of chivalric battle, and the earl promised to meet him the following day. But that night the English attack the camping Scottish forces. Bruce's troops are taken unaware, shattered, and Bruce is nearly captured himself. The battle of Methven is a tragic defeat. Bruce loses many loyal men to the English king's rage and revenge.

August. Legend has it that Bruce went to the shrine of St. Fillan of Glenlochart, and there, did penance and sought absolution for his part in the death of John Comyn.

August through September. For the safety of his wife and sisters, Bruce sends them away from him with his brother Nigel. At Kildrummy Castle, they discover that the Earl of Pembroke is at Aberdeen, waiting for the Prince of Wales to attack. The ladies push northward, but are seized by allies of John Comyn. Nigel valiantly defends Kildrummy, and is only bested from treachery within when a bribed blacksmith sets fire to supplies. Nigel is executed; the blacksmith had molten English gold poured down his throat for his reward. The Bruce women will suffer years of incarceration and humiliation at the hands of their captors.

Autumn. Bruce travels north and is given aid by Christiana, widow of Duncan of Mar, mistress of the lands of Arisaig, Moidart, and Knoydart, and many of the islands. In the highlands of western Scotland, he gathers support.

AD1307: January. Bruce has gathered enough men and supplies to return to Rathlin.

January 29. Edward sends out orders for a fleet to find Bruce in the islands.

January–February. Douglas, sent ahead, ambushes English soldiers and supplies at the Castle of Arran. His attack is fierce and victory is his. But on February 7, Bruce's brothers, Thomas and Alexander, who had been mustering forces in Ireland, are ambushed by the MacDowalls of Galloway, allies of King Edward, as they entered Loch Ryan. They are subsequently hanged, drawn, and quartered. Bruce himself, however, has been awaiting word at Arran, and as his ships arrive at the mainland, he is warned that fires lit at Turnberry Castle were those of Henry Percy, holding the castle. Bruce, trained to chivalric combat, knows that he hasn't the real strength to take the castle. He and his men set silently upon the troops camped before the castle. Henry Percy, behind the walls, certain he is being overrun, gives his men no aid. Almost all are killed, and the Scots go to the mountains of Carrick with a tremendous booty in arms and supplies. Soon after, Douglas lays waste to his hereditary castle where the English have been in residence and Bruce is victorious, with his small party of men, at the battle of Glen Trool and Loudoun Hill.

AD1307:   July 11. King Edward, who had grown so furious with his failing commanders that he had mounted a horse to lead his armies himself, dies at the little village of Burgh-on-Sands, just north of Carlisle. He orders his son to separate his bones from his flesh, and carry the bones with him at the head of the troops, and let them remain with him until Scotland is beaten.

Edward II did not comply. Edward I's body is left at Waltham Abbey, while Edward II marches on to Cumnock, after awaiting the arrival of his banished favorite, Piers Gaveston.